TRAP THE DEVIL

Also by Ben Coes and available from
Center Point Large Print:

First Strike

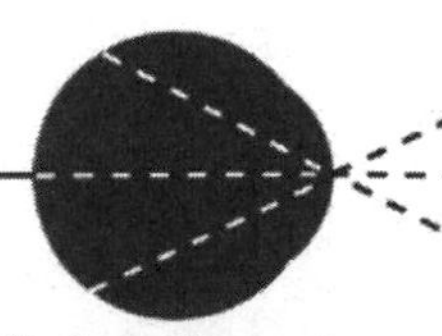

**This Large Print Book carries the
Seal of Approval of N.A.V.H.**

TRAP THE DEVIL

Ben Coes

CENTER POINT LARGE PRINT
THORNDIKE, MAINE

This Center Point Large Print edition
is published in the year 2017 by arrangement with
St. Martin's Press.

This is a work of fiction. All of the characters,
organizations, and events portrayed in this novel are
either products of the author's imagination
or are used fictitiously.

The text of this Large Print edition is unabridged.
In other aspects, this book may vary
from the original edition.
Printed in the United States of America
on permanent paper.
Set in 16-point Times New Roman type.

ISBN: 978-1-68324-602-2

Library of Congress Cataloging-in-Publication Data

Names: Coes, Ben, author.
Title: Trap the devil / Ben Coes.
Description: Center Point Large print edition. | Thorndike, Maine : Center Point Large Print, 2017.
Identifiers: LCCN 2017040854 | ISBN 9781683246022 (hardcover : alk. paper)
Subjects: LCSH: Intelligence officers—Fiction. | Conspiracies—Fiction. | Political fiction. | Large type books. | BISAC: FICTION / Thrillers. | GSAFD: Suspense fiction.
Classification: LCC PS3603.O2996 T73 2017b | DDC 813/.6—dc23
LC record available at https://lccn.loc.gov/2017040854

To my father, Rufus Putnam Coes, Jr.

We'll know our disinformation plan
is complete when everything the
American public believes is false.

—WILLIAM J. CASEY, director,
Central Intelligence Agency, 1981

PROLOGUE

ESTACIÓN DE MADRID ATOCHA
PLAZA DEL EMPERADOR CARLOS V
MADRID, SPAIN
MAY 1979

Can I get a gelato, Daddy?"

Bruner looked down at his daughter and smiled.

"Of course you can, sweetheart."

Bruner reached into his pocket and pulled out some pesetas and handed a bill to her.

"Thanks, Dad!"

"Honestly," said Bruner's wife, Janie, as soon as Molly was on her way to the gelato stand at the far side of the train station. "You spoil her."

"It's the first time I've seen you guys in five months. Of course I'm going to spoil her. Look at her." He pointed at his nine-year-old daughter as she walked across the station. "She's perfect! Have you ever seen something so cute?"

Janie took her husband's hand and pulled him closer, smiling at him.

"Oh, go ahead," she said. "You're right—she *is* perfect. Why not?"

The explosion ripped through the train station with apocalyptic fury. The bomb—a suicide jacket worn by a seventeen-year-old Saudi

Arabian—was detonated inside a T-shirt shop next to the gelato stand. Anything and everything within fifty feet was blown to shreds in a horrible moment of noise and blackness. The ground itself shook, air pushed out, and anyone not in the immediate blast zone was suddenly blown backward, including Bruner and his wife. Bruner reached out his hand as he was punched by the hot air, reaching for the fire and noise and smoke, reaching for his daughter.

"No . . ." he cried, but his word was lost in the wind.

DIRECTOR'S OFFICE
CENTRAL INTELLIGENCE AGENCY
HEADQUARTERS
LANGLEY, VIRGINIA
JUNE 1981

William J. Casey, the director of the Central Intelligence Agency, stepped into his large corner office on the seventh floor. Casey was short and nearly bald. What hair he did have was in a loose ring around the back and sides of his head, white and long. He wore thick glasses and a dark suit, and did not acknowledge the man who was already in the room. Casey carried a manila folder. He walked slowly, with a pronounced limp, and sat down on one of the two beige-colored leather couches.

A visitor, already seated on the other sofa, watched as Casey approached, a blank expression on his face. He'd been waiting nearly fifteen minutes, despite the fact that he was the United States secretary of state. He did not attempt to hide his displeasure at the slight.

"Good morning, Al," said Casey in a clotted mumble. "I apologize for making you wait."

Alexander Haig practically spilled over the couch. He was large, but he accentuated his size by leaning forward, as if expecting to be called upon to tackle someone. Haig had a block of neatly combed brown hair fringed with gray.

"A simple call from your assistant would have been nice," said Haig. "I've been sitting here for fifteen minutes."

"I know," said Casey. "It wasn't intentional. I was in the bathroom. I fell down. I'm afraid my arthritis is getting worse. Nobody came in for quite some time and I had no way of reaching you."

Haig grinned sheepishly.

"I'm sorry, Bill. I didn't know."

Casey waved his hand and gave a rare smile.

"There's no way you could've. Anyway, I'll keep it short."

Haig leaned back and crossed his legs.

"Do you want me to get someone to fetch you a cup of coffee?" asked Casey.

"No," said Haig. "Just tell me why you wanted to meet."

Casey leaned forward and placed the manila folder on the glass coffee table. He flipped back the cover. A black-and-white photo sat atop a thin pile of paper. He handed it to Haig. The photo showed the president of the United States, Ronald Reagan, a few moments before John Hinckley stepped forward in a failed attempt to assassinate him. Several hand-drawn red marks dotted the photo.

Haig studied it for a few moments, then set it back down on the table. He looked at Casey, expecting Casey to begin. But Casey remained silent, watching Haig. Finally, Haig grew uncomfortable with the silence.

"What's the point?" he asked.

"Notice anything wrong?" asked Casey.

Haig paused, glanced at the photo, then looked at Casey.

"Other than the president is about to get shot?" he said facetiously.

Casey smiled giddily and slapped his hand on his knee. "I knew you'd see it!"

Haig grinned. "Honestly, Bill, where are you going with this?"

Casey's grin cut hard to a cold, almost bitter look.

"He was about to get shot," he snarled. "And what's going on? *Nothing*. Incompetence. Sheer, utter incompetence. There was no intelligence. But most worrisome, was there anyone prepared to step in front of the president? Anyone to take the bullet? The only ones who stepped in front of that psycho Hinckley were Brady and Ahearn, a press officer and an advance man, respectively. *This was total and complete mismanagement by the Secret Service agents there to protect him!*"

Haig nodded in agreement. "No doubt. I understand Knight is being fired."

Casey waved his hand dismissively.

"Window dressing! It wasn't his fault. It's a structural issue, Alexander! We have the leader of the free world being protected by glorified security guards. They don't know what they don't know."

Haig sat up straight. He didn't know Casey well, but he knew him. He knew the moment always came, the moment when Casey cut to the chase and put forward an idea that half the time was crazy and the other half was brilliant.

"What are you thinking?" Haig asked quietly.

"A covert program. Housed inside State, because State's so big we can hide it there somewhere, budgetwise I mean. An added layer of protection for the president of the United States in a climate of increased threat and specifically in the aftermath of an assassination attempt that came very close to succeeding. We cull its members exclusively from CIA paramilitary, Delta, and SEALs. ”

“Interesting.”

“It’s a pure strike force—more capable, lethal, and autonomous than anything the U.S. has.”

“Strike force?” said Haig. “That’s beyond the parameters of protecting the president.”

“Is it?” asked Casey.

Haig sat back, thinking.

“Without the restrictions of the CIA or the Pentagon, the unit could operate anywhere, including inside the U.S.,” he said, thinking aloud.

“We’ll stick it inside some ubiquitous but irrelevant office,” said Casey. “I was thinking Consular Operations.”

Haig bit his lip, his initial skepticism morphing into excitement.

Casey continued. “We recruit the country’s most elite soldiers, top operators out of Coronado, Bragg, and the Farm. Protecting the president in a changing and increasingly violent world. They’re embedded in the immediate envelope of the president and are ready to engage at any moment. It also means they’re free to take certain preemptive measures.”

“What do you mean by preemptive measures?” asked Haig.

“There are some threats that need to be dealt with long before any bullets are fired.”

“Are we talking about a kill team?”

"That's right. Black on black. Best of the best. Protecting the most important asset America has, its leader."

Casey sat back, crossed his legs, and folded his hands. He looked at Haig.

"How many operators are we talking about?" said Haig.

"We keep it small. A few dozen at most. They'll get access to intel so that things like John Hinckley don't happen ever again. Most important, we get guys willing to take a bullet. Young Turks with balls of steel."

Haig nodded, a shit-eating grin on his face.

"I fucking love it," he said.

Two doors down from Casey's office, a man was seated at his desk. Other than a pair of telephones, the only thing on the desk was a photograph. It was a photograph of a girl. She was smiling widely and enthusiastically despite the fact that both front teeth were missing. Long brown hair was tied in pigtails. She wore a blue dress with white piping around the collar. The photo was a tad yellowish and a little faded from age. The man stared at it until finally he picked it up and placed it in a cardboard box behind the desk.

He was tall and handsome, with neatly combed brown hair. At thirty-six, Charles Bruner retained the healthy physique of the athlete he had once been, the Special Forces operator he had once been, the CIA paramilitary officer he had once been. But his eyes were dark, including the skin around them; whether it was from age, a chronic lack of sleep, or some undiagnosed disease, it gave him a haunted, vaguely demonic look.

Bruner's eyes were drawn to the glass wall that looked out at his assistant. The stooped, slowly moving figure of William Casey came into view. A few moments later, there was a gentle knock on the door.

"Come in," said Bruner.

Casey stepped inside and shut the door behind him.

"Hi, Charlie," he said enthusiastically.

"Hi, Bill."

"Mind if I sit down?" asked Casey.

"By all means."

Casey sat in one of the chairs in front of Bruner's desk. He flashed Bruner a rare, slightly awkward, heartfelt smile.

"So, you're really doing it?" said Casey.

Bruner nodded. "Yes."

"You're going to be bored out of your mind. You're thirty-six years old, Charles."

"Well, I feel like I'm eighty-six."

"I'm going to ask one more time," said Casey. "For God's sake, don't do it. Take a month. For chrissakes, take a year. But I want you back."

Bruner had a troubled look on his face. He stared at Casey. "She was nine years old. She'd be eleven now. Why was she even there, Bill? Why did I let them come for a visit?"

"Oh, Charlie," said Casey.

Casey stood and walked around the desk. He placed his hand on Bruner's shoulder, trying awkwardly to console him.

"You can't blame yourself," he said. "She was your daughter. Of course you should have her there with you. It wasn't like you took her to Tehran. It was Madrid. Stop beating yourself up, son."

Bruner paused and slowly started to nod.

"I know," he whispered.

"Stay and help defeat these crazy Muslims," said Casey. "Channel your anger. As hard as that is to think about, use that hatred you feel for the Muslim terrorists who killed Molly."

"I've tried," whispered Bruner. "It doesn't work. You know it better than I do. Congressional oversight, rules of engagement, red tape. I wish I could channel it, but it's impossible, even here at Langley, even running NCS."

Bruner looked at Casey, and for a moment Casey seemed to sit up and flinch, as if seeing something darker than what he expected in his deputy.

"Honestly, Bill, I'm afraid of what I might do. I shouldn't be here."

Casey handed Bruner a manila envelope. On the cover was a small label:

ECT: 7
EYES ONLY: DCIA CASEY/DNCS BRUNER/
DDCIA MALONE

Bruner opened the folder and started reading. After a few minutes, he looked up.

"Why are you giving this to me?"

"I want you to run it."

"It's a bunch of glorified bodyguards. No, thanks."

"Keep reading."

Bruner quickly skimmed the five-page document.

> **ORDER 6** establishes a secret paramilitary unit to act as an added layer of protection for the president of the United States in a climate of increased threat and specifically in the aftermath of an assassination attempt on President Reagan that nearly succeeded. **(FINDING US.SCP F776390)**
> **ORDER 6** is a pure strike force and counterterrorism unit, more capable, lethal, and autonomous than anything the United States government has. **(GSI 90-86Y)**
> **ORDER 6** members are selected exclusively from CIA paramilitary, Delta, and SEAL

Team 6 (DEVGRU). **(US HIE/DOD 65.32X)**
ORDER 6 members are not encumbered by the restrictions of the CIA or Pentagon. **(WHS 45)**
ORDER 6 can operate anywhere, including inside the U.S.A. **(GSI 142.29)**
ORDER 6 members are embedded inside the White House and near POTUS. U.S. Secret Service, White House advance team, and U.S. State Department are primary assignments for unit agents, but they are also embedded elsewhere, such as the White House mess and press corps. **(POTUS DIR540.46.8)**
ORDER 6 recruits are selected based on a set of criteria having to do with physical and mental strength. All recruits are unmarried, thus capable of operating without any sort of external personal, emotional, and financial attachments. **(REG US 120.M-45)**

When Bruner finished, he looked up.

"So we get the best operators, embed them near the president as an extra layer of protection, but we can also go after potential threats and enemies?"

"Yes. Anywhere in the world, including here at home."

"Without oversight?"

"There will be some, but it'll be buried inside State," said Casey. "Haig's already agreed to it. There'll be some level of notification and reapproval every year, but that's it. We turn the bureaucracy on its head—*you* turn the bureaucracy on its head. We use the bureaucracy to hide it."

"It's a kill team," said Bruner.

"Precisely," said Casey. "Preemptive, off-the-grid, utterly and totally lethal, undocumented, outside the lines. Black on black. In fact, if there was a color that was darker than black, this would be it."

Bruner nodded and leaned back in his chair, picking up the folder again and looking at the cover sheet.

Casey stood up. "Take your time deciding. But I'll need to know sooner rather than later."

Bruner eyed Casey. "I'll do it," he said.

1

YATES FIELD HOUSE
GEORGETOWN
WASHINGTON, D.C.
TODAY

Dewey Andreas was lying on his back. He stared up at the long steel bar above him, his hands holding it loosely. Attached to each end of the bar were two fifty-pound barbells, two hundred pounds in all. With the bar itself, he was looking at a two-hundred-and-thirty-pound lift.

"You sure you should be doing this?" asked Rob Tacoma, who was standing behind Dewey, ready to spot him. "You're not supposed to do any heavy lifting. That's what Hector told me."

Dewey leaned his head back and looked upside down at Tacoma, shooting him an icy stare.

"From this angle it looks like you were just smiling at me," said Tacoma.

"You mind shutting the hell up?"

Dewey clenched his hands a little tighter around the bar. He took several deep breaths. He pushed up on the steel bar; it moved with a slight wobble up into the air, his arms straightening. The pain in his right shoulder went from a dull ache to electric, like a sharp object was inside.

He grunted as he slowly lowered the bar to his chest, pausing a half second, then pushed it back up.

"Not bad," said Tacoma absentmindedly as Dewey struggled to push the weight up again. "You're using your legs too much, though."

After several wavering seconds, Dewey's arms were straight above his head. He locked his elbows and breathed rapidly. The pain in his shoulder was intense. Yet as much as it told him to stop, he knew he needed to keep going. He had a hundred pounds to go until he was back to the strength level before Sirhan el-Khan stabbed him in the shoulder.

"Please, Rob, shut the fuck up," Dewey groaned.

Tacoma smiled.

Dewey was the only individual who made him understand what it was like to have an older brother. There was no question who was in charge, but that was the way he wanted it, the way he liked it. Sure, there had been other mentors in his life: upperclassmen on the UVA lacrosse team; older SEALs who took him under their wing; after the Navy, other agents within Special Operations Group who helped him out, who showed Tacoma a trick or two. But Dewey was different. He was the only operator Tacoma had ever met whom he knew he could not defeat in battle, unless luck was involved. He was the only man who'd ever made him wish he had an older brother.

The last month had been a blast. Katie was off in Rwanda, spending six weeks volunteering along with a group of six other CIA agents, working to create a more secure route for food shipments into the region. Katie was his business partner, and her hiatus had given Tacoma time to hang out and help Dewey recover from the nearly fatal knife wound.

Dewey enjoyed it too. The problem was, at certain times Tacoma acted like that little brother Dewey never had. Little brothers sometimes couldn't resist the temptation to make things difficult for their older brothers.

Dewey let his arms bend and lowered the barbell, where it touched his chest, harder this time, slamming against his breastplate. He pushed up, grunting loudly, the entire barbell wobbling as if it might at any moment drop like a ton of bricks on top of him.

"Have you ever considered getting a llama, Dewey?" asked Tacoma. "I hear they make great pets."

Dewey's face suddenly contorted as he tried not to laugh, but it was no use. The barbell dropped as his arms went weak. It sank rapidly. Just as it was about to land on his chest, Tacoma leaned down and grabbed it. With relative ease, he lifted it and set it back on the brackets.

Dewey's eyes were closed, his face was bright red, and he fought to catch his breath. Finally, he opened his eyes and looked at Tacoma.

"You're an asshole, you know that?"

Dewey sat up, still trying to catch his breath. He clutched his shoulder.

Tacoma eyed Dewey warily. "Sorry."

"I'm hitting the showers."

"Want me to wait?"

"No."

"Well, actually, Hector wanted me to wait and make sure you went to that appointment."

Dewey glared at Tacoma. "Oh he did, did he?" he snapped.

Tacoma's eyes took on a slight edge, an edge Dewey knew all too well. Beneath Tacoma's disheveled frat boy exterior lurked an altogether different person: an ex–Navy SEAL with martial and paramilitary skills that were rare; a cold, deadly serious, brutally tough individual who'd twice saved Dewey's life.

"Yeah, he did. I'm just the messenger."

2

INDIAN PURCHASE FARM
POOLESVILLE, MARYLAND

Bruner's pants were wet with dew as he moved along a footpath that crossed the twenty-acre field near his home. He watched a flock of Canada geese cut across the blue sky, flying in a near perfect triangle to the south. He stopped walking several hundred feet away from the main house. In the morning light, the rambling, meticulous mansion looked ageless, as pretty as it probably had looked when it was built in 1820. He knew that someday photos of it would be in history books.

There were many reasons Bruner had chosen the path he was now on.

The fields leading up to the home spread in a wheat-colored swath, the long grass fluttering as a slow wind came from the west. Winter was almost here; the field would need to be cut soon. A white horse fence demarcated the boundary between high grass and lawn.

Bruner had on thick but worn Filson tin pants, handed down by his father. If Bruner had had a son, they would have become his. He thought about that son he never had, especially at times like now. He thought about the grandson that his son would have given him. Would he have been out here this day with him? Would he have been standing right beside him at this moment? Would his grandson be to his left, pushing through the high grass with the dogs scampering ahead, a wild smile on his face as he learned the raw joys of nature and the physical world, grass and brambles, soil, streams, rainstorms, and the sun?

Then he thought about the daughter he did have, the daughter he lost so long ago.

Bruner shut his eyes. He squeezed the brow of his nose.

"Don't think about her," he whispered aloud.

Everything I do is for you, sweet Molly. You will see what a father will do to avenge the death of a daughter. The world will see.

The large circular driveway in front of the house was lined with automobiles.

Bruner glanced at his yellow Lab, Ranger, who was standing still, tongue out, panting, looking at Bruner. His expression was a combination of delight after a morning's hard run and the anticipation of a meal.

"Are you ready for breakfast?" asked Bruner, kneeling slightly and reaching out both hands to touch the dog. Ranger wagged his tail.

Several minutes later, Bruner followed Ranger inside the house. He heard conversation coming from the den and walked toward the room, pausing just outside, where a servant stood behind a table. On the table was a silver coffee service.

"Hi, Abe."

"Good morning, sir."

He handed Bruner a cup of coffee.

Bruner stepped into the room. He stood near the double doors, casting his eyes around the vast space. A fire was burning in the hearth. The walls were covered in bookshelves. In front of the bookshelves were fifteen large, deep, comfortable chintz-upholstered armchairs. Closer to the center of the room were three big, old green leather chesterfield sofas. Every seat was occupied.

The voices went silent. Bruner took a sip of coffee as he scanned the men's eyes. He stepped to the large stone fireplace and placed his cup on the mantel.

Gathered before him were the chosen few. Each man had been carefully selected, vetted, approached, and ultimately brought into Bruner's inner sanctum. All had sworn allegiance. Before him sat two members of the Joint Chiefs of Staff, three cabinet secretaries, and more than two dozen high-ranking officials inside the administration of President J. P. Dellenbaugh. But they all shared a secret loyalty, a darker allegiance: to Bruner and, more important, to

Bruner's America, a country they all believed needed to reassert its utter strength and supremacy across the globe. This was the shadow government, painstakingly assembled over more than two decades—and now ready for its bloody harvest.

"The time has come," Bruner announced. "Today, we begin the process of saving the United States of America."

3

MAYEWELL HUNTING CAMPS
OSSABAW ISLAND, GEORGIA

The Speaker of the U.S. House of Representatives, Lowell Benson Trappe Jr., climbed out of a mud-covered silver Ford F-250 pickup truck and scanned the gray horizon above the ocean. It was 5:10 a.m.

Trappe was dressed in hunting apparel. It was well worn and fit the way it was meant to; a Filson coat that had been his father's, thigh-high L.L. Bean boots, canvas pants from Carhartt. At six foot tall and two hundred sixty pounds, Trappe was on the heavy side. He looked older than his fifty-six years, though his hair remained thick and brown and his face ruddy and wrinkled with character. He'd been a member of the House of Representatives since age twenty-five and was elected Speaker at forty. His salary was $223,500 a year, but Trappe, like all Speakers, lived like a king.

The three-day duck-hunting trip to Ossabaw Island was a typically high-end respite from the Capitol. The private lodge was small but lavish in its own way, a camp of sequestered log cabins with bold ocean views, room service, and even a nightly tuck-down by maids who were known to spend more than a few minutes with the guests. This was Trappe's eleventh visit to Ossabaw, and every time it seemed to get better. The ducks were more abundant, the food more delicious, the women more beautiful. It was a trip not even a billionaire could arrange. It was the reward for being Speaker. The fact that the camp was owned by Georgia's largest electric utility was inconsequential. Trappe had backed them and opposed them so many times over the years it was hard to keep track. Pundits and idiots said that money could buy influence, but in Trappe's case it wasn't true. Trappe knew that a politician who allowed his or her decisions to be purchased by the highest bidder was, in fact, of little use to most special interests seeking assistance. What money did buy when it came to Lowell Trappe was honesty and a straightforward, no-bullshit way. People, companies, other politicians, reporters—they all knew where Lowell Trappe stood and they knew why.

The utility's chief lobbyist, Will Scranton, climbed out of the other side of the truck. Like Trappe, Scranton looked at home in his hunting apparel. He stood by the truck, staring off to the shoreline, a cup of coffee in one hand. He lit a cigarette. After a couple of drags, he pointed the cigarette to the shore.

"Looks like Schaller's Bluff'll be good," Scranton said in his deep western Georgia drawl. "Surf ain't too high this morning, Mr. Speaker."

Trappe nodded. "You got better eyes than me, Will."

"I know how much you like to shoot from there, Mr. Speaker."

"Yes, I suppose that's true, isn't it?"

They pulled a pair of duffels out of the pickup.

Two dog crates were also there, each containing a white Labrador retriever. The dogs stood at attention, barely making any noise, though their excitement was obvious by the *whack whack whack* of their tails swinging against the crates.

"So what do you think?" said Trappe, sipping from a stainless steel coffee cup.

"It's early," he said.

"You're the one who wanted to get up at four."

"I mean it's early in the season. It's been warm up north. I'm not sure what we're gonna see, Mr. Speaker."

Trappe smiled and put his hand on Scranton's back.

"That's why I like you, Will. You're just who you are. You don't shine people on."

"Thanks, sir, I try not to. But that being said, we might get lucky. My father put down seven last week over there." He pointed. "You're a pretty good shot. I mean what the hell, even if we don't get anything, it's not like we're up in Washington, right?"

Trappe laughed. He reached to his pocket and took out a copper flask. He unscrewed it and offered it to Scranton.

"Mornin', Mr. Beam," Scranton said to the flask. He raised it to his lips and took a big gulp, then hissed as he swallowed.

"Ah-oooh-ga!" he yelped.

Trappe smiled and took the flask back. He downed a large chug.

"So, any things you guys need up there?" Trappe said. "Been here two days and you ain't said shit 'bout nothin'. What do you got?"

Scranton took the flask and threw back one more.

"No, sir," he said, shrugging. "Session's almost done and we got pretty much what we wanted, which was to be left the hell alone. Besides, let's not ruin a good hunting trip with that stuff. We know you got our back, Lowell."

Scranton let the two dogs out of the crates.

They walked for about a quarter mile along a dirt path that led to the rocky shore, the dogs trotting along behind them, scouring the horizon. Finally, the path opened up to a crescent-shaped inlet, a rough, pretty stretch of coastline, a black sea with flecks of foamy white. In the distance, an orange hue was visible at the horizon as sunrise approached.

"You take the bluff," said Scranton, pointing to the small inlet, a magnet for birds. "I'll go up to Widener's. I'll see y'all at breakfast round eight."

Trappe nodded. "Sounds good."

Scranton whistled twice. One of the dogs leapt toward him as the other moved to Trappe's side.

"Good girls," said Trappe.

Trappe walked the final hundred yards to the water, setting his shotgun on a rock. He took a sip of coffee, then one more swig of bourbon. He picked up his shotgun, plopped a shell in each barrel, slammed the gun shut. He moved to a low, flat rock at water's edge. In the water directly in front of him was a latticework of reeds. Even if he'd been a trained operative, he probably would not have noticed that one of the reeds was not a reed at all.

The frogman was beneath the surface of the water. He'd been there since midnight.

The killer had spent two days studying the hunt from a rise to the east, up the coast. He'd assumed the other man, Scranton, would give the

Speaker the best hunting spot on this, their final day on the island.

Two devices stuck up from below: a breathing apparatus, like a straw, and a pencil-size camera. Both blended into the reeds.

He watched Trappe step down along the craggy waterline. He also observed the dog. He would not have been surprised if the dog picked up his scent through the oxygen tube. Dogs were remarkable. He didn't need or want the dog alerting Trappe that something was amiss. He reached to his wrist and pressed a small button, shutting off the tube, initiating a closed-loop oxygen system that would enable him to breathe underwater for a time. Not long, perhaps ten minutes, but that would be more than enough time.

The dog's eyes darted about wildly.

"What is it, Bodie?" Trappe said to the agitated dog. "You excited?"

Trappe saw the ducks cutting like a shadow across the eastern sky. They were disorganized, mainly because there were so many of them. His heart raced. He raised his shotgun.

But before he could fire, his left boot slipped off the rock. He dropped the shotgun into the water, scrambling to catch himself before he fell, but what he thought was a slippery patch of rock was, in fact, a pair of gloved hands, grabbing his ankle and pulling him below the ocean's surface.

Beneath the water, Trappe opened his eyes, looking for something to grab on to. Instead, he found himself staring straight into the black tint of a scuba glass.

Trappe swung at the dark figure, grazing his chin with a slow-moving punch, which did little to the frogman, who clutched Trappe with viselike hands below the water. Trappe struggled, kicking with his free foot, but it was futile. The diver was too strong. Trappe screamed, even though he knew he couldn't be heard. He made a final, desperate lunge for the frogman's mask, trying to pull it aside, but the killer knocked his arm away. A few seconds later, Trappe had no choice; he needed oxygen. He inhaled. A deluge of water poured down his throat and into his lungs, drowning him.

The diver eased his hands from Trappe's ankle and let the corpse float slowly toward the surface. He watched for a few extra moments and then swam quietly away, the only sounds that of a barking dog and the patter of small waves slapping against the rocks.

4

WINDBLOSEN
RUSWIL, SWITZERLAND

The greenhouse was Romy's favorite place on earth. Their chalet, across the field, was beautiful, of course. It was perched on a languid curve of sloping green heather, with views for miles, but it was the greenhouse she loved. It was hers and hers alone.

Romy had cut back lavender growing in the field below the chalet. Now she was tying the small stalks with their tiny purple flowers into bunches and hanging them to dry over the winter. Carefully, she tied a piece of twine around a bunch and was about to hang it up when she heard a vehicle on the driveway. She paused an extra moment or two, making sure her ears weren't deceiving her. When she heard the squeak of brakes, she turned. She put the flowers on the worktable, removed her gardening gloves, and stepped toward the door.

It was a white van, clean looking and new. Perhaps it was a delivery truck, she thought.

She glanced in a small mirror above the potting table. She thought she was a mess and used her fingers to brush her brown hair out of her face, though in truth she looked stunning. Despite the unbrushed hair and the lack of makeup, her youthful beauty was obvious.

As she reached for the door to go outside, she saw the rear door of the van open. Three men emerged, all dressed in white uniforms. She stood still. She felt her heart racing. Her hands were shaking. She looked at the phone on the wall. She knew she shouldn't have answered the call.

Why? Why did I answer it?

As the men moved toward the main house, one of them looked at the greenhouse. He pointed and said something to the others. Romy backed up as the three men walked toward the greenhouse. Had they seen her? She looked around, panic taking over. She looked for a place to hide, but the men were already at the door. They all looked the same. White single-piece uniforms, pale skin, and bald.

"*Qu'est-ce que vous voulez*?" she said as they came through the door without knocking or saying anything. For the first time, she noticed the light blue gloves on their hands.

Two of the men stepped toward her, their arms extended. They grabbed her arms. The third man opened a thin silver case as they held her, pinching her arms tight.

"My husband is inside!" she screamed. *"Kyrie!"* she yelled. *"Kyrie!"*

The third man removed a hypodermic needle from the case. She watched helplessly as he extended the long needle toward her, a drop of liquid bulging at its tip, then felt a sharp prick as he stabbed it into her neck.

5

QUEEN STREET
TORONTO, CANADA

A green Ford Explorer came to the intersection, moving through the flashing yellow light. The vehicle turned down Queen Street.

It was a working-class neighborhood. The shops were small and utilitarian—a butcher shop next to a dry cleaner, a payday check-cashing store beside a take-out restaurant. They all had something in common: signs in Arabic.

In the middle of the block, in a building that appeared exactly like those around it, was the Hamza Mosque.

The SUV slowed as it came to the mosque, then turned right at the next intersection and parked. Ryan, David, Matthew, and Harun—the four individuals in the SUV—were silent as Ryan turned off the engine and sat back in the driver's seat. He stared straight ahead.

"I have to go to the bathroom," said Harun

from the backseat. “I’m about to wet my pants.”

“Thanks for telling us,” said David.

“I could use something to eat,” added Matthew.

Ryan remained silent. His silence caused the others to stop talking. After several moments, he spoke: “This is your last chance. If any of you want to leave, do it now. Once we go inside, we’re stepping over a line we can never return from. Do you understand?”

The license plates on the SUV were dirt covered. They read MICHIGAN—WORLD’S MOTOR CAPITAL. A faded green-and-white sticker was affixed to the bumper. It showed a cougar, mascot of Northeastern High School in Flint, Michigan, where Ryan, David, Matthew, and Harun were students.

“Why are you saying this now?” asked David.

“Because you have to make your own decision,” said Ryan.

Harun opened the back door and climbed out.

“I’m going in. And it’s not just because I have to go to the bathroom. I believe in what I’m doing. Death to the fucking infidels.”

He slammed the door.

Ryan looked in the rearview mirror at David.

“*Allahu Akbar*,” David whispered, nodding. He reached for the door.

Ryan turned to the passenger seat. He looked at his little brother, Matthew.

“What would I even do?” asked Matthew. “I

don't have my license. How would I get home?"

Ryan reached into his pocket and pulled out a wad of cash.

"You take a bus," he whispered, handing him the money. "Call Father when you get there."

"What would I tell him about you?"

"The truth."

Matthew stared at the green flush of bills. "Will I be able to see Mother? You know, up there?"

Ryan smiled. "I don't know. But she would be very proud of you for asking."

Matthew smiled too. "I want to go."

"And you're willing to die?"

Slowly, Matthew nodded. He reached for the door.

They entered the mosque at the back of the building, just as Mohammed had instructed.

Inside, the hallway was dimly lit. It was stale smelling and decrepit, reeking of body odor. The hallway was crowded with men, all Middle Eastern, seated on the floor, speaking in hushed tones, looking at cell phones. As Ryan, David, Matthew, and Harun entered, they cast weary, distrustful looks in their direction.

One of them stood up and stepped toward them. He scanned them all from head to toe.

"Ryan?" he asked, his accent an odd mixture of Arabic and French.

"I'm Ryan."

The man nodded.

"I'm Mohammed. Welcome. Come with me."

They walked to a set of stairs near the front of the mosque. They climbed up one flight and then went through a door that led to a low-ceilinged hallway. Light emanated from a doorway at the end. The door was slightly ajar.

Mohammed walked in front. When he reached the door, he knocked gently.

"Imam?"

"Yes, Mohammed," came the voice from inside the room. "Are they here?"

"Yes."

"Please, bring them in. I've been waiting to meet them."

On the first floor of the mosque, one of the Arabs, Attah, stood up and looked at the other men seated in the hallway.

"I'm going to the store," he said. "Does anyone want anything?"

"Gatorade," said one of the men. "A red one."

Attah nodded and walked down the hall into the front room, then through the entrance. Outside, he went right, zipping up his coat. As he walked toward the convenience store, his eyes darted to a blue delivery truck parked across the street. He made eye contact with a man in the front seat. Ever so slightly, he nodded at him, then made a beeline for the store at the end of the block.

• • •

Inside the blue delivery truck, the FBI driver turned to the man in the passenger seat, Toby Jones. Jones was in-theater commander of the FBI operation to capture Idi Al-Amin, an imam and known Al Qaeda recruiter, along with his document man, an experienced forger named Basal. The operation, code-named "Red Maple," had been planned for more than a year in conjunction with Canadian law enforcement and with the consent and approval of the U.S. Congress. On foreign soil, FBI agents don't have authority to make arrests except in certain cases where, with the consent of the host country, Congress grants the FBI extraterritorial jurisdiction. In this case, Al-Amin was running a major recruitment route from the U.S. to Pakistan via Canada, and the U.S. government wanted it stopped. It also wanted access to Al-Amin's contacts overseas.

Red Maple was the most important foreign operation the FBI had ever run.

"That was Attah," said the agent in the driver's seat. "It's a go. The students are there."

Jones tapped his earbud and triggered commo.

"One minute, guys," he whispered to the three FBI operators already scattered around the neighborhood.

Jones looked into the back of the truck.

Out of view from the cab and the street were three FBI communications engineers, at work in the back. Each engineer was seated in front of a variety of plasma screens, eavesdropping monitors, and other diagnostic equipment all focused in on the mosque, clunky earphones on their heads. Each of them sat before a console of screens, dials, and other high-tech hardware that appeared like a colorful light display and ran the length of one wall. In addition to the plasmas, smaller CPUs sat in front of each man, along with keyboards. Various control panels and devices were arrayed neatly at the front of the console, enabling the men to manage a host of listening devices and surveillance cameras surrounding the mosque. Behind the engineers and equipment was a fenced-in holding cell, accessed from the rear, large enough for at least a dozen prisoners. The truck was tied in to FBI headquarters in Washington, D.C., specifically to the bureau's Strategic Information & Operations Center (SIOC), the FBI's state-of-the-art operations center.

The closest audio engineer gave Jones a thumbs-up, indicating noise levels were calibrated and commo was functional and live-wired.

Jones opened the door and stepped out of the truck. He walked quickly to the corner, eyeing Hamza Mosque a block away.

The streets were crowded with cars, buses, trucks, taxis. Horns blared every few minutes. The sidewalks were also filled with people, most alone, some walking dogs, a few couples.

He saw Parker first, walking to his right, looking into shop windows. Then the light from the taxicab lit up out of the corner of his eye as Ramirez moved. Looking over his shoulder, Jones spied Giannucci stepping through the door of the small café a half block east.

Jones walked toward the mosque now, in the lead. The four agents were staggered, approaching separately.

Ramirez crossed the street so that he was now alone on the east side of the busy road. The mosque was in front of him only a few hundred feet away.

All four men wore coats that concealed their weapons, two silenced Beretta 9mm semiautomatic handguns. In addition, Jones and Giannucci each had a suppressed submachine gun strapped to his back.

Jones tapped his ear four times, enabling him to close-loop the communication and speak only to his three men.

"One more time," he said. "The stairs are near the back of the building. Me, Jimmy, and Al enter at the back, Tony, you come in through the front door. Watch your fields of fire. Tony and Al remain on the first floor and secure the access points. Don't let anyone leave. Don't let 'em play with their cell phones. Jimmy, me and you go upstairs and find the imam."

"Got it."

"There'll be some teenagers milling about, young jihadis. They shouldn't be armed."

"If they are?"

"On the record, only shoot in self-defense. Off the record, anyone lifts a fucking weapon, you shoot 'em dead. Got it?"

"Yeah, got it," said Parker.

6

QUEEN STREET
TORONTO

A man stood at the window of the third-floor apartment looking out onto Queen Street. He had high-powered thermal vision binoculars against his eyes. He swept the binoculars between Hamza Mosque, a block away, and the FBI surveillance truck that was parked directly in front of the apartment building where he stood.

The man was bowlegged, with a slight stoop. His arms pushed out to the side, though only because he was so packed with muscles. He was six feet tall and somehow loomed larger. His blond hair was pushed back messily, long enough to fall below his ears. Several days' worth of stubble covered his face. What skin did show on the man's face was pale and pockmarked from acne scars. Though he stood still, there was about him an aggressive nature, an implication of purpose and restlessness, even belligerence.

The man's name was Kyrie.

The two-bedroom apartment was empty. Nothing, not even a wastebasket, with the exception of a long duffel bag. It was on the floor behind him, next to Guimar, filled with weapons, ammunition, explosives, and communications gear. It was still zipped.

"Let's go," said Guimar.

Kyrie ignored him, continuing to study the mosque.

Guimar pulled out a submachine gun from the duffel, along with a Glock 21 Gen4 .45-caliber pistol. Mindlessly, the way a blackjack dealer handles cards, Guimar threaded a black cylindrical suppressor into the weapon's muzzle.

"Kyrie," said Guimar again, more insistent. "It's time. They're moving."

Kyrie removed the binoculars but kept his back to Guimar, continuing to look out the third-floor window.

"Shut your fucking mouth or I'll shut it for you."

Kyrie studied the delivery truck, parked directly beneath the window.

"We'll need a VBIED," said Kyrie, referring to a car bomb. "Set the timer to three minutes."

Guimar nodded. He reached for a metal object about the size of a soda can.

"Thank God we finally get to leave this fucking apartment," said Guimar.

Kyrie glanced at Guimar, making rare eye contact, but said nothing. He knelt next to the duffel bag and removed a pair of handguns. Though his movements were slower than the young Guimar's, he threaded the silencers faster. He said nothing as he worked, then, when done, looked at Guimar.

"Keep . . . your . . . fucking . . . mouth . . . shut," Kyrie said quietly. "You have a big mouth. *Keep it shut.* Do you understand?"

"Yes, Kyrie."

Kyrie tucked one of the pistols into a holster beneath his right armpit. He walked out of the apartment door and down the hallway, followed by Guimar, then took the stairs to the lobby. Kyrie pulled the hood of his anorak over his head as he walked outside. He strolled casually to the back of the delivery truck. He stopped just behind the driver's window, out of sight, weapon at his side and out of view.

He looked into the cab of the truck. A lone figure sat in the driver's seat, fidgeting with the steering wheel as he looked straight ahead in the direction of the mosque.

Kyrie tapped lightly on the window. The driver

jerked his head around. An anxious look crossed his face. Kyrie knocked again.

"Just a dollar," Kyrie said loudly through the glass, his face shrouded in part by the anorak hood.

Thinking he was a vagrant, the FBI agent shooed him away with his hand and turned back to the mosque.

"Just a dollar," said Kyrie. "Please, sir."

The driver turned with a hateful look. He knew opening the window was a risk, but it was better than risking the vagrant making a scene. He reached to his pocket for some change, then turned to Kyrie and lowered the window, extending his hand.

Kyrie lurched at the man's wrist and grabbed it with one hand. With his other he swept the gun through the window and trained it on the man's head. Kyrie waited, more intrigued than anything else, watching the FBI agent's mind at work, trying, in that precious half second, to figure out what to do. The agent finally reacted, reaching to his earbud to try and warn the others.

Before the driver could utter even a moan, Kyrie fired. The silenced bullet ripped into his larynx, blowing him back across the seat, killing him. With his other hand, Kyrie reached in through the open window and unlocked the door. Calmly, he opened it, pushed the dead agent over, and climbed in.

Behind the seat was a door. Kyrie grabbed the handle but didn't move it. Glancing over his shoulder, he found Guimar.

In silence, Guimar signaled with his index finger: *The bomb is set.*

Kyrie did not respond. He paused, then slowly opened the door to the back. Bright fluorescent light boomed out. He saw two men, both with headphones on, looking at screens. They looked up and their eyes grew wide. Kyrie fired two quick blasts. Slugs tore into each man's forehead. Kyrie pushed the door all the way in and was face-to-face with the third man, who had a snubnose pistol already out and aimed at him.

"We have a—"

Kyrie fired three quick blasts, three metallic *thwangs* sounding, sending the last man bouncing off his chair in a blood-swirled tumble to the floor.

He inspected the back of the truck, making sure no one else was there, then climbed out, shutting the door.

Guimar was leaning against the truck. He looked at Kyrie.

"Start the timer," said Kyrie.

Guimar nodded.

Kyrie popped the mag from his gun and caught it, sticking it in his pocket and removing a full one. He slammed it in as he eyed the mosque a block away.

• • •

Al-Amin's small office was lit with a table lamp and several candles. Photos of Mecca and religious paintings adorned the walls. The room's two windows had been covered with a blanket nailed into the wall above.

A pair of slightly dilapidated couches occupied the middle of the room.

Al-Amin sat behind a desk at the far side of the room. Across from him, with his back turned, was a rotund man in jeans and a brown T-shirt.

Al-Amin was in his sixties. He was tall, light skinned, with dark, intelligent, suspicious eyes. He had a neatly trimmed beard and mustache. He wore a black hijab.

"Won't you please come in, my sons?" Al-Amin gestured to the couches as he stood and walked around the desk. "And tell me, how was your trip from Michigan?"

Al-Amin stood between the sofas as Ryan, David, Harun, and Matthew tentatively sat down.

Mohammed stood silently inside the door.

"It was good, Imam," said Ryan.

Al-Amin looked at him.

"You must be Ryan?"

Ryan stood and offered his hand, though Al-Amin held up his palm, turning it down, but in a gentle way.

"We do not do that here. It is a Western custom."

"I . . . I'm sorry," Ryan stammered.

"Do not apologize. How could you know? This is what we do."

Al-Amin bowed slightly toward Ryan, then smiled. He looked at Harun, who stood up, soon followed by David and Matthew. Each introduced himself to Al-Amin.

Al-Amin slowly eyed the four students.

"You have each agreed to fight on behalf of Allah. But that was when you were in the safety of your homes. There's no shame in saying you have cold feet. The men you walked by when you came in, all of them will—like you—be leaving tonight for the great struggle. But three of them are here for the second time, having each developed second thoughts when he first came. Yet they are back. I say this to you because I want you to know that when you commit to jihad, it commits to you. I commit to you. Do you understand me, sons?"

The four students said nothing.

Finally, it was Harun who spoke. "I'm ready, Imam."

"I am too," said Ryan.

"Praise Allah, I am committed, Imam," said David.

Matthew, the youngest of the four, swallowed and nodded. "I want to fight, Imam."

Al-Amin laughed.

"The spirit of youth," he said. "It is what will deliver the caliphate to us."

Al-Amin turned to the man at the desk, who was slouched forward, a high-powered halogen light on his head.

"Rufus," said Al-Amin, "are you close?"

The man sat up and turned. He had a pale, ghostly pallor and a maniacal look on his face. Al-Amin and the students had to avert their eyes from the light, which swept across them.

"Yes, Imam, I'm done."

He turned off the light, then grabbed a stack of blue passports. He handed them to Al-Amin, who opened the cover of the first one and examined the photo, then looked at Matthew.

"Here you are," he said.

Al-Amin distributed the other three passports. He looked at Mohammed and nodded almost imperceptibly.

"When do the vans arrive?" he asked.

"In fifteen minutes, Imam."

"Good, good. That is good. Mohammed, would you be so kind as to get warm water with lemon for everyone? We have time to talk for a few minutes before you leave. I would like to hear about life in America."

Three of the four FBI agents charged to the back of the mosque; Giannucci was alone in front.

Parker was first to the back door. He flipped off the safety on the submachine gun, then opened the door, swinging the MP7 in front of him as he stepped inside. He registered a couple dozen men seated on the floor looking up in shock.

Jones and Ramirez entered behind him, passing at a sprint and running up the stairs.

Parker swept the SMG in the air.

"Don't fucking move," he said. "We're not after any of you."

Suddenly, his eyes caught something. Halfway down the hallway, a young-looking Arab leapt to his feet. His arm was out . . .

In stride, Giannucci pulled his MP7 around from his back and charged toward the front entrance of the mosque. He flipped off the safety with his thumb without looking.

As he came to the front door, he paused an extra moment. He heard voices. He yanked open the door, submachine gun raised, finger tight against the ceramic trigger.

The front lobby was shabby, lit with a lone lightbulb that dangled by a wire. A filthy oriental carpet was too small for the space.

Giannucci followed the sound of voices. Off the lobby, to his left, he saw light. He glanced right. The prayer room was empty, its floor covered in cushions and mats.

An abrupt yell came from the corridor. He moved toward the sound, stepping into a hallway filled with young Arab males, all in a panicked uproar. At the far end of the hall stood Parker, his submachine gun visible above the heads.

Giannucci was alone. As he approached from the front, no one noticed him. Their eyes were on Ramirez. Suddenly, Jones and Parker stepped in, guns raised, and sprinted for the stairs.

A flash of steel caught a glint of light. Giannucci's eyes shot left. One of the men was pulling out a handgun and moving it around toward Ramirez, shielding it from view behind another man.

He wore sneakers and a T-shirt. He looked no older than sixteen or seventeen.

Giannucci swept the MP7 toward the young gunman. He locked onto the man just as he completed the sweep, pulsing the trigger. A low metallic thud was the only sound as a bullet tore from the MP7 and ripped into the boy's head. He dropped, falling on top of another man, who suddenly yelled as he realized his friend had been shot. The young man's panicked eyes shot to Giannucci. He was the first to realize they were surrounded.

Upstairs, Jones led down the dimly lit hallway. He stopped at a wooden door near the end of the hall, waiting. He heard voices from inside the room.

He pushed the door in, then leveled his submachine gun and swept it, warning everyone not to move.

Jones quickly counted seven men, all seated on sofas except for Al-Amin as well as another man at a table in the back. They were all drinking from small Styrofoam cups.

Al-Amin was seated in a large leather chair. Jones made eye contact with him as, in the same moment, he trained the tip of the suppressor on the cleric's head.

Ramirez moved into the room, flanking Jones, sidearm out, finger on the trigger. He stepped slowly inside, covering Jones, then trained his weapon on a man standing near the door.

Jones glanced over at the fat man sitting at the desk.

The forger.

"You," Jones barked, pointing at Al-Amin. Then he pointed at the forger. "And you. Let's go. *Now!*"

Kyrie looked at Guimar.

"I'll take the back. Kill the sentry at the front and hold until I signal—and stay out of my field of fire."

Guimar nodded. He understood. It meant Kyrie would take the entire hallway full of jihadis.

"There could be twenty men in there," said Guimar.

"Just stay the fuck out of the way, okay? If I see you in the field of fire, I won't stop shooting."

• • •

Kyrie charged down the sidewalk toward the back of the mosque. He reached the door, paused, raised his handgun, silencer pressed to the seam of the door, then yanked it open. A large man in black was guarding the jihadis in the hallway; Kyrie fired a bullet into the back of his skull, just above his bulletproof vest. As the FBI agent crumpled to the floor, Kyrie opened up the weapon, triggering it as fast as he could, firing at the men in the hallway, hitting one after another as several of them, at the far end, scrambled to duck and hide from the fusillade.

As he killed with his right hand, his left hand reached to his armpit and pulled out the second handgun. Just as the fourteen-round mag clicked empty on the gun in his right hand, Kyrie began firing with his left hand, moving along the walls and annihilating anything that moved. He fired after all signs of life were gone, until the mag was spent.

He snapped his fingers. A second later Guimar appeared at the far end of the corridor, submachine gun out. He surveyed the carnage emotionlessly, stepping between legs and bodies as he moved toward Kyrie.

By the time Guimar had crossed over the piles of dead bodies, Kyrie was gone.

• • •

Kyrie moved up the stairs, popping the empty mags from both guns, pulling two fresh ones from his belt and, one at a time, slamming them into the .45s.

He reached the door to Al-Amin's office. He saw Guimar arrive at the top of the stairs. Kyrie listened as words came from inside the office.

"You! And you! Let's go. *Now!*"

FBI agents, arresting the imam. Keeping him alive. They would no doubt fly Al-Amin to Guantánamo Bay and interrogate him, perhaps even finding out some important information, but he would live. It would be yet another typical U.S. counterterrorism operation, noodling around the edges, cutting out a single blade of grass from a lawn the size of a football field. A disgusted, angry look crossed Kyrie's face. He paused one more moment, looking at his watch, breathing quickly, heart racing . . . waiting.

Guimar approached with his gun out. Kyrie held up his hand, pausing Guimar. Guimar had an impatient look on his face.

Again, Kyrie glanced at his watch. He reached for the door handle just as the air was pulverized in noise. A powerful explosion ripped the air from across the street, shaking the ground as the VBIED detonated beneath the delivery truck. Kyrie pushed the door in, his handguns trained at torso level, and began firing before he was even through the doorway, pulsing the triggers on his weapons—low, metallic *thwack thwack thwack*—as slugs spat from the suppressed muzzles of the .45s. The first man down was an FBI agent to his right, the bullet kicking a dime-size hole in his cheek, dropping him just as Kyrie shot the other FBI agent in the neck. He found the fat man at the desk. Kyrie fired quickly—his bullet puncturing the man's forehead dead center, a pained grunt his last sound as he fell off the chair to the floor. A young Muslim near Al-Amin moved, attempting to run toward the corner, but Kyrie found him and fired. His bullet struck him in the temple and he dropped, pulling a small table with him, cups filled with tea splashing as they were thrown to the floor.

Kyrie paused, staring down the four American students, then fired four fast blasts, one into each of their chests, killing them all.

Suddenly, there were sirens—but they were distant.

Kyrie took another step into the imam's office. He took aim, holding Al-Amin in the path of the suppressor. Al-Amin raised his arms in surrender, but Kyrie pumped the trigger, sending a bullet between Al-Amin's eyes, knocking him backward, his momentum forcing the chair over, spilling Al-Amin to the floor, which was covered in a growing pool of wet crimson.

The sirens grew louder—and closer.

"Kyrie—"

Kyrie turned to Guimar. He looked in Guimar's eyes as he slowly swept one of the guns and aimed it at Guimar. He pumped the trigger. The bullet ripped into Guimar's chest. His mouth gaped open in shock and confusion; his hand reached for his chest. He fell to the floor, his eyes still open. Kyrie stared at him for an extra moment, a cold, maniacal look on his face.

"I told you to shut the fuck up," said Kyrie.

The sirens were getting closer. Kyrie stepped over Guimar and charged down the hallway. He needed to get away before the police arrived.

7

FBI HEADQUARTERS
STRATEGIC INFORMATION & OPERATIONS CENTER (SIOC)
OPERATIONS ROOM 4
WASHINGTON, D.C.

Dave McNaughton, the FBI's director of counterterrorism, stared at a large plasma screen that was flashing black and green. McNaughton had on a headset and was barking into it, repeating himself for the umpteenth time even though he knew it was pointless.

"Jones!" said McNaughton. "Are you there? I

repeat, where are you? *Toronto! Anyone!* What the hell is going on?"

The FBI's massive Strategic Information & Operations Center, usually a hub of activity, fell rapidly into a state of quiet pandemonium.

Nearly every employee in the forty-thousand-square-foot facility—men and women spread out over six crisis action team rooms, five large-scale operations areas, and a variety of conference rooms—converged on Operations Room 4.

All eyes were on the plasma screens. There were four screens in all, each nine feet tall and fifteen feet wide. Two of the screens were flashing black and green, as if broken. A third showed a live video feed taken from a satellite. Though grainy and lacking focus, the image was horrific. It showed where a large explosion had destroyed the FBI's in-theater command post. Flames and smoke billowed from the wreckage.

"Dave," said one of the analysts seated at a workstation near the front of the room, "ETF is almost there. I'm bringing it up right now."

One of the flashing plasma screens abruptly cut out. The screen was fuzzy and red for a few moments, then sharpened. They were seeing through the helmet-mounted camera of a Canadian Emergency Task Force police detective as he entered Hamza Mosque. Inside, the floor was littered with bodies, the walls splattered with blood. The officer wearing the camera stopped and flipped a man over. It was one of the FBI agents. Several people in the room let out gasps. Next, the officer focused in on the face of a dead man near the wall. His face was recognizable: Al-Amin.

McNaughton stared at the screen for a few moments, then turned to look at the room. Normally, the room held approximately two dozen people, but other SIOC analysts, agents, and staff members had moved in. McNaughton didn't want them there, but he also knew now was not the time to start reprimanding people, especially given the fact that most of them knew Jones and the other members of the team in Toronto.

"Everyone," said McNaughton calmly, "as hard as it is to do right now, I need you all to get back to work. I was close to all those guys, and I know you were too. Right now, the most important thing we can do is not think about them. I need my operating team to focus on assessment before the concrete dries, and that's right now, so please, everyone clear out unless you're specifically assigned to Red Maple."

As people moved out of the operations room, a female agent seated at a computer terminal near the back signaled McNaughton.

"What is it, Jennifer?"

"Jesus June is on one for you. He says it's urgent."

McNaughton looked at one of the analysts near the door.

"I want a forensics team in the air within the hour," said McNaughton as he pulled his headset back on. "Someone call Walsh at RCMP and have him close off the scene until we're there." He nodded to Jennifer. "Put Jesus through."

8

NATIONAL SECURITY AGENCY (NSA)
SIGNALS INTELLIGENCE DIRECTORATE (SID)
FORT MEADE, MARYLAND

Jesus June, the senior analyst at the National Security Agency's Signals Intelligence Directorate (SID), stared at his computer screen as his hands typed on a keyboard, pounding the keys slightly hard in frustration. The screen was black except for a small flashing red rectangular box with the words:

> SYSTEM ERROR:
> LOSS PARAMETER
> R33.7Y-0

Something had happened. Something bad. Seventeen minutes into the FBI's Toronto operation, June's screen went black and then flashed an "R33" error. While June didn't know yet what the "33" meant, he knew the "R" indicated massive signals dislocation. A bomb or explosion of some sort.

June walked out of his office into a large room filled with a few dozen men and women at workstations, all SID analysts who worked for him. He focused on a woman close to him, Samantha Stout.

"Toronto?" she said.

"Yeah. My environment went down."

"I'm already on it," said Samantha. "It looks like the main FBI hub went down, and there are reports of some sort of explosion coming out of Canadian police dispatch."

June pulled out his cell and hit a single speed-dial number.

"CENCOM, Mr. June. Voice recognition."

"Harvard Sentences."

"Phrase one, please."

"Oak is strong and also gives shade," said June.

"Affirmative. Go, sir."

"SIOC command center. Alpha V."

"Hold."

June stared impatiently at the floor as he waited to be put through. More than a minute later, the phone clicked.

"SIOC, four, this is Agent Glass."

"Hi, Jennifer, it's Jesus June at NSA SID. I need Dave. It's urgent."

"Let me try and get his attention, Jesus."

"Thanks."

A few moments later, McNaughton came on the line.

"What is it, Jesus?"

"What happened?"

"It's early, but it looks like a bomb detonated beneath Bravo command point," said McNaughton. "Whoever did this blew up the truck, then went inside the mosque and killed everyone, including my agents. We got eight dead in all."

"I'm sorry to hear that," said June, pausing. "Dave, I need immediate access to all SIOC electronic signals, meaning backup, metadata, video, digital, pen tap, anything you have up through the explosion. I need you to provision us into the trunk."

"You got it," said McNaughton. "It'll be on six dash zero."

"Thanks, Dave. One more thing. I need decent head shots and thumb scans of everyone in the mosque. ASAP."

"Done, I'll get them over to you."

June hung up the phone and looked at Samantha.

"I need authorization," she said.

June pulled a chain out from his shirt and lifted it over his head. Attached to the chain was a thick black plastic card the size of a credit card. He held it up against Samantha's computer screen. A moment later, a series of beeps chimed.

"The entry is through six dash zero," June told her.

Samantha started typing.

"I'm in," she said.

"Lock it down," said June. "Run a matrix against the time frame. Everything up until the explosion. You heard what I asked McNaughton for, but include any variables. Run it against ECHELON, DS-300, Stellar Wind, and PRISM."

"What am I looking for?"

"I don't know," said June.

9

1244 PENNSYLVANIA AVENUE WASHINGTON, D.C.

The office building was simple in its lines, austere, elegant, anonymous looking. A sheet of blue shot up in a mirror of shiny glass ten stories high, edged with copper. Dewey entered the building, still clutching an ice bag against his sore shoulder. He was dressed in jeans and a white, red, and black flannel shirt. A pair of men stood behind the security desk in the lobby. Dewey immediately registered that both were armed. He scanned the lobby, counting four security cameras as well as a two-way mirror behind the guards, framed to look like a beautiful wainscot-framed mirror.

He reached for his wallet and removed an ID card. The guard pushed the card against a digital screen.

"Floor ten, Mr. Andreas," said the guard as he handed the thick plastic card back to Dewey.

On the tenth floor, Dewey walked down the hallway to one of the offices. He glanced at the brass letters on the door:

DR. PAMELA PECK

Dewey knocked.

"Come in."

He stepped inside and shut the door behind him.

The room was long and angled, light filled, and, except for a few choice pieces of modern furniture, largely empty. A long chrome and black leather sofa was at the far end of the room. Two white leather Eames chairs sat unoccupied to the left. An identical armchair faced them. Behind it ran an expansive window that showed a dramatic view down Pennsylvania Avenue to the White House. The office's outer walls were glass, and the view was astonishing, especially on this late autumn day. Washington was arrayed in crisp splendor. The Capitol Building was visible in the far distance, as was the Washington Monument. The buildings nearby refracted and the light seemed to glisten in a light blue haze.

A woman was seated in one of the armchairs. She had medium-length auburn hair and wore a stylish black business suit.

Dewey had a blank expression on his face, though it was obvious he was uncomfortable. He said nothing as she stared at him with a neutral, somewhat kindly expression. He glanced around the room, assessing it.

Finally, Dewey acknowledged her. Dr. Peck met Dewey's stare.

"Dewey?" said Peck.

"Yeah."

"I'm Pamela Peck." She pointed toward the chairs. "Sit down, won't you?"

Dewey paused for a few seconds, then reluctantly sat down in one of the leather chairs.

They eyed each other for more than a minute, saying nothing. Finally, Dr. Peck broke the silence.

"Did you hurt your shoulder?"

"It's just sore."

"So, what brings you here?" she asked.

"You know the answer to that."

"What do you mean?"

"I'm being ordered to see you."

"Ordered?" she asked.

"You know it and I know it, so let's get it over with."

Dr. Peck's normally unflustered face broke into a smile.

"You're not being ordered to do anything," she said.

"Hector told me to come here," said Dewey, referring to Hector Calibrisi, the director of the Central Intelligence Agency.

"You're free to leave at any time," she said.

Dewey grinned.

"Sure, I can leave. Then that fact is noted in some file somewhere and at some point is used against me. I know how the system works. So just ask your questions and let's get this over with, Doc."

Peck's smile slowly disappeared.

"You . . . let me get this straight . . . you actually believe what you're saying?" she asked incredulously, leaning forward. "You think I'm going to share my session notes?"

"Are they listening right now?" said Dewey.

She shook her head in disbelief, but still managed a smile.

"What is said here does not leave this room," Peck said indignantly. "I do not share anything at any time with the Central Intelligence Agency—or anybody. My work is doctor-patient privileged and is protected under various laws and professional ethical guidelines, which I adhere to religiously. In addition, you should know that this room is swept for listening devices every morning. If you'd like to sweep the room with your own team prior to appointments, I wouldn't object."

"How much is this?"

"I'm two thousand dollars an hour. The agency is paying for it. You're only the second person Hector has ever sent to me."

"Who was the first?"

Peck smiled.

"So why do they hire you?" Dewey asked.

"Me personally, or a psychotherapist in general?"

"You personally. There are dozens of them at the agency."

She paused. "Because I'm good at what I do."

Dewey watched as, unconsciously, Peck glanced out the window. In the distance, a few blocks away, was the White House.

"I understand the mind of . . . people like you."

"What the hell does that mean, 'people like me'?"

"Cut the shit," she snapped. She let it sink in. "You know damn well what I'm talking about. People under pressure. Pressure that's atypical. Acute stress. Operators. People staring into muzzles all day."

"Did they show you my file?"

"I have top secret clearance," she said. "Yes, they sent it over. It saves time."

“Then you know damn well there’s nothing wrong with me.”

“How many times have you had PTSD, Dewey?”

Dewey was quiet for a few moments. “A few.”

“Three according to the Agency,” said Peck. “Five by my count.”

“I know how to deal with it.”

“Nobody knows how to deal with it,” said Peck, “even me.”

“Are you the one we go to before they suggest we retire?” Dewey said. “You try and take us back from the edge, make us nice guys?”

“No,” she said. “The ugly truth is, the United States government *needs* you to be on the edge. They need operators like you taking Tier One risk and not asking why. Why you like being on the edge, why you need to be on the edge. You’re here because someone cares enough about you to ask.”

Dewey nodded.

“Isn’t it obvious?” he said.

“To me it is,” said Peck.

“And what’s your theory, Doc?”

“No way,” she said. “That’s one you need to figure out. I’ll help you.”

“Sounds like you already know. Why not just write it down and I’ll memorize it. Then we can skip all this.”

“Unfortunately, it doesn’t work like that. *You*

need to understand the *why* on an emotional level. That takes time."

"You still haven't answered why it matters. Why do *I* need to know?"

Dr. Peck nodded. "Because it might save your life."

Dewey shifted uncomfortably in the chair.

"By understanding the why," Peck went on, "you'll be able to make informed choices when you're in-theater."

"I already make informed choices. I don't need your help."

Peck grinned.

"That came out incorrectly," she said. "For Hector to send you here means you're—"

"A 'top asset,' " he said derisively.

"That's not what I was going to say. It means you're important to him. He told me that he loves you like a son. He wants you to be happy. He wants you to live a long life."

"This is about Daisy, isn't it?" said Dewey.

"Who's Daisy?" she said.

Dewey sat back, pausing.

"Hector's daughter," he said. "He's worried I might put her at risk."

"Are you dating her?"

"I'm not sure."

"Tell me about Damascus," said Peck.

"What about it?"

"I read the file. Why did you go to Damascus?"

"Rick Mallory recruited a highly placed source inside ISIS. He had information involving an imminent threat on the United States. The live drop was in Damascus. Damascus exposed a secret arms program sending weapons to ISIS."

"It also led to the capture of a dormitory filled with students," said Peck.

"It led to the death of Tristan Nazir. A hundred times more dangerous than bin Laden. The dorm strike would've happened no matter what. The cell was already inside the U.S."

"You don't know that," said Peck. "If Raditz hadn't been exposed, the ship would've delivered the weapons and that's the end of the story."

"And ISIS would have controlled Syria and Iraq," Dewey shot back. "They'd have a country. Legitimacy."

"What do you care?" she asked. "Do you live over there?"

"No, I don't. But give those fuckheads a country, and the problem goes from bad to worse. They'd have a foundation. A launch point. A recruitment engine. Permanent access to oil and resources. It would be a major problem. The only way to stop them would be with nuclear weapons, and that's not going to happen."

"So you went to Damascus to prevent the escalation of attacks on America?" she said.

Dewey stared at her, saying nothing.

"To prevent them from coming here and killing Americans?"

Dewey shook his head. "Are you saying I was responsible for what happened at Columbia?"

"Not at all," she said. "And to be honest, it's irrelevant to what we're discussing. I'm not a historian, I'm a psychotherapist, and I want to know why you went to Damascus in the first place, Dewey."

"I already told you."

"You had no idea what Damascus would expose or where it would lead."

Dewey sat back. His face took on a cold, hard look.

Dr. Peck glanced down at her notebook.

"Islamabad. Tehran. Beijing. St. Petersburg. Damascus. All were suicide missions."

"Obviously, they weren't."

"Okay. Highly dangerous missions. Tier One exposure."

"So what. It's *my* life."

"What about the people you put at risk?"

Dewey's eyes flared with anger.

"Didn't take you guys long to go there, did it?" he said.

"What guys are you referring to?" said Peck. "I work alone. Who do you think I was referring to?"

"You know damn well who. Jessica."

Dewey shut his eyes and put a hand to his face. In that moment, he saw Jessica. She was in a white blouse, standing across the room in front of the French doors. The doors were open. A gentle wind was blowing from outside, enough to cool off the room and make her shirt ruffle as she turned to him, just as a low, faint *boom* sounded behind her. A second later, Jessica's blouse was interrupted in a splash of red.

Argentina. They'd come for him and somehow he'd let it happen. He'd let her stand there in the doors. Dewey had allowed himself to believe it was all over, that it could be over, that he could escape it all. But the sniper's bullet had awakened him forever from the crazy notion that he could ever get away from the world he lived in.

Informed choices.

Hector was right, of course, he usually was. Dewey had allowed himself to fall in love with Jessica. He'd asked her to marry him. He'd dreamed of the life that had been taken from him so long ago, the life of any man, with a home and children. The life of someone normal. It had been a choice—but it wasn't informed, as the bullet from the Chinese assassin's gun reminded him in that terrible moment.

He felt aching behind his eyes, as if he might cry.

"What is it, Dewey?" she asked gently.

"Nothing."

"Jessica?" she whispered, her eyes showing sorrow and empathy.

"Yeah."

"Killed in Argentina. She died in your arms."

He nodded.

"You blame yourself?"

Dewey opened his eyes. "Who else is there to blame?"

"The man who pulled the trigger, for one," said Peck. "Fao Bhang, who gave the order to kill you, for another."

"I put her in that position."

"Jessica Tanzer was the national security advisor," said Peck. "Before that she was head of counterterrorism at the FBI. She knew the risks."

"No, she didn't. That's a different world from the one I live in."

"You killed Fao Bhang," said Peck. "You killed his brother. That seems to mean nothing to you."

"Should it?" he said.

Dr. Peck was quiet for several moments. She opened a small notepad and scribbled a few things down.

"If you could have that moment back, that day, that trip to Argentina, would you take it?"

An angry look crossed Dewey's face. "What kind of question is that?" he snapped. "Of course I would."

"You thought you could get on a plane and go to Argentina with your fiancée and everything would be normal. Safe."

"If you're trying to make me feel bad, there's

nothing you could say to make me feel any worse than I already do. Is that what you're trying to do?"

"In a way, yes, it is," said Peck.

"Well, that's fucked-up if you ask me."

"There's something there and it's important. A desire to escape, to live a normal life, to fall in love. To have a child. Yet you can't escape."

"I can escape anytime I want."

"Can you? Can you escape the memory of watching Jessica die?"

"Leave me alone," said Dewey.

Peck nodded, leaning forward and looking at Dewey with an intense expression.

"I want to ask you about your wife, Holly?"

Dewey reacted as if he'd just been kicked in the stomach.

"No."

"She committed suicide, didn't she?"

Dewey stared hatefully at Dr. Peck. He struggled to find words.

"Do you want to leave?" she asked.

"Yes."

"Why don't you?"

"Maybe I will. And if I stay it's not because of anything you said."

She smiled. "Oh, really?"

"Yeah, really."

"What is it, then?" she asked.

"You ask a lot of questions."

"That's my job. You never dealt with your post-traumatic stress disorder, no matter what you think."

"Yes, I did."

Peck shook her head back and forth.

"No, you didn't. My guess is, you just filed it away, hid it somewhere. The problem is, it's still there—the anger, the self-hatred, the guilt—and then it becomes part of you. You want a normal life? You'll never have it, Dewey, not until you deal with the trauma you've witnessed. I barely know you, but I'd bet anything you push yourself into taking inhuman risk out of that guilt and self-hatred."

Dewey shook his head.

"You're right: you don't know me."

"I've seen it before," said Dr. Peck. "It's not exactly a suicide wish, but it's related. Why not take the risk? you say to yourself. After all, if they do get me, I deserve it."

"That's ridiculous."

"You're not even aware of it."

Dewey sat forward, a cold look on his face.

"The things I do, the things I've done, it's because I'm a soldier. You could never understand. Sitting here in your fucking office. Everything I've done is because I'm trying to protect this country."

"You do what you're told."

Dewey grinned.

"I do what I think is right."

Peck shook her head. She smiled at Dewey. She took several moments to let the tension in the room dissipate.

"I don't usually start this way," she said softly. "This is not a trial, Dewey. I'm not here to make you feel bad. I'm not a judge. I'll *never* be judgmental. I understand how to help you. How to help someone who's gone through trauma so that the rest of your life isn't just a reaction to that trauma, so that you don't spend the rest of your life trying to run from it, blaming yourself for it, taking unnecessary risks because you—"

"Don't deserve to live," he whispered.

"What did you say?"

"Nothing."

Dr. Peck stood up and walked to the window.

"Can I ask you a few more questions?" said Peck.

Dewey was quiet. He stared at the floor.

"Do you still think about her?"

"Of course."

Peck turned.

"I wasn't talking about Jessica. I want to start at the beginning. Tell me about your wife. Tell me about Holly."

Dewey involuntarily clenched his fists as another kick hit him in the stomach. He knew it would come to this, that this was where they would force him to go. Back to Holly. Back to the day he found her in their apartment near Fort Bragg.

"I won't talk about her," said Dewey. "You can't make me. You can fuck off."

"That's what it all goes back to, doesn't it?" she said from the window. "Holly. You loved her."

"I said fuck off," he whispered hoarsely, grabbing his knee and pinching his skin so hard he saw blood.

Dr. Peck walked toward Dewey and sat down across from him.

Dewey hadn't heard the word come from somebody else's mouth in so long. It was hard to remember the last time.

Holly.

The last image of her exploded in his memory. The morning he found her dead on the bedroom floor. The side of her face destroyed. A pool of crimson like a drowning pool beneath her. In her hand, his service pistol: Colt M1911A1.

Suicide.

He'd found her there after returning from a training run. He knew why that was the memory that always was the first to come into his head, and he hated it. He hated the memory. He'd long ago accepted her tragic death, just as he'd accepted their son Robbie's death six months before, from leukemia. Yes, he'd accepted it long, long ago, but he couldn't shake the memory. He tried to replace the awful picture in his head with a different one. The first time she came to visit him at Boston College. It was his freshman year. Holly was a sophomore at Bowdoin. She'd taken the bus down from Brunswick to Chestnut Hill to visit him. She was supposed to get there on a Friday night and watch the football game against Clemson the next day, but a snowstorm delayed her bus and she missed the game. Whatever frustration and anger Dewey had at Holly missing the game he'd taken out on the Clemson defensive line, rushing that Saturday for 160 yards and three touchdowns. Holly arrived after the game, as he was walking out of the stadium in his coat and tie, his hair still wet. Her long brown hair was braided in a beautiful honeycomb, and her face was red from the wind and so pretty. They were alone together, with no parents or siblings for hundreds of miles. Her smile that moment had been apologetic, conspiratorial, gleeful, and yearning.

Dewey lost himself for those few seconds, staring down at Dr. Peck's hand, but said nothing. His lips formed into the beginning of a word, a sound, but he couldn't talk.

"What are you thinking about?" she said.

But Dewey was silent.

Dr. Peck kept her hand there for a few more

moments, then sat back. She crossed her arms and looked at Dewey.

"I think that's probably enough for today," she said.

10

QUEEN STREET
TORONTO

Special Agent Sean Walsh of the Toronto Police Service steered his black Chevy Tahoe past a police barrier two blocks out from the crime scene. Queen Street was closed off. A large crowd of television reporters, cameramen, and other onlookers were gathered at the barriers.

Within the crime envelope, the area immediately surrounding where the bomb had detonated was now behind a series of stanchions and black plastic, illuminated by portable klieg lights, completely shutting off the grisly scene to anyone outside the area. Walsh drove past the bomb site and parked on the sidewalk near the mosque.

Walsh walked to the rear entrance of the mosque, cutting between several ambulances, police cruisers, sedans, and other vehicles. A team from the Toronto coroner's office was already on-site, though they, like everyone else, had not gone inside the mosque, per Walsh's adamant instructions.

At the back door of the mosque, another black plastic visual barrier had been erected. Walsh stepped through a break in the barrier. A corpse lay awkwardly on the back steps, faceup. It was a man in black tactical gear: one of the FBI agents. A mess of blood and cratered skull marred the back of the man's head.

Walsh knelt next to him and put a cell close to his face, then took several photos. Next, he took the man's right thumb and pressed it against the screen, recording his print.

Walsh looked at one of the coroners.

"I want you to get the slugs out of the bodies STAT," he said. "Do it on-site and have them couriered to ballistics. Make sure you segregate them carefully."

"Yes, sir."

Walsh stepped over the corpse and turned.

"McCarthy, follow me. Hurry up."

A younger uniformed officer trailed Walsh into the hallway, which was a miasma of dead bodies and blood-splattered walls.

"I want head shots of everyone in the hall," said Walsh. "Then get a scan of their right thumb. Make sure everything is clear. Got it?"

"Yes, sir."

Walsh stepped over a dead man to the stairs and climbed up to the second floor. At the end of the hallway he found the second pocket of carnage. He moved methodically through the room, taking photos and thumbprints of every dead man. When he was finished, he hit speed dial.

"ETF base, this is Walsh," he said as he headed for the stairs. "I need a remote upload and then I need you to get these down to FBI SIOC immediately."

Walsh went back downstairs and found McCarthy, who was taking a photo of one of the dead Arabs.

"Second floor is off-limits until the Quantico team gets here," said Walsh.

"Yes, sir."

Outside, Walsh found the lead coroner.

"You guys are clear," said Walsh, "except for the second floor. No one touches it until the FBI gets here."

Walsh walked quickly past the Tahoe to the bomb site. The cab of the truck was on its side and partially destroyed. The back of the truck—what was left of it—was still a smoking carapace of twisted metal, low to the ground, much of it either melted by the heat or burned to ash.

One of the officers approached him. "What do you want us to do?" he asked.

Walsh looked at the officer, then past him to one of the buildings behind the truck. The bottom floor had been blown in by the explosion. Broken glass was everywhere. Even windows on the second and third floors were shattered. Walsh pointed at the building.

"Let's get a TAC team in here. Quarantine the area and then do a room-by-room search of every building that had a sight line to the mosque or the truck. That means everyone in the buildings needs to be relocated. Have TAC logistics handle hotels et cetera. Put detective units at the hotels and process any witnesses."

11

CIA HEADQUARTERS
LANGLEY, VIRGINIA

Dewey climbed into a taxi outside the building.

"Langley," he said. "CIA headquarters."

At the CIA gates, Dewey did not even lower the back window, instead holding his pass against the glass. The green stripe that cut across the top of the small plastic badge told the guards: top priority figure, let him in immediately.

He entered through the main atrium and passed through two more security points, then went to the elevators. On the seventh floor, Dewey stormed off the elevator, his face red. At the armed security perimeter to the director's suite of offices, Dewey did not slow down.

Dewey moved past office after office until he

was at the end of the corridor. The walls became glass and expansive, letting in the sunlight and a view of trees in fall color. Lindsay, Calibrisi's assistant, stood up as he approached.

"Hi, Dewey," she said, a surprised look on her face. "He's with—"

Dewey swept by her and pushed in the door. Calibrisi was standing, clutching a cane. On two leather sofas sat three men, all in suits.

The room went silent. Dewey was dressed in a navy blue Lacoste polo with a slight tear at the midriff, alongside a white paint stain. He had on an old pair of jeans that made the shirt look new by comparison.

"Dewey," said Calibrisi. "Thanks for joining us."

"I need to talk to you."

"Dewey, these are the three senior members of the Senate Intelligence Committee, our oversight committee. Can this wait?"

Dewey glanced at the men.

"No."

Calibrisi turned to the three senators.

"Give me a minute," he said.

Calibrisi led Dewey down the hall to the CIA director's private office, known by only a few. He shut the door behind them.

Dewey stood, arms crossed, staring at him. After almost half a minute, Dewey looked away. He scanned the small office. One wall was books. The other was framed photos of friends and family; Vivian, Vivian and Calibrisi, Vivian, Calibrisi, and Daisy, and then mostly Daisy at every possible age, baby pictures, toddler. Fourth grader, high school, college. Near the window at the far side of the room, a large photo was in a black frame. It showed him and Jessica. They were seated next to each other at an outdoor dinner party. The photo captured the soft light of candles against the summer night. It was before they'd dated, before she'd said yes when he asked her to marry him. But he already loved her, even then.

Dewey stared at it for an extra moment. His arms relaxed and he moved them down to his side.

"What is it?"

"I saw Dr. Peck," said Dewey. "This is about Daisy, isn't it?"

Calibrisi was silent for a second or two.

"It's about you."

Calibrisi moved behind the desk. He stared at Dewey but said nothing.

"Look I get the point," said Dewey. "You think I'm reckless. You think if your daughter likes me, that I'll somehow get her killed. Is that it?"

Calibrisi paused. "Yes."

"Why don't you just forbid me from seeing her?" barked Dewey. "Or fire me?"

"Because it's your choice, Dewey, and her

choice. And I would never fire someone for dating my daughter, even someone I didn't like, and the truth is, I . . ."

Calibrisi paused.

"Well, I just think it might be time for you to consider dialing it back a little. I want you to understand the implications of the risks you take, that's all."

"What exactly does that mean?" said Dewey. "I take a desk job? Are you fucking joking? I'm not meant to sit behind a desk, Hector. You know it and I know it."

"That's why Jessica died."

"Fuck you."

"Dewey," Calibrisi said gently, "I want to know you when you're fifty. Sixty. Seventy. Strategy is just as important as tactical. Maybe more important. I'll make you a deputy director. Your office will be next to mine."

Dewey shot him a look. "Great. Can I get a foosball table too? Maybe I can get a dog and bring it to work with me."

Calibrisi grinned.

"I made my point," he said. "I can see I'm not going to talk you into a job."

"No, you're not."

Calibrisi shook his head.

"You're a stubborn son of a bitch," he said. "Fine. But until that shoulder heals you're doing light duty. The secretary of state called me this morning. He's going to Paris for secret talks with Iran and France. He'll have his State Department security team with him."

"So why are you sending me?"

"There's chatter," said Calibrisi. "He's received a number of death threats. I told him I would send someone to provide an extra layer of protection. You'll be in Paris for a day or two. You're staying at the George Cinq. Hang out, drink some wine, keep an eye on the secretary. Your plane leaves from Andrews at six A.M. tomorrow."

12

INDIAN PURCHASE FARM
POOLESVILLE, MARYLAND

An hour and a half west of Washington, D.C., a black sedan moved along a winding rural road through empty, rolling Maryland farmland. The sedan abruptly slowed and turned left, past a sign that said NO TRESPASSING.

It was Sunday afternoon, and a yellow dusk was settling in over the expansive countryside, green and brown with late autumn's cold.

The car moved down a long gravel driveway, each side lined with a white horse fence. It was a private driveway, its rustic appearance masking the fact that it was embedded with a state-of-the-art security system. The security perimeter was invisible and utilized a variety of technological defenses, including motion detection, visual spectography and, at several demarcation points beneath the surface of the mile-long road, weight sensitivity.

The vehicle passed a thick oak a quarter mile down the driveway and came to a set of steel gates. The driver pulled up to a small black screen attached to a steel pole and lowered the window. He reached out and entered a six-digit code, then stared into an ocular scanner. After a few seconds, the gates swept slowly inward. The driver hit the gas, watching in the rearview mirror as the gates shut.

Two men sat in the backseat. They didn't talk. One of them, Andrew Flaherty, was reading a document, jotting notes on it every few moments. The other man, Harry Black, the U.S. secretary of defense, stared out the window, deep in thought.

A few minutes later, the sedan came to a sprawling farmhouse. It was gray clapboard with light blue shutters, a slate roof, copper gutters, and gardens tucked perfectly across a sweeping front entrance. It was surrounded by waist-high fields that ran far into the distance.

As the sedan came to a stop in the circular driveway before the home's central portico, Flaherty looked up. He tucked the document into the leather pocket on the back of the seat in front of him. He glanced at Black and climbed out.

Black followed Flaherty toward the front door.

Flaherty was in his late fifties, bald, with a bushy mustache. Black was sixty-two, slightly overweight, with thick, black hair.

At the front door, Flaherty knocked. A few moments later, a tall, thin black man opened the door.

"Hello, Mr. Flaherty."

"Good afternoon, Abe."

The two men went inside, passing a middle-aged woman who was cleaning up dishes in the kitchen. The wife of the man Flaherty had come to see.

"Hi, Janie," he said. "How are you?"

She gave him a cold look and didn't answer. She nodded toward the back of the house, indicating that the man Flaherty had come to see—her husband—was out back.

Flaherty and Black found Bruner behind the barn, next to a large pile of wood.

Bruner was older than Flaherty by more than a decade. Yet despite his age, he was chopping wood. Bruner had on jeans and a blue-and-white flannel shirt, tucked in neatly. But even in this attire he looked distinguished.

"Lowell Trappe is dead," said Flaherty.

Bruner said nothing. He registered Black, standing near the barn. Bruner slammed the axe into a large stump and took off his work gloves.

"Were there any complications?" said Bruner.

"No," said Flaherty. "The story hasn't broken yet. The body drifted. They didn't find it until an hour ago. By all accounts it was an accidental drowning. Lynch is back in Atlanta. He'll fly to D.C. tomorrow morning."

"What about Toronto?" said Bruner, wiping sweat from his forehead.

"Flawless. Al-Amin, the forger, all of them were eliminated."

"Have you spoken to Kyrie?"

"No."

Bruner paused.

"Well, that's nothing unusual, is it?" said Bruner. "All that matters is that both operations succeeded. Let's go inside and celebrate."

Flaherty smiled nervously.

"With all due respect, Charles, I'll celebrate when we're done."

Bruner patted the diminutive Flaherty on the shoulder.

"That's your prerogative, Andrew," he said. "But I've learned you have to stop and smell the flowers along the way."

Bruner walked to the barn, where Harry Black was standing.

"Hi, Harry," said Bruner. "Thanks for coming out."

"Charles."

The three men walked to the back door of the large house.

Flaherty and Black followed Bruner to the living room, where a roaring fire crackled. The room was big, with old beams spanning the ceiling and a shiny mahogany floor, golden with age. The walls were lined with bookshelves filled with leather-bound volumes. Two large leather sofas were across from a trio of comfortable-looking, linen-covered club chairs. In the middle of the room was a tufted hassock, a few piles of books sitting on top of it.

Bruner shut the door and flipped a switch near the door whose purpose was to jam any electronic eavesdropping, either inside or outside the room.

"Whiskey, Harry?" asked Bruner as he made his way to a tray in the corner and poured himself a bourbon.

"Yes, please."

"Andrew?"

"No, thanks."

Bruner poured another bourbon and handed it to Black. Bruner sat down in the club chair closest to the fireplace. He took a sip of his bourbon, then looked at Black.

"Well?" he said.

"Last night, I authorized the deployment of eleven *Ohio*-class nuclear-powered ballistic missile submarines into the North Atlantic, Arabian Sea, and Mediterranean as part of a

Prompt Global Strike simulation exercise," said Black. "By the end of the week, the submarines will be in position to strike targets across the Middle East, Africa, and Europe as well as create a preemptive shield in the aftermath of our attack."

"How many missiles are we talking about?" asked Flaherty.

"Each submarine is equipped with twenty-four Trident D5 ballistic missiles. Each missile is carrying four individual nuclear warheads, capable of being independently targeted. That's ninety-six nukes per sub. So by week's end, we'll have more than a thousand nuclear warheads in-theater."

"One thousand fifty-six, to be exact," said Bruner.

"Correct," said Black. "Your target list, Charles, calls for a total of seven hundred and forty missiles."

"*Our* target list, Mr. Secretary."

Black shifted uncomfortably in his seat.

"Yes, of course. *Our* target list. That means the fleet will be left with about three hundred warheads to discourage any counterattacks and respond if necessary. Because London and Paris will both be hit, we certainly should expect either country to counterstrike. It will be incumbent upon us to engage in direct, high-level communications immediately after the attack with the leaders of those countries to not only explain our actions but, more important, to make very clear that any counterstrike by them will result in further damage to their countries."

"What about the targets?" said Flaherty.

"The parameters will be uploaded as part of the simulation exercise," said Black. "Once the president—the new president—orders the strike, the targeting manifest automatically assigns, programs, and targets the individual warheads."

Bruner took a sip of bourbon and smiled. "Excellent."

Black nodded. A thin sheen of perspiration was visible on his forehead. He started to say something, then retreated.

"What is it?" said Bruner.

Black stared icily at Bruner.

"It has to do with Toronto."

"What about it?"

"Federal agents were killed," said Black. "Honestly, did you authorize the killing of FBI agents, Charles? Was it really necessary? After all, we're going to wipe out most of the Muslim world in less than a week. Do we really need to draw suspicion at this hour?"

Tension filled the air. Black was visibly upset. Flaherty shifted uncomfortably in his chair. Bruner glanced at Flaherty, then moved his eyes back to Black.

"Yes, I authorized the operation," Bruner

said matter-of-factly. "There will be casualties, Harry. Innocent people will die. The agents were collateral damage. The purpose of the operation was to kill Al-Amin and anyone around him. Did the agents deserve to die? No, of course not. But then they shouldn't have been there. We shouldn't have had to go up there. The U.S. government should have done long ago what we did in Toronto. *Kill the Muslims.* If we're going to succeed in the larger objective, if we are going to *wipe Islam from the face of the earth,* we cannot think about trivial things like innocent people dying. We're on a mission. We are saving the United States of America." Bruner paused. "We're saving the world."

Black stared at Bruner as he spoke. When Bruner was done, Black looked at the fire.

"I don't give a fuck about the dead agents," said Black. "I care about getting caught. I'm sure Kyrie covered his tracks, but there are always clues left behind."

Flaherty, who was on the other sofa, across from Bruner, cleared his throat. He started to refute Black, but Bruner held up his hand, quieting him.

"Are you having second thoughts, Harry?"

Black gulped down the rest of the whiskey. He stood up and went to the bar, pouring the glass half full with bourbon.

"No," said Black. He leaned toward Bruner,

reaching out with his right hand and pointing at him, a hint of frustration on his face. "I'm the one who's been saying we need to act. I just don't see why we need to obliterate half of Europe."

Bruner stood up. Despite his age, there was speed, even strength in the way he arose from the chair. He took a menacing step toward Black, his teeth flaring.

"Don't raise your voice with me, Mr. Secretary," seethed Bruner, leaning toward him, so that their faces were just a few inches apart.

Black didn't budge.

"I'll raise my voice with whoever the hell I choose!" barked Black, taking his index finger and pressing it into Bruner's chest. "Don't forget, I'm the secretary of defense. I'm one of two people on this earth who have the Gold Codes. You seem to forget that fact! When I'm gone, it's all gone!"

The Gold Codes enabled the president of the United States to use nuclear weapons. It was the defense secretary's job to verify that the person using the codes was in fact the president. It was the president's decision to launch nuclear weapons—but the secretary of defense had to authenticate his identity.

Bruner seized Black's wrist with his right hand in the same moment he grabbed his tie with his left. In one fluid motion, Bruner twisted Black's wrist as he clutched the tie, preventing him from escaping or even falling. A dull snap echoed, though it was drowned out by Black's deep-throated scream. Bruner let him fall to the floor.

"I think we all appreciate the importance of the Gold Codes," said Bruner. He stared down at Black, who was on his knees, holding his broken wrist. "Now tell me, Harry, is that why you came out here, to remind us how important the Gold Codes are?"

"No," said Black, panting and grimacing in pain. "I came to tell you the submarines will be in place by this weekend. Every nuclear-armed submarine the U.S. has will be within firing range of the Middle East."

"Good," said Bruner. He walked to the fireplace and lifted a log, then threw it into the hearth. He grabbed a long iron poker and pushed the log farther into the fire.

A door at the end of the room opened. Two large men entered.

Bruner turned and looked at them.

"Take Mr. Black to the basement," said Bruner. "Put a cast on his wrist. Remove his cell phone and any other devices on his person."

The men lifted Black, grasping his arms. Flaherty went to him and patted him down, finding a small, thick plastic case. Bruner nodded to the guards, who dragged Black from the room.

"Only I know the codes," groaned Black as he was pulled through the door.

"We know, Harry," said Bruner.

When he was gone, Bruner looked to Flaherty, who had a fearful look on his face.

"What's wrong, Andrew?"

"Noth . . . ah . . . nothing," he replied meekly.

"Are you getting nervous?" said Bruner.

"Maybe a little," said Flaherty.

"You should be nervous," said Bruner. "Personally, I give it a one-in-three chance of succeeding." A maniacal smile crept across his lips. "Then again, with Lowell Trappe dead and the nuclear codes in hand, perhaps it's now closer to fifty-fifty."

13

FACILITÉ AU PLEIN-DU-MONTS
LAUTERBRUNNEN, SWITZERLAND

Romy clutched the knife in her left hand, behind her back, keeping the blade tucked inside the sleeve of the straitjacket. The sharp edge of the steel pressed uncomfortably against her skin.

It wasn't actually a knife, but she had to *believe* it was a knife. It was a spoon. A spoon she'd scraped to a dangerously sharp point. For the two hours each day she was allowed out of the straitjacket, she would sit on the ceramic toilet in her cell. She found the small aperture in the underside of the toilet one day and the idea had come to her. A day later she'd taken the spoon from Dr. Courtemanche's desk. Every day since, she sat and slowly scraped the spoon against the concrete wall until it became a weapon.

Your husband is a monster.

Romy knew that now, but had she known it earlier? Had she known what he was capable of?

She closed her eyes, pretending to be asleep. She could hear the soft footsteps of the orderlies as they moved down the rubber-floored hallway of the sanitarium.

For strength, she forced herself to remember the phone call. The one she'd accidentally overheard that day. The one that changed everything.

She'd heard the phone ringing while drying the lavender. She picked up the extension in the greenhouse and heard her husband, Kyrie. At that point, she should've hung up. Why didn't she? Now she was the only one who could stop him, stop the man with the deep voice named Charles.

"Good afternoon, Kyrie."

"Hello, Charles."

"Are you alone?"

"Yes, Romy is out gardening."

"The arrangements for your flight to Toronto are complete, Kyrie. You'll fly under a Consular Operations passport from Stuttgart to Montreal, then move by train. A new set of papers is in the locker at Stuttgart."

"Fine."

"The American students will arrive sometime next week. The FBI knows this and will arrest them. You must be in place before they move in."

"Of course."

Romy sobbed as she replayed the memory, remembering that at this point in the conversation her heart had leapt. For a second she'd actually thought Kyrie was being summoned to Toronto to save the American students.

It was the last innocent thought she would ever have on this earth.

"This time, don't make the same mistake you made in Johannesburg."

"I don't make mistakes. There were children in Johannesburg."

"There can be no witnesses. Every human being in the mosque must die, Kyrie! We're at war."

"I don't kill children."

"You kill whoever is in the mosque. Do you understand?"

"Yes."

I suppose I can find solace in the fact that he doesn't kill children, she thought bitterly. *At least not until someone orders him to.*

The footsteps outside the door grew louder. She heard the orderly fumbling with the keychain, the telltale jingling.

"We're so close now, Kyrie. The Speaker of the House will die this weekend. Toronto will distract the FBI. It must be flawless. Brutal."

"Who will kill him?"

"Lynch. And when Congressman Largent takes his place, we will initiate the final act. The vice president and the president of the United States will be assassinated on Friday. The shadow government will take power. The course of human history will change once and for all and we will reassert America's true agenda."

"I think I hear Romy."

"Ah, yes, Romy. That reminds me, Kyrie. You've had your fun with her, but it's time that we tie off loose ends. It's time to put her down . . ."

The white van had arrived within minutes.

The door to her cell suddenly opened.

"*Bonjour, patiente quatre neuf un trois,*" said the white-suited guard. "*Êtes-vous prêt à vivre un autre jour?*"

Hello, patient four nine one three. Are you ready to live another day?

Romy felt the guard's clammy hands against her wrists as he fumbled with the leather straps that kept them bound tight against her back.

Please don't search. Please, please don't feel the front of my wrist . . .

The orderly's hands on her breasts, then her torso, and finally her crotch, pretending to search her.

"*Elle se mouille à nouveau,*" said the orderly to the man at the door. "*Mettez-le dans le rapport. Ils ont besoin d'abaisser la dose de prochlorpérazine.*"

She wet herself again. Put it in the report. They need to lower the dose of the prochlorperazine.

As much as she hated her husband, she hated this pig of a man even more. She stared blankly into his green eyes, one of which blinked rapidly, a tic.

"*Qu'est-ce que vous faisiez avant de vous rendre fou?*" he whispered as he finished unzipping the straitjacket and freeing her hands. "*J'aimerais savoir. Tu es si belle, il me donne envie de fuir avec vous.*"

What were you like before you went insane? I would like to know. You're so beautiful, it makes me want to run away with you.

"*Je voudrais que*," Romy whispered back.

I would like that.

The orderly's eyes appeared momentarily surprised at her first words since arriving at the sanitarium, even more at their meaning. It was at this moment that she pulled the end of the knife from her left wrist and slashed the blade into the man's neck, puncturing skin and cartilage, and ripping the blade violently through the carotid artery before he could react. Crimson flooded out of the gash as the orderly reached with both hands for his neck, his eyes wide with terror as he dropped to his knees and she pulled the blade out.

The other orderly dropped his clipboard and turned to run. Leaping, she cleaved him halfway down his back, the blade gashing a deep hole through his uniform, into his spine, just above his waist. He tumbled to the ground, letting out a pained moan. Before he could scream, she pulled the knife out and, gripping his hair, slashed it slowly across his neck.

Romy looked around. The sanitarium hallway was eerily quiet. The doors to the other cells were shut, the only adornment the red lights above each door indicating that it was locked.

She pulled the orderly from the hallway into her

room, next to the first man, and wiped her hands on his white pants, to get as much of the blood off as she could. A pool of blood had spread and was growing quickly. She stepped into the hall and pulled the door shut, locking it and watching as the red light came on.

There were doors on either end of the hallway. The one to the right led to the central part of the sanitarium. The other door was Dr. Courtemanche's office.

He had to be in there. He *needed* to be in there, or else . . . or else it was all for naught.

Three knocks. It was what the orderlies did when they brought her.

"What is it? I am with a patient."

Her heart raced as she knocked again.

There were footsteps and then the turning of the doorknob. The door went ajar, a small crack emerged, then Romy leaned back and slammed her foot into the middle of the door, kicking as hard as she could. The door struck Courtemanche in the face, knocking him down, a pained yelp his only noise.

She charged into the room and dived down upon him, slashing his chest with the knife as he yelled and tried to push her off. The blade cut through Courtemanche's shirt and perforated several inches deep, directly into his heart. She stared in horror as his eyes bulged, shocked at what she was capable of, of how easily the blade had severed down through his chest. Blood gushed from his chest in an abrupt hiccup. Romy felt it all over her fingers and hands.

Something caught her attention—she swiveled her head, nearly yelling when she saw a man on Courtemanche's leather couch. He was in a straitjacket, lying down. It was a patient. He was old, with long gray hair. He stared at Romy with insane eyes.

Slowly, her eyes glued to the witness, Romy stood up.

"Don't say or do anything," she whispered.

"Are you the bird lady?" he asked.

Romy went to the office door, locking it. She knelt next to Courtemanche and wiped her hands on his shirt. She rifled through his pockets, removing a large wad of cash, then searched his desk, finding a cell phone, a credit card, and more cash. A pair of sunglasses were on the desk, and she took those too. In the closet, she found a black trench coat and a rain hat.

She glanced one more time at the man on the sofa. His eyes were affixed to Courtemanche, who stared blankly up at the ceiling, his shirt a red riot of wet blood.

Romy opened the window. It was the second floor. She could see the woods of the nature reserve in the distance. She climbed to the windowsill and leaned out, looking left and right and above. She saw no one.

She climbed backward out the window, holding on to the sill, and let herself drop so that, for a brief moment, she was holding on to the sill and dangling. A second later, she let go. She landed on the grass and, without looking back, fell into a desperate run for the woods.

14

NSA
SIGNALS INTELLIGENCE DIRECTORATE
FORT MEADE, MARYLAND

Samantha stared at the computer screen. It displayed a series of four rectangular digital charts in bright white, crossed by bright green wavy lines that zigzagged every few seconds. The four graphs represented signals frequency activity that had occurred during a seventeen-minute period of time in Toronto.

Samantha had isolated the tight geography around the mosque as well as the specific time and run both through a gamut of NSA appliances and software applications that had cataloged the signals activity: every audio, visual, and other electronic activity in and around Toronto involving the FBI agents as well as Al-Amin and anyone in his vicinity. She wasn't looking for the content of the actual conversations. Rather, she was trying to understand the seventeen minutes in terms of the hundreds of frequencies transmitted in order to isolate anomalies.

Samantha had already studied the encryption layer the FBI had used for its in-theater communication. The encryption had held, and Samantha was able to dismiss one possible way the operation might have been compromised. Nobody had hacked into the FBI commo and used it as a road map to penetrate the live operation.

The signals analysis, like the encrypted layer analysis, was designed to weed out possibilities. Much of Samantha's work was exactly that, crossing things off a list until, hopefully, one possibility remained.

Suddenly, her computer pinged loudly. She scanned all four graphs. It was the graph in the lower-right-hand corner. She double-clicked it. It was an obscure application that tracked ultra-high-frequency communications, capturing phone calls made through telecommunications satellites, high-altitude devices rotating in outer space. She assumed Al-Amin didn't have one, and she knew the FBI agents didn't. Yet at the nine-minute mark of the seventeen-minute time span, the graph showed a sudden and sharp spike in a particularly high frequency. Samantha clicked on the long digital registration number and studied it, looking for certain digits that would place the ownership of the satellite. The number wasn't familiar. She pinged the number against a decryption engine and then through a series of directories, looking for a match against any new, unknown, or supposedly obsolete devices. The analysis came back empty. It wasn't that the device was off-grid—that happened all the time. It was the frequency itself. It was as if it had been used for the first time.

Without moving her eyes from the graph, she hit her phone.

"June," came the voice.

"You still here?" Samantha asked.

"Yes."

"I have something."

June hung up the phone and started to leave his office when his eyes caught a photo taped to the wall above his desk. It was a photo of his younger brother, Diego. A sad look settled over June's face.

June was all too familiar with the spectacle of Islamic radicals—terrorists—recruiting young Americans to do their dirty work.

Diego had run away from home and joined Al Qaeda in 2006. June hadn't seen it coming, perhaps because, at the time, he was in Iraq, running communications systems for the Pentagon, learning his tradecraft. Six weeks after arriving in Iraq, Diego had been killed by a smart bomb on a dry plain outside Rawah.

At the time, June was in Baghdad. He could've gone and seen his brother's body, but he didn't, afraid of making people higher up realize he was related to a terrorist. Every night, for many years afterward, June clutched a photo of Diego as he went to bed, muttering tearful apologies to the brother he didn't have the patience to understand or the courage to say good-bye to as he lay dead on a steel platform in a makeshift American morgue.

Toronto had meaning for June. Diego had been one of these boys fooled by the Muslim charlatans. He wanted to know what happened, how it ended. He wanted to understand the boys who'd driven up there and to see who prevented the FBI from finally catching one of the criminals who killed his brother. Al-Amin may not have pulled the trigger. He may not have even been the one who recruited him. But someone like Al-Amin had. June wanted to find out who destroyed the operation.

He walked to the central SID operations room.

"Tell me you found something," he said to Samantha.

"I might have. I was looking at spikes around certain types of frequencies. If there were no unusual spikes around certain frequencies, then we eliminated them."

"Okay."

"But if there was something, it might indicate

unusual activity." Samantha pointed to a chart in the lower right-hand corner.

The chart would have been incomprehensible to almost every person on earth—but not to June. It translated frequency transmissions into a visual spectrograph. The various lines and colors represented SIGINT activity: cell phones, TV, credit cards, anything that emitted electronic signals. The chart indicated there was a problem.

June leaned forward and stared at what appeared to be nothing more than a long V-shaped squiggly line.

"What is it? I've never seen that kind of beta."

"It's superhigh frequency," said Samantha. "Something occurred at the nine-minute mark that absolutely spiked the tracker. This is a military-grade signal, Jesus. We're talking beefed-out SAT phones. If I went off the grid, this is how I'd do it. This is very advanced technology. I didn't expect it to pop, but nine minutes into the Toronto operation, someone made a call using a SAT phone on an uncharted frequency. *Their own frequency.* Their own satellite."

June nodded, thinking.

"What about the FBI?"

"No, I checked," said Samantha. "They weren't using SATs. It was closed loop, operating theater and a hub. Nobody in the mosque had a SAT phone. I thought it might be Canadian Intelligence, but it's not, at least not anything I've ever seen. It's not Iridium or any other network. It's not us, and it's not Langley either. I ran it against NSA Knowledge Base. It's got a different frequency from anything we've seen before. Higher. It's like it's no one. Whoever it is has their own satellite and, more important, their own frequency, a frequency that up until ten minutes ago was unknown."

June's eyes met Samantha's.

"What do you think it means?" she asked.

"It means someone we don't know was in Toronto that night. Inside the theater of operation. Someone with a highly sophisticated, military-grade communications capability set. We're talking about a satellite as powerful as COMSTAR."

June paused, deep in thought. "Is there any way to know who owns the phone?" he asked.

"No."

"Keep digging," he said, turning for the door. He stopped as he was about to leave. "And Samantha?"

"Yeah."

"Don't share this with SIOC. Until we know whose satellite that is, I want to run this quietly. I need to talk to Jim."

When June got back to his desk, an icon on one of his screens was flashing. It was a priority message from McNaughton at SIOC. He clicked it and the screen tiled with photos of the dead men from Toronto as well as thumbprint scans. Typing quickly, June entered a series of NSA applications, including DS-300, Stellar Wind, and PRISM. Each application did different things, though all fell under the general rubric of surveillance and data collection. DS-300 aggregated massive amounts of Internet traffic, storing it, then running sophisticated algorithms against it to mine out relevant activity. PRISM did something similar, but with the ability to capture stored and historical data, a massive trove of information collected from at least nine major U.S. Internet companies. Stellar Wind mined similar forms of electronic activity, such as cell phone calls, financial transactions, and e-mail.

June mirrored each individual program onto its own screen so he could monitor them separately. When he was finished provisioning the photos and thumbprints, he walked down the hallway to the office of his boss, Jim Bruckheimer, the head of SID.

Bruckheimer was on the phone. He held up a finger.

"Hold on, Ken," he said, covering the phone. He looked at June. "What's up?"

"I need permission to appropriate one of the primary satellites."

"Why?"

"I need to take some pictures."

15

4436 PARKRIDGE BOULEVARD
RESTON, VIRGINIA

Hundreds of sleek but nondescript brick-and-glass office buildings scattered concentrically out from Washington, D.C., in cities like Vienna, McLean, Alexandria, Arlington, and Reston. The buildings housed software companies, defense contractors, lobbyists, banks, investment firms, political consultants, hedge funds, law firms, think tanks, newspapers, start-ups, nonprofits, and an endless array of other enterprises, most with some connection to government.

One of them, a seven-story rectangular brick-and-glass office building along Parkridge Boulevard in Reston, looked like all the others. It was anonymous-looking—austere, modern, clean, secure, boring. The building's glass was a forbidding dark blue, impossible to see into. Its bricks were light gray. It didn't stand out at all, and that was the point.

A plastic key was required to get into the lobby. Inside, there were four elevators and two sets of stairs. In order to access any of them, it was necessary to place one's right hand on a scanner, which analyzed and matched fingerprints against a database.

All of the floors of the building were empty except the fifth.

To access the fifth floor, all entrants had to look into an ocular scanner.

Eighty-four individuals were authorized to enter.

A thin mesh of copper, almost invisible to the naked eye, lined every square inch of the building's windows, walls, ceilings, and floors. This prevented electronic eavesdropping.

The fifth floor was quiet. Offices and conference rooms lined the outer walls. All work was done on computers that remained in the building. There were no printers. Paper of any variety was strictly prohibited.

A windowless room near the center of the floor held a state-of-the-art communications center. It was modeled on the White House Situation Room, with a large conference table and walls covered with plasma screens.

Every seat at the long table was filled with men, most in dark suits, a few in military uniforms. There were twenty-four. One man, Kopitar, sat at the far end, a laptop in front of him. Kopitar was overweight, with a long beard and shaved head. He wore jeans and a ratty-looking rugby shirt. It was Kopitar who controlled the various photos, blueprints, and videos that populated the plasma screens along the walls.

The briefing had been going on for more than an hour. Flaherty held the floor.

"What do we know about the vice president's schedule?" he asked.

Flaherty slid the laser pointer across the table to a burly-looking man with black hair and a thick mustache. This was Hooley.

"Thanks, Andrew," said Hooley. He pointed at a screen on the wall behind Flaherty, which lit up. It showed a map of the Hawaiian Islands. Hooley drew a red circle on the screen with the laser.

"The vice president is leaving with his family on vacation Thursday," said Hooley. "He'll be spending five days on the Big Island, here, near Kona. As you might expect, the compound will be heavily fortified, so trying to do anything on the island will be challenging. We've anticipated a western flight path toward the airport and have positioned a team of men here." Hooley pointed to a small dot on the screen. "It's an island about ten miles offshore. The team will employ surface-to-air missiles to take down the vice president's plane."

"As you know, Jim, the timing of this is incredibly important," said Paul Hochman, an older man with short brown hair and glasses. "The death of the vice president must occur *after* Dellenbaugh is assassinated. If it happens beforehand, Dellenbaugh will be locked down."

"Actually, the two deaths must be virtually simultaneous," said Bruner, speaking for the first time. "The same dynamic will exist if President Dellenbaugh is killed before Donato."

Kopitar cleared his throat. "There will be very tight communications protocols between the men in Hawaii and the gunmen at the stadium," he said. "In addition, the team in Hawaii will be in possession of a variety of radio frequency jamming devices, all state-of-the-art. We'll be able to disrupt the communications systems aboard Air Force Two across a period of approximately one to two minutes."

"Finally, FedEx Field," said Flaherty. "Carey?"

A younger-looking man with receding blond hair took the laser pointer. Carey Price pointed it at a screen just over his shoulder. The screen showed a three-dimensional blueprint of FedEx Field, outside Washington, D.C., home field of the Washington Redskins.

"The president will be announcing reelection at approximately twelve fifteen," said Price. "We'll stage two snipers at FedEx tomorrow, embedded long enough to establish points of fire and stow the necessary materials in order to then withstand pre-event scanning, dogs, and other measures that will begin Thursday morning. The gunmen will enter with the crowd on the morning of the announcement and establish position during the event."

A door behind Bruner opened.

"Mr. Bruner," said Benedetti, a tall man in a dark sweater and khakis.

Bruner stood up, eyeing Flaherty as he did so. Flaherty stood and started toward the door.

"Please excuse us," Bruner said to the table.

Bruner stepped outside, shutting the door behind him. Flaherty and Benedetti were waiting.

"I received a call from the sanitarium," said Benedetti quietly. "Romy escaped last night. She's missing."

"What do you mean?" asked Flaherty. "How could she? There's no way."

"She killed Dr. Courtemanche and two orderlies," said Benedetti.

"Where is Kyrie?" said Bruner. "He was supposed to come here directly from Toronto."

"He's not answering calls," said Flaherty. "At least not mine."

Bruner took out his cell.

"Finish the meeting," he said to Flaherty as he dialed. He held the cell to his ear. "She'll need money. Have Kopitar track Courtemanche's credit cards and cell phones. In the meantime, send a team into the theater. When they find her, they can kill her."

16

HÔTEL DE PARIS MONTE-CARLO MONACO

Kyrie's cell vibrated on the credenza. He crawled out of bed and grabbed the phone.

"Hello?"

"Where are you?" said Bruner.

"None of your business."

"I told you to come to Washington."

"I didn't feel like it," said Kyrie. "You don't tell me what to do. You might have everyone else drinking your Kool-Aid, but not me."

"We want the same thing, Kyrie."

"The same thing?"

"A world without Muslims."

Kyrie walked out onto the terrace and stared at the glittering Monaco skyline. Then he went into the kitchen, picking up a bottle of vodka from the counter and taking a large chug. He was bare chested. His muscles were defined, his biceps round and large, his chest thick. He'd been drinking, but he wasn't drunk. Instead, he looked morose, even angry.

"You just had to take her, didn't you?" shouted Kyrie. "It's all about control with you, isn't it, Charles? You just had to take her."

There was a long silence.

"That's why I'm calling," said Bruner. "Romy escaped from the sanitarium. She killed three people. She's on the run. I'm going to ask you this again, Kyrie: Did she overhear our conversation?"

Back out on the terrace, Kyrie dropped the bottle. It shattered, with several pieces of glass tumbling beneath the railing and falling to the ground seven floors below. He moved back inside the hotel suite.

"Why?" he demanded.

"Answer me!" snarled Bruner. "Did she overhear our conversation?"

"Why are you so concerned?" said Kyrie.

"You know why. If she heard us, she could tell someone. Now answer me. *Now!*"

Kyrie shut his eyes, trying to block out the thought of Romy. He didn't answer Bruner.

"I'm going to have Vincent and Knox kill her," said Bruner. "You're too close, Kyrie. You worry me."

"It's not your decision, Charles. She's my wife. I'll kill her."

"Are you questioning my authority?"

"Let me play this out for you," said Kyrie. "If either of those pigs touches her, not only will it be the last thing they do that doesn't involve having their brains blown out, then I'll come for you and your wife. Maybe I'll kill her as you watch. I told you this when we started. We're partners. Don't *ever* fuck with me."

"Since you put it that way," said Bruner quietly.

"You pushed the issue," said Kyrie. "I don't ask for a lot. I do what needs to be done. But on this issue, I'm adamant."

"If you had just done what needed to be done ten years ago," said Bruner, "we wouldn't be in this predicament."

"Why was it that my wife had to die and yours didn't?"

"She wasn't your wife at the time. She wasn't even your fiancée. You knew what we were planning. It was your idea. The operators were to have no attachments! No families! Those were the rules. You wrote them yourself."

Kyrie was quiet for a few moments. "Can Kopitar find her?"

"He's working on it."

"Tell him to get me the tracking information as soon as possible."

"Kyrie, it must be done. No hiding her. No house on some island somewhere. She knows too much."

"I meant what I said, Charles. If anyone lays a finger on Romy, all I can say is, may God help you."

17

CIA HEADQUARTERS
LANGLEY

Dewey took an elevator to the basement level of the building. He walked along an empty corridor to a large black steel door. Next to the door, embedded into the wall, was an ocular scanner. He stood in front of it until the glass lit up. A moment later, there was a click and the door opened.

This was the entrance to a massive suite of conference rooms, offices, training areas, and athletic facilities that belonged to the CIA's Special Operations Group, or SOG, the paramilitary arm of the Agency's Special Activities Division. SOG was responsible for operations that included high-threat military and covert operations, often run in coordination with U.S. Special Forces. Usually, SOG ran operations the government didn't want to be officially associated with.

SOG employed a handful of strategists, logistics coordinators, and mission designers, but most of its people were operators. Of these, all were male and all were culled exclusively from Special Forces units, including Delta Force,

DEVGRU, Force Recon, 24th STS, Green Berets, and Rangers. There were 240 operators inside CIA paramilitary. Thirty were classified as nonofficial cover, or NOC. NOCs didn't carry any objects or clothing that could associate them with the U.S. government and if compromised during a mission were usually on their own, with the Agency and government denying any connection. While SOG recruited operators of the highest caliber, NOCs were a breed apart, men willing to step into foreign countries without any safety net. Only a handful of individuals inside the Agency knew who the NOCs were. Dewey was classified as a nonofficial cover—Tier 1, one of only four given this top designation. Only CIA director Hector Calibrisi and Bill Polk, the head of the Directorate of Operations, commonly referred to as the National Clandestine Service, knew who the four Tier 1s were.

Dewey rarely stepped foot inside SOG's basement. Offices filled one side of the facility. Every office was occupied by an individual wearing a headset, staring at a computer screen. Dewey knew how vitally important they were to the successful planning and management of covert operations all over the world, but seeing them at their desks and workstations gave him an anxious, slightly nauseous feeling. This was what Calibrisi wanted for him. Paris, he guessed, was just the beginning. An easy trip—part of an official delegation—with little responsibility and even less risk.

Had he been one of these desk jockeys two years ago, Jessica would still be alive.

Dewey walked down the brightly lit corridor, passing a spacious sunken gymnasium at least three stories tall, with a suspended track, where dozens of people were working out. Dewey went around the corner, entering a large locker room with carpeted floors. The wooden locker doors each had a brass nameplate. It resembled a locker room at an exclusive country club, though instead of wrinkled old men in bright green golf pants, this room was filled with men who were ripped in muscles, most in their late twenties and early thirties. Dewey walked over to his locker. He didn't recognize any of the men who were there, and no one looked up when he passed.

The lockers themselves were also oversized, about three feet wide, and deep. Inside his locker, shoes and tactical boots sat on the bottom shelf. Several pairs of jeans, tactical pants, T-shirts, and tactical shirts were neatly folded on the next shelf. Above were a variety of tactical jackets and weapons vests, along with a few holsters. The next shelf up held a safe, accessible with a thumbprint. Dewey opened the safe. Inside was a trove of identification for use overseas, all of it counterfeit, including passports, visas, and other documents. The safe also contained stacks of currency—all of it U.S.—along with dozens of credit cards.

Above the safe, at eye level, was a wall of handguns and knives, neatly arranged. While the SOG facility had two entire rooms filled with weapons, each operator liked to keep a few of his own inside his locker. Magazines filled the top shelf.

Dewey put on a leather shoulder holster. He took a Colt M1911A1 .45-caliber semiautomatic from the weapons shelf and tucked it beneath his left armpit. He grabbed as many mags as he could carry and shut the locker.

Dewey walked to the pool area and to a door at the far end. He heard the sound of gunfire in low, dull thumps through the thick walls. He pushed open the steel door and entered the firing range.

There were twenty carrels in all, half of which were occupied. Dewey went to the farthest one. He stuck in earplugs and put on specialized noise-tampering earmuffs. He hit a button at the side of the carrel, moving the target back until it was a hundred yards away. He took the pistol from its holster, slammed in a mag, then took aim at a target. Then Dewey triggered the .45, firing seven bullets in rapid succession. With each bullet, Dewey felt an electric shock run up his arm, like a kick, stinging his injured shoulder. But he kept firing. When the mag was spent, he hit the button on the side of the carrel and the paper target moved toward him. Dewey stared at it for several moments. He'd fired seven bullets but could see only one hole in the paper.

With each mag, his shooting improved as he learned to overcompensate for the kick his injury was causing. After six mags, Dewey stopped. He looked around, seeing if anyone was looking, then winced. He pulled back the collar of his shirt so that he could look down at the scar on the right side of his chest. It was irritated and red. Several small trickles of blood were oozing out from the edges of the scab.

Dewey eventually moved the target out to two hundred yards. For the next several hours, he fired a total of one hundred magazines, fifty with his left hand, fifty with his right.

Dewey was an excellent marksman—because he understood the importance of never assuming his skills. He practiced. More important, when an unforeseen factor potentially affected his ability, such as the still painful knife wound in his chest, he worked to understand it and how it affected him.

The last two targets demonstrated the importance of practice. The last mag fired with his left hand showed two bullet holes where the silhouette's eyes were, a hole in the forehead, one in the neck, one in the center of the chest, and a hole through each shoulder. The last mag with his strong arm—his right—showed only one hole. It sat in the center of the target's forehead. It was bigger than a single hole, as if more than one bullet had passed through. In fact, all seven had.

Back at his locker, he stripped off his polo shirt and threw it away. He took a shower, got dressed, then packed up a small duffel bag to take with him to Paris. As he left the locker room, he glanced at a clock on the wall. It was midnight.

A black Agency sedan dropped Dewey at the corner of Queen and North Royal in Old Town, Alexandria, Virginia. The usually busy streets of one of the prettiest towns in the world were empty. Cars were parked for the night. Lights in the gorgeous, historic town houses were for the most part shut off.

Dewey walked along North Royal until he came to a brick town house with a bright yellow door. A gas lantern affixed to the edifice burned softly next to the door. Dewey glanced at himself in the glass. His hair was still wet. He ran his fingers back through it, then rang the doorbell. He stood for more than a minute until, finally, he saw a light go on somewhere inside. He heard footsteps on the stairs, then the entrance hall lights came on. A figure appeared. It was a woman. She was wearing a dark blue Northwestern long-sleeve T-shirt that came down to the tops of her thighs. She had long brown hair. She walked slowly to the door, a sleepy look on her face. She looked, vaguely, like a movie star, voluptuous and innocent at the same time. She stood behind the door and stared out at Dewey. After a few seconds, she opened the door.

Daisy said nothing. Her expression remained stone. Dewey looked at her for a dozen seconds and then a dozen more. He wanted to say something, but instead he remained quiet and still. Daisy stepped forward and stood on the step above him, so that their eyes were across from each other. He reached out and took her hands.

"Hi," said Dewey.

"I already told you," Daisy whispered, her lips moving closer to his, "I don't need a set of encyclopedias."

18

LA MOTEL DES DEUX FENÊTRES
DIJON, FRANCE

The semitruck rumbled along the rain-crossed highway, its windshield wipers sloshing away the water as fast as they could move, which wasn't fast enough. It was nighttime—or, more accurately, early morning. Very early.

In the distance, a few hundred feet off the

highway, she could see the blinking neon sign of the motel.

"*Ici, monsieur,*" she said to the driver.

"*Oui? Vous-etes positif?*"

"*Oui.*"

The semi slowed down along the side of the two-lane road, and Romy climbed down from the passenger seat.

"*Merci, monsieur,*" she said to the driver before shutting the door.

She'd run for nearly ten miles through the deep woods that ran south from the sanitarium, finally collapsing beneath a copse of wild blueberries. She slept for an hour and then kept moving, walking several miles to Chevenoz, avoiding roads, looking out for people, climbing through the steep hills that led to the small village, where she'd hid behind a church until a truck driver stopped to buy gas next door.

It had been dusk when she approached him at the pumps.

"My car has broken down and I am trying to get to Paris. I have money, monsieur."

"I'm driving as far as Dijon. I can take you there."

The drive had taken nine hours, through the late evening, past midnight, and now dawn approached. The truck driver was an older man, in his fifties, who rambled on for several hours about politics. Finally he put on the radio, a replay of a football match between Lyons and Paris, and then, when that was over, the news. Romy listened to the radio to see if there was any mention of the murders. There was not. Would there be? It was a private hospital, the best, she'd been told by Dr. Courtemanche. A triple homicide would not be good for business. Yes, she was sure they would keep it quiet, at least long enough for her to get away.

She tried not to think about the horrible crimes she'd committed. Unconsciously, she rubbed her hands on the seat, as if they were still covered in blood. The only way to rid her mind of the terrible thoughts and guilt was to think about her husband, Kyrie. That was even worse.

Your husband is a monster.

Who was he speaking to? Who is Charles?

She searched her memory for anyone named Charles.

Were they serious? Had she really heard them discuss killing these people? The president of the United States?

You must tell someone.

But who could she tell? He worked for the government. Anyone she told wouldn't believe her. They would simply ask Kyrie himself.

"She's insane," he would say. "I had to put her in an institution."

And then they would find out what she'd done.

There was nobody she could tell. Even if she did know someone, she had no proof.

The driver stopped at the outskirts of the commercial area. She climbed out of the cab, muttering "*Merci*" as she stepped onto the shoulder of the empty road.

She walked in the dark gray dawn off the highway as the rain continued to fall. She came to a clean-looking motel, but the lobby door was locked. She kept walking, hiding when she saw oncoming lights from a vehicle. The gray of dawn had changed to light yellow, though it was cloudy and shrouded in miserable fog. After a few miles of walking, she came to another motel, a seedy place, but it was open. A small, grubby ATM was in the lobby. She used Courtemanche's credit card and withdrew €500, then got a room.

In her room, she dialed the only person who she knew would believe her, a woman who might be able to help.

The phone rang. A woman answered. Romy's heart raced, and she felt warmth.

"Hello?" came the woman's voice. She was older now; her voice was fragile and soft with age.

Romy had met Hillary Bartholomew walking one day in the small hamlet where she and Kyrie lived. Hillary was a professor in the United States who owned the adjoining farm, where she came every year for the summer. She and Romy became very close, but the day came when Bartholomew was too old to travel overseas, and she sold the estate to a British couple.

"Hillary, it's Romy Banker. Do you remember me? From Ruswil."

There was a long moment of silence. "Romy?"

"Yes, Hillary."

"Oh, my gosh, Romy! How could I be so forgetful?"

Romy started to cry.

"Dear girl, what's wrong? It's been so long. How are you? Is everything all right?"

"No," said Romy, as tears coursed down her cheeks.

"How is your husband? The great soldier. I can never remember his name."

"Kyrie."

"Yes, that's it. Kyrie. Are you calling from Ruswil?"

"No, I'm in . . . in . . ." Something told her not to say more than she had to. "I'm sorry for calling. I'm sorry for losing touch. I'm sorry for so many things. Most of all I'm sorry for what I've done, for the man . . . the monster I married."

"*Monster?* What are you talking about?"

"I need your help."

"Sweet, beautiful Romy. I don't know what I can do, but if there's anything, you know I'm here. Do you need money?"

"No. I need . . . I need you to listen to me. To believe me."

Romy told her everything that happened, everything she heard, even what she'd done at the sanitarium. Everything. She spoke for nearly an hour. When she was done, Professor Hillary Bartholomew, retired professor of Asian Studies at Harvard University, was silent.

"Do you believe me, Hillary?"

The phone remained quiet.

"I don't know what to say. It's all so unbelievable, and now a phone call from someone I haven't spoken to in years. These men are so well protected. I don't think you need to worry. Nobody could just walk up and kill the president of the United States, or the vice president, or even the Speaker of the House, much less all three. Oh, dear, what *has* happened to you? What did you say the name of the institution was where you were staying? Where are you calling me from? I have friends in Paris. I think you need help. I say that as someone who cares about you. Romy, please let me send someone for you . . ."

Romy quickly hung up and stood in the small, musty-smelling motel room staring at the phone. She felt her legs become weak and then she fainted.

19

NSA
SIGNALS INTELLIGENCE DIRECTORATE

With the assistance of an NSA satellite expert, June was soon able to track the precise use of the rogue satellite. The high-frequency signals being generated by the satellite were indeed heretofore unseen, but it didn't mean they were new. Only that they were of a specific wavelength and telemetry not commercially available and, up to now, unknown to the NSA.

That was of little help in determining the owners of the satellite. In order to do this, June would have to use a little advanced geometric theory called triangulation. To see activity running through the device in real time, all he needed was for three activities to occur simultaneously. This would enable him to pinpoint the location of the satellite. If he was then able to photograph the device with one of NSA's own satellites, capable of reading a fingerprint from outer space, he could, in theory, get a photo of the satellite's serial number. The frequency may have been novel, but June knew that there was no way to avoid certain such identification markings—unless its owner also happened to be able to manufacture, and launch, its own satellites. Only the Chinese and Russian governments had this capability.

The challenge June faced was twofold. Not only did he need three phone calls or other transmissions to be crossing the satellite during the same period of time, he needed them to continue long enough for the NSA satellite to lock on to the location and start "filming." Depending on the location of the satellite and the speed at which it was traveling, this moving and retargeting by the NSA computers could take as little as one minute and as long as five.

Thus far, June had spent several hours waiting.

The mystery satellite sat unused. It was, he assumed, used by a very small group of people. There were many times when one instance of activity—a phone call, for example—occurred. A few times there were two calls. There had been seven instances in which three transmissions were on simultaneously. But they weren't long enough for June to triangulate the satellite.

The eighth time, he finally got lucky. He was able to successfully locate the satellite. It was orbiting at twenty-two thousand miles above the Indian Ocean. Two powerful NSA satellites snapped thousands of photos per second, until one particular photo captured the small manufacturer's serial number on one side of it. Once this occurred, June quickly determined that the satellite was a Lockheed Martin A2100X, built in 1982 and launched into geostationary orbit in 1994. Furthermore, he was able to determine that the device was owned jointly by the U.S. State Department and the CIA under a program called Order 6. The problem was, every time June attempted to look farther into what Order 6 was, his computer came back with the same message:

ERROR
PROGRAM ACCESS PROHIBITED

June got up from his desk and walked down the hall to his boss. Jim Bruckheimer was on the phone. June stood in the door. Bruckheimer gave him a look as if to say, "I can't talk—this is really important." June returned the look with one that responded, "I don't care who you're talking to—this takes priority."

After eight years of working together, June's message was clear.

"I'll call you back," said Bruckheimer, hanging up.

He looked at June. "What is it?"

"Have you ever heard of a joint CIA–State Department program called Order 6?"

Bruckheimer thought for a minute, then shook his head. "No, why?"

"The satellite is owned by the program," said June. "They launched it in 1994. I can't get into the database. I've used every access key I know. I can't get in."

"You tried Warrant B?"

"Yes. Redburn. Total-Two-Four. Exegesis. I was turned away."

Bruckheimer leaned back, a confused look on his face.

"I'll call Hector."

20

4436 PARKRIDGE BOULEVARD
RESTON, VIRGINIA

Flaherty's phone rang.

"What is it?"

"You better get down here," said Kopitar.

Kopitar's office was adjacent to the Situation Room. It was windowless and three times the size of the Situation Room. It was hot and stuffy, despite air-conditioning, the heat caused by several tall stacks of high-powered servers that stood in the center of the room as well as a wall full of sophisticated signals intelligence equipment. On one side of the room were tables and computers. Against the opposite wall, several cabinets with glass doors were lined up neatly. The cabinets held a variety of signals-gathering and -dissemination equipment. Kopitar was a former Air Force contractor, an early member of a large team of technologists, hackers, signals experts, and engineers charged with creating America's first ever capability set in the area of cyberwar. He was responsible for creating, maintaining, and protecting the powerful and anonymous system that enabled Bruner and his shadow government to communicate without being caught.

When Flaherty opened the door, Kopitar turned from his computer screen and looked at him with a blank expression that both men knew meant: There's a problem.

"What is it?" asked Flaherty.

"I was able to generate activity logs off Courtemanche's cell phone and credit cards," said Kopitar. "I tracked Romy's movements by looking at purchase records and calls. It appears she's headed for Paris. She made a phone call to someone in the United States."

"Who?"

"A number in Cambridge, Massachusetts. A former Harvard professor. Dr. Hillary Bartholomew."

Flaherty's eyes went wide.

"I don't imagine there's more than one Hillary Bartholomew?" he asked.

"One and the same," said Kopitar. "Professor of Asian Studies. An expert on China and Vietnam. A confidante of every secretary of state since

Henry Kissinger. She used to spend her summers in Switzerland. The same town as Kyrie."

"How long did the call last?"

"Eleven minutes," said Kopitar.

"Do you know if Bartholomew called anyone?"

"I don't know."

"We need to get someone up there," said Flaherty, turning to leave.

"There's something else," said Kopitar.

Flaherty stopped. He turned and looked at Kopitar.

"Someone at NSA is trying to dig into Order Six."

Flaherty's eyes blinked rapidly as his face took on a look of high anxiety.

"Everything is gone from the files, right, Hans?" said Flaherty.

"Yes, of course. That doesn't mean there aren't tiny fingerprints. Everything leaves a fingerprint, Andrew. Even the act of erasing fingerprints leaves a fingerprint."

"How long do we have until they find something?" said Flaherty urgently. "We need a few days, that's all."

"Chances are they'll never find anything," said Kopitar. "Most of the people at NSA are worthless. If I had to bet, they ran into Order Six and kept right on going. If you need to worry, worry about Kyrie's wife."

21

BRATTLE STREET
CAMBRIDGE, MASSACHUSETTS

A light blue police cruiser pulled up in front of a large shingle-style home on Brattle Street. A uniformed officer climbed out and walked to the front door.

It was early afternoon.

The officer rang the doorbell. He heard the faint *ding-dong* inside. A minute later, the door opened. A short, elderly-looking woman slowly opened the door. As she did so, the officer politely removed his visored police cap.

"Good afternoon, ma'am," he said, showing her his badge. "I'm Special Detective Stearns from the State Police. Are you Hillary Bartholomew?"

She looked at the badge for a few seconds and nodded.

"Have I done something wrong?"

"No, ma'am, you haven't. But I'd like to ask you a few questions. I'm acting as part of a joint task force between the FBI and Swiss authorities. They're investigating a homicide and requisitioned me to ask you a few questions."

Bartholomew gasped. "My word. What would I know about that?"

"Perhaps nothing. It occurred in Switzerland."

Bartholomew placed her hand over her mouth in shock.

"Are you all right?" asked the man who called himself Detective Stearns.

"Yes. It's just that . . . It's nothing. Yes, I'm quite all right."

"This shouldn't take long. May I come in?"

"Of course."

Bartholomew opened the door wider and Stearns entered.

"Please," she said, "in the kitchen, if you don't mind."

"If you have guests, ma'am, I could return later."

"No, nothing like that. I was in the middle of eating my lunch."

"My apologies," he said.

They sat down at a large round table. Classical music was playing in the background.

"Two days ago, three individuals were murdered at a hospital in Lauterbrunnen, Switzerland," Stearns explained. "One of the victims was a man named Courtemanche. He was the hospital administrator. According to records, his cell phone was used to call you sometime after the murders were committed."

Bartholomew had a sad expression on her face. Both of her hands moved to the top of the table, pressing down as if holding her steady.

"French authorities believe they know who

did it," Stearns continued. "The reason I'm here is because of that phone call. Did someone call you?"

Bartholomew's hand went to her chest.

"I believe I should get my lawyer?"

"That would be fine, Professor Bartholomew. But please know, this conversation is on background. It cannot be used to incriminate you and can only be used to help find the suspect and perhaps prevent further attacks. We simply want to find her."

"Her?"

"Romy Banker, the patient who escaped."

Bartholomew closed her eyes and started crying.

"She called me," said Bartholomew, as tears moistened her cheeks. "I should have called someone."

"She was in a mental institution," said Stearns, reaching his hand out and placing it gently on hers.

"She said they put her there against her will," said Bartholomew.

"I don't know why she was there, ma'am. Perhaps that's true."

"She told me so many things," said Bartholomew. "I wrote them down. She told me about the men she killed."

"She did?"

"Yes. She also said there was a plot to overthrow the United States government."

Stearns's eyes went wide. "Are you sure?"

"Yes."

"Well, that might help to explain why she was in a mental institution," he said.

"She sounded very rational, Officer."

"I apologize," he said. "It's just . . . well, it's not every day you hear someone talk about a plot to overthrow the government, if you know what I mean."

"Oh, I know," Bartholomew said. "I thought it sounded rather fantastical."

"Did you report it to the authorities?"

"I didn't. I was going to call a former colleague of mine, but I didn't."

"If they find her, my guess is they will ask you that in a more formal setting," said Stearns. "If you could please think hard, Professor Bartholomew. Any help you can provide now will go a long way toward making sure that any discussion of abetting the crime by not turning her in will be just that—discussion."

"You said this was for background."

"And it is. But there will be an investigation. All I'm saying is, nothing we talk about today can hurt you. It can only help. Later, if there are questions as to why you didn't call someone immediately, your complete transparency now can only help. Does that make sense?"

Bartholomew nodded.

"I . . . I didn't call anyone."

"What about e-mail?"

"No. I don't use e-mail anymore. I hate it. After I retired, it was my first luxury, never having to look at another computer screen again for the rest of my life."

Stearns laughed. "I hear you. I feel the same way."

"But I did tell someone."

"Who?"

"Margita, my housekeeper."

Stearns nodded. "Well, that's okay. Is she here?"

Bartholomew shook her head, but as she did she shot Stearns a suspicious look.

"What does it matter if Margita knows? Come to think of it, what does it matter if I told anyone?"

Stearns smiled as, beneath the table, he removed a thin black plastic bag from his pocket, just as Bartholomew's eyes went to his chest, trying to focus on his name tag: *Lancaster*.

A fear-stricken look whitened her face as her eyes grew large. "Didn't you say your name was Stearns?"

She started to push away from the table. The killer stood and held the black bag in both hands. He lurched for her just as she stood, dropping the bag over her head, then cinching it tightly in back. He clutched it with one hand as she swung feebly at him. The sound of choking was soft and lasted just a few seconds. He held tight for a few more moments, wrapping his free hand behind her back as she crumpled. He carried her into the adjacent living room and lowered the old woman's body to the carpet, arranging it to look like she'd been suddenly stricken by some sort of heart attack and making sure she was near the kitchen and visible from it.

His eyes darted methodically around the room. He went to the front door. Seeing no one, he methodically swept through all three floors of the large house, looking for anyone else who might be there. Margita. He found no one.

In a room off the kitchen was Bartholomew's desk. He found a page of handwritten notes labeled CONVERSATION WITH ROMY. He took the page as well as the page beneath it and went to the fireplace, lighting them.

For the next two hours, he sat on a chair in the kitchen, watching the front door.

Just after four in the afternoon, he heard a car pull into the driveway. He put on a pair of leather gloves and went to the front door and opened it, making it look like he'd just gotten there. On the way, he took the receiver from the phone on the wall and dropped it so that it dangled down at Bartholomew's feet. He took a walkie-talkie from his belt and held it up to the side of his head. He didn't turn it on.

"Hillary?" came a soft female voice with a

Hispanic accent. “I’m here! Why are the police here?”

The killer knelt next to the corpse as he listened to the footsteps on the kitchen floor.

“This is Detective Rick Stearns,” he pretended to say into the walkie-talkie. “I’m at the Bartholomew residence—”

The housekeeper let out a gasp as she saw Bartholomew’s body. He turned.

“Send a unit as well as an ambulance,” he said into the walkie-talkie.

The man who called himself Stearns stood up and faced the woman. “Who are you?”

“Margita,” she whispered. She started to move toward the body.

“I’m sorry, Margita. Until forensics gets here, please don’t touch anything.”

“What happened?”

“She had a heart attack. I’m very sorry. Were you friends?”

“Yes. I’ve been Dr. Bartholomew’s housekeeper for twenty-seven years.”

“I’m very sorry. May I ask you a question or two, Margita?”

She nodded.

“During her nine-one-one call, Dr. Bartholomew referred to something a friend had told her. Some sort of plot.”

“Yes,” said Margita. “She told me. I said her friend was loco.”

“Did you happen to tell anyone about it, Margita?”

Margita shook her head.

He grabbed the front of thc housekeeper’s jacket, pulling her close. He removed a silenced Beretta 9mm handgun as she struggled to push his other hand away. Thc killer slammed the tip of the silencer into her mouth, then levered it up and pulled the trigger. A dull spit came as a bullet fired, killing her. He let her drop to the ground, then walked to Bartholomew’s corpse and shot her once in the chest. He unscrewed the silencer and pocketed it, then placed the gun in Margita’s hand.

As he passed through the kitchen, he hung up the phone.

22

HOTEL PROVISIONAIRES
PARIS

Romy relaxed for the first time in days, sitting on the small bed in a dusty hotel room, the TV on. She had it tuned to the local Paris news. On the screen, the story was about the U.S. secretary of state, in Paris for talks with Iran. Romy stared at the screen as they showed the American diplomat climbing into a limousine.

When the commercial came on, she went into the bathroom and took a quick shower. She knew she had to keep moving. She knew what they were capable of. It was only a matter of time until they found her.

She needed to call Hillary. She picked up the cell phone and dialed. After more than a minute, it started ringing.

"Hello?" came a man's voice.

"I'm calling for Professor Bartholomew."

In the background, Romy could hear voices.

"Who is this?" asked the man on the phone.

Pause.

"I just spoke to her—" said Romy.

"Who are you?" asked the man.

"Her daughter," lied Romy.

"I'm afraid I have very bad news for you," he said.

"What did you do to her?" she whispered.

"Ma'am, this is Sergeant Callahan from the Cambridge Police Department. I'm afraid that your mother is dead. I'm sorry to be the one who has to tell you. Are you nearby?"

Romy hung up the phone. She walked slowly to the bed and lay down, putting her head in her hands, trying to remain composed. She had nowhere to go, no one to turn to.

They killed her! I know they did!

Had Professor Bartholomew reached out to the wrong person? God forbid, had Romy gotten her killed?

Romy sobbed, remembering the kind woman who'd befriended her.

"Make it stop," she whispered, her eyes closed.

23

CAFÉ LES DEUX MAGOTS
PARIS

Kyrie's cell beeped. He looked at the number; it was Kopitar.

"What is it?"

"She made a call with the doctor's cell phone a few minutes ago."

"Is she in Paris?"

"Yes."

"Who did she call?"

"A woman in Cambridge, a professor."

Kyrie paused. "Hillary. Our neighbor in Ruswil."

"Romy might know, Kyrie," Kopitar continued.

"Know what?"

"That we killed the woman. That we're searching for her. Someone answered, I assume the police. They must have told her."

"Of course she knows, you fucking idiot," said Kyrie scathingly. "Where is she?"

"Hotel Provisionaires. It's in the fourteenth arrondissement."

"I want to know if she leaves, Hans. I'll be there in ten minutes."

24

HOTEL PROVISIONAIRES
PARIS

Romy forced herself to stop sobbing. She got up from the bed. It was like standing in quicksand, she thought. The world was surrounding her and trying to destroy her.

It's not the world. You must keep fighting.

Romy didn't have children, and yet she felt,

in that moment, like she did. A warm maternal feeling came over her. She imagined that she had a child—a boy—and she needed to fight for him, to show him what it meant to fight, to do what was right, to struggle when no one else was looking. For him. The feeling lasted only a few seconds, but it steeled her. She wiped her eyes with the sleeve of her coat and looked around the dirty hotel room. She had to leave, to move, even though she had nowhere to go. Something inside her told her to move.

Outside the hotel, she hailed a cab.

"*Ou allez-vous, madame*?"

"*L'Hotel George Cinq*," she said. "*À côté*."

She knew it was a long shot. But it was the only shot. It was a crazy gamble. What if he wasn't there? Or what if he was and they shot her before she could tell him?

He won't shoot you. He'll listen. There's no other way.

She was dropped off less than a block from the George V. It was dark and pouring rain. The street in front of the hotel was cordoned off by security personnel and wooden barriers. Guests had to enter through a security screening point just inside the door. She cursed herself for being so naïve.

"Did you honestly think you could just walk inside and take the elevator to his floor and knock on his door?" she muttered to herself.

Keep fighting.

She looked up at the front façade of the George V, trying to think. Here eyes drifted along the roofline to the building next door. A sign above the entrance read PRINCE DE GALLES.

She entered the lobby, her heart beating rapidly.

The Prince de Galles was a boutique hotel, not quite as nice as the George V, but that didn't matter. All that mattered was that the two hotels were next door to each another.

What if he's on a different floor? What if he's already left?

She couldn't think about that now. She had to *try*. She was desperate. It was the only word she could think of. *Desperate.* She had nobody. All she had was . . . Kyrie . . . *a monster!* A monster who right now was hunting her . . .

"*Madame, nous avons une suite disponible à l'étage penthouse. Il est assez cher.*"

Madame, we have one suite available on the penthouse floor. It is pretty expensive.

"*Bien. Le coût est sans souci.*"

Good. The cost doesn't matter.

Kyrie ransacked the small, shabby room at the Hotel Provisonaires, finding nothing. He sat down on the edge of the bed, trying to think. The TV was on. He stared at it for a few moments.

He looked to his left. The pillow was out of

place, as if she had been lying on it at some point. He reached for it and lifted it to his face, hoping to get a whiff of her, perhaps just the faintest aroma of perfume, of her body. He held it there for several moments.

His cell phone vibrated. He looked at the number. It was Kopitar.

"She's not here," seethed Kyrie.

"She changed hotels," said Kopitar. "She used his credit card. It's called the Prince de Galles, near the Champs-Élysées."

Romy entered the suite. It was luxurious, with cool yellow lighting on a pair of large suede sofas that looked inviting. Soft music came from speakers in the ceiling. The bedroom was visible through a door to the right. Straight ahead was the terrace, accessed through French doors. The patter of rain against the glass mingled with the music. It was the first glimpse of comfort she'd seen in weeks, and she wanted nothing more than to have a glass of wine, a warm meal, a bath, and then sit on one of the sofas and forget about it all, forget about everything that had happened.

The bathroom was large and brightly lit, walls and floors of tannish marble, a big freestanding copper bathtub, a glass-enclosed shower big enough for two. She paused as she took it all in. She knew she needed to move, to try to reach the American secretary of state, and yet she was momentarily frozen in thought. If he was there right now, certainly he would be there in thirty minutes? She knew they would be looking for her, Kyrie or someone like him, sent by the man named Charles, but surely she had a few minutes. She needed it, she realized, needed to feel human again, to renew her strength so that she could keep going . . .

She went to the bathtub and turned on both taps, adjusting until the water was almost scalding. Smiling, her eyes closed, she unbuttoned her trench coat and let it fall to the floor.

"Hurry," said Kyrie from the backseat of the Citroën taxicab, hitting the back of the driver's seat.

"I'm going as fast as I can, monsieur."

"Go faster."

Kyrie knew precisely why Romy had gotten a room at the Prince de Galles. He knew it the moment his car pulled up in front and he saw the George V just a stone's throw down the block, walled off with armed security personnel and several limousines in front with American flags.

Lindsay.

Kyrie put his hand in his pocket, feeling his weapon, a silenced Glock .45. He thought about Romy as he unconsciously squeezed the butt of the gun. She was certainly tenacious. Escaping from the sanitarium had been no easy feat. Now she was attempting to contact the U.S. secretary of state.

The taxi pulled up in front of the Prince de Galles. Kyrie had the door open before it came to a full stop, throwing down a hundred-euro note and moving into the rain.

"*Votre monnaie, monsieur*!"

Your change, sir!

But Kyrie was already at the entrance. A doorman had the door open, and he walked quickly to the front desk.

"Good evening, sir," said a woman behind the counter.

"Good evening," he said calmly, a smile on his face. He removed a Swiss license, hastily made by a contact in Paris that afternoon.

"Welcome to the Prince de Galles, Dr. Courtemanche," said the clerk. "Your wife has already checked in."

"Wonderful. When did she arrive?"

"Mrs. Courtemanche arrived half an hour ago. Is this a business trip, or pleasure? A second honeymoon, perhaps?"

"How did you know?" said Kyrie. "Would you be so kind as to tell me our room number?"

"Room nine oh two, a suite on the top floor. May I send up a bottle of champagne, considering the special occasion?"

Kyrie held up his hand politely.

"That's quite all right. An extra key would be all that I need. If I know her, she is taking a bath. I would rather not disturb her."

Romy stared at the coat on the ground, then glanced at the bathtub.

"*Merde*," she said. She had to do what she needed to do.

She put the damp coat back on and moved to the terrace door, not even bothering to turn off the faucets. The wind was driving the rain in sideways swirls against the glass. She tightened her coat and opened the door. She stepped onto the terrace and looked right to the George V. There were two terraces between hers and the tall security fence that separated the hotels. She shut her eyes, feeling a sense of dread and self-doubt. She'd never make it. Yet she had to.

She climbed onto the brick parapet that separated her terrace from the one immediately next to it, lifting her head just enough to peek into the window of her neighbor. The lights were off. She hoisted herself up and over the parapet, carefully dropping onto the terrace, then crouched low. Though the wind and rain were loud enough to cloak any sounds, she crawled silently across the terrace. At the next parapet, she looked into the window. Several people were seated with their backs to her, watching TV.

Romy climbed over the parapet without making a noise, then crawled across the terrace. The tall security fence stood at least six feet above the parapet itself. Iron prongs stuck up into the air, their ends curved slightly toward her.

Romy stood. She lifted herself onto the parapet and grabbed one of the iron prongs.

A sudden noise came from behind her.

Kyrie took the elevator to the ninth floor and moved quickly to the suite. He paused outside the door, removing the gun from his coat pocket and then inserted the card key in the door. When the green light came on, he turned the knob, but the door didn't budge. Romy had dead-bolted it.

Without hesitating, Kyrie put the gun back in his pocket and took his cell phone out. He brought up a specialized application that allowed him to visualize—like an X-ray machine—the internal mechanics of the lock.

Kyrie glanced around, making sure nobody was coming down the hallway. He pressed the cell against the door, above the steel lock plate, looking at the dead bolt's internal machinery. Once he had it, he carefully scratched two small *x*'s on the door approximately three inches apart. He then removed an unusual-looking object from his coat. It was black, rectangular, the size of a pack of cigarettes. Two pointed steel rods were folded against the sides. Kyrie unfolded the rods, transforming the device into something resembling two short screwdrivers that had been soldered together. He placed the sharp tips against the *x* marks and looked around again, then moved a sliding switch on the side of the tool and pressed in hard. The sharp tips bore into the thick wood as they spun, cutting quickly through the wood. A half minute later, he felt steel and heard the dull click of the dead bolt moving. He removed the device and put it back in his pocket. He inserted the key card at the same moment he pulled out the silenced Glock, then turned the latch.

A noise. Romy turned her head. It was the sound of a door lock moving, of a door opening. A tall man in a raincoat was standing in the doorway to the terrace, holding a cigarette, trying to light it, cupping it so that it wouldn't get wet. Romy remained still, hoping, praying that her dark trench coat would blend with the night. Rain dripped down her hands to her wrists and down her arms, soaking her shirt, making the cold feel even more acute.

After nearly a minute, the man turned and stepped back inside, shutting the doors behind him.

Romy glanced down at the street. Orange-and-yellow car lights were obscured by the driving rain. She was so high . . . a shiver made her entire body tremor for a brief moment. She shut her eyes again, finding strength and stability in the cold iron that she gripped as tightly as she could.

Kyrie.

She pictured his face. In that moment, powerful emotions were driving her. She felt strength and purpose, hatred, anger, self-doubt, and regret. She wanted to kill the monster who'd sent her to a mental institution to rot away. All that mattered was stopping him.

With his weapon in his right hand, Kyrie scanned the room, listening for noise. Suddenly, he was drawn to the bedroom.

His eyes went to the open door of the bathroom. He heard water running in the bathtub.

I was only kidding, he thought, recalling what he told the front desk clerk.

He inched to the door, which was half open, the tub behind it. Then he moved. He stepped into the bathroom and swept the weapon to the tub, but Romy wasn't there.

Had she heard him? Had she heard the dead bolt? The drill?

And was she now hiding?

Kyrie did a rapid recon of the suite—searching closets, corners, spaces behind the sofas, behind curtains—but she wasn't there.

He ran to the terrace and out into the driving rain. His eyes shot right—to the roof of the George V. The rain and darkness made it difficult to see, but he saw the small silhouette of a figure, clinging to the security fence that separated the hotels. He stepped closer, to the edge of the terrace, staring at her. She was trying to reach the top of the fence. For several moments, Kyrie watched as she struggled to climb. When she slipped, something inside him moved, as if he were going to catch her, and then her other hand grabbed hold. Again she was slowly moving up the fence as rain and wind pelted her, and him. He gripped the gun in both hands and raised it into the wind, training it on her. He knew it had to be done. As much as he didn't want to, he knew it was over. He had to kill her. It would be an easy shot. He held his finger against the trigger as her legs pushed against the iron grating, struggling to reach the top of the fence. He stood with Romy in the crosshairs for more than a minute, his hands trembling. Yet he couldn't shoot.

Each of Romy's hands grabbed hold of a prong. She clenched her teeth and lifted herself up, using her feet to push against the fence below. Struggling, she pulled her head even with the top. Her arms ached, but she kept pulling with every ounce of strength she had, until she felt like she would scream. Desperately, she held herself up and then swung her left leg up. Her foot made it over the top so that she was now hanging side-ways, dangling, as rain soaked her. She paused in that position, resting for a few precious moments. She used her leg to help raise the rest of her to the top of the fence. Romy inched over the edge, holding the iron, then let her feet slip down the other side. There was no parapet on this side to fall to, so she crabbed down the fence until finally she felt the ground.

She settled onto her knees, breathing rapidly, trying to catch her breath. The roof level of the George V had only two suites, both magnificent glass-and-limestone structures that occupied the two front-facing wings of the hotel. She was on one of the terraces. If the secretary of state was in the suite on the far wing, she would have no way of getting there.

Romy walked to the closer door. The curtain was partially drawn. She could see inside the suite. A man was seated on one of the sofas, alone. He had gray hair and appeared to be just sitting there, doing nothing, and then she saw him lift a book. Romy brushed her sopping-wet hair back out of her eyes, trying to neaten it even though she knew it was an absurd waste of time. She knocked on the glass. The man's head turned, but he didn't get up. She knocked again.

Slowly, the man stood. He had a quizzical look on his face, but she recognized him. It was the man from the news, Tim Lindsay, the secretary of state. He stared at the glass for a few moments, not moving. His eyes were suspicious. He picked up his cell phone and started to dial.

"Help!" she cried.

Lindsay stepped around the sofa and approached the French doors. He pulled the curtain aside and looked out, searching in the darkness and driving rain. Suddenly, his eyes found her and he jerked back. He reached and opened the door.

For several moments, he stood in the door, staring at her. Finally he spoke. "Are you okay?"

"I—" Romy began. "I . . . I'm not sure."

"How did you—" said Lindsay. "Never mind. Come inside. I'll call hotel security."

"No," she said. "I must talk to you and only you."

Lindsay's face became hard and suspicious. "Who the hell are you?"

He pressed a button on his cell as he started to back up.

Romy held her hands up, as if surrendering. Rain poured down her face. She was drenched.

"Please don't. I have information that is of the utmost importance to the United States of America."

"Are you insane? What sort of information?"

"A plot to kill the president."

Lindsay put the cell to his ear.

"This is Secretary Lindsay," he started, looking at her. "Give me a sec."

He covered the mouthpiece.

"Please," she begged. "I risked my life to tell you. There is a plot to assassinate the president of the United States, and the people are inside the U.S. government. *Please, you have to believe me!*"

Lindsay held the phone to his ear a few more moments, studying Romy as she stood in the rain.

"I'll call back," he said, hanging up the phone.

Lindsay stepped toward her. "How do you know this?"

"My husband is one of the conspirators."

Lindsay raised his hand and placed it on her arm.

"Come in," he said.

25

PRINCE DE GALLES
PARIS

Kyrie stepped back inside the suite, thoroughly drenched. He had a distant look, as if he were staring at a mirage, or a memory.

Why? he asked himself. *What is it that you saw, that warm afternoon that changed everything? What is it you see tonight?*

By the time Kyrie met Romy, he'd lost his

ability to feel. It was the reason Bruner had taken him from that jail one dark night so long ago. It was what enabled Kyrie to kill without remorse.

Yet she touched something beyond all hatred and anger. Romy was his one—his only—weakness. Kyrie couldn't kill her.

He looked down at the gun, still dripping water.

Kyrie shut his eyes and put a hand against the wall, steadying himself. His cell awakened him from his thoughts. He looked up, breathing heavily. The wandering look on his face disappeared. His eyes grew sharp, cold, and angry.

It was Kopitar.

"What is it?" said Kyrie.

"Was she there?"

"Yes, but she fled."

"Did you kill her?"

"No, not yet. Call Casales. Tell him I will be coming from the stairs."

"Is she with Secretary of State Lindsay?" asked Kopitar, a shocked tone in his voice. "Should we just have him handle it?"

"Make sure he's on that side of Lindsay's door," said Kyrie, ignoring him. "Tell him *design flank two, one up.* And Hans?"

"Yes."

"If Casales attempts to handle this himself, before I get there, not only will I kill him, but I will come for you next. I will find you, and you will suffer, and then you'll die. Got it?"

"Yes," said Kopitar quietly.

"Now what's the design Casales needs to know?" asked Kyrie, testing him.

"Stair side, flank two, one up."

"Good."

26

HOTEL GEORGE V
PARIS

Romy stepped cautiously inside as Lindsay shut the door behind her.

"What's your name?"

"Romy Banker."

"How did you know I was here?"

"I watched the news. They said you were staying here. I took a chance. I called someone I know, a woman who used to spend summers near us. She was a professor and I thought she could tell someone. I told her what I heard, and they killed her. I didn't know where else to go."

Lindsay looked stunned.

"What was her name?"

"Dr. Bartholomew."

Lindsay's face took on a pained look. "*Hillary* Bartholomew? From Harvard?"

"Yes."

Lindsay went into the bathroom and returned with a towel, which he handed to Romy. She took it and wiped her face and hair. Lindsay motioned to her to sit down.

"Tell me what was said in the conversation you overheard," he said.

"They have someone who is a congressman, a man named Largent."

"Bobby Largent? It's preposterous—"

"They're going to kill the Speaker of the House and the vice president. That's what they said. All that will be left is the president, and then they will kill him too."

Lindsay stared at her. His face flushed red, a perplexed look on it, as if contemplating his next steps. He slowly sat down.

"What is it?" she asked.

"The Speaker of the U.S. House of Representatives died. He drowned."

"When?"

"Yesterday."

Romy let out a soft gasp.

"I need to tell someone," said Lindsay. "Whether it's true or not, we need to bring you in."

"What if you tell the wrong person?" she said.

"What do you mean?"

"They have people everywhere. They're with the president. They have people *with the president.*

With every one of the cabinet members. Maybe even with you."

Lindsay glanced at the door.

"The man's name is Charles," she said. "He didn't say his last name. He mentioned something called Consular Operations."

Lindsay was overcome for a brief moment.

"What did you say?" he asked.

"His name is Charles—"

"No, the other part. Did you say 'Consular Operations'?"

"Yes."

"You're absolutely sure that's what you heard the man say?"

"Yes."

Lindsay put his hand against the wall to steady himself. He looked dumbfounded, upset, even angry.

"His name is Charles Bruner," said Lindsay.

Suddenly, there was a knock at the door.

Lindsay glanced around. Who could he call? If she was telling the truth, the men outside the door could work for Bruner. No, it wasn't possible. He knew each man. It just wasn't . . . possible.

Or was it?

"Get out of sight," he said as he walked to the door.

27

HOTEL GEORGE V
PARIS

It was just after 9 p.m., and Dewey stood in the large marble-floored bathroom in his suite. He was clean shaven. His hair was medium length, thick, and brown. He wore a white turtleneck that showed off his large chest, shoulders, and arms, which were visibly dense with muscles. Wrapped taut across the upper part of his chest was a thin black nylon-and-Kevlar weapons belt. A small ceramic pouch lay tucked beneath his left armpit. Dark silver steel bulged from the holster.

Colt M1911A1 .45-caliber semiautomatic.

The day had been mundane, consisting mainly of waiting around during Lindsay's meetings and accompanying him back to the hotel. Now that the meetings were over, Dewey found himself alone, lost in thoughts about the past. He tried not to think about Paris, about a honeymoon so long ago, a world away, a different time and place.

Dewey stared at his reflection for more than a minute, thinking in silence. A cold, distant look occupied his face.

He had big blue eyes and a large, sharp nose. He looked athletic, even rugged. He was handsome, though that quality was belied somewhat by eyes that showed hardness, coldness, and an underlying sense of anger.

On the marble sink, a half dozen bottles of various luxury items provided by the hotel were neatly arranged—fancy shampoos, conditioners, and body lotions, none of which had been touched. On the counter next to the bottles was an unusual-looking object. Sleek, black, and rectangular.

Osprey H88 silencer.

He unstrapped the holster and pulled out the gun. It was a plain piece of hardware. Its steel was covered in scratches and patchwork hue from years of use: gun oil, cleaning fluid, salt water, grime, and just plain old wear and tear. It had been used to kill more people than he could remember; to break glass and to smash skulls; it was a gun used for its intended purpose and a few its manufacturer couldn't have envisioned. Dewey knew it the way a boy knows his own baseball mitt.

Its one fanciful aspect, if it could be called that, was the sidearm's grip. Wrapped in black hockey tape, also worn-out and marked by age and, above all, use.

Originally issued to him more than a decade before upon his commissioning as a lieutenant junior class in 1st Special Forces Operational Detachment, known at the time by its nickname, Delta.

Dewey felt perhaps he should've enjoyed himself more in Paris, but Paris was just about the last place he wanted to be.

He stepped into the bedroom and walked to the window. It was raining outside. He could see the Champs-Élysées in the distance. The lights of cars twinkled in yellows, reds, and blues as they moved down the boulevard.

He went to the minibar and took out a bottle of whiskey and a beer. He uncapped the whiskey and drank it in one gulp, then pulled off the cap of the beer and drank it in a few hearty chugs. If he drank too much now, he would only turn inward and lose himself in his thoughts. Yet he couldn't help it. He took two more bottles of whiskey and drank them, then opened another beer. He chugged it even faster than the first. He felt the warmth of the alcohol descend on him, its familiar comfort taking over.

Dewey pulled on his raincoat. In the pocket was a small, thick laminated ID card. It allowed Dewey access to wherever the secretary of state was, a so-called body nick. He put the identification around his neck and stepped into the bathroom. He started to reach for his sidearm, but hesitated. He wouldn't need it.

Out in the hallway, a few doors down, two young agents from the State Department flanked the door to Lindsay's suite. They were dressed in suits, with no ties. Each man clutched a submachine gun, trained at the floor. The guards eyed Dewey as he approached. He stepped past them, not saying hello, paused for a moment, then knocked. A few moments later, the door opened. Lindsay's face appeared.

"Hi, Dewey," said Lindsay. "What can I do for you?"

"Sorry to disturb you, sir. I need a word."

Lindsay paused. "Come in."

The suite had a long entrance hallway. Lindsay stood between Dewey and the rest of the suite, subtly blocking him.

"I apologize for intruding."

Behind Lindsay, Dewey saw movement. A mirror on the wall at the end of the hallway reflected into the large living room. It was just a flash of movement—a woman's face—then she disappeared.

"You're not intruding," said Lindsay. "What's up?"

"I was thinking of going out for a bite to eat," said Dewey. "I wanted to make sure that was all right with you."

"You don't report to me," said Lindsay.

"Whether I report to you or not is irrelevant.

I just want to clear it with you. If you were considering going out yourself, even to the bar in the lobby, I don't want to go out."

Behind Lindsay, he saw it again. This time, the person remained in the frame of the mirror. She had long brown hair. She was seated on one of the couches in the suite. Dewey tried to look without making Lindsay aware that he saw the woman. She looked plain. Her hair was tousled and wet. Then she turned.

Dewey felt a bolt of adrenaline spike as her face became visible.

Lindsay had a nervous smile on his face.

"I'm in for the evening," he said. "Thanks for checking."

As Lindsay was about to close the door, Dewey put his hand out and stopped it.

"Is everything okay, Mr. Secretary?" he asked.

Lindsay patted Dewey on the shoulder.

"It's fine. Go enjoy yourself."

As soon as the door shut, Romy went to the French doors that led to the terrace.

"Where are you going?" asked Lindsay.

"Who was he?" she asked.

"A man who works for the CIA."

"You know this for a fact?"

Lindsay paused. "Yes. I trust him."

"Does he usually travel with you?"

"No. No, he doesn't."

Romy opened the door and stepped outside.

Lindsay came out onto the terrace. "Where can I reach you?" he asked.

Romy was already at the parapet, climbing up and grabbing the steel fence as cold rain poured down. She said nothing as she lifted herself up on top of the fence and then scuttled over to the other side.

Dewey took the elevator to the hotel lobby.

In addition to a few bellmen and other assorted hotel staff, a few people remained there, milling about. Soft laughter echoed down the corridor from Le Cinq, the hotel's restaurant. Dewey scanned the lobby, looking for anything unusual. Two gendarmes decked out in tactical military gear flanked the large glass front doors, both men clutching carbines. At the side wall, another CONS OP agent stood watch. Dewey glanced at his watch. It was 9:30.

A doorman pulled one of the doors open.

"*Bonsoir, monsieur*."

"*Bonsoir*," said Dewey.

"*Une parapluie, monsieur*?" asked the doorman. The tuxedoed man held out an umbrella.

"*Non, merci*," said Dewey.

Outside, beneath a glass-and-iron canopy, Dewey buttoned up his trench coat and looked around. It was still raining hard. The October night had a chill to it. The semicircular drive in front of the George V was filled with idling limousines.

"Do you need a taxi, monsieur?" asked one of the valets.

"Sure."

Dewey climbed into the back of the taxi, a sleek Citroën with a female driver.

"*Bonsoir*," she said. "Where to, monsieur?"

"I'd like to get something to eat," said Dewey.

"Nearby?"

"Whatever. Just something good."

"Do you like fancy good or good good, monsieur?"

"Good good."

"I'm happy you say this. I know just the place."

Romy was drenched by the time she made it back to her suite. Climbing to Lindsay's hotel had been difficult, perhaps the hardest thing she'd ever done, but getting back was harder. Somehow she thought that after she told him, it would be all over. But when she heard Dewey's voice, something about it told her to trust no one.

Think, Romy!

"My God," she said.

Her hands went to her pocket. She removed the cell phone and credit card, staring at the name along the bottom of the card:

Slowly, as if in a dream, she sat down on the sofa and picked up the phone. She called the front desk.

"Good evening, Mrs. Courtemanche."

"Hello."

"I trust you and Mr. Courtemanche are enjoying the hotel?"

"Mr. Courtemanche?"

"I checked him in myself. Such a kind man."

Romy couldn't speak for several moments. She willed herself to go on.

"Yes, yes, he arrived. I forget myself. He is a doctor, so when I heard 'mister' it confused me. I apologize."

"How may I help you, madame?"

"Is it possible for the hotel to place a call for me? I don't know the number."

"Of course. Who would you like us to ring for you?"

"It's a hospital in Switzerland," said Romy. "It's called Au Plein-du-Monts. I don't know the town."

"One moment, Mrs. Courtemanche."

As Romy waited for the call to go through, she looked desperately around the suite, trying to think. Her eyes went to the ceiling. She studied the recessed lights. Then she focused on the sprinkler heads tucked into the ceiling.

"Ah, yes, here it is," said the hotel clerk. "One moment, please."

A few seconds later, she heard the phone ringing. A female voice came on the line.

"Facilité Au Plein-du-Monts, how may I direct your call?"

"I would like to speak to Dr. Courtemanche," said Romy.

"I'm afraid Dr. Courtemanche isn't here right now."

"I must speak with him, please."

"What is your name?"

Romy paused.

"Romy Banker. I was a patient of his."

"Hold on," said the woman. "Banker. I'm afraid I don't have any record of a patient with that name. Is there another name it might have been under?"

"He was my doctor," said Romy. "I must speak with him. It's imperative. Is there a number he can be reached at?"

"Dr. Courtemanche will not be available for some time," said the woman. "He has decided to take an extended leave of absence. He left specific instructions that he not be disturbed. Would you like me to suggest one of our other professionals, madame?"

Romy hung up the phone. She knew what it meant. They'd somehow hidden what she did at the sanitarium—the murder of Courtemanche, the murders of the orderlies, everything. It was the only explanation for why she hadn't been arrested the moment she checked in to the hotel. They were following her . . . and she'd led them right to her. Courtemanche's credit card had led them directly to her.

And she'd led them to Lindsay.

She stood up from the sofa. She put the cell phone on the floor and smashed it with her foot, stomping on it. She ripped out the small pieces of circuit, wire, and plastic, stomping on them until they were small bits and particles in a messy pile. She started to bend the credit card—but then she stopped. She knew she might need it. As perilous as it was, it was not as perilous as being on the run without money.

Run, Romy! You must leave, now!

Kyrie went down a back alley and waited outside the entrance to the hotel's parking garage, crouching behind a Dumpster. His cell chimed. It was Kopitar.

"Casales is set. There is an incremental layer of security, someone from Langley. He just left, but Casales didn't know where he was going."

Kyrie hung up as the mechanical clanking of the steel gate caught his ear. He waited for a vehicle to emerge. After it was out of sight, he slipped inside just before the gate shut.

He climbed the stairs to the top floor of the

hotel, pulling on a pair of leather gloves as he ascended.

He felt nothing now but purpose and duty. They had found her, and now he needed to do what Bruner had wanted him to do for a decade. He had to kill his own wife. He had to kill Romy.

He opened the door to the penthouse floor and saw two figures in the distance, guarding Lindsay's door. One of them was Casales; he was closer. When he saw Kyrie, he walked toward him.

Kyrie pulled the small canister of spray paint from his coat pocket and held it up to the red security camera, blasting it with a quick spray.

He nodded at Casales, who turned and fired a silenced slug into the other agent's chest, dropping him.

"Has the Agency man come back?"

"No."

"Was he wearing a raincoat?"

"Yes."

"Do you have a key to his room?"

"Here," said Casales, handing Kyrie a key and pointing to the door.

Kyrie entered the room and looked quickly around, finding the CIA agent's gun in the bathroom. A Colt M1911A1. He picked it up, then saw the suppressor, which he screwed into the muzzle.

In the hallway, Kyrie moved toward Lindsay's suite, where Casales was waiting.

"I'm sorry," said Kyrie, "but it is necessary to make them believe the CIA man did it."

"What's necessary?" asked Casales.

"This."

Kyrie swept the weapon toward Casales and pumped the trigger, sending a bullet at nearly point-blank range into Casales's forehead.

Kyrie knocked on the door. After nearly half a minute, the secretary of state opened it.

"What is it?" asked Lindsay, before the door was fully open, before he could see the stranger now standing in the door frame, weapon in hand.

Kyrie trained the pistol on Lindsay's head.

"You're the one!" said Lindsay.

"Where is she?" asked Kyrie, stepping into the suite and forcing Lindsay backward, the gun trained at all times on his head.

"She's gone," said Lindsay. *"It's too late!"*

Kyrie fired. The bullet struck Lindsay in the shoulder, knocking him to thc floor.

"Where is she?"

"You won't get away with this!" groaned Lindsay. "It's Bruner, isn't it?"

He looked at Lindsay.

"Yes, it's Bruner. Unfortunately, you won't be around to tell anyone."

"Why?" groaned Lindsay, grimacing, holding his shoulder.

"Because of men like you and Dellenbaugh. Pacifists, content to watch Islam spread like cancer across the globe."

"Then help us fight them," said Lindsay, his shoulder now covered in blood. "Join us."

Kyrie laughed.

"How? When they blow up a bus, all you do is issue a press release. After nine/eleven we should've eradicated the Muslims from the face of the earth. Instead, we started two wars that have only made them stronger. Our weakness emboldens these animals. We let them into our country, and when they blow up a school or kill innocent Americans we talk about the need for tolerance and gun control."

"You don't get rid of cancer by killing the patient. You remove the tumor."

Kyrie looked hatefully at Lindsay. "And that's where we'll have to agree to disagree. We're willing to kill the patient in order to get rid of the cancer."

"You're insane!"

"No!" shouted Kyrie. "Insane is to shackle oneself in morals as you fight people who don't have any."

He trained the gun on Lindsay and fired another slug directly into his chest, killing him.

Kyrie searched the suite, looking everywhere for Romy—but she was gone.

A laptop was tucked in Lindsay's briefcase.

It was cold and appeared unused. He found Lindsay's cell phone and checked for calls he had placed. There hadn't been a call made in half an hour, and the one half an hour ago had lasted less than fifteen seconds. Finally, he went to the hotel phone and dialed the operator.

"Operator, Mr. Lindsay. How may I help you?"

"Please tell me the last outside call I made from this phone."

"Yes, Mr. Lindsay. According to my records, this phone has not been used to make outside calls, only room service."

"Thank you."

Kyrie dropped the gun to the floor and left the suite, taking the stairs to the ground floor. He exited the hotel and was less than a block away when he heard the first shouts—then a high-pitched alarm coming from the George V.

Romy heard the sirens just as she finished disposing of the cell phone. She ran across the bedroom, through the living room, then back out onto the terrace. Rain continued to howl down. She went to the edge of the terrace and looked down. She watched in horror as first one, then two Paris Métro police cruisers pulled up to the front of the George V. Despite the cold rain, she felt as if she couldn't move. Several more police cars, ambulances, and dark sedans rushed to the hotel, and soon the exterior was mayhem. She looked to her right, trying to see the suite where Lindsay was, but the parapets were too high—and she dared not try to get a better view.

She replayed the conversation:

"I'm not sure I believe you, but I am obligated to pass this along to the highest levels of my government," said Lindsay.

Are they looking for me? Did the U.S. secretary of state turn me in?

No. Had he turned her in, the police would be in front of the Prince de Galles and not the George V. There would be no ambulances.

Why are they here?

She shook her head, trying to make the answer go away, but she knew something was horribly wrong. She went back inside the suite and shut the doors. For several moments, she stood against them as water dripped from her body onto the floor.

They killed him. Just like they killed Hillary.

"No," she said. "It couldn't be. There's no way. There is too much security."

Romy was desperate. From a drawer in the bar, she found a box of matches. She took the newspaper from the table and lit the corner. Soon, billows of smoke lifted from the burning paper, and then flames. She moved the burning paper beneath the sprinkler head and held it there as the room grew choked with thick smoke. After less than a minute, she heard a loud snap. Suddenly the entire room was consumed in a furious deluge of water as every sprinkler came to life. At the same time, the piercing horns of the hotel's fire alarms rang out.

Romy moved to the door, dropping the newspaper, which was quickly doused by the sprinklers. She looked out the peephole and saw hotel guests filing from their rooms, most dressed only in nightclothes. She stepped out into the small crowd, falling in line as they proceeded to the emergency stairs.

28

LA CLOSERIE DES LILAS
PARIS

Dewey sat alone on a high leather-back seat in the brasserie section of the restaurant. He was almost done with his steak frites when his phone beeped, breaking the silence.

Emergency priority.

He looked at the cell phone.

555SCOM

Dewey charged from the restaurant, not even pausing to pay his bill, and tried to hail a cab, but there were none. He was on the opposite side of the city. He started running, then saw a sign for the Métro. He descended into the station just as a train pulled in. He jumped the turnstile as a pair of chimes rang out, indicating the train was getting ready to depart, sprinting the final yards and getting onto the crowded train.

He went to the city map and scanned it quickly. The train would take him a block away from the hotel.

He was wet from the rain. He looked around the car for the first time, realizing people were staring at him. He took out his cell, but there was no reception.

555SCOM: an alarm triggered by Secretary of State Lindsay himself, a small device on a necklace every cabinet member wore.

555 meant imminent danger.

After what felt like an eternity, the train stopped at the George V station and Dewey got off, sprinting for the exit. But as he went through the turnstiles, he saw her. It was the woman from Lindsay's suite.

"Stop!" he yelled.

She turned, saw Dewey, and ran.

Another train was arriving.

Dewey leapt the turnstile and ran for the train. The woman got on. He pushed people aside, trying to get to the doors before they closed.

The woman was standing in the corner of the last car, drenched, her face flushed with fear. She looked up just as the doors closed and the train started to move. Her eyes met Dewey's; their eyes locked. He recognized her. From some long forgotten part of his past, he'd seen that look before. Who was she?

As the train moved faster toward the tunnel, Dewey broke into a sprint. He passed the last car and reached the closed doors, trying to pull them apart as, at the same time, he ran to keep up with the train, which accelerated faster and faster toward the tunnel. He yanked with all his strength, but they didn't budge. Instinctively, still running, he reached inside his jacket for his gun, but it wasn't there. A memory flashed. The hotel room, the marble sink. He'd left it back at the hotel.

The train rumbled into the tunnel. Suddenly, the woman stepped into the frame of the window and stared at Dewey, as if searching for something. Dewey looked into her eyes one last time, just a couple of feet away. Then the train disappeared.

Dewey stood, breathing hard, his hand against the concrete abutment of the tunnel. He glanced around the brightly lit station. Across the tracks, a crowd of waiting passengers stared at him as if he were insane. Behind him, on his side of the tracks, a few people had arrived for the next train. They averted their eyes; one older couple walked quickly back toward the exit.

Dewey's mind swirled. He looked frantically

about the platform, his eyes darting wildly. He had to think.

Who was the woman?

Dewey ran across the platform to the Métro map. He quickly counted eleven stations in the path of the train. But three of those stations intersected with other lines, and those lines went in both directions across Paris. And in the path of those lines lay yet more intersecting lines. The possibilities were endless.

She could be going anywhere. Even if he knew the station, what could he do? What *would* he do?

The ground shook as a train pulled into the station on the opposite side of the tracks. People got off the train and ambled toward the exits.

He waited, for how long he lost track. Finally, another train rumbled in. He climbed on. He rode to the next station. He scanned the crowd, looking at people getting off along with him, at others pushing their way on, at empty benches. She wasn't there.

He climbed back on the train. He rode to the end of the line, checking at every stop, searching for the woman—but she wasn't there. He crossed to the other side of the tracks and took the return train back to the George V stop. He felt lost and confused, his mind gripped by a sense of longing—not so much for her but for information, as if he'd accidentally stumbled onto something. But what?

Outside, the rain was coming down hard, but he didn't seem to notice or care. He stumbled back to the hotel, dazed.

He saw the lights from two blocks away and broke into a hard run.

The George V was in a state of pandemonium. Several ambulances were out front, along with at least a dozen police vehicles and even more dark sedans. A perimeter of soldiers clutching carbines formed a semicircle in front of the hotel entrance.

Dewey pushed his way through the small crowd of onlookers and journalists outside the security perimeter. He came to one of the soldiers and showed his diplomatic passport along with the State Department special ID granting him access to the secretary of state at all times.

"No one gets in," said the soldier dismissively, not even bothering to look at the ID.

"This ID grants me access to Secretary of State Lindsay at all times," said Dewey, holding up the laminated plastic. "Get your commander. You by law cannot refuse to let me in."

"Yes, I can," said the French soldier, a sneer on his face.

"No, you can't," said Dewey. "Get your commander, *now*."

The soldier looked at the soldier to his left, an older officer, who stepped to Dewey and examined the card.

"He's right," said the senior officer, nodding at the card. He looked at Dewey. "Mr. Andreas, I understand what this means. But I will need to still get sign-off."

"That's fine. Hurry."

The soldier moved toward the hotel entrance. Looking through the glass doors, Dewey saw a swarm of people.

A minute later the officer returned, accompanied by a short man in a dark suit, holding an umbrella. He said nothing. He took the card from Dewey's hand and examined it. He turned to the younger soldier. "Idiot," he said.

He looked at Dewey. "You work for the secretary of state?"

"Yes."

"What do you do for the secretary of state?"

"None of your business," said Dewey. "Who are you?"

"I'm Detective Bastian with DGSI."

The lobby was chaos. It had been taken over by police, soldiers, and men in dark suits. Dewey searched for a pair of familiar eyes, perhaps from the State Department, but saw no one. He followed Bastian to the elevators, which were guarded by armed soldiers, as he dialed his SAT phone. He and Bastian climbed onto the elevator as his phone started to ring.

"Control eye-zero-two."

"Requesting voice RECOG," Dewey whispered. "Level Two."

"Go."

"Alpha-bravo-four-one."

Pause.

Then a computer-generated female voice, soft. "Confirming: Andreas, Dewey, nine-zero-nine-two-alpha. Status active. This is a Level Two confirmation."

Control: "Who do you need, Andreas?"

"Calibrisi."

"Hold for a sec."

Dewey glanced at the French detective as the elevator climbed to the seventh floor. The Frenchman kept his eyes affixed to the dark, polished wood of the elevator walls. When the elevator stopped, Dewey stepped off first and looked right, the phone against his ear as he waited for Langley Control to patch in Calibrisi.

He felt a cold sensation that hit his lower spine, then spread—a visceral feeling of shock, like walking from a warm house out into a winter blizzard. The floor was crowded with agents, EMTs, and other first responders; the mood was tense and spectral, eerily quiet except for a single male voice, speaking in French. Dewey's eyes focused. He was dressed in a thin white medical robe, hands purple due to the gloves.

Coroner.

Dewey saw movement to his left. His room. The door was ajar. A uniformed agent stood outside looking in, his hand holding a pistol. Dewey moved toward Lindsay's suite, not quite at a run but quickly. A crowd was gathered. As he came closer, his eyes were drawn to the floor, behind white tape: outside in the hall, flanking the door on each side, lay two bodies; the walls behind each man were splashed crimson, still shimmering wet, fresh and untouched—the State Department security team.

It's an operation.

Both men were dead. Each had a bullet hole in the forehead.

Double tap.

The agent closer to Dewey was lying on his back. His face was covered in blood. He stared up to the ceiling, eyes open, a blank, empty expression on his face. There was a dime-size black puncture just above his right eye; his chest had also been hit and was drenched in red. Dewey's eyes moved to the other agent. He was wedged awkwardly against the wall, a puddle of wet blood beneath his head. A medical technician was laying down a strip of white tape to separate the contorted corpse from the agents, coroners, and police gathered at the door. Yet other than this man, no one paid any attention to the dead CONS OP agents. They were secondary. All other eyes and attention were focused toward the inside of Lindsay's suite.

Dewey came to the edge of the gathered men. A plainclothes guard, clutching a pistol, held up his hand.

"*Arretez!*"

Stop!

Dewey pushed the man aside with his left hand as, with his right, he raised his ID.

"Move," he barked, as the agent attempted to grab his arm, which Dewey threw off with a hard elbow; the agent went tumbling sideways, off balance.

Other men tried to stop him entering Lindsay's suite. Arms grabbed him from behind, which he tried to push off. Someone else grabbed his legs. As he pushed forward, he felt the sudden pain of steel against his head; he dropped to the floor as several men tackled him.

As the throng of DGSI agents struggled to restrain Dewey, he fought to stand up, but it was no use. He searched through the legs of policemen and agents. Standing inside the long entrance hallway inside Lindsay's suite was a pair of older-looking men in suits along with several EMTs and coroners. Where the corridor opened up into the large living room, a bright yellow strip of tape cordoned off the room. Blood spatters covered the white walls above the sofa. In front of the sofa, on the floor, sprawled on his back, was Lindsay. His white shirt was ruined in blood. A massive red pancake covered the chest. The oriental carpet beneath him was blood-soaked.

Then Dewey saw something that made him lose his breath.

On the floor, a few feet from Lindsay, was a gun. Black hockey tape was wrapped around the butt. A silver Osprey silencer stuck out from the end.

Then he heard the words: *"Arrest that man!"*

29

NSA
SIGNALS INTELLIGENCE DIRECTORATE

Jesus June walked through the large analyst-filled room where his SID team was trying to learn more about a program called Order 6, to no avail. He stopped at Samantha's desk.

"Nothing?" he said, frustrated.

"Nothing. I found a few files in an old SQL directory, but it was scraped clean of everything, down to the metadata. Whatever it was, it's gone."

"Then why is the satellite still being used?"

Samantha shrugged. "Maybe it's not such a nefarious explanation. What if they launched it, disbanded the program, and reassigned the satellite?"

"What about the frequency?" he said. "They basically created a new signal range. There's only one explanation."

"Which is what?"

"Someone wanted to hide something. Someone *is* hiding something."

"I'm tracking activity that goes through the satellite now. If and when it's used, we should be able to pinpoint the location of the callers."

June went back to his office. A grid of photos was arrayed across the screen in front of him. Twenty-three individuals had been killed inside Hamza Mosque. June had pushed the photos against a broad spectrum of top secret NSA and U.S. government programs, including DS-300, Stellar Wind, and PRISM. June had intentionally not applied any "smart" metadata to the photos, choosing instead to see what NSA's computers could come up with based on facial recognition and thumbprints alone. After several hours, there were no surprises. The dead FBI agents spiked the grid first. The powerful computers matched the agents' photos quickly and then assembled comprehensive individual files with detailed background information. The four dead American high school students flashed soon thereafter. All were from Flint, Michigan: Ryan and Matthew Balthus, David Black, and Harun Johnson. Because the NSA programs had the ability to pore through e-mails and social media, the students' files clearly showed their collective radicalization over the past year, as well as the sophisticated courting done by Al-Amin and his group in order to convince them to come to Canada and join jihad. June stared an extra few moments at the youngest of the four, Matthew Balthus. He looked as if he was barely in his teens, innocent and clean-cut.

It took the computers longer to synthesize the dozen dead Muslims. Al-Amin's file completed first; he was well known and the file was large. The man known as "the forger," the one young Muslim who'd been working as a confidential informant for the FBI, and the rest of the young jihadis took longer to place. Eventually, however, they were all positively identified: a motley collection of men, most from Canada, but two—the forger and another, named Mohammed—from Germany.

June read through every file, looking for clues to a mystery the outlines of which he couldn't even begin to understand.

For some reason, however, one of the dead men had yet to produce any matches within DS-300, Stellar Wind, PRISM, or any other program based on his photo or thumbprint.

The photo showed a good-looking olive-skinned man with short, curly black hair, in his twenties.

June stared at the man's face for several seconds, then found the scan of his thumbprint. He magnified the print over and over, until he was looking at the individual ridges, each an inch or so wide. At the edge of the scan, he saw something that made his mouth drop open. It was an extremely fine line—a scar—running along the man's thumb.

June raised Dave McNaughton on the phone.

"Is your TAC team there yet?"

"Yeah," said McNaughton. "I know you want the contents of Al-Amin's computer, but we're still quarantining it, making sure it's not set up to erase itself."

"There's something more important," June told him. "There's a man there, one of the dead ones. I'm sending you his photo. I need a forensic coroner to examine his fingers closely. His fingerprints."

"What are we looking for?"

"Skin grafts."

30

PARIS

Kyrie stood beneath an awning across the street and half a block away from the George V, watching the chaos along with dozens of other curious onlookers.

He felt a kind of inner conflict he'd felt only once before in his life, when duty ran directly against what he knew to be right. The feeling of having to kill someone he loved.

He retraced his steps in his mind, searching for the flaws that might have delivered him to the hotel a few minutes earlier, in time to catch her and kill her before she escaped.

Now she was gone. Bruner would be apoplectic, not that he cared, but it mattered. But could it be helpful? The fact is, the chaos created by Lindsay's death was a thousand times more powerful than the attack on the mosque in Toronto. The White House would be consumed by the tragedy and the aftermath, mourning the country's top diplomat, searching for the killer. Security around the president and vice president would be a hundred times tighter.

The CIA man he'd framed would be locked up, but Kyrie knew it wouldn't last. No one, no matter how stupid or sloppy, would leave a gun on the floor like that. It was a move intended simply to create a mild impediment to the one man in Lindsay's vicinity who might be capable of finding him, a simple bump in the road to buy Kyrie time to get away.

He turned and walked away from the scene, opening his umbrella, then removing his cell phone. He dialed Flaherty.

"Is it done?"

"No," Kyrie said as he continued to walk. "She was gone by the time I got there."

"Did you kill him?"

"Yes. He knew."

"Good," said Flaherty. "She no doubt told him everything."

"I had to kill Casales too," said Kyrie. "If he lived, I thought there would be too much suspicion. He would be interrogated, tortured. There would be pharmaceuticals. I didn't want to take the risk. He could expose everything."

"Agreed," said Flaherty. "Where are you now?"

"Still in Paris. What's his reaction?"

Flaherty paused, clearing his throat.

"He'll understand, but it's going to cause complications," he said. "Security will tighten dramatically around the president and the vice president. Until they know it's not part of a broader sanction, getting the necessary opportunity for action is going to be more difficult."

"We have men inside the immediate envelope of both of them," said Kyrie.

"True," said Flaherty, "but not all the time and, most important, it must be coordinated, planned, and executed. If protocols are altered, schedules changed, that sort of thing, it will throw everything off. The real problem is, with Romy still . . ."

Kyrie winced as he listened.

". . . alive, it forces our hand. There is no optionality. We can't delay a thing. We have to act now, before the plot is somehow discovered. Right now, Romy is desperate, on the run, an escaped mental patient who murdered three people. But she'll find someone who believes her. Our options become more limited the longer she's alive. I know you don't want to hear that, Kyrie, and I'm sorry."

"I'll handle her," he whispered.

Kyrie walked for several blocks, listening to Flaherty. As he walked, he caught something, a reflection in the darkened windows of a shop. Half a block behind him, a sedan was following.

"She leaves us with no choice," continued Flaherty. "We take over the government now, before she finds someone who believes her and can do something to stop us. If she lives and the plot is uncovered, every single one of us will be killed. But more important, Islam will win. There will be nobody to eradicate these people—

this cancer—from the earth. Finding and killing Romy could be the difference between saving the United States of America and destroying it forever."

Kyrie stopped beneath an awning. He stared at the sedan. After a few moments, it sped up and passed him.

"Spare me your speeches, Andrew. After tonight, she'll realize the cell phone and credit card led us to her. Tell Kopitar he needs to find another way to track her. I said I would find her. Then I'll kill her."

31

PARIS

Dewey lay on the floor, staring into Lindsay's hotel suite, the weight of several men on top of him. A kneecap was jabbing into his upper back, pinning him down. Hands gripped his ankles.

"Don't be fucking idiots," he barked as his arms were yanked behind his back.

A boot pressed against his cheek, twisting his head sideways, pressing his face into the carpet.

"Whoever killed them is still out there!"

He felt sudden pressure around his ankles. He let out a pained grunt as both his ankles and wrists were bound with flex-cuffs.

"Call Calibrisi!" he shouted just as a rubber bite block was jammed between his teeth and chained tight around his head, preventing him from talking.

He was lifted to his feet and led to a service elevator, which descended to the hotel basement, where he was placed in the back of a van. There were no seats, only a steel floor. He couldn't speak and he could barely move. A steel partition separated the front of the van from the rear. The van had no windows. A single light on the ceiling cast an eerie green hue. A flashing red light in the corner indicated that the men in front were watching him as the van sped away from the George V.

It was impossible to know if the media had picked up on Lindsay's assassination yet, but when they did, all-out hell would break loose.

Dewey could only assume he was in the custody of DGSI. He knew the Direction Générale de la Sécurité Intérieure, France's internal security and intelligence agency, by reputation only. Smart, tough, competent, and effective, but dogged by rumors of torture and other acts of violence. DGSI was increasingly the place France's best soldiers ended up. But the agency was considered unreliable and wavering. The CIA had been badly burned the year before when it sought DGSI's assistance in tracking down a Yemeni woman—a graduate student at the Sorbonne—suspected of being a conduit for funds to Al Qaeda in Yemen. The sources of funding were what Langley were after. DGSI grabbed the girl and within two days she was dead, asphyxiated by accident inside a DGSI interrogation cell. The betrayal snuffed out an intelligence operation that had been in process for almost three years.

Dewey wasn't thinking about DGSI at that moment, however. He was thinking about the woman.

32

EAU PALM BEACH RESORT & SPA
MANALAPAN, FLORIDA

The motorcade was made up of eighteen vehicles. Two black Suburbans, one in front, the other at the back, held armed security personnel from the Secret Service. Four men in each vehicle were dressed in tactical military gear. Two agents in the middle bench seat clutched M4 carbines, muzzles trained at all times toward the outside, prepared to engage any sort of external threat. A third agent in the back of the SUV had a shoulder-mounted surface-to-air missile, trained at the window in back, which was black-tinted so that bystanders watching the motorcade couldn't see in.

A fourth man was in the front passenger seat. He held an HK MP7A1 submachine gun, a weapon designed for close-quarters combat. This was the point man, the first to engage any bystander threat in the immediate envelope of the motorcade.

A third Suburban held a cameraman and photographer from the White House press corps, so-called pool photographers, both of whom stood on the open back door of the SUV, harnesses around their waists, one filming, the other snapping pics.

A half dozen black sedans were filled with White House staff, a second layer of security personnel, and various major donors and VIPs from the Florida Republican Party, including U.S. Senator Stephen Vilas, running for reelection; Vilas was the reason the motorcade was in town.

The fund-raiser for Vilas was a dinner with the president of the United States.

A swarm of Palm Beach police, including several officers on motorcycles, were out in the lead, blue-and-red lights flashing as they barreled down Ocean Boulevard.

They were there because of one particular vehicle in the motorcade—a heavily customized Cadillac limousine whose every inch was composed of bulletproof and bombproof materials. This vehicle carried President J. P. Dellenbaugh, who waved absentmindedly at the hundreds of Floridians standing in the warm sunshine, holding signs and placards, waving and cheering back at the wildly popular first-term president.

Inside the limousine, the mood was calm, the shouting and cheering from the outside barely registering through the thick glass and reinforced steel. Dellenbaugh sat next to his wife, Amy. Across from them were a young, skinny man with somewhat shaggy, dirty-blond hair and droopy eyes: Holden Weese, the president's personal aide, and Mike Murphy, the president's senior political strategist. Murphy, who was scanning a thick document, was slightly overweight, disheveled, and handsome, with glasses. He was wearing jeans and an untucked black-and-red polo shirt.

"Vilas is in trouble," said Murphy, referring to the senior senator from Florida, for whom the president was in town to raise money. Murphy was reading numbers from a recent poll. "He's eight points down with three weeks to go."

"Well, hopefully this dinner will help close the gap," said Dellenbaugh.

Murphy stared sardonically out the window.

"Yeah, maybe, but I doubt it. If I'm reading the crosstabs right, he's losing Jewish retirees by a three-to-one margin. They're the ones who elected him."

"*Vilas?* He's one of Israel's top supporters."

Murphy shook his head. “It isn’t about Israel with Jewish retirees, Mr. President. It’s about erectile dysfunction.”

Dellenbaugh shot Murphy a baffled look.

“This should be good,” said Dellenbaugh.

“Vilas voted against the Medicaid prescription bill,” Murphy explained. “Jewish retirees have to pay for Viagra now.”

Dellenbaugh laughed.

“Everyone is always saying the cost of elections is going up,” Murphy went on. “In Florida, the cost of erections is going up. This election is about Viagra.”

“That’s preposterous,” said Dellenbaugh, shaking his head, but still laughing.

Outside, someone was holding a large sign that read WHEN WILL THE GOVERNMENT TELL US THE TRUTH ABOUT MARTIANS?

Murphy stared at the sign.

“God, I hate Florida,” he said. “If it weren’t for all the votes down here, I’d advocate for cutting it off and letting it crash into Cuba.”

Dellenbaugh grinned. “I thought you hated Massachusetts most?”

“That was last week. I mean, look at these people!” Murphy pointed out the window. “Elderly shut-ins, beach bums, bus passengers who ran out of money, swamp people, and pirates. Besides, I hate every state, sir. You have to in order to do what I do.”

Dellenbaugh raised one eyebrow and shook his head. But Dellenbaugh loved Murphy. His legendary rants were largely an act. Murphy loved America and its people. After dropping out of Georgetown freshman year to run his first Senate campaign, Murphy had established an incomparable win-loss record in the numerous statewide races and the three presidential elections he'd run. He knew every state, city, county, and nearly every town in America, and if he ripped on them it was because he liked making people laugh, the more powerful the person laughing, the more Murphy liked it. For those, like Dellenbaugh, used to existing in a cocoon of flattery and politeness, Murphy's withering, hilarious discourses were a sign of something important in a political strategist: honesty.

"Have you heard Florida's new motto?" added Murphy. "Florida: If you think we don't know how to vote, wait 'til you see us drive."

More laughter.

"Florida: if you don't like us, move to one of the other fifty-six states."

The motorcade slowed as it rounded the final corner before arriving at the Eau Palm Beach.

"Holden, how many people will be at the dinner?" the president asked, glancing at Weese.

"Seventeen hundred and thirty-two, sir."

"How much money will it raise?" asked Dellenbaugh.

"Ten million, one hundred and seventeen thousand dollars, Mr. President."

"If Vilas was smart, he'd take all that money and buy everyone Viagra," offered Murphy. " 'Vote for Vilas! Free Viagra!' He'd win in a landslide."

Amy Dellenbaugh, who had tried not to laugh, was now bright red, cackling as Murphy went on.

But her laughter was suddenly interrupted by a loud, piercing squawk, which pealed from every speaker in the limo. It was followed by the flashing red light on one of three phones along the limo door.

Two Secret Service Suburbans immediately flanked the presidential limousine.

The driver turned, holding his ear, indicating he was hearing something over his communications device.

"Sir, we have a situation. We need to get you to the airport."

Dellenbaugh glanced at his wife, then Murphy, both faces blank. Weese grabbed the phone from the console next to him and extended it to Dellenbaugh just as the limousine abruptly launched left, outside the line of the motorcade, and sped up, a Suburban out in front and another close behind.

"President Dellenbaugh, this is Control," came a female voice, the urgency obvious.

"Go ahead, Control."

"Hold for Josh Brubaker, Mr. President."

The phone clicked twice, then the national security advisor came on the line.

"Mr. President?"

"What is it, Josh?"

"It's Paris. Tim Lindsay is dead. He was murdered inside his hotel suite approximately twenty minutes ago."

Dellenbaugh watched through the front window as the limousine blazed left, following one of the Suburbans. He was quiet for a moment, glancing at Murphy.

"My God," whispered the president.

Multiple sirens pierced the quiet of the limo as the small convoy moved at high speed down a side street, where it fell into line behind a swarm of police cars.

Dellenbaugh looked at his wife, then Murphy, and finally Weese.

"Tim Lindsay was killed in Paris," he said.

"Per protocol, Mr. President," said Brubaker, "we're removing you from your present location and getting you airborne. Adrian is letting Senator Vilas know."

Adrian King was the White House chief of staff.

"Has anyone spoken with Debbie Lindsay?" said President Dellenbaugh.

"Yes," said Brubaker. "Vice President Donato called her."

"Has it leaked?"

"No, sir," said Brubaker.

"Get John on this immediately. I want a statement in my hands within the next ten minutes. Keep it short." John Schmidt was the president's communications director.

"Yes, sir."

"Now tell me everything we know, Josh."

"Hector has been the point of contact with French authorities. He's going to join us as soon as he gets off the line with them. It should be momentarily, Mr. President."

33

CIA HEADQUARTERS
LANGLEY

Hector Calibrisi stood behind his desk on the seventh floor of CIA headquarters, tucked into the corner of the building, its walls made almost entirely of glass. Four individuals were with him. Luke Brennan, Langley's general counsel, was seated on one of two chairs in front of Calibrisi's desk. On the couch against the wall, Bill Polk, head of National Clandestine Services, was next to one of his two deputies, Mack Perry, who ran the Special Operations Group. Angie Poole, the other NCS deputy, who oversaw the Special

Activities Division, was standing near the window, pacing back and forth. In her hand was a cell phone, which she was listening to with her hand over the microphone.

A large rectangular phone sat atop Calibrisi's desk, its speaker on.

Calibrisi was on a call with Bernard Cazanove, the head of DGSI. It was their third conversation in the last hour.

France's internal security and intelligence wing was similar to the FBI, charged with safeguarding France from all manner of threat. For the most part, this meant terrorism. DGSI was at the front edge of France's efforts to stem the tidal wave of radical Islamists inside its own borders. It was a battle the country was losing. France, and Paris in particular, had become a vital entry point for jihadis intent on penetrating Europe, the UK, and, eventually, Canada. America, of course, was the ultimate objective, but America was accessed through Canada, and Canada through France.

Angie Poole was linked into White House Control, where Josh Brubaker was patched into the limousine carrying President Dellenbaugh.

Calibrisi's tie was loosened and his top shirt button undone. The atmosphere in the office was tense; everyone was in shock, not only at Lindsay's murder but also at the accusation being leveled by Cazanove, namely, that Dewey Andreas was involved.

Cazanove was speaking, his French accent lilting and aristocratic.

"It was his sidearm. A Colt .45 M1911A1, with some kind of tape wrapped around the butt."

Calibrisi shook his head.

"Have you run the prints? Ballistics?" he asked.

"It happened less than an hour ago, Hector. We will run the prints, the ballistics, and every other bit of evidence we find. In the meantime, Andreas is in our custody and we're going to ask him some questions."

"Someone is setting him up. He wouldn't kill Tim Lindsay."

"People change," said Cazanove.

"Bernard, it might be his gun, and you might think you have proof. But Dewey wouldn't kill the secretary of state. We need to investigate. I need to speak with him. And I need to do it before DGSI starts going crazy on him."

"Insulting DGSI investigative tactics is not going to be productive."

Angie Poole leaned toward the phone. "Where's he being held, Mr. Director?" she asked.

"Why is this relevant?"

"It's no secret that Branch Four has had a series of incidents," said Poole. "At the very least, please assure us you have Dewey inside the central facility at DGSI headquarters and not Branch Four."

"I make no such assurances. You all seem to

forget the simple fact that right now he is the prime suspect in the murder of the United States secretary of state."

"Is he at Branch Four?" she persisted.

"Yes," Cazanove acknowledged.

Poole looked at Calibrisi. She had a concerned expression on her face.

Suddenly, Polk snapped his fingers, pointing at his phone, indicating the president was waiting. Calibrisi nodded and held up a finger: *one more minute.*

He turned back. "When can I speak with Dewey?" he said.

"He's being interrogated as we speak."

"Interrupt your men."

"No," said Cazanove, "I won't. There is a process. Even you should want to see that justice is done."

"You know damn well I want to get to the bottom of it, Bernard. But Dewey didn't do it."

"All evidence indicates that he did."

Calibrisi glanced at Polk. His face was red with anger.

"Goddammit!" Calibrisi erupted. "*Stop fucking around!* That's *our* dead secretary of state. That's *my* agent and someone I know and trust personally! Someone the president trusts!"

"I'm sure Tim Lindsay was someone the president trusted as well, Hector," Cazanove replied tartly.

"This is a U.S. issue. It just happened to have occurred on French soil."

"If it happened at the embassy, I would agree. But it didn't. It's French jurisdiction. DGSI is running it. As you Americans say, period, end of statement."

"You're not going to let me speak with him?"

"No." Cazanove paused. "Not yet, anyway. We need to let justice take its course."

Calibrisi shook his head. He was irate.

"By the way," continued Cazanove, "as part of our investigation, I have asked, through our American ambassador, for access to any and all files involving Andreas that are in your possession. We are more than willing to read them inside Langley with all various protective measures in place to ensure secrecy and whatnot. I assume this will not be a problem."

Calibrisi's red face turned a shade redder, but Polk got his attention, waving his finger across his neck like a guillotine, telling Calibrisi to end the call before he said something he would regret. Calibrisi shut his eyes and nodded, taking a deep breath.

"Are you there, Hector?" asked Cazanove. "Can we avoid some of the administrative steps that tend to take so much time—"

Calibrisi didn't wait for Cazanove to complete his sentence, hanging up the phone.

"You need to stop the search warrant before it's

executed," said Calibrisi to Brennan. "National security. We do not want DGSI reading Dewey's files."

Brennan stood and moved to the door.

Calibrisi looked at Poole and nodded. A green light lit up on the phone console. Calibrisi hit the speaker button.

"Sorry, Mr. President," said Calibrisi.

"What the hell is going on?" asked Dellenbaugh.

"DGSI has Dewey in custody," said Calibrisi. "They think he killed Lindsay."

"What?" Dellenbaugh asked incredulously.

"They apparently have evidence, sir. His sidearm was used in the murders."

"Oh, Christ," said Dellenbaugh.

"It's not possible. We both know Dewey would never do anything like this."

"Have you spoken with him?"

"No. They won't let me."

Dellenbaugh was silent for a few moments.

"I actually think that might be a good thing," the president said.

"What do you mean?"

There was another long pause.

"We have a dead secretary of state. We need to get our ducks in a row. Of course I don't think Dewey did it, but more important than getting him out right now is the fact that America's highest-ranking diplomat was assassinated. We need to ensure this isn't a broader attack and that it doesn't somehow inadvertently signal our enemies or sideline some of the initiatives we're working on."

Calibrisi was quiet. On some level, he knew Dellenbaugh was right. But it rankled him nevertheless.

"You're right, Mr. President," said Calibrisi. "But Dewey is in the middle of it. The reason we need to speak with him is that he's closest to what happened. We need to determine why someone killed Lindsay and whether it's part of a broader sanction."

"And you think we need to speak to Dewey to do that?"

"It certainly would help, Mr. President."

"Is there some sort of flash brief on this by DGSI?"

"Yes. I'll send it to you."

"I'll be back in two hours," said Dellenbaugh. "I want your people running hard at this. I want updates on the way."

"Yes, sir." Calibrisi pressed the speaker button and hung up the phone. He knew Dellenbaugh was right, but still, something ate away at him. The focus needed to be one hundred percent on Lindsay. First he would call Jim Bruckheimer at NSA and get his team of cryptologists and eavesdroppers charging ahead. Next he'd coordinate a call with Derek Chalmers at MI6 and Mossad.

But he couldn't help thinking there was something else going on.

"The president is right," said Calibrisi, looking at Polk, then Perry, and Angie. "I want our best Europe and CT analysts on this, same with field personnel. We need to find out what happened and why. I'll call Jim Bruckheimer and get them hunting down the death threats, chatter, and whatever other intel might be related to the killings. Let's reconvene in thirty minutes."

Calibrisi picked up the phone, shooing them away.

"Get me Jim Bruckheimer at Fort Meade. Tell him it's urgent."

34

DIRECTION GÉNÉRALE DE LA SÉCURITÉ INTÉRIEURE (DGSI)
BRANCH FOUR
PARIS

The van arrived at a nondescript warehouse behind Gare Montparnasse, the massive train station in south-central Paris. This was Branch Four, one of three high-security DGSI intake centers used for temporary incarceration and interrogation of suspected terrorists.

Dewey was pulled from the van and led down

a brightly lit corridor. The walls were made of corrugated steel, the floor was concrete. A faint aroma of oil was in the air. Dewey passed through a doorway into a line of cellblocks. The individual cells were unnerving and different from any other incarceration units he'd ever seen. The front was a wall of Plexiglas, with overhead lights so bright as to sting the eyes.

He glanced inside the units as he passed by. The first few were empty. In the third, a bald man in an orange prison jumpsuit was asleep on a concrete platform. His head was covered in a bizarre-looking tattoo, some sort of geometric pattern in black-and-red ink. Suddenly, the man's eyes shot open. He stared at Dewey and then at the guards. He stood and ran toward the Plexiglas wall, screaming angrily, then launched himself against it. The wall didn't move, and even his words were impossible to hear; the cell was soundproof.

Dewey's world was on fire.

Focus. Stay calm.

Yet as much as he tried to remain in the present, as much as he tried to register the concrete and steel walls all around him, all he could think about was the woman on the train—the woman he saw in Lindsay's suite. He couldn't make sense of any of it. He needed to speak with someone. He needed Calibrisi, and not just to get him out of jail. He needed to tell someone about the woman.

He knew one thing with overwhelming certainty: he had to find the woman who murdered Lindsay.

Unless . . .

Unless she didn't do it. But who else could've done it? One of the agents? They were both dead. It made no sense. It *had* to be her. If it wasn't, wouldn't she be dead too?

Dewey pictured his gun on the floor of Lindsay's room. Whoever did it had access to his room. That was a small group—Lindsay himself, the CONS OP detail, and certain hotel employees who'd been extensively vetted and were allowed in only with permission. Whoever did it also knew he was packing a weapon. How could they have gotten into the room without getting stopped by Lindsay's security team?

There were too many variables. It was impossible to make sense of it all.

Dewey tried to sift through it by imagining the operation:

Lindsay in the suite with the woman.

Two agents in the hallway.

She exits, door closes, she guns down the two agents.

She finds a key to his room on one of the agents. Retrieves his gun and returns to Lindsay's suite, knocks on his door, kills him, drops the gun.

But why go through the complication of framing him? It made no sense. If she had a gun to kill the agents, why not simply use it to shoot Lindsay too? Why the theatrics of setting him up? To frame him? Certainly there were people who wanted Dewey dead, enemies, people like the Fortunas. Dewey's enemies didn't want him in jail. They wanted him dead.

Could it have been a hotel employee, an embedded operative from another intelligence service—China, Russia, Iran—posing as a chamber maid? She shows up to clean the room, takes his weapon, kills both guards, then Lindsay. The woman who was in the room isn't killed because she had already left.

That made more sense. Then again, it didn't. Every hotel employee had been thoroughly vetted against every CIA, State, NSA, and INTERPOL database that existed. In addition, the only employees allowed on the floor had to have been working at the hotel a minimum of twenty years. A hotel employee would've been easy. Too easy.

The woman.

Then he remembered the words from training:

The minutes immediately after lethal action are the most important. Successful lethal action is not just about removing a target. Just as important is the freeing up of time for escape from the overwhelming suspicion, movement, and reaction that will come in the seconds and minutes after it's done.

The words were Delta, but Delta didn't have a monopoly on how to successfully sanitize a targeted killing. The tactic was universal.

Distraction, confusion, and misdirection must be built into the planning of any assassination. They are as powerful a weapon as the one that is used to kill.

Yes, that's what they did—what *she* did. Created a distraction. *He* was the distraction. At this very moment, Dewey should've been moving to find her, and yet here he was in a DGSI terror unit. In all likelihood, he would be interrogated for days, maybe weeks.

The U.S. secretary of state had been murdered on French soil. It would be a huge black eye for France and DGSI specifically. Even with Calibrisi's assistance, he would likely remain in DGSI custody for weeks or even months. There would be pharmaceuticals. It had been years since he'd endured them. Indeed, if only for the intelligence value of what was inside Dewey's head, DGSI would put him through a gauntlet of physical and mental torture. They wouldn't kill him . . . unless.

He recalled his trial so many years ago, after Holly was found dead. Then, too, it had been his gun that shot the fatal bullet. Her face was beyond recognition. He knew it was suicide, of course. But then he got his first lesson in the American justice system. He was falsely accused of murdering her. The local DA had him locked up and put him on trial.

Dewey also learned then about being abandoned by the very people he needed most, the U.S. military, the people he worked for, sacrificed for, risked his life for. The military abandoned him to the justice system, washed their hands of the entire thing. Dewey vowed to never again allow himself to be placed at the whim of those above him. It was happening all over again.

Hector isn't like the others. He'll know what to do.

But would he?

Calibrisi had been back at his desk at Langley for less than a week when he sent Dewey to Paris. His recovery from a massive heart attack had taken months. It weakened him physically and mentally. More important, it weakened Calibrisi within the cutthroat ranks of U.S. intelligence. Others asserted themselves in places that were the purview of the CIA. Even inside Langley, the rumors of Calibrisi's possible retirement were rampant.

And then it struck Dewey. Even with the full weight of the U.S. government pushing for his release, he'd be lucky to come out the other end alive. Not because the French would intentionally kill him, but being in a French prison would. His identity would be on INTERPOL within hours. Every enemy he'd ever made would know where he was. It would not be hard for someone to hire the right people—inmates or guards—to stick a knife in Dewey's back while he slept.

He felt his heart beating faster. It was a feeling of futility and helplessness.

Why did you do this? Who are you?!

The agents brought Dewey into a small, windowless, and dimly lit interrogation room. A lone chair sat in the middle of the room, a small table in front of it. Dark bloodstains were spattered on the concrete floor. Dewey was pushed to the chair and shoved onto the seat. His legs and wrists were cuffed tight to the chair, which was bolted to the floor. A two-way mirror took up half a wall off to the side.

The door opened and two men entered. One—a blond-haired man with a long nose—was dressed in jeans and a T-shirt. He looked to be in his late twenties. The other man was tall, with longish brown hair, dressed in a green corduroy suit and no tie. He appeared to be around forty.

"I am Detective Beauxchamps," said the older man, with only a hint of a French accent. "This is Detective Rousse. You are Dewey Andreas, yes?"

35

SAINT-DENIS—UNIVERSITÉ

Romy got off at the next station and switched trains. There were too many people wondering why the large man was chasing her. She switched trains again, not knowing where she was going. After almost an hour, she came to Saint-Denis—Université and got off, climbing the stairs to the streets above.

She found a drugstore a few blocks from the Métro station. She walked down several aisles until she found scissors. In the back of the drugstore were restrooms. She went inside the women's room and locked the door.

Romy stood before the mirror and grabbed a handful of hair, lifting it above her head, holding it taut. With her other hand, she took the scissors and started cutting her hair as close to her scalp as she could. Slowly, over the course of the next few minutes, she cut her hair as short as possible, leaving only a thin, patchy layer of hair. She took as much of the hair as she could and flushed it down the toilet, then quickly left the drugstore.

Outside, the rain was pouring down harder than before. She started walking, not knowing where she would go, concentrating only on the cold raindrops as they hit her scalp and ran down her face, mixing with tears that wouldn't stop falling from empty, shell-shocked eyes.

36

NSA

A loud chime sounded from Samantha's workstation. She turned to one of three large computer screens that spanned her desk. An icon on the middle screen was flashing.

She hit her speakerphone, raising June.

"We have a hit," Samantha told him.

She clicked the icon and the screen opened into a black map with bright green lines. The screen sharpened and focused as it zeroed down on the map, as if aiming for something. Within seconds, the screen stopped above a street grid of Paris, with a single flashing light.

June came into the large bullpen of workstations and went to Samantha's desk.

"I just triangulated a call through the satellite," she said. "You're not going to believe this."

"Where was it made from?" said June.

"Paris," she said. "Hotel George Cinq."

37

DGSI BRANCH FOUR
PARIS

Dewey stared at the two agents but said nothing.

The younger agent, Rousse, clutched Dewey's ID badge. He tossed it onto the table in front of Dewey. He walked behind Dewey and unhooked the mouth gag around his head.

"Who are you?" Rousse asked. Unlike the older Beauxchamps, Rousse's accent was thick and gruff.

"I want to speak with Hector Calibrisi," Dewey said calmly.

Rousse stared blankly back at him.

"You killed three people," he said matter-of-factly. "Put aside for a moment the fact that one of those three individuals was the United States secretary of state. *You killed three people.*"

"I didn't kill anyone."

"You did it on French soil. This is not some sort of operation where you suddenly get magically whisked away by the Central Intelligence Agency."

"Go fuck yourself," said Dewey.

"This is a multiple homicide on French soil.

It is a matter for the French government now. Hector Calibrisi can't help you."

"I didn't do it. Whoever did do it is walking around free while you two nitwits stand here wasting time. I need to speak to Hector Calibrisi."

Rousse looked at Beauxchamps, who stood quietly against the wall, allowing Rousse to lead the interrogation. Rousse came closer to Dewey, across the table from him. He leaned down so that his face was only a few inches from Dewey's.

"Did you not hear me?" he said.

"I heard you. Now either let me go or get me Calibrisi. *I didn't do it.* You and I both know that."

"I don't know that at all," said Rousse. "How would I know that?"

"Because by now you've run my profile. Does that look like the record of a traitor?"

"Times change. People change."

"Even if I did change, would I leave my gun next to the body?"

"I've seen stupider things."

Dewey glared at the blond. He turned to the brown-haired detective, Beauxchamps.

"Please," Dewey asked politely. "Let me speak to Calibrisi. Or at least get Chiesa in here."

Chiesa was Langley's Paris chief of station.

"Your sidearm was next to the body," said Rousse. "Your fingerprints are all over the gun.

The ballistics aren't back yet, but who's kidding who? You and I both know they will match."

Dewey stared daggers at Rousse. "Listen, you stupid son of a bitch, I didn't do it. Why would I kill Tim Lindsay?"

"Who knows? Perhaps for money? It's almost always about money, isn't it?"

"I didn't do it. Somebody, however, *did* do it. That person, those people, whoever it is, they're walking free right now. Meanwhile, you idiots are losing whatever trail they left behind."

"We're running four teams against this," said Beauxchamps. "Two of those teams are working on the assumption that, in fact, you *didn't* do it. Not because we think that, but because that is the way we run forensics on a murder like this. The problem is, we have a weapon."

"I was at a restaurant when Tim Lindsay was killed."

"Did you pay?"

"No. I received the alert and ran. I got on the Métro."

Dewey glanced at the two-way mirror to his right.

"You film inside the Métro stations, right?" he asked.

"We have examined the video," said Beauxchamps. "You were filmed at the station approximately twenty minutes after Lindsay was murdered. You ran to the train and tried to pry the doors open as it was leaving. Why? Were you trying to get away?"

"Fuck you," Dewey said.

"Why did you run to the train?" persisted Beauxchamps. "Why did you attempt to pry the doors open?"

"That, by the way, is also a felony," added Rousse.

"Answer the question," said Beauxchamps.

Dewey stared at him with a cold, blank expression.

"I'm not answering any questions until I speak with Calibrisi."

Rousse stepped forward and swung his open hand through the air, striking Dewey viciously across the cheek. Dewey absorbed it; he felt the harsh sting but barely moved.

"Why were you trying to get away?" asked Beauxchamps.

"I wasn't trying to get away. Do you think if I killed the secretary of state, or anyone, for that matter, I'd escape on the fucking Métro? And even if I did, do you think I'd make such a spectacle of myself?"

"Someone who dropped his weapon would," said Rousse.

Dewey stared straight ahead, at the wall, past Rousse, who was in his face. Again, Dewey pictured the woman from the hotel suite.

"Did you see someone?" asked Beauxchamps.

Dewey remained silent.

"Answer him," said Rousse.

He swung again, harder this time, with a closed fist across Dewey's mouth. The punch jerked Dewey's head sideways. He tasted blood.

"Stop hitting me," said Dewey, more annoyed than anything. "I didn't kill Lindsay."

"Why were you running?" asked Beauxchamps. "Who did you see?"

Dewey shook his head, saying nothing.

"Who?" yelled Rousse.

This time, he unleashed a violent kick to Dewey's knee. Involuntarily, Dewey lurched forward, straining against the chair. Before he could straighten again, Rousse hit him in the stomach, knocking the wind out of him.

It took awhile for Dewey to catch his breath. When he did, he looked up, an angry expression on his face. He spat a mouthful of blood-crossed saliva onto the table.

"So much for French hospitality," he said, a shit-eating grin taking over his face just as blood began dribbling down his chin.

"Why wouldn't you want us to know the reason why you were trying to get on the train?" asked Beauxchamps.

"Because I don't trust you."

Rousse leaned in again. With a smile on his face, he slapped Dewey with the back of his hand. He turned to Beauxchamps.

"It's an internal hit," said Rousse to Beauxchamps. "As much as it appears that it would have to be an idiot who did it the way it was done, the truth is, I think it was him."

"Think what you want," said Dewey. "Get Calibrisi on the phone. I get one call."

Rousse laughed. "A phone call?"

"Yes, a phone call."

"You must have learned that on some American TV show. You don't get any calls."

"Call him," Dewey said to Beauxchamps.

Another slap sent blood splattering across the floor to Dewey's left. He could tell that his lip was swelling up badly. He looked at both men, his eyes moving methodically between them.

"I didn't do it, you French fuckheads. You can break every bone in my body, you can kill me, but my story won't change. I didn't kill Tim Lindsay."

Rousse rubbed his fist, which was sore from hitting him.

"Fuckhead?" he said, then swung again.

Dewey anticipated it.

As Rousse's hand cut through the air, Dewey turned toward it. He opened his mouth, teeth bared, and lurched at Rousse's fist. The strike from Rousse came in the same instant Dewey clamped down, biting whatever he could find. Rousse's punch sent Dewey's head sideways, but he had Rousse's thumb between his teeth. Dewey bit down hard, breaking skin, reaching the bone.

The detective screamed. *"Let go! Stop! Let go!"*

Rousse tried to extricate himself, yanking his arm, but Dewey just bit down harder, then twisted, nearly breaking his thumb. Rousse let out a pained yelp. After a few seconds, he stopped struggling, realizing it was making it worse and that he could easily lose a finger.

Beauxchamps watched the entire sequence, barely moving.

"Let him go," he said calmly. "You're only going to make matters worse."

Dewey looked up at the older agent. There was a calm expression on his face. He nodded toward his handcuffs.

Rousse suddenly yanked his hand again, trying to pull his thumb out of Dewey's mouth. Dewey bit down harder, eliciting another pained groan.

Beauxchamps stepped forward, pulling keys from his pocket.

"You're still shackled to the chair," he said as he unlocked the left flex-cuff. "Don't forget that. I'll unlock your hands, but that's all. Trust me when I say this: that's it."

Dewey eyed Beauxchamps as he moved to Dewey's right. As Dewey felt the right flex-cuff releasing, he slashed his elbow into Beaux-champs's kidney—sending him backward—then grabbed Rousse at the elbow, twisting viciously, pulling Rousse closer. Dewey swung his left arm around Rousse's neck and clenched tight. He had the agent in a death hold.

The door burst open. Two gunmen charged into the room. Each agent carried a handgun, which they had trained out in front of their bodies, aimed at Dewey.

"If you shoot, hc dies too," said Dewey. "I know what I'm doing."

Dewey stared at Beauxchamps, who was bent over, holding his side in pain.

"I'm not going to hurt him," continued Dewey, "unless you do something stupid."

"You're not leaving, if that's what you think. He'll die before I authorize your release. What do you want?"

Dewey registered the two muzzles now aimed at his head.

"I want what I asked for. A phone call."

Beauxchamps stepped to the wall, staring at Dewey.

"Fine," he said, exhaling. He took a cell from his pockct and placed it down in front of Dewey. Beauxchamps waved his hand at the gunmen, dismissing them. He glanced to the two-way mirror, making a gesture to his ear.

Record it.

Slowly, Dewey leaned forward and picked up the cell phone. He dialed a six-digit number and waited for it to ring, all the while clutching Rousse's neck in a vise.

A computer-generated female voice came on the line.

> Identify.

"E.N.C. one-six-nine-four-pharaoh," said Dewey.

Dewey's command caused the CIA computer on the other end of the line to do two things: enable it to identify Dewey by voice recognition alone and not by the usual method, which would've required Dewey to voice his non-official cover identification number and encrypt and digitally scramble the call he was about to make, channeled via a CIA satellite.

Several low beeps could be heard as Dewey continued to hold Rousse. Finally, the female voice came on the line.

> Affirmative pharaoh, dock eight-one-eight-alpha-eight.

Dewey punched in Calibrisi's number, but as he was about to hit Send, he paused, staring at Beauxchamps. In his head, Dewey replayed the sight of the woman on the train, as if in a movie, over and over again. Who was she? Who did she remind him of?

Dewey had stared into the eyes of a man who tried to detonate a nuclear bomb in the heart of

New York City. He'd felt the edge of a knife at his neck, held there by an ISIS terrorist as he was about to cut his head off. There was no limit to the evil in the world, or the darkness that drove men to do unspeakable things. For some reason, he felt the same sense of dread about the woman he'd seen. He felt an unshakable coldness, and the worst part about it was he didn't know why.

Who are you? Who sent you? Why did you kill Tim Lindsay?

And then he heard his own thoughts coalesce into a single question: *Why me?*

"Hurry up," groaned Rousse.

The words stirred him from his thoughts. Dewey yanked up, wrenching the smaller man hard, lifting him from the ground and causing him to cough painfully. Then Dewey let him go. Rousse stumbled slightly as he practically jumped away from Dewey. His face was bright red. His hand was bleeding. Rousse removed a gun from his shoulder holster and aimed it at Dewey.

"Drop the phone!"

"Leave him alone," Beauxchamps said calmly. "Go get two cups of coffee. Now."

Dewey said nothing as Rousse went for the door, cursing under his breath. He looked down at the phone and cleared Calibrisi's number, then dialed another number he knew by heart. He hit

Send and waited. Several clicks sounded. Then someone answered.

"What is it?" came a perturbed voice. The accent was German. "Who is it? Do you know what time it is? How did you get this number?"

"Hi, Rolf."

There was a long pause.

"Ah, yes," said Borchardt, suddenly alert. "Let's see . . . a call at four in the morning from a sanitized Lotus-caliber switch. A dead secretary of state. It must be Dewey Andreas. Let me guess: You need my help?"

"I don't have time for this. You can gloat later."

"Are you alone?"

"No."

"Okay, fine. Hold on."

"I can't," said Dewey, glancing at the brown-haired agent.

"Trust me. Hold on."

Several clicks echoed from the phone. Then came a low buzzing noise. Finally, Borchardt returned. "Speak," he said.

"What was that?"

"A jamming device, just in case whatever one you routed through doesn't hold. We'll have about three minutes. Where are you?"

"DGSI. Someone set me up."

"Or you did it."

"I didn't do it."

"No, I know you didn't," said Borchardt. "The

question is, who is framing you, and why did they kill Tim Lindsay? Now, personally I never liked the man. Too much of a pacifist. But his plantation in South Carolina was always fun to visit. I shouldn't bite the hand that feeds me. In fact, remind me to inquire as to whether or not it's for sale, will you?"

"You're a demented little bastard."

"Careful, prisoner soixante-neuf."

"It's not funny."

Borchardt cleared his throat. "No, it's not. I apologize."

"Who did it?" said Dewey.

Borchardt was silent for a few seconds, then spoke in an oddly soft, curious voice.

"There are certainly a few groups that would like to kill the U.S. secretary of state, no matter who it is. The part that doesn't make sense is that no one is taking credit. Instead they're pinning it on you."

Dewey felt a chill. "What are you talking about?"

"How did they get your gun and, more important, why? Why not just kill the man?"

"I don't know."

"Lindsay knew something," said Borchardt. "There's no other explanation."

The cold chill emanated from Dewey's spine and spread. The woman. Did she kill Lindsay, or . . .

He tried to imagine a scenario in which she, in fact, hadn't killed Lindsay. Why? Did she tell Lindsay something, something so explosive that whoever was behind it had no choice but to put a bullet in him?

"I need to get out of here."

"You should consider the fact that you might be safer inside a DGSI cell than out on the streets."

"Can you help me or not?"

Pause.

"Yes, but it won't be easy. We're about to lose the encryption layer. Let me speak quickly. The cells when you first entered. Were there bars?"

"No, Plexiglas."

"Okay, you're at a DGSI terror unit called Branch Four. Now this is important. Do they have you in one of those units or in something more old school?"

"All I've seen is the inside of an interrogation room."

"If they bring you to one of the Plexiglas units, there's nothing I can do. But I'm guessing they'll bring you to an isolation cell in the basement."

"How will I know?"

"It'll be a concrete box, no glass. The Plexiglas cells are for after they've broken someone. Before that, they hold prisoners in the basement. So obviously, don't break."

"I didn't do it."

"Fine, fine," said Borchardt. "First of all, don't

eat anything. Dinner, breakfast. *Nothing*. It will be drugged and you won't wake up for a long time. The French have been experimenting with certain combinations of drugs to elicit confessions, and apparently it's very powerful stuff. You might not have done it, but knowing DGSI, they will coerce other valuable information out of you. That's the last thing you want."

"Keep going."

"There's a small digital lock on the back of every door. It uses a ten-digit combination. It's designed for certain exigencies such as prison riots or takeovers. The guards and agents can lock themselves in and get out when they choose."

"What's the combination?" said Dewey.

"It changes every twenty-four hours, and every cell has a different number. I will arrange to have someone place the combination on your breakfast tray tomorrow morning. It will be a slip of paper. It could be hidden in the eggs, taped to the bottom of the plate, or somewhere else."

"What about monitors?" Dewey eyed Beaux-champs.

"There aren't any, not on that corridor. That's why Branch Four has such a bad reputation. A number of human rights groups have sued the French government. With nothing recording what happens, a lot can happen."

"How do you know all this?"

"I've seen the designs of DGSI's terror intake units, including the one you're in. There are a number of structural weaknesses in the schematic. Now listen carefully: if you get the door open, you'll have less than a minute before they come. There's an abandoned stairwell. It will not be easy to find, but you *need* to find it. It will be behind a cabinet or will be painted over, but there is access to it on each floor. Go to the basement and go out the door. There'll be a car parked across the street. The key will be in it."

"What kind of car?"

"Something fast."

38

U.S. CAPITOL
WASHINGTON, D.C.

The Capitol steps were crowded with reporters. At least a dozen different cameramen were positioned at various points along the sweeping granite portico, shoulder-held cameras trained on a posse of network reporters doing live feeds, all focused on the death of Lowell Trappe, Speaker of the United States House of Representatives, an accidental drowning while on a hunting trip in Georgia.

In front of the Capitol dome, a large American flag hung at half-staff, its red, white, and blue canvas snapping in the autumn wind.

Sprinkled among the cameramen and reporters were several members of Congress, available for on-air interviews to discuss their esteemed colleague. Most were speaking not only as colleagues but also as friends, reminiscing about a man who was almost universally respected.

Trappe's drowning had left a vacancy at the apex of Congress, a position that was third in line to the presidency of the most powerful nation on earth. Most of the congressmen and congresswomen availing themselves of the media exposure were messaging a deeper intent, showing the press corps, and the country, that they were considering running for the coveted position.

One of them—a good-looking, sandy-haired man in a dark suit—was surrounded by reporters. This was Congressman Ned Carroll of Pennsylvania, the Republican majority leader in the House, second in line to Trappe. As everyone knew, the speakership was Carroll's if he wanted it.

"Ladies and gentleman," said Carroll with a somber look on his face. "Now is not the time, nor is this the place, to discuss what shall happen in regard to the speakership. Like everyone who knew Lowell Trappe, I'm a friend today and that's all. A very sad friend. Lowell Trappe was a mentor to me and to . . ."

A black sedan idled at the corner of Northwest Drive and Delaware Avenue.

Virtually unnoticed amid the hubbub on the steps, a tall man in a brown suit emerged from a side door atop to the left of the conflagrations of reporters, cameramen, and politicians. His name was Bobby Largent.

Largent had on a dark trench coat and a baseball hat. He walked quickly down the steps, avoiding reporters and colleagues. A seven-term congressman from Oklahoma, Largent was the Republican House Whip, third in seniority in the House of Representatives behind the Speaker of the House and the House Majority leader, the man now pontificating to reporters.

Largent approached the idling sedan via a sidewalk filled with tourists. He scanned the vicinity of the sedan. He swept his eyes in a casual, lackadaisical way, but his intent was anything but. The moment Lowell Trappe was reported dead, Bobby Largent knew the hour was upon him. Every moment from here on out had to be executed with the utmost precision and care. Every second had to be mistake-proof.

He saw nothing unusual as he took the final steps to the sedan. He opened the back door and climbed in.

Bruner stared at Largent. He had an emotionless expression on his face.

Then he spoke: "It's begun."

Largent nodded.

"I'm not sure I have the votes, Charles. Ned Carroll called me last night and said if I don't back him by lunchtime, he'll run someone against me."

Bruner glanced into the rearview mirror. The sedan began to move.

"Carroll is not your concern," Bruner said calmly. "He will be taken care of. The important thing is that you do exactly as you're told."

Largent nodded. "Of course, Charles."

"Suspicion and paranoia could start to take over the government's reaction to recent events," said Bruner. "Lowell Trappe's death is one thing. But if the White House or CIA starts to get suspicious about other developments, it would necessitate a more urgent time line."

"Developments?"

"I'm afraid the inner sanctum has been punctured."

"There's no way—"

"A trip wire was initiated," said Bruner. "The operation in Toronto. Langley and the NSA are digging in very hard. In addition, we have a possible security breach."

"What do you mean, security breach?"

"Romy."

Largent looked out the window, a look of mild anger on his face. He shook his head in disgust.

"I told you she needed to die," he said, seething. "Everyone told you."

Bruner listened, nodding politely, as Largent railed.

"Yet you allowed Kyrie to keep his trophy, didn't you?" continued Largent.

"Has Kyrie been granted privileges?" Bruner said calmly. "Yes, he has. But so have you. Without Kyrie, we would not be where we are today."

Largent looked away from Bruner. He lowered his head slightly and rubbed his eyes.

"What happened?"

"She found out," said Bruner. "She told someone. In fact, she told two people. A woman in Massachusetts and—"

Bruner looked out the window as the sedan cruised along Constitution Avenue. Several blocks ahead in the distance was the front of the U.S. State Department. He pointed. Largent's eyes followed Bruner's finger. His mouth went wide in disbelief.

"Do you mean—"

Bruner studied Largent's eyes, without emotion.

"Do I mean what?" he said calmly.

"Lindsay? . . . The . . . *secretary of state?*"

"Yes, that's precisely what I mean."

Largent's eyes shot to the door, as if he was contemplating trying to run.

"Go ahead," said Bruner.

"You'd have me killed."

"I wouldn't have to," said Bruner as the limo came to a stop across the street from the entrance to the State Department.

"What do you mean?"

"We're in a race against time now, Bobby. Either we find Romy and kill her, or she will expose the entire conspiracy. If that happens, we are *all* dead. She told Lindsay, and Kyrie was able to eliminate him before he told anyone. But every hour she lives increases the risk that she'll succeed in betraying us. That's why we must act *now.*"

Largent stared at the seat in front of him.

"If we don't take over the United States government, you'll be caught along with me and everybody else. I don't need to tell you what happens next, but I guarantee you it doesn't involve a jury," said Bruner, his voice quietly seething.

"Don't forget what this is about," he continued, calmer now. "You're a patriot, Bobby. We're all patriots, and together we're going to save America. *Don't be afraid.* You'll be in history books and it will be because you were instrumental in stopping the Nazism of our time, Islam."

"You're right," said Largent, making a fist and lightly hitting his knee. "You're absolutely right. I'm ready, Charles."

"I know you are."

Bruner climbed out and shut the door, then tapped on the back window. Largent lowered it a few inches. The slits of Bruner's dark eyes were the only things visible as Largent looked at him.

"We've all made sacrifices," said Bruner. "You perhaps more than anyone. I would like to tell you that it all ends up evening out, but that's child's talk and we both know it."

Bruner had an intense look in his eyes as he stared in at Largent.

"We're playing a man's game now," he said, a hint of threat in his voice. "In a matter of hours, you'll be the youngest Speaker of the House in American history. Soon after that, if everything goes according to plan, you'll be president of the United States of America. Are you ready?"

"I was born ready."

39

CIA HEADQUARTERS
LANGLEY

Calibrisi entered his office, shut the door, and sat down behind his desk. He ran his hand back through his thick, slightly shaggy black hair. Mack Perry and Angie Poole were already seated.

"Let's get started," said Calibrisi, looking at Perry on the sofa. "Mack, take us through the time line."

Perry looked at Angie and nodded. She tossed him a remote. He synced it with his laptop computer and then clicked a button. A large plasma screen descended from the ceiling in the middle of the office. Perry typed and the screen filled with a grainy photo of a hallway. It was footage from a video, which was paused.

"This is video from the hotel security camera down the hall from Lindsay's suite," said Perry. "Start time is in the lower right of the frame, so this is at eight oh five P.M. Paris time."

He hit the remote and the video started playing. Two men were standing in the hallway near Lindsay's door. It was hard to tell what they looked like due to the angle.

"The close agent is Tim Casales," said Perry.

"The other agent is Rex Cline. Both CONS OP, Cline a little over a decade, Casales, eight years."

Suddenly, a dark figure entered the frame of the camera, only his back visible. He was wearing a polo shirt. He was large, his frame wide and muscled. He had longish dark hair. He silhouetted in the hazy light of the security camera but was unmistakable. He walked with an athletic, menacing air.

"That's Dewey," said Perry.

Onscreen, Dewey moved past Casales to Lindsay's door and knocked. He stood in front of the door for several moments, waiting. Then the door opened. Dewey stepped inside, though the door remained ajar. The video showed the two agents glancing to Lindsay's door but saying nothing. Less than a minute after entering, Dewey emerged from the suite and shut the door. He walked down the hallway in the opposite direction from where he'd come.

"Where's he going?" asked Calibrisi.

"Elevators," said Perry.

He clicked the remote several times, bringing up a series of photos of Dewey, exiting an elevator on the ground floor, passing through the front entrance, then, from an outdoor camera, moving along a wet sidewalk as rain pelted down.

"What about footage from around the time Lindsay was shot?" asked Calibrisi.

Perry hit the remote. “This is twenty-two minutes after Dewey exited the hotel,” he said.

The screen cut back to the security camera in the hallway outside Lindsay’s suite. The two agents were still standing guard. The closer man, Casales, turned his head toward the camera. A second later, the screen went dark.

“That’s the last footage we have,” said Perry. “The camera was still active, but someone hit it with black spray paint.”

“Let me guess,” said Calibrisi. “They found the paint in Dewey’s garbage can.”

Perry nodded.

“So they covered up the camera,” said Calibrisi. “We don’t know what happened next?”

“We don’t have visual reconnaissance on it,” said Perry. “We do know that within the next four minutes both guards were terminated, as was Secretary of State Lindsay.”

“Play it again,” said Calibrisi.

Perry reran the video four times, each time eliciting the same reaction from Calibrisi, squinting, as if he was trying to see something that wasn’t visible.

Finally, Calibrisi leaned forward. “What about ballistics?”

“They sent the report about twenty minutes ago. The slugs matched the hits. Colt M1911A1, the gun found on the ground near Lindsay’s corpse. The slugs that killed Lindsay were fired by that gun. It was Dewey's sidearm. They were all the same: .45 ACP, Kevlar tipped."

The door opened and Polk walked in. He was carrying some papers. "Sorry I'm late."

"I analyzed the footage from the hotel security camera," Perry continued. "From the moment Lindsay left the suite in the morning until the camera went dark, two people entered the room. Both were hotel service staff. They were in there about an hour, then they left. I did a back-pull on the two ladies, ran their identification cards through INTERPOL as well as our databases. They were clean. Other than that, no one entered the suite except for Lindsay . . . and then Dewey."

"Go back farther," said Polk. "Someone could've entered the day before. The week before. Look for entries and exits. If you get clear visual frame on a face, send it to Jesus."

"Is the goal here to find Lindsay's killer?" asked Perry. "Or prove Dewey's innocent?"

Polk shot Calibrisi a look.

"Dewey *is* innocent," he said. "We don't need to prove it. But there's something going on here and we need to know what. I'm not sure I care who killed Lindsay. But I want to know *why* he was killed, and *why* Dewey was put in the middle of it."

Perry nodded, although he looked as if he didn't one hundred percent agree.

"You disagree, Mack?" asked Calibrisi. "You're allowed to disagree. What you're not allowed to do is disagree and keep it to yourself. That does us no good."

"If you're sure he's innocent, why don't we try and get him out?" asked Perry. "He's at Branch Four. They kill people there, Hector."

"I'm trying. You heard me."

"Let's design something," said Perry.

"A prison break?" Calibrisi asked facetiously. "Even if it could be done, which I highly doubt, it'd only make matters worse. Cazanove will go out of his way to try and railroad Dewey and prove he's guilty. Dewey can handle Branch Four. We need to get to the bottom of what happened, and we need to do it quickly."

Lindsay, Calibrisi's assistant, came to the door. "Jim Bruckheimer is on one."

"Put him on."

Calibrisi's phone beeped. He hit Speaker.

"Hi, Jim. What do you got?"

"I'm putting this up on your screen," said Bruckheimer. "It involves one of Lindsay's Consular Operations agents. These are the guys with immediate body detail to the secretary."

A photo shot to the screen. It showed Lindsay at an airport, walking along a red carpet and shaking hands at an arrival ceremony somewhere.

"The first photo's from Lindsay's trip to Vietnam last May," said Bruckheimer.

A red circle appeared around a man walking behind Lindsay. He had a rugged-looking face, a mustache, and short black hair. He appeared to be in his late thirties or early forties.

"Tim Casales," said Bruckheimer. "He was one of the agents killed in the hotel."

Another photo appeared. This one showed the same man, Casales, up close. He looked younger, his mustache slightly bushier, with fewer wrinkles around his eyes. He had a hard, unapproachable look, with no attempt to smile or appear in any way kind.

"This is Casales's first file photo from the State Department. He joined CONS OP eight years ago. Before State he was in the Secret Service, which he joined right after graduating from USC. Majored in government, played on the USC soccer team. Grew up in Bakersfield, California. Never married. We're digging in deeper, but it all seems pretty straightforward."

"What's the point, Jim?" asked Calibrisi.

"Well, PRISM has a facial recognition module called LayerX," said Bruckheimer. "It's an algorithm based on underlying physical characteristics. Basically, the algorithm breaks down an individual's subdermal physical characteristics into metadata. A person's face is translated into data—bone structure, eye socket width and depth, mouth, skull size, all of it. Your face basically becomes a collection of zeros and ones, thus allowing the program to match photos based on a very precise set of data that is specific only to that individual. Now this is important: LayerX is designed to err on the side of what we call 'extreme accuracy.' So it misses connections all the time. For whatever reason, the metadata doesn't match because someone can look or appear different at various times. But when it hits—when a photo matches—LayerX is nearly one hundred percent accurate."

On the screen, a black-and-white photo of a young man in a dark blue military shirt appeared. He had dirty-blond hair and was tan. He looked like he was a teenager. He was tough-looking but wore a friendly smile.

"Who is it?" asked Calibrisi.

"You tell me," said Bruckheimer. "According to the Pentagon, his name was Jeff Tindall. Tindall was a Navy SEAL, killed during a helicopter accident in 2003. Prior to that he was a highly decorated operator, a demolitions expert. He was part of the initial SPECOPS manpower we sent into Afghanistan after nine/eleven. DEVGRU. We're talking about a badass. According to his file, he went to Chapel Hill and played football. Grew up in Wyndmoor, Pennsylvania. This is a top secret pre-mission photo taken in 2004."

Casales's State Department photo appeared next to the black-and-white one. The two men looked different, though certain similarities existed. Both had similar muscular foreheads and prominent cheekbones.

"What's that have to do with Casales?"

"According to LayerX, it's the same guy."

Polk stood up, as did Calibrisi. Both men moved to the screen, studying the two photographs.

"Did you rerun it?" asked Polk.

"Twice."

"Why didn't PRISM ever flag this before?" asked Polk.

"It's the first time we've ever run him against PRISM," said Bruckheimer. "We don't run State Department employees against it, except foreigners, of course. The consular judge had to sign off on the FISA warrant. He allowed us to run everyone on Lindsay's trip. Casales popped the grid."

"I'm confused," said Perry. "Did this guy actually die? I mean, did the SEAL die?"

"I read Tindall's obituary, death records, and the after-action report," said Bruckheimer. "We even spoke to his father. Tindall's dead—or at least everyone thinks he is."

Calibrisi moved back to his desk, rubbing the bridge of his nose, deep in thought. He looked at Polk. They appeared equally confused.

"There's a first for everything, and this could be the first time LayerX screws up," said Bruckheimer. "But I doubt it."

Calibrisi looked at Poole. "Get a FISA warrant prepared," he told him. "I want to run all Consular Operations employees against PRISM, Stellar Wind, and DS-300."

"That's going to be a tough warrant," said Poole. "Judge Wetherbee doesn't like it when NSA technology is aimed at Americans."

"You know Wetherbee, Bill," Calibrisi said to Polk. "Hand-deliver the warrant request yourself. Let's get it over there immediately."

"Roger."

"There's one other thing, chief," said Bruckheimer. "Take me off speaker."

Calibrisi picked up the phone. "What is it?"

"It's about Toronto."

"Jim, Toronto's going to have to wait."

"Just listen."

"Fine. Make it quick."

"We picked up unusual activity leading up to the attack on the mosque. Electronic signals activity in the immediate vicinity of the mosque. It was running through an unknown frequency."

"What the hell does that mean?"

"Someone was making phone calls on a SAT phone with its own satellite," said Bruckheimer. "A military-grade Lockheed Martin device with a heretofore unknown frequency."

"What does that have to do with the CIA?" said Calibrisi.

"It's your satellite," said Bruckheimer. "Launched in 1994 under a 1981 joint State Department–CIA program called 'Order Six.' "

"So access the files."

"They're gone. Purged, sanitized, including metadata. Level with me, Hector: Have you heard of it?"

"No," said Calibrisi, "and right now, trying to find some file on an ancient interagency program is about the last thing I'm going to do, Jim. We have a dead secretary of state—"

"Earlier tonight," interrupted Bruckheimer, "we triangulated another call that was made through the satellite. The call originated from the Hotel George Cinq approximately five minutes after Lindsay was gunned down."

40

DGSI BRANCH FOUR
PARIS

Dewey was led to a cell by two prison guards. The front of his shirt was spattered in blood. His left eye was black and blue. His lower lip was puffed up and cut down the middle. It hurt to close his mouth, and so blood continued to seep over the damaged lip and down his chin. They closed the cell door behind him. He went to the concrete slab that stuck out from the wall, the cell's bed. Dewey lay down and fell asleep.

He didn't know how long he'd been asleep when he was awakened. It was a bucket of cold water that stirred him, thrown by a guard. Dewey didn't move, not until a second bucket was thrown. Beauxchamps was standing behind the guard.

"*Glacé*," Beauxchamps said.

A guard left the cell and returned a few minutes later with a plastic bag filled with ice. Beauxchamps handed it to Dewey. Dewey put it up against his lip.

"Water," said Dewey.

"*De l'eau*," said the agent.

The guard left again. He returned with a large plastic jug full of water. Dewey sat up and started chugging, losing much of it down his chin. He drank—or spilled—the entire jug. He threw it down and looked up at Beauxchamps.

"Whiskey," said Dewey.

"Do you think I have whiskey in here?" said Beauxchamps, shaking his head in disbelief. "Do you think this is a hotel?"

Dewey skewed his head sideways so that he could see better.

"What do you want?" asked Dewey.

Beauxchamps closed the cell door most of the way. He leaned against the wall.

"What happened?" asked Beauxchamps sincerely. "What did you see?"

Dewey stared at Beauxchamps for several moments.

"I got an alert from Lindsay," said Dewey. "I left the restaurant. It was raining and there weren't any taxis so I got on the Métro and took it back to the hotel. I saw a woman on the train at the station near the hotel. It was the same woman I saw in Lindsay's suite before I left. I tried to follow her. That's why I ran. It's why I tried to pry open the doors. I would've smashed the glass if I could've, but she got away. When I got back to the hotel, you dumbasses arrested me."

"Then how did your gun end up on the floor of the suite?"

"I don't know. I don't have an explanation."

"Who do you think it could've been?"

"You figure it out," said Dewey. "Why don't you get off your ass and do some work? How the fuck do you expect me to figure who put it there? I can barely see, thanks to you dickheads. I'm locked in a cell. Stop being so fucking lazy and incompetent."

Dewey clutched the ice against his head. "What time is it?" he asked.

"Why?"

"I want to know how long you fuckheads have had me in this place."

"It's a little after one in the morning."

"Has anyone attempted to get me out of here?"

"Calibrisi has phoned my boss several times."

"So why can't I speak with him?"

"You'd have to ask my boss."

Beauxchamps reached for the door but didn't open it. He turned to Dewey.

"I began my career at DGSI back when it had another name," he said. "I started in the code bureau. I learned how to write codes, break codes, that sort of thing. It's now called the bureau of cryptographic activity."

"What's your point?" asked Dewey.

"We were able to decrypt the recording of your phone call," said Beauxchamps. "Trust me, there will be no 'slip of paper' in your eggs tomorrow morning."

Dewey paused for a half second, long enough to create a lull in the conversation, then moved with ferocious speed, dropping the bag of ice as his right hand swept behind his back. He tore a gun from between his belt and back and swung it toward Beauxchamps, stopping when the muzzle was aimed at his head.

"Don't move," said Dewey quietly. "Do exactly as I say and I won't kill you."

Beauxchamps had a surprised look on his face as his arms went up in the air.

"How the hell did you get that—"

"Shut up," said Dewey, standing up, holding

Beauxchamps in the crosshairs, moving closer. "Put your arms directly out in front of you, take two steps to your right, face the wall, and get down on your knees."

Dewey went to the cell door, shutting it most of the way but leaving a small crack. He stepped behind Beauxchamps.

"Remove your belt and your shirt, now."

Beauxchamps unbuttoned his shirt and tossed it toward Dewey. He did the same thing with his belt.

"How did you get the gun?" said Beauxchamps.

"Your partner. In addition to being an asshole, he's sloppy. Put your hands behind your back."

Dewey put the gun on the ground and took Beauxchamps's hands, looping the belt around them at the wrists. He forced them down behind Beauxchamps and looped the belt around his ankles as well. It was a struggle, and Beauxchamps groaned in pain as Dewey tightened the belt. Once the belt was very tight, Dewey pushed Beauxchamps down on his side. He tumbled over, grimacing at the awkward position, arms behind his back, tied tight to his ankles. He couldn't move.

"Has anyone ever escaped from here?" asked Dewey.

"Yes," Beauxchamps said, coughing. "Two years ago in a garbage truck."

Dewey patted him down, removing a cell phone.

"What floor are we on?"

"Five."

"Where's the abandoned stairwell?"

Beauxchamps was silent.

"Tell me," said Dewey. "Right now."

"I don't know."

Dewey slammed his fist into Beauxchamps's stomach. Beauxchamps grunted in pain.

"Where?"

"The end of the hall. Behind the guard station."

"How many guards are there on the floor?"

"One man."

Dewey tore Beauxchamps's shirt in half. He twisted one half together and wrapped it around Beauxchamps's head, pulling it through his mouth, tying it tight, gagging him.

Dewey leaned down and looked into Beauxchamps's eyes.

"Totally unnecessary," said Dewey, shaking his head in disdain. "Totally *unfucking* necessary. It's your own dumbass fault. I didn't shoot Lindsay. I'm breaking out of here to find out who did."

Dewey opened the cell door. He took Beaux champs's cell and turned on the camera, making sure the flash was off. He knelt down and stuck the phone on the ground, inching it out into the hallway, aiming it left. He snapped a photo, then flipped it over, taking one of the hallway to the right. He pulled the phone back inside, moved the door almost shut, and examined the two photos.

The hallway was empty to the right. To the left, a uniformed guard stood behind some sort of counter.

Dewey went back and knelt beside Beauxchamps.

"I'm going to give you an opportunity to save a man's life," he said. He showed Beauxchamps the photo of the guard.

"Do you know him?"

Beauxchamps nodded.

"I can either go out there and shoot him," said Dewey, "or you can ask him to come down here, in which case I'm simply going to knock him out and leave him with you."

Beauxchamps didn't move.

"Well?"

Slowly, Beauxchamps nodded. Dewey untied the gag.

"I know what you're thinking," said Dewey.

"How much I hate Americans?" muttered Beauxchamps.

Dewey grinned.

"I'm sure you have protocols," he said. "You can get him down here, like I asked, or you can warn him somehow, some code word. I'll know if that happens. Sirens will go off, a bunch of other people will come running. I want to be very clear. If that happens, you're a dead man. Do you understand?"

"Yes."

"Tell him you need a bandage, some more ice, whatever."

Beauxchamps nodded.

"How do you communicate?"

"Turn on the phone," said Beauxchamps. "The code is one-one-four-three."

Dewey entered the code and brought up the main screen.

"Speed-dial six."

Dewey hit the speed dial, then held it to Beauxchamps's ear. With his other hand, Dewey stuck the muzzle of the gun against the Frenchman's temple.

"Norman," said Beauxchamps. "The first-aid kit. Do you have one at the station?"

"*Oui*, Jean."

"Can you bring it down here?"

"*Bien sûr*."

Dewey hung up the phone and retied the gag. He grabbed a section of the restraining belt and dragged Beauxchamps across the floor so that he was behind the door, out of sight. Dewey pulled the door slightly ajar, as Beauxchamps had had it. He stood behind the door, listening. He heard footsteps coming down the hallway. The door suddenly pushed open and the guard stepped inside, holding a white box. He looked around and was met by the sight of Dewey's gun, aimed at his head.

Dewey slammed the pistol into the guard's chin, knocking him sideways and down, then kicked him hard in the stomach, knocking the wind out of him. Dewey pushed the door almost closed, then pounced on the guard and turned him onto his stomach, pressed his face into the concrete, and put his knee onto the back of the guard's neck. He reached down with both hands and choked the guard until he lost consciousness.

Dewey stripped the man's gun, walkie-talkie, and cell phone, tossing them out of reach. He took the other strip of material and tied it around his head, gagging him, then removed his belt and tied him up like Beauxchamps.

Dewey pocketed both cell phones and picked up the two guns. He stepped to the door and moved it slightly ajar.

He felt warmth now, a feeling he knew well, the rush of adrenaline. He took several deep breaths, and all pain was pushed away. He glanced back, making sure Beauxchamps and the guard couldn't move so much as an inch.

He raised the muzzles of the two firearms into the air, clutching them, not too tight, index fingers on the triggers. He knew he would have only a short period of time before the guard would be discovered missing.

Then he moved.

He stepped into the hallway, shutting the cell door behind him. He charged down the hall to the guard station and leapt over it. Behind the desk was a large cabinet. Dewey pushed it aside. Behind it was a door. If Borchardt was correct, it led to an abandoned stairwell.

A warning sign in bright yellow read *NE PAS ENTRER*!

Dewey kicked the latch and the door went flying in at the same moment a loud alarm bell started ringing and a bright red emergency light began flashing on and off, dousing the corridor in chaos. He heard shouting from somewhere behind him.

The shouting grew louder, then he heard boots, running. He looked, but still, no one had entered the hallway.

Dewey stepped to the abandoned stairwell. It was pitch-black. He took one of the cell phones and turned on the flashlight, shining it down. It was empty. Whatever stairs had been there were now gone.

He heard shouting, in French, along with the tapping of steel-toed boots on linoleum.

He peered down into the stairwell. All that was left was a dark shaft, windowless and black.

Dewey swept the light across the air again, quickly. The guards would be in range in a matter of seconds. He searched desperately. Below, attached to the wall, he saw a fire extinguisher, covered in rust.

Dewey turned and saw gunmen. The boot steps were like thunder on the hard floor. He tucked both guns into the small of his back, beneath his belt, then charged toward the dark stairwell. He took two big steps as automatic weapon fire erupted, his right boot striking the ledge just as bullets ripped the air above his head. He leapt out into the air, legs kicking, aiming for the wall below. Dewey shut his eyes, feeling with his hands and feet. He braced for the impact.

Above, more gunfire.

He slammed into the wall, right foot first, followed by his outstretched right hand, forearm, shoulder, like being checked without padding into the boards, trying not to let out a grunt as the full force of his two-hundred-and-twenty-five-pound frame at full speed struck the prison wall. Bullets ripped closer, several submachine guns, weaving slugs into the wall as Dewey clawed along the concrete, scratching his hand in total darkness, desperately searching for the fire extinguisher. He dropped the instant after he hit the wall, feeling weightlessness in his spine, then pure terror. A half second later, his boot hit the fire extinguisher.

Dewey shot his hands out, reaching frantically for it as he plunged faster and faster toward the ground.

His right hand found the hard steel of the old fire extinguisher, grabbing the top. It immediately bent down, creaking, yet somehow held.

Dewey looked up at the opening. He registered the flash of muzzles through the dark, clotted air. With his left hand, Dewey removed one of the guns and swung it toward the opening above, firing. His first slug hit a gunman in the stomach; he groaned and fell forward, into the shaft, screaming as he dropped. Then the fire extinguisher broke from the wall.

Dewey was now in free fall. He felt nothing but air, rushing up at him, and a sense of weightlessness. He kicked against the wall as he plunged, pushing out, launching into the middle of the shaft, then simply dropped until, a second and a half later, his legs struck, landing atop the guard, who groaned as Dewey fell on him, then rolled off.

Dewey crawled toward the wall as bullets rained down. He held his fire, knowing the flash of his muzzle would alert them to his location. He found the wall. He moved along the cold concrete, feeling with his hands for something, anything, in the musty, damp darkness. He found a doorknob and turned it. The door creaked open. He pushed it forward. He was in an alley. He heard the alarm bells screeching from inside the prison, then, in the distance, sirens.

Across the alleyway, a bright green Lamborghini

Aventador was parked. He ran to it and pulled at the door handle. The door moved up into the air, like a razor. He climbed in, searching for the keys as the door slid back down. He saw a small bright red plastic object between the two seats and lifted it. Beneath was the Power button. Dewey pushed it and the Aventador roared to life, its engine grumbling like an angry beast. He slammed the gas pedal and the Lamborghini broke into a wild sprint down the alley.

41

INDIAN PURCHASE FARM
POOLESVILLE, MARYLAND

Bruner had to bend over in order to descend the rickety wooden stairs that led to the basement. He went past the furnace and then beneath a single lightbulb, glaring brightly beneath the musty beams. He opened a door at the back, into what looked like a closet, unlit, with clothes hanging. He pushed the clothing aside. A touchpad screen was incongruously attached to the wall. He pressed his thumb to the screen. After a series of low beeps, the back of the closet opened.

Bruner entered the small, cold room. A cheap floor lamp cast a foggy, greenish light across the room. The floor was concrete, the room windowless. Lying on a single bed in the corner was a shirtless man. He was out of shape, slightly obese, and his hair was disheveled. One of his wrists was shackled to the bed with a chain. The other was in a cast and tied down with rope to the bed. He was scrunched up in a fetal position, trying to stay warm.

Bruner walked across the room and stopped when he was next to the bed.

"Harry," said Bruner.

There was no response.

"Harry!" Bruner barked.

Harry Black's eyes opened. It took him awhile to focus. Finally, he registered Bruner. His face flushed and he lurched toward Bruner, but the chain and the rope held him back. He yelped in pain, looking at his wrist in the cast.

"You son of a bitch, let me out!" he screamed. "Who the fuck do you think you are?"

Bruner stared down at Black, saying nothing.

Black ranted on. *"Let me out! They'll know! The secretary of defense cannot go missing!"*

"You've taken a short vacation," Bruner said calmly. "It's already been reported. In fact, someone on *Hannity* was speculating as to why you might be going on vacation the week of President Dellenbaugh's announcement for reelection. Speculation about a possible illness."

Black stared at Bruner, a pained look on his face.

"You'll never get the codes from me," said Black, sweat pouring down his face, which was beet red. "I'll die before I tell you."

"I told you, we don't need you for the codes," said Bruner. "We needed you to move the submarines into the European theater. You did that. The codes are irrelevant. Once Bobby is sworn in as president, he can appoint whomever he would like as secretary of defense."

Black suddenly relaxed, laying his head back on the bed. He glared hatefully at Bruner.

"I sacrificed everything," said Black. "Despite your vile . . . your evil treatment, *I believe in what we're doing!*"

"I know you do, Harry," said Bruner.

"Then let me out of these chains."

"No."

Black again lurched up at Bruner, though this time he swung his feet out, trying to kick him.

"Then kill me."

"No, Harry, we still need you."

"Why? What for? I'll never do anything else for you!"

Bruner had an empathetic expression on his face.

"We need you to be the secretary of defense," Bruner said quietly. "It's what we've always needed you to do. You're the best secretary of defense America has ever had."

Black was taken aback. "What do you mean, you need me?"

"You heard me," said Bruner. "You're here because the pressure has gotten to you. It's understandable. This is a stressful time. Only a few of us have ever known this kind of pressure. But it will soon be over, and when it is, you will be the secretary of defense—that is, if you would like to be. If you wish to retire, you can do that too. But we need you there. America—a new America—needs you there."

Bruner swept his arm across the basement.

"You will forget all of this," he said. "Trust me. You will be hailed as one of the people who saved our country. I don't expect you to thank me, but someday I hope you'll understand why I did it."

Bruner turned and walked to the door.

"I'll have blankets brought in," he said.

42

THE WHITE HOUSE
WASHINGTON, D.C.

The Diplomatic Reception Room was packed with reporters. Every network in America and across the world was ready and waiting. Within the hour, every single one of them would cut away from their prime-time programming to carry the U.S. president's press conference live.

A low din of conversation permeated the stunningly beautiful room, with its antique wallpaper and period furniture. Bright klieg lights from two platforms—one against the back left wall, one the right, made the room bright with camera-perfect light.

At 8:11 P.M., a tall, husky man with thick brown hair and glasses stepped to the podium. He wore a friendly smile and was dressed in a blue business suit. Everyone knew who he was: John Schmidt, the White House director of communications.

"Good evening, everyone," he said. "The ground rules are simple. The president will be making a brief statement. He will *not* be taking questions, so don't ask." Schmidt stared at a female reporter seated in the front row. "That means you, April."

"BBC is reporting they have someone in custody, John," said a reporter from the back of the room. Schmidt shot him a look but remained quiet.

"John—" asked another reporter, a female seated near the middle of the room.

"Kelly, I'm not getting into it."

"Will anyone from the administration be available for questions?" she asked.

"Is it true there were threats made to the secretary of state before the trip?" another reporter called out.

Soon, reporters were talking over one another, shouting questions. Schmidt didn't respond to any of them.

Finally, he held up his hand, telling everyone to be quiet. It took nearly a minute for the reporters in the room to settle down. During this time, Schmidt looked down at the lectern, then at his watch, waiting patiently. Finally, Schmidt looked up.

"We're twenty minutes out," he said. "Let your producers know: we go live at eight twenty-five. That means do your pre's before then. I want dead silence at eight twenty-four. And anyone who asks the president a question is going to have a shit storm on their hands, got it?"

Schmidt nodded politely, then turned and

walked down the long, ornate hallway, enveloped by the sound of yet more questions coming after him. He moved around the corner, aiming for the West Wing.

The formality of the central part of the White House transitioned into the comfortable elegance of the West Wing, where the day-to-day work of the president and his senior staff took place. The halls closed in slightly, the ceilings lowered, the lighting, provided by beautiful sconces on the walls, had a warm, golden hue. The West Wing had an old New England feel to it: preppy and aristocratic, like a mansion in Chestnut Hill. Lush wall-to-wall carpeting covered the floors, its pattern a rich red-and-tan matrix. The walls were decorated in white-and-silver Farrow & Ball wallpaper. Large photos of President Dellenbaugh in recent settings—with the British prime minister, the annual pardoning of a turkey at Thanksgiving, a speech before thousands of supporters—hung along the walls every few feet.

Despite the late hour, the West Wing was a buzz of activity. It was the epicenter of all that was going on. Sadness was on the faces of White House staff and senior government officials, all of whom knew Tim Lindsay both professionally and personally.

As Schmidt approached the closed door of the Oval Office, a tall, thin man with glasses emerged from an office just down the hallway, sleeves rolled up, clutching some papers.

"Hey, John," he said.

"Hi, Cory."

Cory Tilley was the head of White House Speechwriting. Schmidt followed him to the door.

"Is that the statement?" asked Schmidt, pointing at the papers.

"Yeah."

"Let me see it before we go in."

Tilley handed over the pages. Schmidt scanned them.

" 'Murdered'? " he said.

"What else would you call it?" said Tilley. "Besides, it's already out there."

"I know it's out there. Assassinated is what we should probably call it. Anyway, let's let him make the call."

"He said he wanted to use it," said Tilley.

Schmidt looked up, a quizzical look on his face. "He did?"

"Yeah."

"Okay. Forget it. Go with it."

Schmidt opened the door to the Oval Office.

President Dellenbaugh was seated on one of the two tan leather chesterfield sofas in the center of the room. A small group of people were with him: Hector Calibrisi, the director of the Central Intelligence Agency; Adrian King, the White

House chief of staff; Josh Brubaker, the national security advisor; Jacqui Murray, secretary of the treasury; Arden Mason, head of Homeland Security; Vice President Danny Donato; George Kratovil, the FBI director; along with certain key White House staff.

Three plasma screens on the far wall were tuned to news coverage—all *Special Reports* preempting regular programming to focus on the death of U.S. Secretary of State Tim Lindsay. Two of the stations—CBS and BBC—had reporters outside the George V, still a hub of activity—flashing blue lights of police cars, several ambulances, crowds of reporters. The third screen, tuned to Fox News, had cut to the White House and showed the room where President Dellenbaugh would soon speak. All three TVs were muted.

It was clear from the body language in the room that an argument had been taking place. Calibrisi had an angry look on his face, as did the vice president.

Dellenbaugh turned.

"Should we come back?" Schmidt said.

"No," said Dellenbaugh. "Is that the statement?" he said, nodding to Tilley.

"Yes, sir."

Tilley handed the papers to the president, who read it quickly.

"How much time until I need to get out there?"

"Twelve minutes, Mr. President."

Dellenbaugh nodded, motioning for Schmidt and Tilley to sit down.

"Where were we?" said Dellenbaugh.

"Forensics," said Kratovil. "The bullets came from Andreas's gun. His prints are on the gun as well as the doorknob."

"Where's Dewey now?" asked Brubaker.

"A DGSI holding facility in Paris. They're saying nothing and they're not giving us access."

"Has anybody spoken to him?" asked Dellenbaugh.

"No," said Calibrisi. "DGSI isn't letting us speak with him, nor will they allow our station chief to see him."

"Why was he there?" asked Brubaker pointedly.

"I sent him," said Calibrisi. "There was chatter coming through NSA regarding Lindsay's trip."

"What is DGSI saying?" asked Dellenbaugh.

"They see the evidence as being, at least circumstantially, airtight, sir," said Calibrisi. "Dewey's hotel suite was adjacent to Lindsay's. He comes out of his room, kills the two agents, enters Lindsay's suite and shoots him. Drops his gun and takes off."

"Why would he come back to the scene of the crime?" asked King. "I mean . . . this is Dewey, guys."

"I agree, why would he drop his gun?" added Donato. "It doesn't add up. Dewey shoots him and then drops the weapon? It's absurd. We should demand his immediate release."

"No," said Calibrisi.

All eyes shot to Calibrisi.

"Did you just say no?" asked Adrian King.

"Yeah."

"Hector, why the hell would we not twist those bastards' arms a little and get him out?" said King, who was pacing near the wall. "He's obviously innocent."

"We can twist arms all we want," said Calibrisi. "Until they complete their investigation, Dewey isn't leaving."

"The bigger issue is, why would someone kill Tim Lindsay?" said Dellenbaugh. "That's what we need to focus on. Dewey wouldn't kill him. It's absurd. Let France complete their investigation. Get Ambassador George involved. Let's make sure the investigation is aboveboard. In the meantime, we need to find out who killed Tim and why."

Schmidt cleared his throat, getting Dellenbaugh's attention.

"We're five minutes out, sir."

"Let's push it back ten minutes," said Dellenbaugh.

"Fine," said Schmidt, standing up.

"I wouldn't do that," said Calibrisi.

"Why?"

"Because someone is going to leak the fact that

their main suspect is an American. The moment it gets out there, it'll be pandemonium. Frankly, I wouldn't be doing a press conference at all. Just release the statement."

"I'm addressing the American people. They need to hear from their commander in chief."

"Then, with all due respect, let's get it over with. And by God, don't take any questions."

"I've already laid down the ground rules," said Schmidt. He took a few steps toward the door.

Dellenbaugh stood up. He looked around the room.

"The main question is, why Lindsay?" he said. "I'm going to give the statement and then go upstairs and read to my daughter. I want to reconvene at ten thirty tonight. I want to know why someone would want to kill America's top diplomat."

Dellenbaugh walked to the door. Calibrisi got up as well, following the president into the hallway.

"Mr. President," said Calibrisi.

Dellenbaugh stopped outside the door.

"Give us a minute," the president said to Schmidt.

Schmidt walked ahead, giving Calibrisi and the president room to speak in confidence.

Dellenbaugh started rubbing the bridge of his nose as he closed his eyes for a moment. He looked at Calibrisi. "What is it?"

"The NSA has uncovered anomalies leading up to the event," said Calibrisi.

"What do you mean by anomalies?"

"First, a direct link between Lindsay's murder and the Toronto mosque massacre. In addition, one of the dead State Department guards might have been some sort of sleeper agent. Deep cover. There were, at most, six people who knew Dewey was in Paris. Who knew he had a weapon, that he was staying on the same floor as Lindsay."

"Do we know who he was working for? A foreign government?"

"That's the thing," said Calibrisi. "At this point it all ties back to us, that is, the U.S. government. The ties to Toronto, the sleeper—it's all internal."

Dellenbaugh took a deep breath. "What are you thinking?"

"I'm not sure," said Calibrisi. "In order to do what they did, they would've needed to know Dewey was there. He wasn't on any advance team manifests. It was Lindsay, his security team, me, and a few people at NCS. There was no forced entry into his room either. It has the markings of an inside job, someone we know, someone with access to a very tight stream of information. Something deeper was going on."

The lectern stood empty. A low mumble of voices filled the room. Suddenly, President Dellenbaugh emerged from the West Wing and walked down the red carpet to the lectern. Cameras rolled, flashbulbs flashed, yet other than those sounds, the room was as quiet as a library, or a morgue.

Dellenbaugh looked down at the lectern, averting his eyes from the gathered press corps. After almost half a minute, he looked up. He squinted slightly as his eyes scanned the room. It was as if he was in pain, or angry, or a combination, but whatever distractions had perhaps existed until that point in time within the audience, they disappeared. He held the reporters—and by extension the hundreds of millions of people watching across the globe—in rapt attention, as they all waited for him to begin.

"It is my sad duty to report to you that Secretary of State Tim Lindsay died earlier this evening while on a diplomatic mission in Paris," said the president. "As has been reported, Secretary Lindsay did not die of natural causes. He was murdered. We don't know who was responsible for this heinous crime, but we will find out. Anyone involved will be brought to justice, and make no mistake: American retribution will be severe. Despite reports that seem to indicate law enforcement has an idea who committed this crime, the investigation has only just begun and as of now we don't know who did it, and we certainly don't know why. But whoever was behind it will pay dearly."

Dellenbaugh paused. He looked down at the lectern, and then his eyes moved to the camera.

"Tim Lindsay was appointed secretary of state by my predecessor, President Rob Allaire. During the three years since I took the oath of office, Secretary Lindsay has been a valued advisor, and a trusted friend. His time in the Navy, where he retired as a rear admiral, taught him toughness, determination, and a deep understanding of the strategic challenges that face the United States of America. He understood the problems that exist in our troubled world. It was Tim's calm under fire—and the way he built relationships across ideological divides—that defined him. Godspeed, Timothy Josiah Lindsay."

Calibrisi watched the president's speech inside the office of Adrian King. But his mind was elsewhere. All he could think about was what Bruckheimer had told him: an extant CIA program called Order 6.

Calibrisi had been at the CIA in the early 1990s. Like most agents, he had little exposure to the sort of governing orders under which the Agency operated. Those were the purview of a select few in the upper hierarchy. If the original order was memorialized in 1981, as Bruckheimer said, finding out information now would be complicated and potentially dangerous. Most of the senior ranking officers from that time were gone—either retired or dead. But there were a few, he knew, who could be brought in and questioned. And that was where the dangerous part came in. If Order 6 had never been shut down and was, in fact, still active, asking questions about it might tip off the very people—the insiders—now at work.

His phone vibrated. It was a text from Polk.

WETHERBEE:
NO

Frustrated, Calibrisi glanced at the television, absentmindedly scanning the news ticker along the bottom of the screen.

SOURCE: HOUSE MAJORITY WHIP
BOBBY LARGENT EMERGES AS
LEADING CANDIDATE TO REPLACE
TRAPPE AS SPEAKER

Calibrisi speed-dialed Polk.

"You got my text?" Polk asked.

"Yeah. But that's not why I'm calling. We need to find someone who was at the Agency in 1981. Someone we can trust. And it must be done extremely carefully."

"Why?"

"I'll explain later," said Calibrisi. "Right now,

I need you to figure out who was there—and in the immediate vicinity of the director."

"That would've been Bill Casey."

"Exactly. This is important: Do it yourself. Right now, this stays between you and me."

43

NSA

Samantha Stout spent several hours studying the mysterious satellite. She had two of her fellow analysts examining the frequency, trying to determine how they'd been able to do it. Samantha's interest, however, was drawn to one of the photos: a close-up of the manufacturer's plate on the side of the satellite.

She heard a loud whistle. It was Zachary Follett, another analyst who was sifting through State Department, OMB, and other U.S. government purchase records trying to find transaction records on the satellite.

"What?" said Samantha.

"I found the record." Follett pointed at his screen.

She stood and walked behind him. On his screen was a slightly lopsided PDF of an old document.

"What is it?"
"It's a State Department purchase record."
Samantha stared at the screen.

FORM NUMBER: SD6502
TITLE: EQUIPMENT—VARIOUS
VENDOR: LOCKHEED, GmbH

EDITION DATE: 199461001
CANCELLATION DATE: 199484001
FORMATS:
PLEASE BE ADVISED: No link under "FORMATS" indicates no electronic format is available.
To obtain copies of forms, contact YOUR Military Service or Component Forms Manager. Canceled forms are not available.

REMARKS:
ISSUANCES: AR-783-1
NAVSUPINST 6443.128D
ADJMAN 63-1297(I)
MCO 10630.2D
SPONSOR / POC:
SUB-SPONSOR:
NUMBER OF PAGES: 1
USERS: NA
PRESCRIBED OR ADOPTED?: P
DISPOSITION:

SUBJECT GROUP: 6 (ORDER SD126)
FORM CONTROLLED:
MANDATORY PRINT
SPECIFICATIONS: Y

RCS:
IRCN:
OMB:
PRIVACY ACT IMPLICATIONS: Y

"What does all that stuff mean?"

"It's administrative language," said Follett. "Who pays what, what budget it comes out of, that sort of crap. The satellite was purchased by the State Department through Lockheed's German subsidiary. More important, it came out of an appropriation for the same entity: Order Six."

"Is that it?" she said. "We knew that. There's nothing there. Was that really worth whistling for?"

Follett looked slightly peeved. "It confirms it."

"We don't need confirmation, Zach. We need a lead."

"It was the only transaction between the State Department and Lockheed in 1994 and, for that matter, the only one for five years in either direction," said Follett. "I did a macro on every sales executive at Lockheed Martin in 1994 and ran the entire manifest against Langley knowledge base, PRISM, DS-300, Stellar Wind, and ECHELON. There was a CIA operation in 1994 that went badly south. Two agents were killed. It happened in Bonn. These guys were all gunned down in a nightclub. The reason it was flagged is because a senior vice president from Lockheed Martin was also killed at the nightclub."

Samantha nodded, deep in thought.

"You think it's related?" she said.

Follett crossed his arms and looked up at her.

"I have no idea," he said. "But when I tried to access the Langley files, there was nothing there. They were cleaned out."

"We already knew that."

"I did find something, however," said Follett. "The CIA chief of station at the time in Bonn. He's retired, lives in Virginia. I was going to call him, but I didn't know if maybe someone more senior should do it."

"What's his name?"

"Andrew Flaherty."

44

BOULEVARD DU MONTPARNASSE
PARIS

Dewey was picked up by two Paris Métro police cruisers on Boulevard du Montparnasse moments after he sped out of the alley, ripping onto the boulevard at seventy miles per hour. A few blocks later he cut right onto Boulevard Raspail, heading south, away from the center of the city. He floored it even as the squeal of the tires pierced the calm evening, causing every pedestrian within a quarter mile to turn their heads. The police cruisers gave chase, tearing onto Raspail behind Dewey one after the other. The high-pitched whine of the sirens mixed with the throaty, breathtaking roar of the Lamborghini's engine as cars and pedestrians fought to get out of the way of the chaotic scene.

The police cars were quickly on his tail, coming from behind him at high speed, closing the gap. Dewey floored it—narrowly missing a taxi that was crossing Raspail—and got separation from the police cars. He floored it for a few more moments, then jacked the wheel hard and worked the brakes—swinging into a one-eighty—and hit the gas again, charging directly at the cruisers.

By the time he reached them, he was moving at a hundred miles per hour. With precious little distance to go before they collided, Dewey swerved left, as if he would try and pass them on that side, but it was a feint. With just feet to spare, he slammed the brakes for a half second as he spun the steering wheel clockwise. The back of the Lamborghini fishtailed out from behind him to the left side—in front of the oncoming cruisers—then Dewey whipped the steering wheel counterclockwise and slammed his foot on the gas. The car swerved right, passing just inches to the left of the closer police car. He tore past the pair of sedans, as the screech of their brakes mixed with the sound of sirens.

He picked up Beauxchamps's cell and dialed in the code, then called Borchardt.

"Who is this?"

"It's me," said Dewey.

In the rearview mirror he counted four police cars, sirens roaring, lights flashing.

"Where are you?"

"I don't know," Dewey said calmly. He looked for a street sign. "Raspail."

"Good. Stay on Raspail, it will lead you to the Seine."

"They're swarming," said Dewey. "I'm not going to last long."

"Get to the Louvre," said Borchardt. "The Pyramid. We're in the air. DGSI is going to shut down airspace any minute. We can hover at most five minutes—after that, you're on your own."

"Fine."

Dewey tossed the phone to the seat and grabbed the steering wheel.

After passing the two police cruisers, Dewey was alone on Boulevard Raspail, heading north. The road was already shut off by police. He used that emptiness to push the Lamborghini as hard as he could. He saw an intersection ahead but kept the Lamborghini floored, crossing Rue de Sèvres at a hundred and thirty miles per hour. The police cars behind him grew smaller in the rearview mirror. Then, suddenly, bright lights hit him from ahead, like a flash. A pair of dark police sedans had been parked ahead, lying in wait, lights off. Dewey swerved right onto Rue du Bac, which led to the Seine. He again hit the gas, looking in the rearview mirror. Suddenly, another wall of bright lights appeared. He jerked backward, adjusting his eyes. There were two large tactical vehicles—Humvees—moving toward him from the top of Rue du Bac. As he came closer, they stopped and made a V-formation in the road ahead, cutting Dewey off.

Dewey scanned for a side street, but he was midblock and there were no escape routes. Several gunmen climbed out of the Humvees, setting up, preparing to fire.

Dewey slammed the brakes, holding his foot

hard against the floor, and spun the steering wheel. The Lamborghini swerved into a cacophonous one-eighty, tires screeching as gunfire erupted from the dark sedans. He heard several dull thumps as slugs hit the back glass of the sports car. It was bulletproof.

As the tail of the Lamborghini swept across the tar in front of the Humvees, Dewey again floored it, tearing away in the opposite direction—down Rue du Bac—where the first police cruisers were now fast approaching. The first pair of cruisers had been joined by two more, and all four—sirens wailing, lights strobing—came at him abreast, taking up the entire width of the street. The gunfire behind him stopped—the gunmen no doubt realizing that they could easily miss and hit one of the police cruisers.

Dewey scanned both sides of the street, looking in between the Lamborghini and the oncoming police cars, desperate for an escape route, but there was none, only sidewalks, not wide enough for the car, and stores behind, shut for the night.

With no choice left, Dewey cut right and ripped the car toward the sidewalk. Ahead, he eyed the front window of a bank, now closed. He slammed the gas and surged into the window, smashing through the glass. He kept moving, flooring it, cutting across the bank's large unlit atrium, past tellers' stations, pulverizing chairs, desks, and everything else in his way. At the far end of the atrium was another window, and Dewey kept accelerating, glancing in the rearview mirror as a police cruiser, then two, entered the bank in hot pursuit.

Through the window ahead, Dewey saw the lights of another street. He pushed the pedal again to the max. The Lamborghini smashed into the wall of glass then went airborne for several seconds, hitting the sidewalk, then tearing for the busy Quai Voltaire, which ran along the Seine.

In the distance, across the Seine, he scanned for the Louvre, seeing it to his right, behind him. In the rearview mirror, he saw bright klieg lights from a roadblock in back of him. Ahead, Dewey picked up the Pont de la Concorde, the nearest bridge over the Seine. He needed to cross it to get to the Louvre. But a massive roadblock stood at the bridge's entrance. Klieg lights, Humvees, police vans, cruisers, and armed SWAT agents too numerous to count prepared for the oncoming Lamborghini.

He looked again in the rearview mirror, counting five police cruisers trying to keep up the savage pace.

Dewey was boxed in. He looked to his left for a side street, but all he saw was the large stone edifice of the Musée d'Orsay, looming like a phantom.

He looked right, scanning the wall above the river. A few hundred feet away, he caught a flash of light coming from the wall as, in front of him, the muzzle flash of weapons lit the air like firecrackers, followed by the thuds of bullets ripping into the bulletproof windshield.

It was a small light, illuminating the entrance to an old staircase that led down to water's edge. Dewey spun the wheel and gunned the now badly damaged Lamborghini toward the sidewalk, jumping a few feet as he hit the side of the curb. He buckled his seat belt as, at the same moment, he slammed the gas, sending the car to a hundred twenty as gunfire continued from the roadblock ahead.

The entrance was too small for the Lamborghini. Both sides were made of granite several feet high. But Dewey didn't have a choice. He kept his foot hard to the floor.

Yards became feet, then inches, minutes became seconds, and then the Lamborghini slammed into the opening at the top of the stairs. It hit with such force that both sides of the wall cratered. At the same time, the front of the car crushed in and folded backward. The sound was horrible, metal meeting rock, but the car's momentum won out. It toppled the stones and slowed, but it was still moving, and it suddenly hit open air, flying out toward the Seine. A moment later, the car crashed into the dark water, then plunged beneath.

Calmly, Dewey unbuckled the seat belt as

cold water rushed into the car. He kicked at the door, but it was bent inward. That, and the pressure from the water, made it impossible to open. As the last bubble of air inside the car became filled with water, he took a final breath, then put his feet up against the windshield, intact but cracked in several places. A sudden bump shook the car as it landed on the bottom of the river. Pressing himself against the seat, he pushed his feet against the glass, kicking as hard as he could. Slowly, the seam at the top of the glass inched out. The water overhead went from pitch-black to green and brown as, somewhere above, searchlights scanned the river, looking for him. He kept kicking until part of the glass was separated from the frame of the car. He climbed out through the opening, pushed off from what was left of the hood, and swam. He kicked his legs furiously, grasping for distance from the place where the car had entered, where soon police divers would swarm.

Dewey held his breath as long as he could, stroking his arms and kicking his legs in a desperate frenzy. He forced himself to hold his breath even longer, counting the seconds as his arms and legs cycled through the frigid Seine. When he reached one hundred and twenty seconds, he felt as if he might breathe in the water, and yet he kept swimming beneath the surface, protected by the blackness. At three minutes, he finally breached—quietly, without a splash—and looked up. A wall of lights shone down several hundred yards away from where the Lamborghini had entered the river.

Dewey let the current take him farther downriver, until he passed beneath the Pont de la Concorde. He side-paddled to the right bank and climbed up a wall of rock, getting out within the dark shadow of the bridge. He studied the banks of the river in both directions, seeing nobody.

Dewey didn't want to risk going to street level by one of the stairways, which he assumed were guarded. He skulked along the bank, away from the bright klieg lights now visible upstream, shining down eerily from the left bank. At some point, he climbed up the granite wall to street level. He peeked his head over the embankment. Beyond was the Jardin des Tuileries, its gardens now dark and abandoned, the outlines of trees silhouetted by ambient light.

At the far end of the Tuileries, Dewey could see the golden triangle of light that was the Pyramid, marking the entrance to the Louvre. He started running along a row of trees, his pants chafing as he moved, his boots sloshing with water. Suddenly, he heard the telltale high-pitched whirr of a helicopter.

He scanned the sky as he continued his run. In the air above the Louvre, he caught the small red lights of a chopper as it cut through the night air toward the Pyramid. He came to the edge of the Tuileries, where the Place du Carrousel cut between the gardens and the Louvre. He waited behind a tree for a break in traffic, looking for signs of law enforcement. All he could see were the klieg lights in the distance. When there were no cars on the road, he charged out from behind the tree and sprinted across the last stretch between him and the Louvre. To his right, he heard sirens.

Dewey leapt onto the sidewalk, running toward the descending chopper, a sleek black Panther AS-403. The chopper settled onto the grass next to the Pyramid just as searchlights crisscrossed the air as sirens grew louder.

Dewey jumped inside just as the pilot slammed the choke and took off, soaring into the sky. Catching his breath, Dewey looked out the window. Paris had descended into chaos, a city scorched by a night's violence. But from the air it became simply another collection of small lights.

"Hello, Dewey," came a voice from the shadows.

Dewey turned. The lights in the cabin were extinguished. For the first time he saw Borchardt.

"Hi, Rolf."

"How's my car?"

"It's been better."

"You know that cost me nearly a million dollars? I hadn't even driven it yet."

"Well, for what it's worth, it was a little stiff," said Dewey. "Where are we going?"

"Away from Paris," said Borchardt. "DGSI will have an INTERPOL out on you any time now. You're a wanted man. You need to get away."

Dewey nodded, pushing his hand back through his wet hair.

"We need to find her," said Dewey.

"Who?"

"The woman who killed Lindsay."

"Don't be so sure she did it," said Borchardt. "Don't trust your eyes. They can deceive you."

45

HOTEL GEORGE V
PARIS

Beauxchamps stepped off the elevator. He was alone. He rubbed his mouth, which was sore from the gag that had been wrapped around his head. His shoulders ached. He'd been tied up, he guessed, only ten minutes. Still, it left him feeling like he'd been beat up. Mostly, he was embarrassed. But he wasn't angry. Everyone else at DGSI was, especially his boss, Cazanove. For some reason, that was precisely why he wasn't mad.

When Andreas offered to spare the life of the

guard, a thought was born inside him, a feeling that now had grown into certitude.

Andreas didn't kill Lindsay.

Instead of going to his apartment and getting some sleep, or a glass—or two—of wine, he went to the George V. The penthouse floor was empty, dimly lit, and eerily quiet. The hallway carpet was gone and the rough plywood underboard sat bare and ugly. Yellow police tape crossed both sides of the hall in front of the elevator, prohibiting access. He went right and lifted the tape and went beneath it. He walked toward Lindsay's suite. The door was propped open. Beauxchamps stood outside, looking in, trying to think.

He formed his right hand into an imaginary pistol. He aimed it to the left side of the door, where one of Lindsay's guards had been shot.

"Boom," he said, pretending to shoot. He swept his hand to the right and fired at the second guard. "Boom."

Beauxchamps walked into the suite. "Boom boom," he said quietly, aiming at the far wall, imagining what the killer did when he shot Lindsay. He paused for nearly a minute, staring at the wall. It was clean now, the blood scrubbed off, though a small crater was carved out of it where one of his men had found the casing from the bullet that traveled through Lindsay's body.

Beauxchamps picked up his cell and hit speed dial.

"Saint-Phalle."

"It's me," said Beauxchamps. "How many bullets did we take from the scene?"

"Three."

"Three? Or four?"

"Three. One was in Lindsay's chest, one was in the wall, one was in one of the guards' heads."

"What about the fourth bullet?" Beauxchamps asked impatiently.

"What do you mean?"

"That's three bullets. There were four shots fired, Marc. Two into Lindsay, one into one guard's head, one into the other guard's chest. Was it in the other guard's chest?"

"No," said Saint-Phalle.

"Did you look for it?"

Saint-Phalle coughed.

"Ah, no, Jean. I guess I figured they all came from the same weapon and didn't bother."

"They probably *did* come from the same weapon," said Beauxchamps. "You still should've run it down."

"Yes, you're right. I apologize. I'll go over to the hotel right now."

"No, I'm already here. Did you run the ballistics on the three bullets you did find?"

"Yes. All came from the same gun, the Colt M1911A1."

Beauxchamps hung up. He went back to the hallway, taking a left. He moved to within inches of the wall and inspected it, running his hand along it. He turned on a small, powerful flashlight. He shone it at the wall and moved slowly away from the suite, sweeping the light up and down the wall, searching. He kept moving, searching for the slug. From the way the corpse had been positioned on the ground, it was impossible to surmise anything about where it had landed other than that it was in this direction. When he got to the far wall, at the end of the hallway, he saw it immediately: a head-high hole in the wall next to a painting. He took a knife from his coat pocket and stabbed it hard into the wall above the hole, cutting through wallpaper and Sheetrock, then dragging it down, eviscerating a line in the wall with the knife's serrated edge. He worked around the hole until he had the small section that contained the slug. He popped it out, blew dust and silt from it. It was badly misshapen, with black tinges from dried blood compacted into the dull white gypsum powder from the Sheetrock. There was no question, however, that it was a .45-caliber slug. He put it in his pocket and went back to Lindsay's suite.

A small army of forensics experts had already scoured the suite several times, dusting for fingerprints and other evidence. All the furniture had been removed, along with the carpeting and any paintings that had been hanging on the walls, and was now in a DGSI laboratory at the agency's headquarters building for further examination. He went into the large bedroom. It, too, was stripped, even though the crime envelope hadn't contaminated the room.

Beauxchamps wanted his team to determine two things. First, if there was any physical evidence inside the suite other than the gun that was tied to Dewey. Second, if, in fact, a woman had been inside the room, as Andreas claimed. Several dozen hairs were found throughout the suite, embedded into carpet, along edges of walls, so small they were, for the most part, too hard to see. Because it was a hotel room, the hairs were probably useless, accounted for by previous visitors or chambermaids. Andreas's DNA had been run against all of the hairs found; none matched.

Beauxchamps went around the rooms, studying and thinking. Saint-Phalle's oversight rattled him, though he understood why the young detective made the mistake. In all likelihood, the slug in his pocket would in fact be a match to the others.

After more than an hour, he opened the doors to the terrace. It was a sunny day, a bit brisk, with a stiff wind that tousled his hair. He walked to the edge of the terrace and looked out on Paris. At times like these, he craved a cigarette. It had been two and a half years since he'd quit, and yet at least once a day he felt the urge to have one, especially at times like this, when he was alone, outdoors, with an interesting, even beautiful view, thinking, trying to figure something out.

A child's laughter came from somewhere to his left. Casually, he walked to the side of the large terrace. Below, on a small terrace that belonged to the building next to the George V, he saw two young girls throwing a tennis ball to each other. He watched for several seconds.

Back inside, he shut the doors and looked out one more time, his eyes cutting to a small object that was stuck to the fence. He went back out to the side of the terrace that overlooked the two girls. Between the George V and the next building was a tall, forbidding-looking fence, with thick steel prongs that jutted up high above both buildings. On top of one of the iron prongs was a small patch of black material.

He dragged a chair to the side of the terrace. He climbed on top of the brick wall that formed the edge of the terrace, reached up, and removed the swatch of material.

As he walked quickly back to the elevator, he dialed Saint-Phalle.

"I have the slug and I'll be there in twenty minutes. Have ballistics standing by."

"Yes, sir."

"In the meantime, I want the guest list for everyone who was staying at the Prince de Galles the night Lindsay was murdered, separated by floors."

46

NSA

Follett dialed the number for the third time. This time, instead of going to voice mail, someone picked up.

"Yes?" came the voice. Nasal, slightly soft.

"Mr. Flaherty?" said Follett. "Andrew Flaherty?"

"Yes. Who is this?"

"My name is Zachary Follett, sir. Um, I work for a government agency. I have a few questions I wanted to ask you."

"What agency?" said Flaherty.

"The National Security Agency."

"I'll call you back."

"Yes, of course."

Flaherty got the NSA's main number from directory assistance. A few minutes later, Follett's phone beeped.

"Zach Follett," he said.

"So you do work for the NSA," said Flaherty. "What do you want? Do I need a lawyer?"

"No, nothing like that, sir. I just am trying to get some information on an incident that occurred when you were, ah, working in Germany."

"That was a long time ago."

"I know. I was hoping you might remember or perhaps have an old file or two."

"By law, I'm not permitted to retain any files from my service. I'm surprised you don't know that."

"Well, I . . . I work at a different agency, of course. I just didn't know. Now that you mention it, of course I should've known that."

"It's fine," said Flaherty. "I can barely remember what I had for dinner last night, Mr. Follett, much less something more than two decades ago, so I'm not sure I'd be much help. Now, if you don't mind, I'm taking my wife out to lunch. It was nice talking with you—"

"The incident," interrupted Follett.

"Oh, yes, the incident. What are you referring to?"

"Bonn, 1994. Two of your agents were killed at a nightclub along with an executive from Lockheed Martin. Well, the thing is, I was wondering if you had any recollection of that or of something called Order Six?"

Flaherty was in Reston, seated inside the windowless conference room on the fifth floor of the office building. He clutched his phone as he listened to the young NSA analyst, Follett. His face remained placid and emotionless, but his eyes shot to Bruner, who was seated across the conference table from him.

A large plasma screen on the wall had CNN on—a live report from Capitol Hill, where Congressman Bobby Largent had just been elected Speaker of the House of Representatives. Bruner was watching the report, though when Flaherty looked at him, he stopped watching TV and turned to Flaherty.

Flaherty sat up in the chair. He pushed his horn-rimmed glasses higher on his head. "I believe I do recall the incident," he said. "Yes, it was a very sad night for all of us."

"Could you explain what happened exactly?"

"I'd be glad to try," said Flaherty. "I'd prefer to meet in person, however. I don't trust all these newfangled listening devices and recording tools. I'm a retiree. I'll try and tell you what I can."

"Can you meet tonight?" asked Follett.

Flaherty knew he needed to buy time. He also knew he couldn't say no. Whoever Follett was, he spoke and acted inexperienced. Were the suspicions real, it wouldn't have been a phone call Flaherty received.

"I can't meet tonight," he said. "Would next week work for you?"

"I'm afraid our investigation is more active

than that," said Follett. "What about tomorrow? Breakfast?"

"I can meet in the afternoon," said Flaherty. "There's a restaurant in Great Falls. It's called L'Auberge Chez François."

"I know where it is," said Follett. "How about one o'clock?"

"That would be excellent."

"Great. Thank you, Mr. Flaherty."

"Please, call me Andrew."

"Of course, Mr., ah, Andrew. One o'clock at L'Auberge Chez François."

Flaherty hung up his phone. He gazed at Bruner with a hollow, distant look.

"What's wrong, Andrew?" said Bruner. "Bobby was just elected Speaker. You should be very happy. Soon, I have no doubt, Romy will be eliminated. We're getting closer."

"They found Order Six."

47

CIA

Calibrisi entered his officc, looking around at a half dozen men and women, all of whom had their eyes glued to the plasma screen in the middle of the room. The television was tuned to a French news channel. The screen showed a pair of cranes on the banks of the Seine, illuminated by bright klieg lights. Dozens of police cars and other emergency vehicles lined the banks, blue and white light bars flashing in the night.

Calibrisi stared at the screen for a few moments, then went to the TV and turned it off. He turned to the group, a stern look on his face.

"What happened?"

Angie Poole spoke first. "Dewey escaped from the DGSI holding facility," she said. "There was a high-speed chase through the city, culminating in Dewey's car plunging into the Seine."

"We need to stop the French authorities before they go to INTERPOL," said Calibrisi. "Any sort of notice that mentions Dewey will alert his enemies that he's on the run."

"It's too late. France is about to issue a Diffusion to all countries in Europe," said Poole, referring to a specific type of INTERPOL alert seeking help in arresting a known fugitive. "I'd expect INTERPOL will follow up with a Red Notice any time now."

She handed Calibrisi a piece of paper, which he quickly scanned.

"He had to have had help," said Calibrisi, his voice rising with frustration. "We need to speak with him."

The room was silent.

"He'll need money. I want every asset we have in-theater focusing on this. That means they need to expect Dewey moving to one of the safe houses."

"And if he doesn't?" said Mack Perry.

Calibrisi shot him a look.

"We can't control his actions," he said, "only ours. If he moves to one of the safe houses, I want him locked down. Shoot him up with tranquilizers. Whatever we need to do to get him off-grid before Hezbollah or someone else reads this." He held up the INTERPOL alert. "We'll extract him later."

"Angie, did you get a make on the car he was driving?" said Polk.

"Lamborghini," said Poole. "Aventador. Brand-new."

Polk glanced at Calibrisi. "Borchardt," he said.

48

VILLA BLANCHE
SAINT-TROPEZ, FRANCE

Borchardt's property was set on a hill a few miles from the center of Saint-Tropez, playground of the rich. Although there were people in the area with extraordinary amounts of wealth, ready and willing to spend it on virtually anything, only one could possess Villa Blanche.

Borchardt normally would've flown to Southern France on one of his private jets, but French authorities would be searching all flights out of Paris. He chose instead to make the trip in his chauffeur-driven Maybach. He knew they were looking for him—in particular for his cargo: a two-hundred-and-twenty-five-pound, headache-inducing individual who sat across from him in the back of thc limo.

It was morning. They had driven through the night. The sky was bright blue, though clouds interrupted from time to time. The road was a narrow two-lane that meandered up from the bustle of Saint-Tropez to the countryside that ringed the ocean from above. The higher the road climbed, the more beautiful grew the views of the Mediterranean.

"Have you been to Saint-Tropez before?" asked Borchardt.

Dewey was staring out the window. He didn't say anything.

"It's quite nice this time of year," continued Borchardt. "Fewer tourists. Most people who do not live here are away. It's the only time I come, to be honest."

Dewey turned to Borchardt. His normal look—of confidence, even coldness—was not there. Instead, Borchardt saw a different expression. Dewey's eyelids drooped slightly. He was slouched in the leather seat. Borchardt saw sadness.

"I know you don't want to talk about it," said Borchardt, "but you need to. I can help. I already did help."

"My question is, why?" asked Dewey, his first words since leaving Paris.

"Why what? Why did they kill Lindsay?"

Dewey shook his head.

"Why did they frame you?" said Borchardt.

"No. Why did you help me?" muttered Dewey.

Borchardt was silent for several moments, then sat back with a wry smile. He pushed a button on the door. A piece of black titanium arose behind him until it reached the ceiling, separating and sealing the back of the limo from the driver.

"It's a fair question," said Borchardt, his

German accent sharp and authoritative. "I know you think it was calculated, that I have some sort of ulterior motive, but the truth is, I don't. You called and my first instinct was to help you. To protect you."

Dewey studied Borchardt for several moments.

"Who's waiting at your villa?" he askcd. "Did you sell me back to the French government?"

Borchardt's expression grew cold.

"Why would I help you escape from the prison if only to sell you?"

"We both know the answer to that," said Dewey. "Money. Self-interest. Being the center of attention. You sold me once to the Fortunas and once to the Chinese. You'd do it again and we both know it."

"Perhaps, but not today. People change."

Dewey stared into Borchardt's eyes. Borchardt looked slightly hurt.

"I helped you escape because you're about the closest thing I have to family in this ludicrous world, as insane as that may sound."

Dewey shook his head.

"You've eloquently cataloged all the times I betrayed you, but what about Iran?" continued Borchardt. "Without me, you never would have penetrated the country. I also got you into China. Then there was Russia last year, a totally clean insertion with no back-pull. Do you think that was easy?" Borchardt was pointing at Dewey as he spoke. His face turned red and his voice grew loud. "And now I seem to recall a certain French jailhouse I may or may not have helped you escape from a few hours ago."

Dewey laughed.

"Okay. I apologize for questioning your motives, Rolf. Just remember what I'll do to you if you're lying."

The country road was lined on both sides by a succession of majestic, fanciful iron gates behind which ran long driveways that swept away and into the distance, out of sight. Overgrown lilacs in full violet bloom spread in clusters near the road. Stands of old birch, dogwood, and apple trees covered the olive-colored hills on both sides.

The Maybach eased into a pebble stone lane. A hundred feet ahead was a pair of dark green security gates. As the vehicle came close, the gates slowly opened.

As the limousine passed through the gates, Dewey glanced back. The ten-foot-tall gates swung shut. He saw nothing, and yet he continued to watch. Just as the Maybach turned the corner and the gates were almost out of sight, he caught a glimpse of a man standing just to the side of one of the brick stanchions that supported the gates. He was dressed in tan camouflage and clutched a submachine gun.

The pebble stone drive continued through a gorgeous estate of apple, pear, and lemon trees for nearly a half mile. A final stretch was elongated through a dark stand of perfectly manicured fir trees. Then Borchardt's villa appeared. It was the largest house Dewey had ever seen. As much as he wanted to, he could not hide his momentary shock. Columns punctuated the front of the mansion, like an English country estate, but instead of limestone or brick, the house was constructed in white marble. It appeared as white as if freshly snowed upon. What wasn't white was glass. It spread as far as the eye could see and was three stories tall. Green ivy grew in flourishes across several walls of the massive villa.

Dewey stared at the house as they drove closer. When the limo came to a stop, he continued to stare. Past the house, the dark waters of the Mediterranean Sea looked stunning, with diamonds of refracted sunlight dancing across the surface.

"What do you think?" asked Borchardt.

"Not bad," said Dewey. "Reminds me of my dad's toolshed back in Castine."

49

JETÉE KHÄIR-EDDINE
SOUSTARA, ALGERIA
NORTH AFRICA

The apartment building was nine stories high. Because it sat on top of a jetty that reached out into the ocean, every window in the building offered bold ocean views in virtually every direction. Yet it was a forlorn-looking building, its white concrete stained with age, windows on every floor smashed, a few of them boarded up with wood that had already started to rot. But if the exterior was neglected, the interior was even worse. When it was constructed in 1962, it was one of Algiers' most exclusive apartment buildings. Now the apartments were seedy remnants of what had once been. Floor after floor, apartment after apartment, were covered in dirt and filth, broken glass and chunks of crumbling concrete. Only a few apartment doors remained, the others long since torn from hinges by vagrants. Toilets—those few that were left—were backed up. Whole rooms were burnt out, black soot covering walls and ceilings like wallpaper. It was a wasteland.

If exclusivity had to do with beautiful views

and luxurious amenities, 2 Khäir-Eddine epitomized the very opposite. If exclusivity had to do with how difficult it was to gain entrance, however, it was the most exclusive building in all of Algiers and perhaps all of North Africa.

Armed gunmen patrolled the property twenty-four hours a day, seven days a week. No one came within a quarter mile of the building unless invited. Those who were invited moved in and out of 2 Khäir-Eddine with nihilistic swagger. Most were young, some still in their teens. They lived and worked in the building, sleeping on floors, rarely bathing, even when the water worked.

All of them were Arab. All were jihadis.

For three years, 2 Khäir-Eddine had served as the primary staging ground before infiltration into Europe by Al Qaeda recruits. Most of the young Arabs were bomb makers. A few were suicide bombers. Some were document specialists. A handful were propagandists proficient with technology. All were coming from one of Al Qaeda's camps in North Africa, traveling via Algiers on the road of jihad.

The first floor of the building was empty except for gunmen, positioned at the entrances as well as in several rooms, constantly looking outside to survey the surroundings. The next four floors were used to make IEDs, which were then packed into vessels of every size, shape, and color, always pulling up to the jetty in the dead of night. Those vessels then departed before daylight with a fresh batch of bombs and jihadis bound for Al Qaeda affiliates in Lebanon, Turkey, Syria, and Egypt. Floors six and seven were where the young Arabs slept and ate. There were no beds, only blankets and mats, and none were reserved. They slept where they could find a place. The eighth floor was largely empty, save for the last third of the floor, closest to the city. The walls had been torn out with sledgehammers, leaving an open area haphazardly arranged with desks and tables. This was where a dozen hand-picked, carefully screened men performed three key functions: forging documents, such as travel visas; monitoring news and manufacturing propaganda; and managing finances. For despite the group's appearance, and the general squalor of the surroundings, they had plenty of money.

The top floor—the ninth—was shut off to all except for a handful of men. This was the one floor that looked at least somewhat habitable. Like the eighth floor, a large section had been cleared of its walls, only it had been done by a local Algerian carpenter. A steel wall separated that private area from the rest of the floor, which sat empty. The private area occupied the part of the floor closest to the Mediterranean and could be entered only through a single armored door that had an electronic security code as well as two gunmen positioned outside at all times.

Inside the private, walled-off section was a loftlike space that included a luxurious bedroom, a kitchen and dining room, and a large open living room with bold views of the ocean in every direction. On the interior wall, two large poster-size photographs were taped. Both showed the same man. In one of the photos, a color photo, the man had thick, unruly brown hair, a wide, muscular face covered in a thick beard and mustache, and wore a dark blazer and button-down shirt, but no tie. The other photo was black and white and much older. It showed the same man. His hair was cut short and he was clean shaven. He wore a dark T-shirt and a tactical weapons vest, a patch of the American flag visible on the front of the vest. Beneath the man's eyes were two thick stripes of eye black. In his right hand, he clutched an assault rifle, pointed up at the sky. This photo captured the look in the man's eyes as he stared at the camera. It was a cold look, menacing, even threatening, as if he was preparing to swing the rifle down and fire. The word ANDREAS was handwritten across the photo.

It was noon on a clear day. The sun made the sea sparkle in luxurious black, light blue, white, and silver refractions, undulating with the breeze and the currents.

Asleep in the middle of the king-size bed was a naked man. His legs and body were muscled like an athlete's. His hair was medium length, black, and stylish. Like his father, like his younger brother, he was remarkably good-looking, a gift from two famously attractive parents, both now dead.

On each side of him, also asleep, and also naked, were women. On the left was a black woman who was lying on her stomach, her large, voluptuous posterior beneath the man's hand. On the right was an Algerian woman with light skin, a startling beauty with long black hair cut in bangs across the top of her eyebrows, with large breasts and her legs draped over the man's.

On a glass table next to the bed was a humongous pile of cocaine, like a half-eaten birthday cake.

The black woman stirred, turned her head, and looked at the man. She reached her hand out and lightly rubbed his cheek.

"*Veux-tu que je te fasse du café, Nebuchar*?" she said.

Do you want me to make you coffee, Nebuchar?

Fortuna opened his eyes. He stared at her for several moments but said nothing.

Nebuchar Fortuna never wanted to fight the war in which his brother and father had died fighting.

Alexander, his younger brother, was the second most notorious terrorist in modern history, behind Osama bin Laden. Alexander had been embedded inside the United States as a young boy, raised by a couple in Maryland and secretly indoctrinated from the youngest age into jihad. He'd gone to Princeton and then entered the world of finance, rising to its pinnacles and amassing great wealth along the way, all the while biding his time, planning, and ultimately unleashing the greatest single attack on American soil since 9/11 through a carefully designed network of sleeper cells. Yet most of Alexander's plot was stopped before it truly hit—stopped by one man, a disgraced former Delta named Dewey Andreas, who killed Nebuchar's brother on a snowy evening at Alexander's seaside mansion in East Hampton.

Nebuchar's father, Aswan, was despondent when Alexander was killed. Aswan vowed revenge, spending millions in order to find and kill the man who killed his son. Aswan's men scoured the earth for Andreas, finding him in a remote town in Australia, where, one night, a team of highly trained mercenaries ambushed Andreas in a crowded bar, unleashing a bloody and protracted attack. But Andreas proved yet again that he was a formidable opponent, killing every member of Aswan Fortuna's team but one, then escaping. This bitter failure only made

Aswan angrier, and after Andreas led a coup in Pakistan, Aswan bribed the newly installed Pakistani president into handing Andreas over. Andreas was tied up and thrown into a cargo plane bound for Beirut, where Aswan's men were waiting. This time, it was a brigade of Israeli Special Forces soldiers from Shayetet 13 who denied Aswan the satisfaction of avenging his son, saving Andreas from certain death. A few months later, Andreas found Aswan at his mountaintop lair above Beirut and shot him in cold blood.

For Nebuchar, the hard, tortured history of his father and brother was something he tried to forget, to ignore, to leave behind. He had inherited more than $3 billion after his father died, and he spent years living a life of luxury and hedonism, fueled by alcohol and cocaine, women and fast cars. Then, one day, Nebuchar awoke with a start and knew that everything had changed. Like a fever, the feeling swept through his insides and left him breathless and dizzy. He would outdo his brother. He would inflict more damage on the west than even Alexander had.

And someday, Nebuchar knew, he would outdo his father as well. *He* would be the one to avenge the deaths that destroyed the Fortuna family. He would be the one to at long last kill Dewey Andreas.

Nebuchar had sold most of his belongings.

The mansions, chalets, and apartments he'd given to his younger sister, Maddie, without any explanation. He'd made contact with AQAP through an intermediary, ultimately spending more than a month with Al Qaeda's leadership council in southern Yemen. Nebuchar madc his commitment. He would help in the effort to hurt the West, rooting them out of the Middle East, as well as aid in the gradual overtake of Europe. But he would answer to no one. If he ever got tired of it, he could walk away.

Nebuchar hadn't gotten tired of it. Instead, he grew hungrier, angrier, and frighteningly more effective. He turned Algiers into a key thoroughfare, pouring millions into bombs, recruitment, and the training of fighters. He hated Algiers. He missed Beirut. He missed his life of luxury. But he knew he could never go back, not now. What started as a calling thrust upon him by his father and brother—a cause at one time he disagreed with and scoffed at—had turned into his very lifeblood. He knew his father had loved Alexander more than him. He knew Alexander was smarter than him. When they were alive, and even in the years immediately following their deaths, he hated them both. But at some point, time healed Nebuchar's wounds. The fire of hatred was transformed into emptiness, loss, then love. He understood that the reason he shunned them so and fought against his true calling was precisely because of how much he did still love them.

In turn, that love fueled the bitter hatred that now guided his actions against the West. And within that hatred was the image of Dewey Andreas.

A floor below Nebuchar, a twenty-two-year-old Egyptian named Hosni stared at his computer screen, his mouth growing wide. His eyes scanned back and forth across the screen several times.

Hosni looked around the room. Mustafah and Jerome weren't there. He hit Print and quickly pulled off the paper as it finished. He ran up the stairs to the top floor. He charged along the empty floor until he came to the pair of gunmen standing outside the entrance to Fortuna's apartment. Without even acknowledging them, Hosni entered the six-digit security code.

"Nebuchar!" he barked as he entered, before he had even noticed Fortuna and the two women. "Nebuchar, wake up!"

It took Nebuchar a few seconds to open his eyes and then process what was going on. When he finally did, he reached beneath his pillow and pulled out a Glock G19 semiautomatic handgun, then whipped it around, training it on Hosni.

"Oh, for fuck's sake, Hosni," he groaned.

"It's important!"

Fortuna stared angrily at Hosni. He dropped the gun and put his hand to his face, rubbing his eyes. He looked at the Algerian woman next to him, then at the black woman.

"Get out," he ordered. *"Now!"*

The two women slunk from the bed, grabbing clothing—a shoe here, panties there, a shirt, another shoe—as they ran toward the door.

Nebuchar climbed out of bed, doing nothing to hide his naked body from Hosni. He stepped to a bureau and pulled out a pair of jeans and slipped them on. On top of the dresser was a pack of cigarettes. He pulled one out and grabbed for a lighter. He took a long puff and finally turned to Hosni.

"What do you want?"

Nebuchar leaned forward and dipped his right index finger in the pile of cocaine on the table, brought it to his right nostril, and snorted it. He repeated the act with his left.

"Look, Nebuchar!" said Hosni, stepping closer to Fortuna, his hand extending a piece of paper. "It was just released by INTERPOL."

Fortuna stared at it for several seconds, then leaned down and snorted another scoop of white powder.

He stared at the photo in the middle of the sheet of paper.

"When did this come out?"
"Five minutes ago."

INTERPOL Ω
DIFFUSION NOTICE
—WANTED—
ANDREAS, DEWEY

ARREST WARRANT: GREEN CODE 1
ISSUING AUTHORITY: DGSI/FRANCE (UU8-8)
CIRC. 863-23055G
CITIZENSHIP: USA
WHEREABOUTS: FRANCE/EU

FLASH SUMMARY (18:09:11 GST):
ANDREAS is primary suspect in the murder of United States Secretary of State Tim Lindsay and two other U.S. State Department employees. ANDREAS was apprehended following commission of the crime and brought into DGSI subsection 4 (Paris 08W-4). ANDREAS escaped DGSI facility and is at large and believed to be in France. ANDREAS should be considered armed and extremely dangerous.
DO NOT ATTEMPT TO APPROACH ANDREAS ALONE.
If ANDREAS is sighted, local and

federal law enforcement should
be called immediately followed by
INTERPOL central station:
72-331-1-786-8690.

Fortuna handed the piece of paper back to Hosni. A malevolent smile spread across his face. He placed his hands on the youth's shoulders, grinning from ear to ear in glee. Tentatively, Hosni smiled. Then Fortuna slapped him viciously across the face, a sadistic look on his face.

"Excellent work," said Fortuna, flicking his lit cigarette casually onto the floor.

"What was that for?" yelped Hosni.

"That was my way of saying, thank you," said Fortuna. "Go get Jerome and Mustafah. There is work to be done."

"What do you mean?" said Hosni.

"Andreas is on the run. He's a flushed bird, out in the open. He's a wanted man. This is our opportunity to kill the man who killed my father and my brother. Now go. *Go!*"

50

INDIAN PURCHASE FARM
POOLESVILLE, MARYLAND

The large, low-ceilinged master bedroom was cozy and elegant, with bookshelves, exposed wooden beams, and a large bed. A fire burned warmly across from the bed, casting the room in a diffuse orange hue. Above the mantel was a large oil painting of a young girl no more than ten.

Bruner moved slowly, his mind consumed with Flaherty's words.

They found Order Six.

It was what started it all, and yet he hadn't heard the words in so long. Perhaps mistakenly, Bruner had thought he would never have to hear the words again. He knew the files were gone, that there was no way for anyone to know what Order 6 was, and so his mood had nothing to do with the fear of being caught. The truth was, getting caught was the farthest thing from his mind. No, what ailed him this night was the memory. The thought of what had driven him to do what he was now just days, just hours, from finally accomplishing.

Don't think about it. Not now.

He looked at his wife, Janie, who was asleep.

He glanced at the fire, making sure it was under control enough for him to go to sleep. Then, against his better judgment, Bruner looked again at the painting of his daughter. He tried to look away, yet the girl's eyes seemed to hold his attention.

His wife, who he thought asleep, suddenly spoke. "Are you all right, Charles?"

Bruner's hands were trembling. He looked at his wife and then at the painting. His face contorted into a pained, infinitely sad look. Tears started to fall down his cheeks.

"Oh, Charles," she said calmly, reaching for him.

But he didn't hear her words. Instead, his thoughts were on the painting and the girl. He stumbled, reaching for the corner of the bed as the vision came on, holding the wooden post so that he wouldn't fall to the ground.

"No," he cried as he fell to the bed, a low, animal sobbing coming from deep within as the memory took him over.

He pictured Molly in that last moment. He remembered her hand as he let it go, filled with money for the gelato. The pain took him over as if he were back there that day, that terrible day in Madrid. Like a movie, the final moments of his daughter's life played and replayed again and again until finally he passed into a state of eerie calm.

• • •

Bruner didn't know how many hours had passed when he awoke. The fire was almost out. Janie was asleep. He forced himself up from the bed. He went to the painting, lifting it from its hook. He placed it against the wall.

The painting had covered a safe. Bruner turned the dial several times, then pulled down the steel latch.

The bottom half of the safe was filled with neat stacks of hundred-dollar bills. On a shelf above the cash was a wall of solid gold bricks.

Stashed atop the gold was an old manila folder. With trembling hands, Bruner reached for it. He looked at the small label affixed to the folder:

DSAT: ORDER 6
VXW-OPS: SB 6609-H
NEVSTUP: 167.8 A TSIL: 699/T

Bruner put another log on the fire. He sat down in an armchair next to the painting of his daughter. He slowly opened the folder, as if he were back there that day, that fateful day when he understood what he had to do in order to save the world.

It was 3 A.M. when Bruner finally stopped staring at the papers, stopped remembering Madrid and William Casey, stopped feeling the clutches of the past. Slowly, he arose and took the folder, with the document inside, and set it in the fireplace. A few moments later, the corner of the folder started smoking and then caught fire, burning brightly as Bruner watched from above.

51

CENTRAL BUS AND RAIL TERMINAL MARSEILLE, FRANCE

Romy climbed off the bus, carrying only what was in her pockets, which was €455 and a pack of gum—the only thing she'd eaten in twenty-four hours.

In the crowded terminal, she found the women's room. An older woman was washing her hands. Romy went to the farthest stall and shut the door. She didn't sit down, but rather stood, eyes shut. She started sobbing. She put her arms across her chest as she cried for several minutes, as if holding herself. She tried to push away the thoughts of what she'd done, the sight of the two dead orderlies covered in blood, Dr. Courtemanche clutching his chest, blood spilling from his mouth and nose. She let her tears blanket her in some way, protect her, wash her mind of the terrible memories. Romy knew she would never be the same again, that she could never forgive herself, even though all she wanted to do was warn an unsuspecting world of the monsters that were coming. That were here already.

She longed, at this lonely moment, for a memory somewhere in the recesses of her mind, any memory, of anything, as long as it was from before the trauma that caused her amnesia. All Romy had was the memory of Kyrie as he lifted her from the ground. She'd long ago stopped asking herself where she was that first day of her new life, stopped trying to see the pictures on the walls, the furniture. It was now just a hollow abyss, but her tears made her feel as if there had been a day, long ago, before it all. When she was happy, when she was kind, when there was someone there to hold her the way she held herself in that bathroom stall, soothing her and assuring her, "It's going to be all right."

When she finally left the stall, she went to the sink and looked at her reflection in the mirror. Her head had only a thin, patchy layer of hair and it looked shocking and strange. But the lack of hair also made pure the striking beauty of her face, her sharp, tanned nose, her high cheekbones, and her dark eyes. For several seconds she didn't recognize herself, and though she knew that was the point, her eyes welled up again. But she didn't cry. Instead, she looked into her own eyes, searching for the person who was in there, looking for that person to somehow say something or do something.

"It's going to be all right," she whispered to her reflection.

She splashed water on her face to clean away the tears.

An icon on Kopitar's laptop started blinking. He double-clicked it. His screen opened into a map. A red circle flashed in the middle of the screen. The map zoomed in closer and closer until he saw the name of the city, then the name of the street.

A quizzical look was on Kopitar's face. The signal was being emitted by the credit card Romy had taken from Courtemanche. He was dumbfounded for two reasons. First, because she hadn't thrown it away. Second, because it was telling him where she was, even though she hadn't used it.

"Stupid woman."

Credit cards emit certain low-frequency electronic signals at all times, but only the credit card companies themselves have the ability to look at the signals. By law, they were required to keep this ability turned off. Someone—probably French law enforcement—had placed some sort of legal order on the card company itself, thus turning on the card's location.

Kopitar picked up his phone and dialed Kyrie.

"I found her. She's in Marseille, at the train station."

"I'm hours away," said Kyrie. "She'll be gone by the time I get there."

"I think I can track her."

"Don't tell anyone, Hans. Do you hear me? You tell someone, and I promise you I will stick a fucking metal spike into one ear and push it out the other one. I've done it. It's surprisingly easy."

"I won't tell anyone, Kyrie."

Flaherty, who was seated at the other end of the conference table, glanced at Kopitar.

"Who do we have near Marseille, Hans?"

Kopitar paused, his loyalties torn, but only for a moment. He tapped on his keyboard.

"Felix Jackson," he said. "He's in Nice."

Flaherty picked up his cell and dialed.

"This is Jackson," came the voice.

"It's Andrew. We need your help and we need it immediately."

"Where?"

"Marseille. The train station."

"Who is it?"

"Kyrie's wife."

There was a pause. "Fine. Send me a photo. Rendition?"

"Termination."

• • •

In the central terminal, Romy found a newsstand and picked up a paper. She knew what it would say, but she needed to see it anyway.

The headlines screamed across the top of the page:

LINDSAY, U.S. SECRETARY OF STATE, ASSASSINATED IN PARIS
TWO OTHERS ALSO KILLED AT HOTEL GEORGE V
AMERICAN SPY WANTED AND AT LARGE AFTER ESCAPING FRENCH JAIL
HIGH-SPEED CAR CHASE ACROSS PARIS

Below were two photos. On the left was a profile photo of Lindsay, his gray hair combed neatly back, a large smile on his face. The photo on the right made her gasp and bring a hand to her mouth. A warm tingling sensation burst somewhere inside her, shooting down her back like electricity. She felt fear. The photo showed a much younger man, in his thirties, with longish brown hair parted roughly down the middle. He was handsome, but more than that he was rugged, like an athlete, with several days of stubble across his face, and eyes that looked as if he had no feelings, blank and distant. The eyes, she thought, of a killer.

The name beneath the photo read DEWEY ANDREAS.

Her hands shaking, Romy reached into her pocket and retrieved some money. She paid for the newspaper and walked to an empty section of the station and sat down.

> PARIS—U.S. Secretary of State Tim Lindsay, 68, was assassinated last night in his suite at the Hotel George V, where he was staying during meetings with French and Iranian officials. Two other State Department employees were also killed in the attack at Paris's most elegant hotel. Sources inside DGSI described the scene at the hotel as a "killing field." All three men were gunned down at close range.
>
> Lindsay was a well-respected diplomat who was in his third year as secretary of state. Leaders from across the globe expressed their shock at his death. Chinese premier Li Keqiang called Lindsay "a man of strong convictions who was not afraid to compromise in the pursuit of greater good." French president François Hollande said, "I was with Tim this morning. I now know what it must feel like to watch a friend die on the battlefield."

American president J. P. Dellenbaugh praised Lindsay during an emotional speech at the White House, calling him "a valued advisor and a trusted friend." Dellenbaugh vowed to bring his killer to justice, saying "whoever was behind it will pay dearly."

In a startling development, DGSI revealed that the main suspect in the murders is an employee of the Central Intelligence Agency. According to sources, Dewey Andreas was in Paris with Lindsay and may have "gotten into an argument" with him. Andreas, according to sources, gunned down the two State Department security officials who were in the hall outside Lindsay's suite before entering and shooting Lindsay. Andreas was apprehended at the hotel and brought to a DGSI intake unit in southwestern Paris, where he escaped.

Multiple witnesses reported seeing a high-speed car chase around midnight near the DGSI facility that ended when a vehicle drove through an embankment near Pont Royal and plunged into the Seine. An unnamed source inside Paris Métro police confirmed that the driver of the vehicle was Andreas and that he has not been found.

> DGSI officials refused to comment on how Andreas was able to escape the high-security facility known as Branch 4. DGSI issued an all-points bulletin warrant for Andreas's arrest. INTERPOL is expected to issue a declaratory warrant within the next hour.

Other photos were below the fold, including several of Lindsay with foreign leaders. One photo showed the automobile involved in the car chase as it was being lifted by crane out of the Seine, green, smashed, and dented, dangling in the air as water poured from various holes and cracks in the car's frame.

Suddenly, Romy's eyes were drawn to a man who was walking through the crowded terminal. He was bald and wore a black sweater. He didn't act the way most people at a train station do, either rushing to get to their train, leaving the station, or wandering around as they waited. Somehow this man appeared as if he was hunting. His eyes swept the terminal slowly and methodically, but it was not the look of someone trying to find a loved one, a restroom, a gate. This man looked as if he wanted to kill someone. He walked with his legs spread, eyeing each person in the station for a half second as if registering them in his head, then moving on. He was coming toward her. She realized now that she'd made a mistake; she should have found a seat in a more crowded area of the terminal. Here she stood out.

She felt her heart racing.

Romy wanted to stand up and move. She wanted to run. But she knew it would only make it worse. It would focus the man's attention on her. She remembered her haircut. There was a reason she did it. Unless . . . unless cutting off one's hair was the move of an amateur. What if they're looking for a woman with a shaved head?

You're being paranoid. It's just a creepy-looking guy.

As the man drew closer, Romy kept her eyes focused on the newspaper but didn't hide. She tried to act natural—bored at having to wait for her train, passing the time like everybody else. Then she remembered Zurich. The Park Hyatt with Kyrie. He'd gone to the bar to get drinks while she waited near the window. A man was standing alone at the bar. As Kyrie waited for the drinks, they exchanged words. This was the same man.

As he came closer, Romy felt his eyes on her. He was still several feet away, standing at the end of a row of seats. Romy didn't look up. Instead she continued to read. It was all she could do not to scream in terror.

After a few moments, the man moved away, stalking toward the next section of seating. Romy shut her eyes and exhaled. She was either being paranoid, or her change in appearance had worked. Either way, she felt a momentary sense of relief.

When she looked up, she saw the man standing at the far side of the terminal, a cell phone to his ear, staring at her.

"No!" she cried softly.

She stood up and moved. He was across the large space, standing beneath the entrance to a set of tracks. She looked to the right where the newsstand, restaurant, and a few other shops were located. Beyond them was the main entrance to the station. Romy started walking toward the shops and exit—away from the man. But as she did, he moved also, aiming in a line for the shops, cutting diagonally across the terminal.

Romy weaved in between people, children with parents, senior citizens in wheelchairs, moving as quickly as she could without running. She heard a scream to her left. She glanced over. There was a small commotion. A woman lay on the ground, toppled by someone rushing across the station—the man in the black sweater.

Romy glanced between the man and the exit. She realized that even if she started running, he would be able to cut her off before she got there. She broke into a sprint. She cut down through the terminal, sidestepping people, even jumping onto an empty seat in order to get around a large group, running desperately toward a small, crowded restaurant. She took a last look as she was about to enter the restaurant. He was ten feet behind her and to her left. He had a weapon in his hand, a handgun with a long black silencer jutting from the muzzle.

Romy charged into the restaurant, past a hostess who started yelling, cutting between tables toward the back. The hostess screamed as the man entered behind Romy, followed by the sound of a table being knocked over, breaking glass, yelling.

Romy charged through the swinging door at the back of the room and down a short corridor. A waiter was talking on his cell phone. He looked up in shock, then held up his hand and yelled for her to stop, but she lurched past him. She saw another swinging door and surged toward it, hands out, pushing through and diving just as the air was cut by the dull *thwack thwack* of suppressed gunfire and the *thump thump* of the door being struck just behind her. A moment later, a painful groan came from the hallway—the waiter being killed.

Romy was in the restaurant's kitchen. She had only seconds to act. A sweat-covered cook was standing over a large stove with a spatula in his hand as several hamburgers fried. Romy looked desperately around, searching for a door, a window, anything that would allow her to escape. But there was nothing, nowhere to run, nowhere to turn, nowhere to hide. She caught a glimpse of something behind the cook. She ran toward him. He reached both arms out, trying to grab her, but Romy ducked, dropped to her knees, scurried along the floor, and then stood, grabbing for the object, a large knife on the counter, then turned.

She didn't have any more time. A second or two at most. As the cook lurched at her, hate in his eyes, Romy leapt to the stovetop, running full speed across the hot surface toward the door, raising the blade and diving into the air just as the door flew open and the killer started firing. Bullets spat from the gun, but they were beneath her, and by the time he could react she was on him with the blade, hacking a ferocious cut into the center of his chest. He fell backward, his eyes wide, a haunted, surprised look, as Romy landed on top of him along with the blade, which sank all the way through his chest and spine, and into the floor.

Romy climbed up from the killer. The cook was on the ground, a quarter-size hole in his forehead.

Romy quickly searched the killer's pockets. She found a money clip stuffed with bills and took it, along with a set of car keys. She heard voices from inside the restaurant. She ran down the corridor, jumping over the dead waiter just as a woman entered and, seeing the body, screamed. She pushed by her and charged back into the restaurant, running out into the main terminal. She ran toward the most crowded section, where a line of passengers was standing. As she came to the conductor, he asked for her ticket.

"I don't have a ticket. May I buy one from you?"

"Yes. Where are you going?"

"To the last stop."

"Frankfurt? That is two hundred and twenty euros for a coach ticket."

Romy looked behind her at the row of passengers. She glanced past them, searching for anyone who might've been following. She didn't see anyone—but she did see a growing commotion across the station at the restaurant.

"Is there anything quieter, more private?"

"Well, yes, first class. You will have a semi-private compartment, but it's not too crowded today. However, I must warn you, it's much more expensive, madame."

"It's fine," she said.

"Four hundred twenty euros," he said, writing out a ticket. "You are in Compartment four. I believe there is only one other person in the compartment, so you will have privacy."

Romy handed him bills from the killer's wad, took the ticket, and climbed aboard. Two armed policemen were standing at the entrance to the car. They checked her ticket and let her through.

Romy walked through the car, passing an elegant dining area where several people were already seated and enjoying drinks. Compartments lined both sides of the car after the dining area, glass and wood, doors shut. Many of the passengers had already pulled down curtains so that passersby couldn't peer in. She found Compartment 4 and opened the door. There were two leather bench seats that spanned the width of the compartment, enough room for four people. An elderly woman was seated on one of them, already asleep. Romy quietly pulled down the curtains on the door and sat down across from the woman. As the train began to move, she stared at her reflection in the glass. She was still breathing rapidly.

They were coming after her. They would do anything to stop her. She knew their terrible plans. Their secrets. But whom could she tell? Who would believe her?

A small, triumphant grin—too small to notice even if someone was looking—crossed her lips. She had known nothing but fear since the moment she heard the man's voice talking to her husband while she was out in the greenhouse, tying together bunches of lavender. *Bruner*. But right now, Romy Banker felt nothing but elation. Three times they had tried to stop her, but she continued to elude them, and today, she killed one of them. She noticed dried blood on her right hand. She put her hand in her pocket just as the train emerged from the tunnel and a splash of warm sunlight washed across her face.

52

DGSI HEADQUARTERS
LEVALLOIS-PERRET, FRANCE

Beauxchamps entered his office. When Saint-Phalle saw him, he stood up from his desk and grabbed a folder.

"Ballistics?" Beauxchamps asked.

"Yes," said Saint-Phalle. "A different gun was used to kill one of the guards."

He handed a paper to Beauxchamps. He scanned the document quickly. The ballistics on the Colt .45 matched the bullets found in Lindsay and one of the guards. A Glock 17 had been used to shoot the second agent outside the suite.

"What about the Prince de Galles?" asked Beauxchamps.

"The guest registry listed a 'Madame Courtemanche.' A suite on the top floor, next to the Cinq. The last name matched the credit card she used. She checked in on the ninth, an hour and a half before Lindsay was killed."

"Has there been any other activity on the card?"

"No. But I placed a lien on the credit card company. We now have access to real-time location information."

"Where is she?" asked Beauxchamps.

"Marseille."

53

ALGIERS

Nebuchar Fortuna had his laptop open to Al Jazeera TV. He was smoking a cigarette, watching as an Al Jazeera reporter on assignment in Paris described a high-speed car chase by an American who French authorities believe assassinated the U.S. secretary of state.

Andreas.

It was 6:08 A.M. Fortuna had yet to go to bed. Instead he was fueled by small handfuls of cocaine and cigarettes.

The particular section of the video he kept watching was of a car dangling from a crane. It was the car Andreas had led Paris law enforcement on in a wild chase across the Left Bank.

He picked up a rolled-up hundred-dollar bill. He snorted three lines of cocaine and then reached out and hit a button on his laptop, pausing the news video. Frozen on the screen was a close-up photo of the destroyed car as it was hoisted from the Seine.

"Aventador," barked Fortuna, pumping a fist, a triumphant smile on his face. "I knew I'd figure it out."

Hosni came closer. He looked at the image.

"What about it?"

"Who drives a Lamborghini?" asked Fortuna.

"You do," said Jerome. "At least you used to."

Fortuna shook his head in disgust. "Stupid fuck. Who escapes from jail and has a Lamborghini waiting for him? No one! No one, that's who!"

The others came over.

"Obviously the CIA put it there," said Mustafah. "It's some sort of prearranged escape strategy if you're a CIA agent and get caught."

Fortuna shook his head.

"No!" he screamed, staring at his men. "The CIA would put a fucking piece of shit there. They would never put a decent car there and certainly not a Lamborghini. Maybe a Ford Taurus."

The group stared at Fortuna. Slowly, Fortuna's anger transformed into a large smile.

"Someone left it there," said Fortuna. "Someone who can stick a Lamborghini somewhere and not care if he ever sees it again. Most important, someone who is close to Andreas."

"Borchardt," said Mustafah.

"Who knows a man on Borchardt's security team?"

"I do," said Hosni. "His name is Yaron. A rough guy. But Nebuchar, Borchardt pays them handsomely for their loyalty. I don't think he would betray Borchardt."

"Everybody has a price," said Fortuna. "Besides, we're not asking him to be disloyal to Borchardt. We're asking for information about someone else, with the promise that this information will not hurt Borchardt."

"If I can get word," said Hosni, "what should I ask?"

"Does he have a guest with him?" said Fortuna, his nostrils flaring with excitement. "Is this guest a big fucking American? If the answer is yes, where is he? That's it."

"What if he says no?"

Fortuna turned angrily and stepped closer to Hosni.

"You fucking idiot," he seethed. "You don't take no for an answer. You tell him either he tells us and becomes a very rich man, or he dies!"

Fortuna pulled on a T-shirt.

"Dewey Andreas is out in the open. Today—this moment—right now is our chance to kill him and avenge the deaths of my father and my brother."

"How much are we willing to pay, Nebuchar?"

"Anything," said Fortuna. "Tell him to name his price. Just get it done."

54

INDIAN PURCHASE FARM
POOLESVILLE, MARYLAND

It was midnight, more than two hours after Flaherty said he would be there. But everything had started to go decidedly not as planned.

Flaherty turned onto the dirt driveway, knowing that his car, at that instant, set off a security system. The vehicle, and him specifically, were being photographed, scanned, and run against a database. Had he not been expected, one of the six gunmen who patrolled Bruner's estate would soon be standing in the middle of the road, blocking his path, assault rifle targeted at him, while at least one other gunman flanked from left or right, ready to kill. Flaherty didn't know precisely what would happen if someone uninvited made it past the first gunman, but he knew he wouldn't make it to Bruner's farmhouse—not in one piece, anyway.

Flaherty couldn't see them, but they were there. Six trained operators, sworn to protect Bruner. In his many times visiting Bruner, Flaherty had seen one of them once, a chance reflection in the night, headlight hitting the glass of night optics off in a field. He knew who they were. Flaherty had vetted each man, knew their backgrounds almost as well as they did. Each man shared the same general Special Forces background. It was Flaherty's job to go beyond that, however, and that was the art, for what they were doing was treason and he had to find those young, elite soldiers willing to commit it. Beyond his organizational brilliance, what Andrew Flaherty knew how to do was separate the patriots from the disaffected, the elite soldiers prepared to defend America at any cost and the young men who believed America had gone bad.

Once broken, a horse will never ride wild again. Once a man had committed to treason, there was no turning back. Most of them never had doubts. They were committed, as committed as they had once been to the United States of America, because they believed that they were fighting a second revolution. It was Flaherty's job to carefully select them. It wasn't the ones who were blindly loyal. It was the rebel, the naysayer, the one with a checkered, even violent incident in his past. Each man was, on some deep level, angry. Flaherty found them, but it was Bruner who quietly harnessed that anger and channeled it toward the days to come.

Two men in the nearly thirty-year history of the covert group known only as Order 6 had ever tried to run. Both were dead within hours, their bodies never found, their names, faces, and records purged. It was as if they never existed.

Flaherty parked in the driveway and grabbed a folder from the passenger seat.

Bruner met him at the front door. He was wearing a flannel shirt and jeans. He said nothing as he held the door open. Flaherty followed him to the den, where Bruner went to a small tray in the corner of the room, on top of which was a collection of bottles, glasses, and a silver ice bucket. Flaherty sat on one of the leather sofas. A fire was dying out though still warm, providing a lovely shade of crescent orange and the occasional crackle of sparks.

"I'm having a bourbon," said Bruner as he poured himself a drink. "I believe I know what you're going to say, which is, 'No, thank you,' but I'll ask it anyway."

"Yes," said Flaherty. "Neat."

Bruner stared at Flaherty for a few moments, arching one of his eyebrows. "Well, I guess this is important, isn't it?"

He handed a drink to Flaherty, then sat down on the couch opposite him. He reached his glass out to Flaherty and clinked glasses.

Flaherty handed Bruner a folder.

It contained a series of photos. They all showed the same man. He was bald, tanned, and muscular. He was in his late thirties but still a remarkable physical specimen. The man was dead. In the middle of his chest, a knife handle stuck up into the air. Blood was everywhere.

"Marseille," said Flaherty. "Two hours ago. Felix Jackson."

Bruner remembered him. He was one of the first recruits. Bruner was there when they killed Jackson's wife and son. Jackson never found out. But it served its purpose. Losing his family turned Jackson into an animal, devoid of feeling. Now he was dead.

"Romy is proving to be a worthy adversary," said Bruner.

"She innovated," said Flaherty as Bruner stared at the photos. "She marked him when he entered the station. When she understood what he was there for, she ran. It may have been luck, but she demonstrated adept skills."

Bruner held up a photo. It was a close-up of the large kitchen knife jammed into the dead man's chest.

"She killed a man not many people on the planet could kill," he said. "She knows our plans. Romy knows precisely why Tim Lindsay died—she told him, and then we eliminated him. She endangers *everything!*"

He swung his arm out and struck a lamp, which smashed to the floor. Bruner's face took on a reddish hue, his nostrils flaring in anger.

"There's something else." Flaherty tossed a sheet of paper onto the table between them. It was a black-and-white photo of a young man with short, dark hair. He had on a T-shirt. In his right hand, he held a carbine, which was aimed at the sky. Thick stripes of eye black ran beneath his eyes, which stared menacingly into the camera.

Bruner took another sip and looked at Flaherty.

"The man Kyrie framed for Lindsay's murder," said Flaherty.

"What about him?"

"His name is Dewey Andreas. Does that ring a bell, Charles?"

Bruner paused, contemplating the question. He took a sip from his glass, then slowly shook his head.

"No, I'm afraid not."

"It should. He was one of the first Deltas we targeted for recruitment. Kyrie was sent to bring him in."

Flaherty extended a folder. It was formal-looking, light tan with diagonal green stripes, with a fanciful black ribbon for tying it closed, a green border around its edges. On one side, a small box in bright yellow read:

CATEGORY 4
EYES ONLY

Bruner shot Flaherty a look.

"I thought I was the only member of Special Operations Group in history to have a green-bordered file?" he said, taking the folder.

"So did I," said Flaherty. "It was awarded to him in September after stopping the attack on the dormitory at Columbia."

Bruner opened the file.

ANDREAS, DEWEY
ACCESS 14
Non-Official Cover

[Warning: Release of information illegal under Article(s) 239.A, 56-1.C, and FFR 42, Section 5]

CIT: United States of America

HOMES: Castine, ME
Washington, D.C. (current)

EDUCATION: Boston College
English B.A. 3.1 GPA
Varsity Football (captain)

MILTARY SERVICE:
U.S. Army: enlistment Jun
U.S. Army Rangers, Fort Benning, GA
Graduate Winter School: Jan–Mar

RANK: 1 in class of 188
1st Special Forces Operational Detachment, aka Delta Force

CAREER (known):

- Lisbon, POR: Jan–Mar: (mission unknown)
- San Isidro de El General, COS: Oct-Jan: Anti-narcotic: NIC, COL, VEN
- London, ENG: Apr: Assassination (attempted) Subhi al-Tufayli/Hezbollah (mission failure)
- Munich, GER: Apr: Exfiltration Constantine Vargarin (wanted by GUR-RUS) (mission success)
- Buenos Aires, ARG: Sep–Dec: Anti-narcotic: ARG, COL, CHI, BOL
- Montreal, CAN: Jan: Assassination Constantine Vargarin (mission success)
- Lisbon, POR: Mar: Assassination Frances Vibohr (Siemens VIP suspect in sale of TS info to SAU) (mission success)
- Bali, IND: Aug: Assassination of Rumallah Khomeini (mission success)
- Jun 00–Dec 11: (nonmilitary) roles offshore oil & gas industry
Aberdeen, SCO
Edinburgh, SCO
Belfast, IRE
Cardiff, WAL
Valparaiso, CHI
Buenaventura, COL
- East Hampton, NY: Dec: Andreas kills

Alexander Fortuna (sanction: believed to be unofficial)

- Washington, DC: Jan: U.S. Presidential Medal of Freedom and U.S. Congressional Medal of Honor
- Islamabad, PAK: Jun: Overthrow of Omar El-Khayab (sanction: assumed to be official JSOC/CIA)
- Broumana, LEB: Jul: Assassination of Aswan Fortuna (sanction: believed to be unofficial)
- Mahdishahr, IRA: Oct 12: Infiltration/theft nuclear device (sanction: unknown)

ACTIVE FILE(s):

- VEVAK Tehran, IRA
  05–08: (inactive: kill or capture)
  12–pres: (active: kill or capture)
  IRG Tehran, IRA: 12–pres: (active: capture)
- AL-MUQAWAMA/Hezbollah
  Tehran, IRA: 98–01: (inactive: kill or capture)
  Tehran, IRA: 11–pres: (active: kill or capture)
  Damascus, SYR: 12–pres: (active: kill or capture)
- HAMAS
  Gaza, ISR: 12–pres: (active: objective unknown)

- GRU
  Moscow, RUS: 04: (inactive: capture)

MISC:
- Fort Bragg, NC: Wife (Holly) dies: Andreas charged with murder
- Arlington, VA: Discharged from 1st Special Forces Operational Detachment, U.S. Army, and stripped of all honors
- Fort Bragg, NC: Acquittal on all charges
- Nov 12: Engagement to U.S. National Security Advisor Jessica Tanzer
- Date of marriage: (unknown)

For the next ten minutes, Bruner read through the file without saying anything. When he was done, he put it down. For the first time, Bruner showed the slightest hint of sharpness in his eyes. He sat forward, locking eyes with Flaherty.

"Andreas was one of the recruits?"

"Yes," said Flaherty. "He was Delta. He had a wife. Her name was Holly. As with the others, Kyrie killed her and made it appear to be a suicide. Andreas was to be the fourth member of the team."

Bruner nodded. He remembered. It was one of the darkest secrets in the history of Order 6. Bruner insisted on single males only, unencumbered by personal attachments. If someone was promising, that individual's family disappeared.

Andreas was deemed so potentially valuable that Bruner ordered that his wife be killed and staged to look like a suicide, freeing Andreas to join the unit. But Holly Andreas's murder ended up being pointless. Andreas was arrested immediately and charged with the murder. After his acquittal, he fled the United States.

"Warn Kyrie," said Bruner. "Right now Andreas has no idea what just happened. But he will. He's going to scour the earth to find Romy. If he finds her before us, it's over."

55

BEIT-E RAHBARI (RESIDENCE OF THE SUPREME LEADER OF IRAN)
TEHRAN

The visitor walked down the empty corridor, past armed gunmen who stood at attention every ten feet, compact submachine guns clutched in their arms, trained to the side. The floor was wood, but it appeared like glass, varnished to a beautiful golden hue and yet worn with years, and with history.

At the end of the hallway, behind a large door, the supreme leader of Iran, Ali Suleiman, lay asleep.

The visitor, Abu Paria, walked without a care for the noise his steel-toed boots caused. He was big, at least six-five, and needed to hold his arms slightly out to the side because of the size of his biceps. He wore a military uniform: tan khaki pants, a matching shirt adorned with rows of medals and other insignia on both sides, and atop his shoulder epaulets in gold and red, signifying the man's accomplishment at age thirty-two, becoming the youngest general in Iranian history. Now, ten years later, he wore it not to project confidence. Paria had all the confidence he needed. As head of VEVAK, Iranian intelligence and military affairs, as well as the KUDS Force, an elite paramilitary division of the Islamic Revolutionary Guard, Paria was a role model. He wore his old ribbons to say to a younger generation: you too can do this. Those young animals will see my chest of medals and will want to beat me. That is how we will become the strongest, most feared country in the Middle East.

Paria came to the door and nodded at one of the guards, telling him silently to open it. His hand lurched for the door, obeying the second most powerful man in Iran.

Paria stepped inside. The room wasn't dark,

but it was dimly lit. A fireplace gave off an orange-ish dome of light that reached the massive bed. A single lamp was on the table next to the bed. On the red sheets, an old man was sound asleep. He had a grayish beard and his skin was pock-marked.

Paria walked to the side of the bed and the sleeping imam. He paused for a few seconds, then reached out and placed his large paw of a hand on the tiny old man's shoulder. Ever so gently, Paria shook his shoulder.

"Imam," said Paria, shaking for several moments, until Suleiman opened his eyes.

It took Suleiman a while to focus. He reached for the side table and found his eyeglasses and put them on.

"Who is it . . . at this hour . . ."

"Imam, it is Abu. I apologize for waking you, but it's important."

Suleiman sat up against the headboard, finally becoming alert.

"Abu," he said, nodding. "What is it, son?"

"You said to disturb you if we ever were in a position to kill the man who stole the nuclear weapon," said Paria.

"Andreas," snarled Suleiman.

"Yes, Imam. Dewey Andreas, the American."

Paria handed him the INTERPOL Red Notice. It was in Arabic. In the middle of the page was a head shot of Dewey.

Suleiman read the notice several times.

"What does it mean, Abu?"

"He's on the run," said Paria, his nostrils flaring. "The man who stole our nuclear weapon is on the run! He escaped from a French jail and is now trying to get out of the country. He's in France. It's our chance, Imam."

A small grin crept across Suleiman's lips.

"He's a flushed bird," he said. "Isn't that the expression?"

"Yes, exactly. He's exposed."

"So what do you need from me?" asked Suleiman.

"I want your permission to move some people into France in order to kill Andreas. He won't be flying. My guess is, he went south—Nice, Monaco, someplace where he can blend in. Perhaps Spain. He speaks Spanish. The important thing is, this could be our only chance."

Suleiman was silent for several moments, looking away from Paria, deep in thought. Finally, he turned back to Paria.

"Capture him if you can. But kill him if you must, Abu."

In a dark apartment across the wide boulevard from Beit-e Rahbari, a man with binoculars watched Paria's vehicle depart from the Supreme Leader's residence.

The apartment had been carefully selected. In addition to offering a view of the entrance to Beit-e Rahbari, with binoculars, the bedroom of the Supreme Leader was visible.

The man picked up his phone and dialed a long number.

"Perry," came the voice. "Who is this?"

"Mack, it's Abdullah," whispered the man.

"Abdullah, is something wrong? What time is it there?"

Perry, the head of Special Operations Group, had recruited Abdullah in London, when Perry was London chief of station and Abdullah was a graduate student at the London School of Economics. Perry had met Abdullah playing tennis at the Hurlingham Club and they became friends. At some point, Perry trusted the young Iranian enough to confide in him and ultimately ask him to return to Tehran and become an asset for the United States. On the surface, Abdullah was a loyal Iranian subject who worked in the finance department of National Iranian Oil Company, the state oil monopoly. But beneath the surface, he hated the religious dictatorship in Iran and wanted to be one of the ones who someday helped take it down and bring democracy to Iran.

"A little before four in the morning," said Abdullah. "Listen to me. Abu Paria arrived at Beit-e Rahbari thirty-six minutes ago. He left just now. Just after he arrived, the lights in Suleiman's apartment went on."

There was a long pause, and finally Perry spoke.

"The INTERPOL," said Perry. "There's no other explanation. Good work, Abbie."

56

BIRCH HILL FARM
MCLEAN, VIRGINIA

Bill Polk was on his way to Calibrisi's house when Perry's call came through.

"The Iranian informant just called me," he said. "Paria visited Suleiman a few minutes ago. Four in the morning Tehran time. Woke him up. I assume they got the Red Notice."

"The Iranians are going to try and kill him," said Polk. "Has Dewey made contact?"

"No."

"And Borchardt—"

"—is ignoring the calls, or else we have a wrong number."

"Okay. Let me speak with Hector. In the meantime, I want any assets in-theater alerted to the situation and briefed up," said Polk. "We don't know where Dewey went, so draw a wide perimeter. France, Spain, Italy, Germany, et cetera. Get them prepared to move if and when we find out where he is."

"You got it."

Polk was too tired to drive to Calibrisi's home. He was senior enough at the Agency to be driven by a security team every day, but he liked to drive. This night, however, he felt an unusual, dark mood coming over him. He'd known Lindsay personally. Beyond that, Lowell Trappe had been a close friend; Polk had been a congressional staff member on the House Intelligence Committee when Trappe recommended him for a job at the CIA. Over the years, the two had become confidants. His drowning saddened Polk.

But the truth was, neither Lindsay's murder nor Trappe's drowning was really on Polk's mind. All he could think about was Dewey.

They had a rough relationship. Technically, Dewey reported to him. But try and tell Dewey that. Dewey tolerated Polk; he spoke with Polk when Calibrisi wasn't available. The thing is, it didn't rankle Polk. If speaking directly with Calibrisi was what was necessary to have Dewey at Langley, it was a small price to pay.

Polk's mind was swirling. Why had Dewey been set up to take the fall for killing Lindsay? Polk knew Dewey didn't do it. What worried him wasn't whether France would recapture him and lock him up. No, what bothered Polk was the simple fact that when things began to spiral out of control, and Dewey was involved, it was always a bad sign. Fortuna. Cloud. Tristan Nazir. Dewey was like fly paper; he attracted the worst situations. Now the Iranians were coming into the picture.

All he could do was stare out the window as they passed through the quiet mansion-filled town of McLean.

The Suburban pulled through the gates at Calibrisi's six-acre estate, the driver waving to the pair of gunman positioned just inside the gates.

Calibrisi was inside, sitting at the kitchen table, cell phone clutched to his ear. He eyed Polk as he entered. Polk glanced at the clock on the wall above the AGA stove. It was eleven.

"Keep trying," said Calibrisi, and slammed the phone down.

Polk sat down across from him.

"What is it?"

"What the fuck do you think?" said Calibrisi. "Dewey."

Polk smiled and nodded. "He's mad he had to break out of the jail."

"Clearly," said Calibrisi. "You have the files?"

Polk placed a manila folder on the table and opened it. A small stack of paper was inside. He put the top sheet in front of Calibrisi.

"These are the individuals who worked at Langley in 1981 and who had direct access to William Casey," said Polk, "and who, as of an hour ago, were still alive. As you can see, it's a small list."

There were seven names on the list:

GRANGER, NICHOLAS
611-N9
Arizona State Univ.
ROTC
Marines/Force Recon
CIA

PANDOLFO, JAY
622-K8
Boston Univ.
U.S. Army—Delta Force
CIA
Exxon Mobil Corp.

DE VRIES, WILLIAM
390-H1
Univ. of Utah
U.S. Navy SEALs
White House—NSA
CIA

ABERNATHY, WARREN
72V-70

Harvard
Marines
Dept. of Defense—DIA
CIA
IBM Corp.

FLAHERTY, ANDREW
864-IG
Stanford
Harvard Law
U.S. Navy—Intelligence
CIA

BRUNER, CHARLES
462-A8
Yale
ROTC
Harvard Law School
U.S. Army Rangers
CIA
Dept. of State—Cons Op.

WHITE, MICHAEL
09-G45
Univ. of Michigan
Wharton
Goldman Sachs
CIA
Appaloosa LLC

"These are the men who would know about Order Six," said Polk.

"Do you know any of them?" said Calibrisi.

"No," said Polk. "I mean, I'm sure I've met some of them at some alumni function, but they were here almost forty years ago."

"Bruner went from here to State," said Calibrisi. "Let's bring him in. Do it carefully."

"If you don't want him to suspect anything, we should run it through the White House."

"Adrian," said Calibrisi.

"I'll handle it," said Polk, closing the folder.

He started to get up, but then stopped.

"There's something else," he said. "Abu Paria was seen entering Beit-e Rahbari at four in the morning. He visited with Suleiman."

"Oh, for fuck's sake," said Calibrisi.

"I have Mack briefing up every asset we have in-theater."

"So they read the INTERPOL and now want revenge. Those fucking French. I'm going to make those bastards pay for this."

"Right now, we need to keep cool," said Polk. "Look, this could end up being relatively simple. We find him, bring him home, end of story."

Calibrisi smiled. "Wishful thinking."

The phone on the wall, with Calibrisi's unlisted home number, rang. Calibrisi looked at his watch—then reached for the phone.

"Hello?"

There was a long pause.

"Hello? Who's there?"

"It's Dewey."

Calibrisi took a deep breath. "Hi, Dewey."

Calibrisi waited for Dewey to speak, but the silence went on and on.

"Where are you?"

"At the moment, not in a French jail. In case you didn't hear, they accused me of killing Lindsay. By the way, thanks for the junket."

"Borchardt?"

"It's nice to have friends who are willing to go out on a limb for you."

"Must be nice," said Calibrisi.

"Fuck you," snapped Dewey.

"What did you expect me to do?"

"Get me the hell out of that prison is what!"

"I'm not the goddam tooth fairy, Dewey! You think I didn't try? They believe you did it. That trumps any kind of pull the U.S. government might have."

"Whatever," said Dewey. "It doesn't matter. I called because there was a woman hiding in Lindsay's suite right before he was killed. I saw her later on the Métro but she got away. She's the one who killed Lindsay. Now I need some intelligence work. I assume I'm calling the right place."

"Drop the attitude," said Calibrisi. "I'm putting you on speaker. Bill is here."

"Hi, Dewey."

Dewey said nothing.

Calibrisi cut to the chase. "It's time to extract you."

"I need to find the woman."

"She's gone. Whoever she is, she's gone. Obviously, she was an agent. Probably Russia. But you're not going to find her now. She has hours on you. They extracted her."

There was a long pause.

"Then why the Métro?" Dewey said.

"Public transportation is the optimal escape protocol," said Polk. "You know that. Anonymity."

"How are you going to find her?" said Calibrisi.

"How the hell should I know? That's why I called you."

"Do you have any photos?"

"No," said Dewey. "They sort of have this policy at the DGSI *terror intake unit* about the amount of Wi-Fi a prisoner is allowed, so they deleted my photos."

Polk issued a rare grin.

"No, I don't have any fucking photos. I just escaped from jail, for chrissakes."

"What did she look like?" said Calibrisi.

"She was beautiful."

"That narrows it down," said Polk.

"Paris," said Calibrisi. "There aren't many beautiful women. We'll have a name and an address in a few minutes."

Dewey's soft laughter could be heard over the phone.

"I don't know," said Dewey. "She looked like that girl on *Game of Thrones*, with the blond hair, except it's brown."

Calibrisi shrugged.

"And how do we get in touch with you?" said Polk.

"I don't know," said Dewey. "I'll call you every few hours."

"We need a number."

"No. Not until I know you're not going to try and extract me."

Polk glanced at Calibrisi.

"We're not going to try and extract you," said Calibrisi.

"I want it in writing," said Dewey.

Calibrisi shook his head with annoyance. "Are you questioning my integrity?"

"Yes."

"Goddammit, Dewey!" he barked. "When I say I'm going to do something, I'm going to goddam well do it!"

"Really? Like that time you stuffed the dead Israeli into a box and sent him to the Chinese premier, even though I asked you not to?" said Dewey.

Calibrisi put his hand against the wall, steadying himself. His anger washed away and a look of deep sadness came to his face.

It had been Calibrisi's action—unbeknownst to Dewey—that triggered a violent series of events that culminated in the accidental death of Dewey's fiancée, Jessica. While Dewey got his own form of revenge, Jessica was still gone.

Jessica had been like a daughter to Calibrisi. A trusted colleague. His best friend, despite their age difference. A meteor of Irish beauty and brains.

Hers was a loss both men felt deeply.

"I'll put it in writing," said Calibrisi.

"Here's the number," Dewey said calmly, a hint of apology in his voice. He read off the number. "I'm in Saint-Tropez."

Over the next half hour, Calibrisi and Polk told Dewey everything they knew—Toronto, the satellite, and Order 6.

"So she does know something," said Dewey. "She must. She told Lindsay, they killed him."

"That's a big leap," said Polk.

"Maybe. It's my decision."

"There's something else," said Polk.

"What?"

"We believe Iran is coming for you. The Red Notice alerted them. Your old friend Abu Paria."

Dewey was quiet.

"I have every paramilitary asset in-theater briefed up and waiting for me to tell them to come and get you," said Polk. "It's time to come back here before someone finds you and puts a bullet in you."

"Bill, I appreciate it. So don't take this the wrong way. If I want to escape from Europe, I know how to do it. I don't want to escape. I want to find the woman. She knows something. Either she killed Lindsay or she told him something. Either way, we need to find her. That doesn't involve me going back to the United States. Not yet."

The phone went dead.

Calibrisi and Polk stared at each other for a few moments.

"He's right," said Calibrisi.

"Let's at least move some men toward southern France."

"I have a better idea," said Calibrisi, reaching for his phone.

57

CORAL BEACH CLUB
BERMUDA

Tacoma's cell rang. Katie was sitting beside him on a bench next to the tennis court. She looked over, holding a finger to her lips, telling him to shut off the ringer.

Rob Tacoma and Katie Foxx were watching a slightly overweight couple play tennis under the bright lights of the Coral Beach Club. It was almost midnight, but they were on a job.

RISCON, the security firm they owned together, was the preeminent company to hire if money was no object and you needed something done in the dark world of international business. They dealt with situations like hostage takings, protecting corporate chieftains while they visited subsidiaries in trouble spots. Their fees were exorbitant. A five-year retainer was required for all clients, its annual cost tailored to the specific client, though no retainer was less than $1 million a month, plus expenses. A very wealthy few hired them for personal security, a job both hated and for which they charged double.

The man in tennis whites was worth, according to *Forbes*, more than $25 billion.

For a long weekend in Bermuda making sure the man and his wife weren't kidnapped, Rob and Katie would earn a cool $2.5 million.

"Yeah?" Tacoma whispered into his cell.

"Where are you?" It was Calibrisi.

"Bermuda."

"I'll have a plane there in an hour. Are you with Katie?"

"Yeah."

"I need you two in Europe."

"What for?"

There was a long pause. "Dewey."

Tacoma was quiet. "Where is he?"

"France. I'll brief you guys in the air."

Tacoma looked at Katie.

"We're kind of on a job," he told Calibrisi.

"Tell your client we're sending over a team. They'll be on the plane. The CIA will watch them until you two get back."

58

FEDEX FIELD
LANDOVER, MARYLAND

FedEx Field, home to the Washington Redskins, sat quiet on a chilly, cloudless night. Exterior lights were on, enough to illuminate the side of the massive facility and the enormous parking area surrounding it.

At 2:44 A.M., a white-and-blue police sedan patrolled slowly around the circumference of the stadium. The vehicle looked exactly like a Landover police cruiser, making its normal rounds, but it was not.

A man dressed in a police uniform was driving. Two men dressed in all-black tactical gear sat in back. The men had on ski masks and carried black weapons rucks strapped tightly to their backs.

On the car's second circuit of the large stadium, the driver held up five fingers, lowering one finger at a time with each passing second, signaling that they would soon be at the drop-off point, a place the driver felt was the darkest point along the route. When the driver's thumb went down, indicating the count was up, the back doors opened and the two men ducked out, hitting the ground in a half roll, then leaping up and sprinting toward a steel gate—a delivery entrance to the stadium—as the cruiser kept on going.

The snipers quickly scanned the side of the stadium, one of them pointing to a section of steel fence thirty feet up the wall above the large portico of the delivery entrance. They began a rapid, silent ascent, gripping small edges of the steel and concrete, tearing up next to one another like tarantulas. They came to the small section of fence that offered a way in. One of the snipers, Ellsbury, used wire cutters to cut through one of the spans of steel. The two men climbed inside, one after the other. Law, the other sniper, jumped, landing almost silently on the concrete below, while Ellsbury remained at the cut in the fence. He removed a piece of steel rod that looked exactly like the fence, then took pliers from his vest and squeezed both ends of the wire to the two ends of the steel that he'd just cut, effectively hiding the incision. He put the pliers back in his vest and leapt into the pitch-black of the stadium, landing on his feet with barely a grunt.

Ellsbury and Law pulled night optics down over their heads.

Law led a fast jog toward the low part of the roof, where the seats closest to the field sat just above. He went counterclockwise for several hundred feet until he came to a green door. Inside was a windowless stairwell. Law and Ellsbury charged up the stairs. The night optics—because there was no ambient light—were useless, but they moved quickly to the first floor. Ellsbury opened the stair door and went out, followed by Law.

They jogged around the wide-open concessions area. Ellsbury came to Section 211. To the right, across the empty concourse, he eyed a men's room.

"Wait here," he said.

Ellsbury entered the restroom and moved to the line of sinks, going to the last one. He unzipped a pocket of his weapons pack and removed a black nylon pouch. He crawled beneath the sinks and flipped over onto his back. He held up the pouch in front of the night optic. On the side of the pouch was a strip of tape, covered in nonstick plastic. He peeled off the tape and pressed the pouch against the underside of the counter, holding it in place until he was sure it was tight. He crawled out, throwing the plastic in a trash can, then went to join Law.

They charged back to the stairs and climbed until they arrived at the floor where the stadium's luxury suites were located.

Ellsbury handed Law a key.

"Twenty-six," said Ellsbury, referring to the suite number.

Law nodded and moved along the concourse toward Suite 26, on the other side of the stadium, as Ellsbury went in the opposite direction. Several hundred yards along the dark concourse, Ellsbury came to Suite 2. He removed a key from his pocket and went quietly inside.

The suite had a dining area, a wet bar, a restroom, and, behind a wall of glass, three rows of seats on an elevated deck that overlooked the stadium. He stepped to the glass and carefully slid the door open. A strong wind blew in. Ellsbury pushed his night optics back up onto the top of his head and stared down, studying the empty stadium. The half-moon was bright, as were the stars. The light bounced atop the eighty-two thousand empty seats, making the interior of the stadium seem to glow.

He went back inside and shut the glass door. He took off his backpack and removed the pieces of a firearm. It was a Remington 700 Long Action rifle with a Lilja Precision 26.5" 1:10 barrel, a McMillan A-2 tactical stock with a saddle-type adjustable cheek piece, a McCann Industries Integrated Rail System (MIRS) rifle mount, a Nightforce 20 MOA Picatinny rail as well as Nightforce High Rings and an NXS 8-32x56 Riflescope. Screwed into the muzzle was a Knights Armament Mk11 suppressor. The rifle also had a Harris 6–9" swivel bipod. He inserted a magazine and went into the bathroom.

He climbed onto the sink, then pushed up on a ceiling tile and moved it aside. He put the rifle in the space and moved the tile back into place.

He went back to the suite, to the seating area. He took a powerful night monocular from his jacket. Putting it to his right eye, he stared down at the football field, finding the Redskins logo at midfield, the optic so powerful that he could see individual blades of grass.

Ellsbury ran to the stairs. Soon he was climbing through the hole he'd cut below in the fence, patching it up, then dropping. Law was already there waiting.

"You good?" said Ellsbury.

"Yes," said Law. "All set."

59

11 RUE SUBAIN
PARIS

Beauxchamps entered his apartment. In the small galley kitchen, he uncorked a half-empty bottle of wine, poured a glass, and took a sip.

Beauxchamps hadn't slept in a day and a half, yet he wasn't tired. He went to his desk and opened the top drawer, removing a cell phone. It was an old phone, a small flip model, but it worked, and he had it for just such occasions, when he wanted to make a call unbeknownst to DGSI. He looked at his wrist, where he'd written the number with a ballpoint pen, and dialed.

A series of clicks ensued, followed by a low ring. He took a few more sips as he waited for someone to answer.

"Hello?" came the voice, slightly Germanic, groggy, annoyed at being woken up. "Who is this? How did you get this number?"

"My name is Beauxchamps. I'm a detective for the General Directorate for Internal Security. I apologize for interrupting you, sir."

"How did you get this number?" seethed Borchardt.

"It was the number Dewey Andreas called from Branch Four, Monsieur Borchardt."

"If you're simply trying to buy time so you can initiate some sort of geographic trace, you're wasting your time, Beauxchamps."

"No, I assure you. I'm using my personal cell phone. I want DGSI to know about this conversation about as much as you do."

"What do you want?"

"To speak with him. It's important."

"He's not interested."

Beauxchamps's phone went dead. He pressed a button on the side of the phone. A map came onto the screen. It showed a wide spectrographic of Europe, then slowly zoomed in.

He hit speed dial.

"I need a helicopter," said Beauxchamps. "Pick me up in the park."

The silver-and-black Panther AS440 cut sideways and swept over a last stretch of dark land at the outskirts of Saint-Tropez. It was past midnight. The pilot brought the Panther over the mansion, then hovered low and dropped slowly onto a stretch of grass near a back terrace.

Beauxchamps hit a button near the left side of the cabin. A hydraulic sound mixed with the echo of the slowing rotors. The door slowly opened and swept toward the grass.

"Wait here," Beauxchamps told the pilot.

He stepped down the helicopter's stairs onto the grass. In his right hand, he held a manila folder. He stared at the ground as he walked but didn't look up. He came to a curving marble stairway that led up to the terrace. He sprinted up the steps. Seated on a chaise lounge was Dewey. He had on jeans, no shirt, and was barefoot. A few empty beer bottles were on the table to his left. He was staring at Beauxchamps. In his hands was a pump-action 12-gauge shotgun. It was aimed at Beauxchamps.

"A shotgun?" said Beauxchamps. "Interesting choice."

"What do you want?" said Dewey.

"To speak with you."

"Really? Let me guess, you'd like to invite me to a special ceremony and award me a ribbon?"

"I'm sorry for how the questioning went."

"If I ever see Rousse again, I'm going to kill him," said Dewey. "You can tell him that."

"You need to put aside your anger for a few minutes and listen," said Beauxchamps. "It's important."

There was a pregnant pause.

"You have one minute," said Dewey. "Then I blow your right kneecap off."

"I reran the ballistics on the slugs." Beauxchamps took a step forward and extended the folder to Dewey. "The first analysis was run only on the ones that killed Lindsay, the presumption being that whoever killed Lindsay also killed the guards. Your gun *was* used to kill Lindsay and one of the guards, but the other agent came back with a different ballistic. There were two weapons used."

Dewey took the folder but didn't open it.

"It could mean anything. Maybe I had an extra gun."

"Someone else was there. My guess is, you were framed to distract everyone, including you, but also DGSI and the United States government. There's one other thing. You say you saw a woman in the room. We found evidence of a woman matching the description you gave. She checked into the hotel adjacent to the George

Cinq a little while before Lindsay was killed. There's a photo."

Now Dewey opened the folder, flipping papers until he found one with a photo. He kept the muzzle of the shotgun trained on Beauxchamps as he stared at the photo under the dim light from the mansion.

"How'd she get in the suite?"

"She climbed," said Beauxchamps. "I found a piece of her coat on the steel fence separating the two properties."

"And you think she killed him?"

"Maybe. Probably. Maybe not. Who knows? If she did, it seems clear that she was either hired or sent by an intelligence agency, perhaps Russia. But perhaps she didn't kill him. Maybe Lindsay was killed because of something she told him. The bottom line is, we need to find her."

"And how do you suggest we do that?"

"I know where she is."

Dewey was quiet for a few moments. He put the paper down and picked up a beer, downing it in two big gulps.

"We're tracking the credit card she used," said Beauxchamps.

"Are you guys going to try and find her?"

"No," said Beauxchamps. "No one knows, other than someone who works for me, a man I trust. I don't think you did it. But something's going on and we have to find her. If she's a foreign agent, we need to get her before she leaves the country."

"I don't work with people who don't know what they're doing."

"I deserve that," said Beauxchamps. "But I do know what I'm doing. I found you, didn't I? Besides, you don't have a choice."

There was a long pause as Dewey stared at Beauxchamps.

"I'll let you tag along, Beauxchamps, but if I find her, she's America's property. This has to do with *our* secretary of state."

Beauxchamps nodded.

"Fine. She arrived in Marseille last night. An hour ago, she got aboard the overnight train from Marseille to Frankfurt. We'll get aboard at a later station, Lyon or Chalon-sur-Saône."

"Okay. Can your guy give us a lift?"

"Yes. But you need a disguise. INTERPOL issued a Red Notice a few hours ago. Your photo is everywhere."

60

NSA
SIGNALS INTELLIGENCE DIRECTORATE

Samantha and Follett were seated in Bruckheimer's office. June was standing before a whiteboard. He picked up a black marker and quickly diagrammed the information that was known to them at that point. It looked like a spider, with lines coming off of a central body: Order 6.

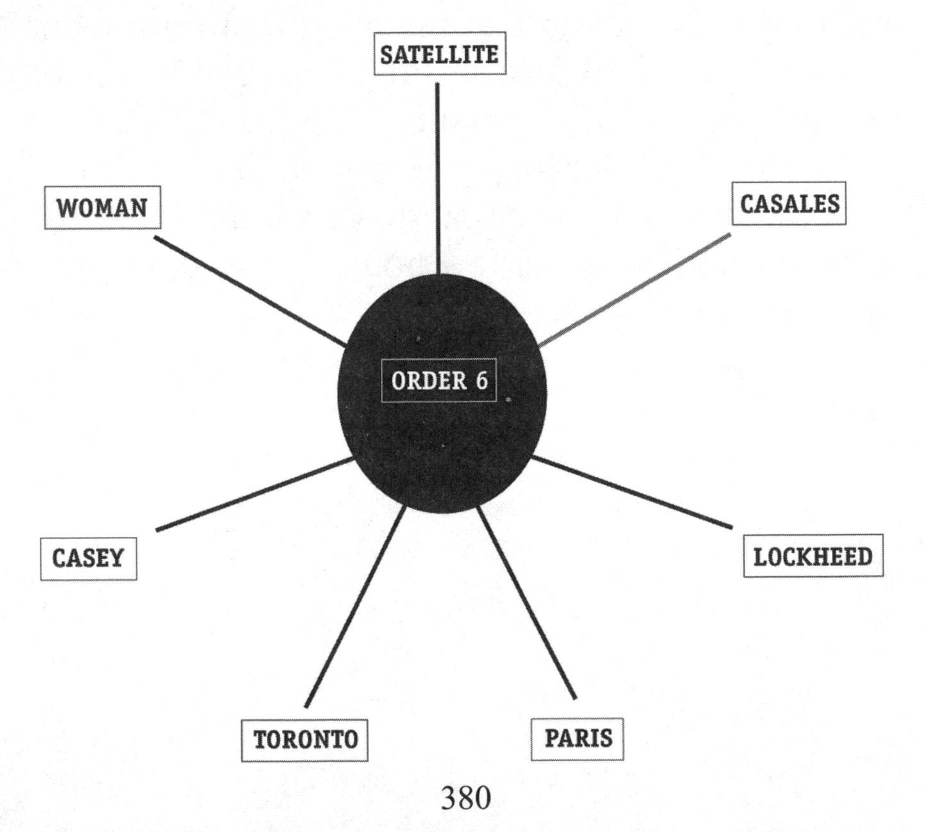

June had used a black marker for every word but one: Casales, the dead Consular Operations agent was in red.

On speakerphone were Calibrisi, Polk, Perry, and a few others from the CIA, as well as Josh Brubaker, national security advisor, and White House chief of staff Adrian King. The two agencies were sharing notes about the investigation into Order 6, which everyone felt was critical to figuring out who killed Tim Lindsay.

That afternoon, Charles Bruner, the former head of the National Clandestine Service under William Casey, was meeting with King at the White House. Bruner, they all believed, knew something about Order 6, having left Langley for the State Department, where he ran Consular Operations.

In addition, Follett was meeting with another individual on the list of people who might know about Order 6, Andrew Flaherty.

But June believed they needed to do more.

"We need to run Consular Operations employees against PRISM, DS-300, and Stellar Wind," he said, referring to three of NSA's key software programs.

"I previewed it with Judge Wetherbee at the FISA court," said Polk. "He was very opposed to the idea of simply running every Consular Operations employee through the NSA ringer. He called it a fishing expedition. You're going to need to background them another way, Jesus."

"We've looked at goddam everything," said June.

"Actually, there is a way," said Brubaker. "Title 50 of the U.S. Code. Specifically, Chapter 36, Subchapter I, Paragraph 1805. If the U.S. attorney general determines that an emergency exists, he may authorize the use of electronic surveillance *before* obtaining the necessary authorization from the Foreign Intelligence Surveillance Court. As long as the AG or his designee notifies a judge of the court at the time of authorization and applies for a warrant within seven days, it's legal."

"I'll call the attorney general," said King.

61

VILLA BLANCHE
SAINT-TROPEZ, FRANCE

One of Borchardt's staff members, a woman named Lynette, cut Dewey's hair—not too short, but short enough to look nothing like the photos of Dewey splashed across the newspapers and European news channels. She then colored it a very light gray, almost white. Lynette also made Dewey shave and then applied a deep base of light-colored makeup, which made his skin appear very pale.

For his wardrobe, Dewey found a hideous cardigan sweater in Borchardt's closet. He also found a pair of eyeglasses with no prescription—designed to simply alter his appearance. They were horn-rimmed and oversized. He took a wooden walking stick from Borchardt. He didn't want to project an old man, but rather someone in his early sixties—a skier who'd twisted his knee one too many times.

Someone who knew Dewey—or a highly trained professional—might be able to recognize him, but most would not. He looked like a wealthy European on his way to the Alps for some very slow skiing. Wealthy, a bit bookish, and odd.

He and Beauxchamps walked quickly to the waiting Panther, its rotors already slashing the air, creating a din and blowing a hard wind over Borchardt's lawn. They passed one of Borchardt's security men nearby, Dewey nodding at him as he took the final steps toward the open door of the helicopter.

Yaron watched from the lawn as the helicopter carrying Andreas lifted off and cut into the darkening sky. He opened his cell phone and signed into his bank account, then removed another phone, a cheap disposable one he'd bought the night before. He dialed.

"Hello?"

"It's me," Yaron said, his British accent sharp and rough, Cockney.

"Hold on."

A moment later, another person came on the line. "This is Nebuchar Fortuna. Where's Andreas?"

"He just left."

"Do you know where he's going?"

"Yes. I know precisely where he's going."

"Well, *where?*"

"I'm staring at my bank account," said Yaron. "I'm not saying anything else until I see the wire hit."

"Understood. Hold on."

The phone was silent for nearly a minute.

"Try now," said Fortuna.

Yaron refreshed the bank app on his phone. Suddenly the number jumped.

$5,000,000.00

"I want the rest of the money now. I don't trust you."

"We had a deal."

"We still do. You want to know where Dewey Andreas is going, you pay me. Same deal, we're just going to alter the terms of payment a little."

"Fine," snapped Fortuna. "Hold on."

Again, a long pause. Finally, Fortuna came back on.

"Look again."

Yaron refreshed the bank app again. The

number indicating how much money he had in the account made an abrupt jump.

$10,000,000.00

"He's on his way to a train station," said Yaron. "He's catching the Marseille overnight train to Frankfurt."

62

LAYSAN
NORTHWESTERN HAWAIIAN ISLANDS
PACIFIC OCEAN

A white-and-red go-fast boat ripped across the dark waters at eighty miles an hour. The boat had departed from a private dock a few miles from Honolulu that morning. The boat had no running lights as it roared across the deep Pacific.

There were two men on the boat, both in their late twenties, both former U.S. Navy SEALs. They wore similar-looking outfits: jeans and dark T-shirts. The driver, Rogers, was smoking a cigarette despite the warm wind. He had night optics, but they were around his neck and turned off. The boat's NAV system and the stars above were enough for him to see.

They reached Laysan at midnight. Laysan was

one of the ten islands and atolls in the uninhabited Northwestern Hawaiian Islands.

They worked at night, removing several long steel weapons cases from the boat, along with sleeping bags, food, and communications equipment. When they were done unloading, they covered the boat with a camouflaged tarp so that anyone flying overhead, or searching via satellite, would see nothing.

The weapons cases held MANPADs, man-portable air-defense systems—shoulder-held surface-to-air missiles. There were ten missiles in all, all of them Stingers.

They set up their tents a few hundred yards inland, eating cold bread and sliced steak beneath a starry sky.

Rogers turned on the communications equipment before he went to sleep. He dialed a phone number.

"Hello?" came the voice.

"Mr. Flaherty, it's Tommy," said Rogers. "Joe and I are here and in position."

"The flight course will be automatically uploaded directly into the firing sequence," said Flaherty. "You simply need to press the trigger. However, I want in-theater redundancy."

"We'll both be firing," said Rogers. "Joe's MANPAD will be the one you guys control. I'll target the plane on my own."

63

MARSEILLE, FRANCE

The train moved out of Marseille as an early winter storm, predicted to blanket Europe in at least two feet of new snow, cast the first lazy flakes across a hazy sky, turning gray as night approached.

Romy looked at the clock above the door of the compartment. It was 10 P.M. She studied the train schedule. They would arrive in Frankfurt just before 6.

She'd been to Frankfurt many times. It was a city that would enable her to figure out her next steps. Large enough to hide.

But she was tired. The thought of running anymore made her eyes moisten again with tears. She sat and stared out thc window at the passing countryside, eventually feeling her eyes grow heavy. She wanted to stay awake. She needed to think. What if she simply called the White House and told the operator everything she knew? Most likely, the operator would hang up on her, but there was a chance. Maybe they had to write down all messages? Surely if she said she was with Lindsay before he died, that a man named

Charles Bruner was behind it all, they would report it to someone?

She could try, even though she knew it would be a waste of time. If they didn't hang up on her, the message would be laughed at in some junior-level staffer's office.

"Just stop thinking about it for a few minutes," she told herself. "Rest. You need it."

Even beyond the need to warn somebody about Bruner was the simple fact that she didn't know where she was going or what she would do when she got there. She had no direction. She'd chosen the train arbitrarily, the first one leaving Marseille after she killed the man in the restaurant. She had no future. She had no past. She had the memory of Kyrie and that was all, a memory that was destroyed, her entire life ruined by a man she now realized was a stranger—a monster. She shut her eyes and drifted off to sleep.

64

LYON, FRANCE

The Panther descended from the sky, swirling the heavy snowflakes in a white eddy. Nighttime had settled like a dark quilt, black, white, and violent. The front edge of the blizzard announced itself in a line of snowfall, blown by fierce crosswinds, which the pilot struggled to navigate.

Dewey and Beauxchamps sat in the cabin, not saying much. A backpack on the seat held two sets of forged documents for Dewey, one Swiss, the other U.S., prepared by a contact of Borchardt's and designed to withstand examination at border crossings or by police. They would deliver a clean back-pull when pushed against INTERPOL.

In a compartment at the bottom of the backpack were several magazines filled with bullets, along with a spare .45 pistol. Around his neck, a leather cord was looped through the trigger of a silenced Colt M1911A1. Dewey's fixed-blade Gerber was sheathed to his left calf.

The chopper landed behind a large warehouse on the outskirts of Lyon, where Borchardt maintained a storage facility. Dewey and

Beauxchamps climbed out and walked to a black van, idling, steam billowing from its tailpipe. They hopped in the back. One of Borchardt's men was waiting in the driver's seat.

"Philippe?"

"Hi, Dewey. We need to move quickly if you're going to make the train."

"Were you able to get skis and boots in my size?"

Philippe nodded toward the back. "It wasn't easy. You have big feet. I also put a jacket in there and some decent gloves."

"I need you to carry them on the train for me," Dewey said to Beauxchamps. "A man with a walking stick doesn't carry skis."

"I'll put them on the train for you. Where do you want them?"

"Near the front. A seat on the right. Put the boot bag on the seat and the skis on the rack at the front of the car."

Dewey went into the station, walking slowly with the aid of the walking stick, entering through a different door than Beauxchamps. He bought a ticket and sat down, pulling out a book he'd grabbed from Borchardt's library. He pretended to read as his eyes slowly scanned the station.

At some point, Dewey heard a hum, so faint that most people wouldn't have noticed. It was a chopper. Exactly five minutes later, a gorgeous blond-haired woman came in through the main entrance, dressed in a shiny red-and-blue Bogner ski jacket and black leather pants, with fur boots up to her knees.

Katie.

Just then, through a side entrance, another figure appeared. He had medium-length brown hair, tousled, and a week's worth of stubble. He had on jeans, worn Timberland boots, and a bright orange Patagonia jacket. He was lugging a large snowboard bag. He looked to be in his twenties, maybe a college student or someone who'd just graduated. Though nighttime, he wore white-framed sunglasses.

Several females turned when he walked in.

Tacoma.

Tacoma dropped his gear, then scanned the station. His eyes passed Dewey once, then twice, each time hovering for a while longer. Finally, he grinned and walked over to the bench. A shit-eating grin crossed his lips.

"*Bonjour*, *monsieur*," he said, sitting down next to Dewey.

Dewey pretended not to notice, trying to sew a bit of doubt into Tacoma's assumption that he'd found him, despite the disguise.

"Monsieur," said Tacoma, "I'm from the local newspaper. I'm writing an article on the sexual proclivities of old people, and I'd like to interview you."

"You're sick," Dewey whispered under his breath. "Shut the fuck up."

"Laughing's good for you, Dewey," Tacoma said quietly. "Isn't that what the doc told you?"

"How the fuck do you know what the 'doc' told me, asshole?" Dewey leaned back, seething. "I knew they shouldn't have sent you. This isn't a fucking joke."

A woman came over the loudspeaker, announcing the arrival of the overnight train to Frankfurt. A few minutes later, the low grumble of the arriving train could be heard. Dewey stood up and went outside, Tacoma following. There were several dozen people waiting for the train, most carrying ski equipment. Dewey noted Beauxchamps, farther down the platform, waiting to board.

The smooth bullet-shaped nose of the train swept down the tracks. The train pushed the falling snow into violent swirls of white as it came sliding in front of the platform and halted.

"I know it's not a joke," said Tacoma.

Tacoma looked around and then opened his parka. A compact MP7A1 was strapped inside. An M1911 was also visible, its muzzle extended by a long, thin silencer. A combat blade was sheathed just below. He quickly shut the jacket.

"Just don't kill the woman," said Dewey. "Or me."

Dewey moved down the platform to the back of the train, meandering toward Katie along the way.

"Nice coat," said Dewey quietly.

As he walked by, Katie handed him what looked like a pack of gum.

"Don't distract me," said Katie in a businesslike manner. "You think I want to be in France right now, in a blizzard, hunting for VEVAK agents? Just find her and we get off at the next stop, hopefully before the Iranians start shooting."

"All I said was 'nice coat,' " said Dewey. "It looks good."

"My God," she whispered. "You were in jail for like an hour. You're acting like you were there for a decade. I do *not* look good. I bought this shit in Bermuda on the way to the airport."

"Okay, whatever."

Dewey kept ambling to the rear of the platform. He was the last person to climb aboard and barely got inside before the doors shut. A loud beep sounded, and the train started moving. He was in the last car.

Dewey waited for passengers to take their seats and then moved slowly down the aisle, slightly stooped over, walking stick in one hand, the other hand on the seat backs for stability.

Dewey had spent months learning surveillance and discovery: How to look for someone who knows he's being looked for without being seen or noticed. How to spot unusual behavior. Inconsistencies vs. aberrations and how to differentiate between the two, inconsistencies indicating possible intentional concealment, aberrations simply part of the human condition. A man pretending to be old with a brand-new cane was an inconsistency. An actual man in need of a cane would have a worn one or, more likely, something like a walking stick, something to make the process of decline and aging personal, even enjoyable. Had Dewey been using a new cane, a metal one, for example, he could've been marked easily.

He scanned each row for the woman. A black man, a child, a group of teenagers off to ski—these didn't have to be examined. Others did.

She wasn't there.

Dewey moved through ten passenger cars. As he came to the car just behind the first-class car, he noted Tacoma seated near the back and Katie half a dozen rows in front of him.

When he reached the front, he looked through the passageway to the first-class car ahead, the car closest to the locomotive. A pair of uniformed policemen stood at the entrance to the car, preventing access to anyone who hadn't paid the exorbitant price for a first-class ticket.

Dewey turned around and meandered back down the aisle. Halfway back, he saw the seat with the boot bag on it. The other seat was empty.

Across the aisle, one row back, sat Beauxchamps. Dewey placed the bag in the overhead compartment and took off his backpack, putting it on the floor, then sat down. He removed the book and started reading. After a few minutes, he looked over to Beauxchamps, who was looking at his cell. Ever so subtly, Beauxchamps glanced forward—to the first-class car. His look revealed an important message: She was on board.

65

CHALON-SUR-SAÔNE, FRANCE

Fortuna, Mustafah, Hosni, and Jerome entered Chalon-sur-Saône's train station through separate doors, pretending not to know each other.

Even though he wasn't expecting an attack from his past, Andreas would be looking for everything. The greatest likelihood for success was blending in, then attacking with speed and brutality. The plan was to start looking two hours into the train ride. Even if someone suspected that a passenger was Andreas, they were to do nothing. Fortuna knew it was the only way. Andreas obviously understood not only how to blend in but also how to mark someone who didn't. Andreas's liability was his size. It was impossible to hide. Fortuna had two liabilities that posed risk of detection. One was his face. He had the same ability to make a room full of people turn to see his face. He was as handsome as a model.

His second liability was the fact that he and his team were Arab. Airports, with the exception of Israel, didn't profile. They didn't cull out, the way Israel did, specific groups based on the color of their skin, their nationality. It was the greatest gift America and the West gave to terrorists. But Andreas would be different. There was no question that he profiled. Like a filter, Andreas would sift out the obvious non-possibilities. Then he would cull through the remnants, looking for suspicious behavior—something as trivial as how a man's pants fit, knowing that a pair that looked unnatural on someone probably was, that they'd been given them on the way to the airport or were concealing something.

The plan was simple. After settling aboard the train, Mustafah, Hosni, and Jerome would search for Andreas while Fortuna remained seated and out of the way. Fortuna had never met him, but he knew Andreas might recognize similarities between himself and his father or brother. The element of surprise was paramount.

Mustafah and Jerome carried snowboard bags. Each bag contained a snowboard, boots, and, in hidden pockets, weapons and ammo. Mustafah had an Uzi and a Glock 38. Jerome was carrying an MP7 and a Walther PPK.

Hosni had a large suitcase. Inside was clothing and, in a secret compartment, enough explosives to blow up the train, along with a Glock 38.

Fortuna had two bags. Onc was a smaller boot bag, which held a pair of ski boots stuffed with 8-gauge shotgun shells. A long, thin ski bag was strapped to his back. Inside was a pair of skis and Fortuna's weapon of choice, a sawed-off pump-action Benelli 12-gauge shotgun.

All four men carried knives as well as concealed handguns.

They purchased tickets from separate windows, then moved to the platform to await the train's arrival. Fortuna took a slight detour, heading into a bathroom, locking the door, and removing a ziplock bag filled with cocaine from his pocket. He took several fingertips' worth and snorted it sloppily into both nostrils. He checked himself in the mirror, wiping his nose and getting rid of any traces of coke, then went to the platform just as the overnight Marseille train was coming into the station.

An hour into the train ride, Katie removed a small prescription bottle from her jacket pocket. Inside was a tiny silver object the size of a Tic Tac. She placed it in her ear, then tapped twice.

“Rob,” she whispered.

“Yeah,” said Tacoma. “You’re late.”

“Sorry. Can you hear me okay?”

“Yeah, loud and clear.”

“Is Dewey on COMMS?”

“No.”

Katie stood up and went to the restroom, bolting the door. She dialed the international switch for Special Operations Group, looking for Polk, Mack Perry, or anyone else monitoring the operation. It was Perry who picked up in one of the operating theaters. A former member of the Air Force’s 24th Special Tactics Squadron, referred to as 24th STS, Perry had been recruited to the CIA by Katie when she ran SOG.

“This is Perry.”

“It’s me,” she said.

“Are you on the train?”

“Yeah. I can’t talk. Lock me in, phone and watch, then I need something.”

“Hold on.”

Katie waited for the familiar beeps as Perry initiated a tracking protocol from Langley, based off her cell phone and watch, enabling Langley to track her in real time and impose her location on a digital map in the theater.

“Okay, we got you,” said Perry. “What do you need?”

“Do the trains have cameras inside?”

“No.”

“The train is packed,” said Katie. “We need to weed it down. Do we at least know how many there are?”

“Negative.”

“KUDS Force? VEVAK? It couldn’t be Hezbollah, could it?”

“We don’t know,” said Perry.

“Try scanning the manifests,” said Katie. “Arabic-sounding names.”

“I’ll try, but you’re in Europe. There are going to be plenty of Arabic-sounding names.”

“Just look for something.”

“I will. By the way, we have a chopper en route. It’s a Trauma Hawk, so we can use it for extraction or if anyone gets hurt.”

“When will it be in position?” said Katie.

“Belfort,” said Perry. “You’re coming into Chalon-sur-Saône, so you have another hour and a half or so until we’ll be in position to pull you out. The snowstorm is wreaking havoc.”

Dewey read quietly as the train moved north, occasionally leaning back and staring out the window. Snow was so thick it was hard to see more than a few feet. The white billows of snowflakes were illuminated by the train’s running lights. For a few moments, Dewey thought about what it must have been like to be going skiing this night with a family, traveling north, going away for a weekend or a week.

Then he remembered the package. He reached in his pocket and removed a small, thin green-and-white box that said TRIDENT on the side. He opened it up and pulled out the earbud, sticking it in his ear, then tapping twice.

"Hey, guys," he whispered. "You hear me okay?"

"Yes," said Katie.

"I hear you," said Tacoma.

"She's in the first-class car," said Dewey, "which unfortunately has a couple of gunmen guarding it."

"When do you want to get her?" said Tacoma.

"The sooner the better," said Dewey. "I doubt Paria beat us getting on board, so let's get her off before those nutjobs show up and spoil the party. Ideally, we grab her and get out of here with no loss of life."

"A chopper is en route," Katie said quietly. "We'll be able to extract once we get to Belfort. That's an hour and a half, maybe two hours from now."

As the train pulled into the next station, Dewey scanned the crowds of people waiting to get on. The platform was more crowded, and a large sign on the side of the station announced CHALON-SUR-SAÔNE.

As the train stopped, his eyes fell on a young man with short black hair. He was wearing a green ski jacket with white stripes down the arms. A bulky snowboard bag was slung over his back. The man was tall, with dark skin: Arab. There was no reason to consider the man in any way. Dewey was on the train to find the woman, and that was all. His main concern was DGSI, and thus far he hadn't seen any signs of law enforcement other than the two officers guarding the first-class car. Yet something about the Arab in the green jacket triggered an instinct inside Dewey. He felt a chill in the back of his head that spread down his spine.

Fortuna looked down the Chalon-sur-Saône platform. He made eye contact with each man. Fortuna was closest to the rear of the train. Hosni was waiting at the next car. Mustafah was in front of him a car forward, followed by Jerome.

As the doors opened, Fortuna stepped inside, quickly scanning for anyone who might be looking at him. But there was no one, just some teenagers grabbing a cigarette in the small area at the end of the car. Fortuna walked down the aisle until he found an open window seat. He put his ski bag in the overhead compartment and looked at the passenger in the aisle seat, a pretty blond woman.

"*Pardon*, *mademoiselle*," he said politely. "*Est-ce-que c'est pris*?"

She looked up at Fortuna, unhappy that she had to give up the empty seat, but then as she took him in with her eyes, a smile appeared on her lips.

"*S'il vous plaît*," she said, standing up and stepping into the aisle to let him by. "Sit down. It's not taken."

The new group of passengers flooded onto the train. A family of four settled into empty seats near Dewey, the father taking the seat next to him. They were French. The man nodded politely to Dewey as he sat down. Dewey smiled back, nodding warmly, saying nothing as his eyes continued to scan the front of the car, where he knew the man in the green jacket would be entering.

Dewey watched him move down the aisle, his jacket reflecting in the glass, allowing Dewey to follow his movements without looking away from the window. He sat down a few rows in front of Dewey, across the aisle, stowing his bag overhead, along with his jacket.

Dewey needed to figure out a way to get into the first-class car, but now his mind started to drift, watching the young man as he got comfortable. He stuck earbuds in his ears, then plugged them into his cell phone. He didn't look back once, not even to check out his immediate vicinity. Instead, he tilted his seat back as far as it would go and shut his eyes.

Dewey slouched back into his seat, lodging

his head in the corner near the window. He crossed his arms and shut his eyes most of the way, keeping them just the slightest bit open, remaining alert. An hour passed, along with a few more stops, and Dewey continued to study the Arab, who napped, woke up, and went to the café car one car back, returning with a bottle of water, which he drank as he read a magazine.

You're being paranoid.

But who could blame him? Every law enforcement official in France wanted him captured. More than a handful wanted him dead. Thanks to the INTERPOL alert, DGSI had alerted every country in Europe, and they, too, would be looking. Dewey finally picked up the book again, opening to a random page. At some point, the young Arab stood up and walked toward the front of the car. He knocked on the bathroom door and entered.

Dewey got to his feet.

"I'm sorry," said Dewey to the man next to him. "I left something in my bag."

Dewey walked to the empty seat across the aisle and opened the overhead compartment. He searched with his hand, feeling for the zipper, then unzipped the snowboard bag. Inside, he felt a smooth snowboard, boots and, beneath the snowboard, a submachine gun. Dewey quickly zipped it back up and shut the compartment door.

He glanced back at Beauxchamps and almost

imperceptibly shook his head. The meaning was clear: Dewey was not going for the woman yet.

Dewey walked to the front of the car, the walking stick in his left hand. As he got there, he put the stick on a shelf next to the ski rack. He stepped close to the door, glancing back, making sure no one was coming, and put his hand under his sweater and gripped the butt of his handgun. The lock on the bathroom door clicked. As the Arab started to slide the door open, Dewey stepped in the way and moved in, raising the silenced Colt .45 and training it on the Arab as he shut the door with his other hand. The Arab looked utterly shocked, but instead of fear, he seemed angry.

"On your knees," Dewey said quietly. *"Now."*

The Arab glanced behind Dewey, then looked at the window. But he didn't move. Dewey remained still. Suddenly the Arab lurched forward, slashing his right arm through the air. Dewey blocked it with his left forearm and kicked viciously, striking him in the groin. He dropped to the ground, clutching his groin, heaving for air.

"Who are you?" said Dewey.

"No one," groaned the Arab. "Mustafah. I'm a student at the Sorbonne. I'm meeting my girlfriend in Vienna."

"Why the weapons?"

"What weapons?"

Dewey stepped forward and kicked him hard in the knee. He let out a pained yelp.

"If you want to live, answer my questions. Why the weapons?"

The train jerked slightly as brakes were applied. They were slowing down.

"I always carry something," said Mustafah. "Are you fucking kidding? Watch the news sometimes. These fucking jihadis are everywhere. I'll tell you right now, if I'm on a train or at a nightclub, I'm packing, and I'll go out in a hail of bullets before I let one of these fucking towel-head nutjobs kill me."

Dewey trained his gun on Mustafah, who remained prone on the floor. Dewey crouched and jabbed the end of the suppressor into Mustafah's right eye.

"I wouldn't move if I were you," he said.

The speakers crackled and a woman spoke: "*Besançon, quatre minutes*!"

They were coming into a station.

Dewey patted him down. He found a gun sheathed to his left calf, a knife tucked into a concealed holster at his waist, and another gun tied to a piece of string around his neck. He took all three weapons, stepped to the window, gun trained at all times on Mustafah, pulled the window open, and threw them out.

"That's a lot of firepower for someone worried about a random attack," said Dewey.

Mustafah looked up.

"Please," he begged, becoming distraught, even emotional. "I'm just an amateur. I'm a fool. The only time I've even fired one of these is at the range. My father, he's a successful lawyer. Please don't kill me. Look."

Mustafah held out his arm. On the wrist was a gold watch. "If I was a jihadi, would I have a Rolex?"

"*Besançon, deux minutes*!"

Dewey stared at the young Arab lying pathetically on the floor. He was lying. The concealed weapons proved it. Yet his explanation was believable. Was this man guilty simply because Dewey was on edge? Had his elevated sense of threat unwittingly sentenced an innocent man to die?

More important, killing him would create an unnecessary hassle. There would be blood, plus the need to dump his body out the window.

"Stand up," said Dewey.

Mustafah slowly got to his feet just as the train slowed to a crawl. They were at the station.

"You're getting off right now," said Dewey. "The alternative is, I shoot you and throw your body out the window. I know you're lying, but I don't care. Stand up."

Mustafah stared at Dewey. His eyes moved to the floor as he considered what to do. He nodded his head.

"I open the door. I step out first. You follow me. You take a left, then go straight out the door onto the platform."

"It's a blizzard," he said, pointing at his T-shirt. "Can I get my jacket?"

Dewey ignored his question. "You keep walking toward the station. I'll be standing in the doorway. You take a step back toward the train, I'll kill you, and nobody will know where the bullet came from. You signal somebody, a hand gesture, I'll kill you. If you wait until the doors close and signal somebody, I'll pry the door open and put one in your head. Are we clear?"

"Yes."

A few seconds later, the train came to a stop. Dewey put his hand beneath his sweater, concealing the weapon, but made sure Mustafah understood that the end of the silencer was aimed at him. He opened the door to the bathroom and stepped out, followed by Mustafah, who went left toward the exit. He walked slowly onto the platform, limping. Dewey followed him and stopped in the doorway, with his finger on the trigger of the gun. Snow blanketed the air. The cold air stung Dewey's face. The terrorist blended in with the crowd of passengers waiting to get on. Soon, the doors slid shut and the train started to move as Dewey watched Mustafah, looking for some sort of signal, but he saw none.

• • •

Dewey also didn't see the two individuals waiting on the platform several cars back. One of them, a woman, saw him, however.

Her long black hair was braided and dangled slightly over one shoulder, jutting out from beneath a fur cap. She was tall, dressed in a white down jacket, and wheeled a black suitcase behind her. Her passport was French, her name, according to the document: Manon des Vosges. Her real name was Reema.

At a train car behind her was a short, older man. He wore grubby clothing, covered in a layer of silt and dirt, along with beat-up work boots. He carried a tool satchel. His face was stubbly and pale, weathered by years of being outdoors and fighting the elements. This was a working-class man, perhaps a mason, who appeared to be in his fifties. He, too, carried a French passport. According to the passport, his name was Michel Bertrand. His real name was Sangar.

Reema and Sangar were Iranian, both highly decorated agents in Iran's secretive and powerful intelligence service, VEVAK.

It was Sangar who spotted Dewey—or, rather, who spotted an older man standing in the doorway of the train. What Sangar noticed was the size of him, that and the way he stood in the frame of the door, watching as a young jacketless Arab moved cautiously across the platform. Sangar was reasonably sure he'd marked the man they'd been sent to kill. The man called Dewey Andreas.

66

FIRST-CLASS CAR
BESANÇON, FRANCE

Romy awoke with a start. She was breathing quickly. Her shirt was drenched in perspiration. She looked at the woman in the seat across from her. She was very old, with a scarf that held her white hair in place.

"*Allo*," said Romy.

"*Bonjour*, *mademoiselle*," the old woman said, smiling.

What was she dreaming about? There was something there, just outside her ability to reach. She shut her eyes, trying to remember. But it was useless. It always was.

The train was stopped. Outside, snow was falling in heavy sheets of white. The storm was blinding. She loved snowstorms. She felt warm and safe on the train. How long had she been asleep?

"*Ou sommes-nous*, *madame*?" Romy asked.

"Besançon."

Romy looked out the window as the train began to move. A man in a T-shirt was standing on the platform. He walked slowly toward the station. He didn't have luggage or even a coat. It made no sense.

She looked back at the old woman. Her eyes were closed and she was leaning against the corner.

"*Madame*," said Romy, reaching out and lightly touching her arm. "*Pourquoi ne vous mentez pas vers le bas*? *Il n'y a pas d'autre à venir dans notre compartiment*."

Why don't you lie down? There is no one else coming into our compartment.

Romy assisted the woman as she reclined across the leather bench seat. For the first time in days, Romy felt hunger pangs. She would go to the dining area and get something to eat. But her mind was drawn again to the station, escaping now in the distance, and the man—a young man of Middle Eastern descent—walking away in a T-shirt.

A chill made her shiver for a brief moment.

Not everything is related to you, she thought, smiling.

Slowly, she stood up and opened the door. She peeked out, looking in both directions down the corridor. She saw no one. She started walking toward the dining area.

• • •

As the train began to crawl out of Besançon, a tall man in a black Moncler down jacket stared out the window.

He was in the last car, near the very back of the train. He'd gotten on board in Avignon.

The man's hair was dirty blond. He was darkly handsome, even rugged-looking, his nose sharp, with a big jaw. He had several days' worth of stubble. He avoided eye contact assiduously. He watched a young man walk across the platform, as snow fluttered down.

Kyrie had stolen a car outside of Paris and driven across eastern France, the last hours through blizzard conditions. Kopitar had guessed which train Romy was on based on the time of Felix Jackson's death. It was the only train departing Marseille within an hour and a half of the attack. But the truth was, he had no idea if she was on board.

Kyrie had long ago lost any sense of proportion. Any sense of reality. He inhabited a different place altogether now, a world hidden from all but a few. The mundane aspects of Kyrie's life were all taken care of for him. He was very wealthy; Bruner saw to that. All Kyrie had to worry about was killing. That was what his world was. Killing people.

It had been Bruner who found him and saved him more than two decades before. Kyrie had been in Riyadh, a day after closing out an operation in Kuwait. Kyrie was a paramilitary officer within Special Operations Group. The operation in Kuwait, like all of Kyrie's operations, had gone flawlessly. The morning he was scheduled to depart from Riyadh, Kyrie had walked into a mosque with a submachine gun and killed thirty-four people. Everyone in the building. Half an hour later, he was on a plane back to Virginia.

When he landed, Kyrie confessed to the massacre. He was sent to a CIA facility in West Virginia to await a military tribunal, and likely spend the rest of his life in Leavenworth.

Bruner had visited him the day after he confessed. Kyrie would always remember it.

"My name is Charles Bruner."

Bruner had reached into his pocket and removed a small black device, placing it on the table. *"It's a signals-jamming device. They're not recording, but even if they were it wouldn't matter."*

"I know what it is," Kyrie said. *"Record it all you want, I really don't fucking care anymore. I know where I'm going."*

"Where's that?"

"Leavenworth."

"Why did you do it?"

"Who are you?"

"I work for the State Department."

"I'll never apologize, if that's why you're here. I'm glad I did it. Fuck them. Whoever you are, you just don't understand. You have no clue."

"No clue about what, Kyrie?"

"About the cancer that's out there."

"Cancer?"

"Islam. It's coming, and if we don't start dealing with them now, they're going to take over the fucking world. That's not racism, it's the truth, coming from someone who's seen them up close. They better send me to Leavenworth, because if they let me out, I'll do it all over again."

An hour later, Kyrie had climbed into the back of a dark sedan and, together with Bruner, designed a secret war to stop Islam.

Something snapped that day so long ago when he killed the Muslims. What it was, even he didn't know, but it changed him. Had Bruner not come along, Kyrie had no doubt he would still be locked away in prison—or dead. Bruner saved him. More important, Bruncr also gave him a license to kill. Now Kyrie was a hollow shell, a single-purpose entity. After so many years, he was nothing but a pure, relentless killer.

So why did Romy love him? What had she seen? The question ate away at him until he felt he would go insane. She saw something . . . and now he had to kill her.

Kyrie was in the second to last row in the last

car on the train, in a window seat, alone. He stared out at the man crossing the platform. He was young, Arab, and . . . wore only a T-shirt. It didn't make sense.

As the young Arab walked through the driving snow, away from the train, Kyrie's mind rapidly analyzed the enigma and solved it almost as quickly.

The INTERPOL alert. Dewey Andreas had done a great deal of damage over the course of his career. The Red Notice had undoubtedly been read in a lot of places where he'd left his brutal mark. The smart ones understood. He was a flushed bird, out in the open, there for the taking. This might be the only chance they got to go after the man on their terms.

It was a rare opportunity to even an old score.

So who is it? Kyrie asked himself.

Obviously, they're Arab. Kyrie ran through a list of possible entities.

Pakistan, where Andreas had led a coup d'état, deposing a radical cleric who'd been elected president.

ISIS, whose attack on the dormitory at Columbia University Andreas had stopped.

Iran.

Of course, it had to be Iran. VEVAK or KUDS or perhaps even Hezbollah. Andreas's theft of Iran's first nuclear weapon was a sore spot for the country still.

And then Kyrie realized how stupid he was being. The name practically screamed out to him: *Fortuna*.

Kyrie shook his head and smiled, amazed that he'd overlooked the most obvious choice. Fortuna. Of course. Aswan. Alexander. The only one left, Nebuchar.

Kyrie remembered the man who got on in Chalon-sur-Saône. He'd walked down the aisle to a seat two rows in front of him.

It was obvious. The man was not going skiing.

Kyrie sat upright. He saw the back of the man's head—a block of dark hair.

For the next half hour, Kyrie studied the man. He moved too often. He was too alert. Even as he tried to nap, he would lurch ever so slightly at passengers getting up from their seats.

Kyrie stood up and opened the overhead compartment, getting a better look. The man was a spitting image of Alexander Fortuna, though more rugged-looking. A handsome man.

Kyrie suddenly realized he was seated two rows behind Nebuchar Fortuna, whose team was on the train for one single purpose: find Dewey Andreas and kill him. It was a trip of vengeance.

It meant Andreas was on board. Which meant Romy was on board.

He smiled as he tapped the woman seated next to Fortuna on the shoulder. It would be an entertaining train trip. Fortuna added a layer of complication Kyrie could use to his advantage.

"*Pardon, madame*," he said quietly, nodding toward Fortuna. "*Peut-on changer de place*? *Un vieil ami. Vous aurez deux sièges pour vous tout seul.*"

Excuse me, madame, could we switch seats? An old friend. You will have two seats all to yourself.

The woman got up and Kyrie sat down next to Fortuna.

Fortuna appraised Kyrie. "Who are you?"

"My name is Kyrie."

"What do you want?"

"Nebuchar, correct?" Kyrie whispered. "If I wanted you dead you'd be dead already. And that's your problem. You're here for Dewey Andreas, but you don't know what you're doing."

Fortuna swung his left hand across the air. A blade thrust out, but Kyrie calmly grabbed Fortuna's wrist and held it, the tip of the blade a few inches from his throat.

"Do you realize you're already down one man?" asked Kyrie as he continued to clutch Fortuna's wrist in his left hand. Kyrie nodded toward his right hand. Fortuna glanced down. Kyrie was holding a suppressed handgun, aimed at Fortuna's chest.

"What are you talking about?"

"Andreas kicked one of your men off at the last station. An Arab."

"There are plenty of Arabs."

"In a T-shirt? No bags? A gold Rolex on his wrist?"

Kyrie let go of Fortuna's wrist. Fortuna paused and then withdrew the switchblade, putting it back in his pocket.

"I'm willing to help you," said Kyrie. "If you think you can mosey onto a train and find Dewey Andreas and then kill him, you're mad. He's already eliminated one of your men. How many more do you have?"

"Two," said Fortuna. "What do you want? Money?"

Kyrie shook his head.

"No. I want you to succeed. I'm not after Dewey Andreas. But I am after what he's after. Our interests are aligned. I thought I would have to kill him myself. I'd much rather have you do it. But you'll never manage without my help."

When Dewey arrived back at his seat, he waited several minutes and then hit his earbud.

"A man got on at one of the stations," he said. "Arab. Something about him bothered me. I searched his bag when he was in the bathroom. He had weapons, a submachine gun."

"What did you do?" said Katie.

"I kicked him off the train."

"Isn't it obvious?" Katie said quietly, but with urgency. "Iran."

"He didn't look Shia."

"Everyone who wants you dead knows you're in France. You're being hunted. Maybe it wasn't Paria. You need to get off at the next stop. You don't even know if she knows anything. You're a sitting duck. If you really want her, we can stay and extract her."

"She does know something," insisted Dewey. "It's why she went to Lindsay. They killed Lindsay because she told him something."

"That's conjecture."

"Call it whatever you want. I'm going to find out what she told Lindsay."

"You're a stupid, stubborn son of a bitch," said Katie. "If he wasn't Shia, it means someone else has men on this train. We have a bigger problem than we realized."

67

THE WHITE HOUSE
WASHINGTON, D.C.

Bruner knew precisely why he'd been invited to the White House. He had no reason to be there. It was obvious.

Order 6.

They'd scanned Langley manifests and found the ones who worked for Casey. They, including himself, were the ones who might know something, perhaps about the satellite or something else. A camera shot of Kyrie in Paris, somehow matching an NSA facial recognition program? Who knows? But they found something, and now they were on a fishing expedition. If they knew more, he'd already be locked up.

They were close. *So close.*

"One more day," he whispered to himself.

As Bruner's driver turned into the gates of the White House, he picked up his cell. He hit speed dial.

"Nathaniel?" he said.

"Yes, Mr. Bruner."

"Are you at the restaurant?"

"Yes."

"And has he arrived?"

"Yes, he has."

"I trust everything will be done appropriately."

"Of course, Mr. Bruner. I'll begin immediately."

"One more thing," said Bruner. "Have they assigned manpower for the event on Friday?"

"Yes," said Nathaniel. "I was detailed this morning."

The West Wing of the White House usually surprised first-time visitors. It was an intimate place, as if the offices of the president's senior staff as well as that of the president had been set inside an elegant old New England mansion. The ceilings were low, the floors carpeted in thick, gorgeous patterned rugs, and the lighting cast a warm, informal light that felt familiar. It was a design that harkened back to an era before computers and nuclear weapons, a simpler time. Everyone who walked its hallways knew that the West Wing was the epicenter of the most powerful government on earth—the most powerful government in the history of earth—and yet its informality and plain beauty reminded all that America's history was young. It was the history of a people who had come by its power in the most human and colonial of ways.

Perhaps no office in the West Wing was as intimate and stylishly informal as that of the chief of staff, Adrian King. It sat a few feet away from the Oval Office and was separated by a short private hallway. Bookshelves lined two of the walls. A large desk was at the far side of the office and took up most of the space. A big, comfortable George Smith leather chesterfield sofa ran the length of almost an entire wall, beneath bookshelves that were half filled with leather-bound legal books and half filled with cardboard boxes containing various detritus from King's career. The one wall that didn't have bookshelves on it was decorated not with the usual Washington, D.C., collection of photos with various world leaders and politicians. Instead, a large framed photograph hung in the middle of the wall. It showed King in camouflage hunting attire, a squalid-looking beard and mustache covering his face, a rifle in his hand, standing over a dead grizzly bear, which he'd shot in Idaho. The photo sent an unmistakable message.

If I can kill this grizzly, imagine what I can do to you.

In King's office, history and present day were perfectly aligned. Here, the down-to-earth lack of pretentiousness of the West Wing's surroundings was at all times married to the wielding of the government's utmost power, sometimes in the rawest of ways. King was a fearless, relentless, no-holds-barred administrator who made sure

President Dellenbaugh's wishes were executed. When they weren't, he was the one who kicked the proverbial teeth in.

King was dressed in a navy blue Brooks Brothers suit and cordovan wingtips. He was five-eight with brown hair so thick it looked like it needed a chain saw to cut it. His most distinctive feature was a set of wild-eyed eyebrows, which he didn't trim. White House chiefs of staff were seldom hired for their looks.

King had an Irish temper, which he controlled, for the most part, with the slash-eyed, ruthless calm he'd inherited from his Sicilian mother. King had risen in large part based on an indefatigable work ethic, a big brain, a fiery temper, and a willingness to speak—and sometimes shout—his opinion.

King was alone in his office. He was poring through files on the four individuals who were under consideration to replace Tim Lindsay as secretary of state. The cover sheet listed the people Dellenbaugh had selected following the death of Lindsay:

- Kevin Rennie, senior senator from Connecticut
- John Wrigley, junior senator from Arizona
- Laura Touche, ambassador to Russia

- Charles Bruner, deputy secretary of state

King was lying on the floor. To his right, next to his head, was one stack of papers. To his left was an even higher stack. He was holding up a piece of paper and reading it.

The door opened. One of King's two deputies, Lewis Canfield, walked in. At first, he didn't see King. Then he looked down.

"What the hell are you doing?" asked Canfield.

King continued to read.

"Adrian?"

"What does it look like I'm doing? I'm working."

"I meant, why are you lying on the floor?"

"I fucked up my back. Got a problem with that?"

"How'd you do that?"

King moved the paper to the side and looked at Canfield.

"Are you trying to annoy me?" he asked. "I get about one hour a day where I'm not in a meeting or on the phone and that's right now and I'm reading. Now get the hell out unless you have something important to tell me."

"Charles Bruner is here."

"You don't think you should've told me that when you walked in?"

"Ah, let 'em wait a few minutes," said

Canfield. "The longer you make them wait, the more powerful they think you are."

King slowly shifted to his right side. He reached up and grabbed the edge of the desk and lifted himself to his knees, then stood.

"You really are a nitwit, aren't you?" said King. "Where'd you get that from, the *Dummies Guide to Running the White House*?"

"It's true."

"Okay, whatever. Send Bruner in."

Adrian King had never liked Tim Lindsay, but that didn't mean he wasn't angry at what had happened in Paris. Having to deal with the selection of a new secretary of state was a nightmare, and he was in charge of it all.

After Lindsay was killed, the phone calls started coming in as politicians, diplomats, and even a few corporate CEOs attempted to position themselves for consideration. King had received, at last count, more than one hundred calls on behalf of fifty-nine different individuals who wanted to be secretary of state.

None of the calls or e-mails mattered. Rennie, Wrigley, and Touche were already on a special contingency list. King kept the same list for every cabinet member in case something ever happened, updated monthly with Dellenbaugh and kept locked in a safe in King's office.

King's job was vetting them. This meant

digging into each person's background and trying to find anything that could come out later and embarrass the administration. It also meant making damn sure whoever it was could act in lockstep with Dellenbaugh's decisions.

That morning, King had spent three hours with Senator Kevin Rennie from Connecticut, the ranking minority member of the Senate Foreign Relations Committee. Rennie, King thought, was brilliant—a Stanford-educated intellectual with a patrician's charm, who'd been elected to the Senate at age thirty-two.

Bruner had been a late addition to the list, courtesy of Hector Calibrisi.

There was a knock on the door and Bruner entered.

"Adrian," said Bruner, closing the door behind him.

King was behind his desk, standing. He looked at Bruner with a blank expression.

"Hi, Charles. Thanks for coming. Have a seat."

Bruner sat down in a leather side chair in front of King's desk. He wore a brown double-breasted suit, a white handkerchief stuffed in the chest pocket. His full head of white hair was combed neatly back. He looked dashing, urbane, and above all sophisticated.

Bruner looked around the office.

"I've never been in the chief of staff's office," he said. "It's nice."

King nodded.

"Do you know why you're here?" asked King.

Bruner paused, then shrugged his shoulders. "I assume it has to do with Tim."

"That's right."

Bruner was quiet. So was King. It was Bruner who finally spoke.

"Beyond that, you're going to have to give me a clue, Adrian."

"You're on a short list to replace him," said King.

Bruner leaned back. "Really? Well, that's certainly not what I expected."

"What did you expect?"

"Not that. Maybe you wanted to run some names by me or something to that effect. I can tell you right now, I wouldn't be the best choice."

King stepped around from behind his desk. He took a seat in the chair across from Bruner.

"Are you saying you have no interest?" said King.

"First of all, I should say I'm honored," Bruner said. "Thank you."

"Don't thank me, thank the president. I'm vetting you."

"Adrian, let me start with the obvious. I'm too old to be secretary of state."

"Tim was seventy. You're seventy-four."

"I would say Tim was too old, too. I'm not trying to criticize him."

"I don't give a damn if you criticize him," said King. "Lindsay was a pacifist, in my opinion."

Bruner grinned. "I heard you had a direct style."

"What do you think happened?" asked King.

Bruner shrugged nonchalantly.

"I don't know. The manner in which it happened doesn't seem to fit with the notion that terrorists did it. As for this individual, Dewey Andreas, that seems equally hard to fathom."

"Why do you say that?"

"He's a patriot," said Bruner. "But I don't need to tell you that."

King said nothing.

"What do you think happened?" asked Bruner. "You're a former prosecutor. I assume you've investigated murders."

"I don't know what happened, but we're going to find out."

King flipped through the file on his lap.

"You went to the State Department after the CIA," he said. "Why?"

"I wanted a more peaceful life," said Bruner. "My daughter was killed. It affected me. It still does."

"You were director of operations. What'd they call it then?" said King.

"Director of the National Clandestine Service."

"Young too. Right there with William Casey."

Bruner nodded.

"Yes. But titles didn't mean a great deal to me. I wanted a different kind of life. We bought a farm in Maryland. We rebuilt ourselves after losing . . . Molly."

King held up a piece of paper. "You submitted your resignation. You were going to retire."

Bruner paused.

"After my daughter died, I had a very hard time. Bill Casey convinced me to remain in government," he said.

"But Consular Operations?" said King. "Forgive me for saying this, but it's a backwater. Processing passports and various other important but boring things. Going from Casey's inner circle to Consular Operations must have been like trading in a Maserati for a station wagon."

Bruner smiled.

"Exactly."

Inside the Oval Office, Calibrisi, Polk, and President Dellenbaugh watched King's slow taking apart of Bruner on a screen set up on the president's desk. The camera was behind the grizzly's eye, and it offered a clear view of the chief of staff's office.

"He's pretty good," said Polk.

Dellenbaugh was silent, arms crossed, a hard look on his face.

Calibrisi had come up with the strategy. Put Bruner on the short list, bring him into the

White House, then ask him about Order 6. If he was involved with Order 6, they needed to see his reaction. They needed to ask him bluntly: What was going on in Toronto? In Paris? But do it at the White House, his guard down, his judgment perhaps skewed by the flattery of being considered by the president for secretary of state.

They needed to see his reaction.

"He's very good," said Calibrisi. "He ran the clandestine service, just like you, Bill. But he's lying."

"He hasn't asked him yet."

"I'm just saying, he turned the interrogation back onto Adrian. He inserted his daughter and took control. Which means he's acting. He knows something."

"So, if you were secretary of state, what would be your top priority?" said King.

Bruner caught King's look and understood then. They were watching.

Bruner knew they added his name to the list for this specific purpose. He knew it even before King asked the innocuous question. But he saw it in King's eyes.

He found the camera a moment later: a pinhead-size shimmer of silver in the photo of the bear.

He knew what was coming. He didn't want to do what he was about to do. But he had to.

"My priorities would be set by the president," said Bruner. "I would view myself as a servant to the foreign policy agenda as set out by the president, duly elected by the American people."

"In 1983, a month before you moved from Langley to Foggy Bottom, a covert program was opened up," said King. "It was called Order Six. A joint program between the CIA and the State Department."

"Yes," said Bruner, nodding. "I remember. What would you like to know about it?"

68

L'AUBERGE CHEZ FRANÇOIS
GREAT FALLS, VIRGINIA

Flaherty arrived at the restaurant at 5 P.M., thirty minutes early. He took a seat at the bar and ordered a coffee while carefully scanning the restaurant for agents who might have been sent ahead of Follett, the young NSA analyst Flaherty was meeting with.

Flaherty didn't know where the eavesdroppers and hackers from the NSA had found Order 6, but the mere fact that Follett called was significant. The fact that it had been a phone call requesting an interview versus an outright abduction showed that they had little or no hard information. That the call was from a clearly midlevel person at NSA was further proof as to the government's cluelessness. The agencies were getting closer, no doubt, but they needed to be kept in the dark for only one more day.

One day.

Flaherty wasn't worried. NSA had no sentries at the restaurant, Follett sounded young and inexperienced, and most important, Flaherty knew more about deception than almost anybody else on earth. Many of Flaherty's methods for spotting and avoiding detection, methods he pioneered while at the CIA, were still taught to young agents.

Still, he felt uneasy.

He saw Follett enter. He looked about thirty, with a big dirty-blond Afro, glasses, and a scholarly-looking face. Flaherty remained seated and watched as Follett looked around the room, searching for him. When he finally saw Flaherty, Follett smiled and nodded.

"Andrew," said Follett as he approached, hand extended. "Zach Follett. Nice to meet you, sir. Thanks for coming."

Flaherty shook his hand but said nothing.

A hostess approached. "Here for an early dinner, gentlemen?"

"Just drinks," said Flaherty. "A booth, if its available."

The hostess led Flaherty and Follett to a table

in the far corner of the restaurant. After they were seated, Flaherty cut to the chase.

"So," he said, "what do you want?"

Flaherty was aggressive, staking out a hard wall in the conversation.

"As I mentioned," Follett said, "I want to ask you about Order Six."

"What about it?"

"What was it? I mean, what was in the order?"

Mistake number one, Flaherty thought. Revealing he doesn't know what Order 6 even means. Kopitar may have sanitized it, but Follett shouldn't have let on to the fact that they hadn't found anything. There was always the chance Kopitar missed something. Unless Follett was using some of the new NSA interrogation tactics, trying to manipulate Flaherty by leading him down a tree of seemingly innocuous, even naïve, questions.

"There were many orders, Zach," said Flaherty.

"I was able to piece together the fact that Order Six had a two-hundred-million-dollar annual budget its first three years," said Follett. "Then the program disappeared. It was buried inside the State Department."

Flaherty nodded nonchalantly.

"That could very well be," he said. "There were a number of orders."

"I was reading somewhere that the orders were usually three digits, like Order 521. These usually came from line-level deputies. The double-digit orders were more important, usually assigned by the director of operations. I think it was called the Clandestine Service when you were there."

"Yes," said Flaherty, now realizing Follett was better prepared than he had anticipated. "That's what they called it."

"And the single-digit orders were from the director himself," Follett continued. "This order—Order Six—would have come from Director Casey, I believe. In fact, it would have come exactly one week before Mr. Bruner left for the State Department. You, at that point, were Bruner's deputy, according to various records. I believe you were made interim head of the Clandestine Service after Mr. Bruner moved to State."

Flaherty shifted ever so slightly, despite the fact that he knew he shouldn't, that shifting was the first indicator of anxiety in an interrogation. Anxiety correlated directly to dishonesty, according to multiple clinical trials Flaherty himself had overseen. Yet he had shifted.

"That's right."

"It was the only order issued under William Casey, I believe," said Follett. "As head of NCS, I would think this would have been somewhat of a milestone."

"Yes."

"So do you remember Order Six, Andrew?" Follett said innocently, leaning back, a hint of violence in his gaze.

"I think I remember it. Since you mentioned it. It was a long time ago."

"Why is an extant CIA program still utilizing a communications satellite? I mean, how did you guys even afford it?"

Follett let it sink in.

"Afford?" Flaherty said calmly. "There are so many government expenditures, Zach. I don't remember any specific satellites, but there were many."

"The satellite uses a heretofore nonexistent frequency," continued Follett, a baffled look on his face. "I'm not sure I even understand the mathematics behind the frequency, and I have a Ph.D. in math. It was used in Toronto the day of the mosque murders and from inside the Hotel George Cinq five minutes after Secretary of State Lindsay was assassinated."

Follett paused. Flaherty saw the waitress approaching and subtly held up his hand, turning her away.

"Order Six was an early attempt to infiltrate Islamist extremist groups," said Flaherty, lying. "Collaboration between State Department diplomats and in-theater Agency personnel. It didn't work. I was the one who shut it down. I don't know why the satellite is still functional. It wasn't my decision, but the assumption all along was that it would be transferred somewhere within the Agency. As for the frequency, you're talking to someone who barely understands how to get his e-mail."

"Can I ask you about your time as Berlin chief of station?" said Follett.

"If you must."

Nathaniel waited until the parking lot was full. He climbed out of the car and moved down several aisles. He came to the black Mercedes. He looked around, making sure no one was looking, then went down on the ground, flipped onto his back, and moved beneath the car. The S550 was a complicated vehicle. Cutting its brakes was largely a technical exercise, versus the old-fashioned method of simply snipping the brake lines, though he did that too. He was under the car for almost eight minutes. When he finished, he looked across the parking lot, seeing no one.

Nathaniel climbed into his car, a blue Mustang, and drove quickly away.

69

NORTH OF BESANÇON FRANCE

The lights were dimmed in the train car, allowing passengers to sleep. The man beside Dewey was snoring lightly, his head resting on a down jacket that he was using as a pillow.

Dewey tapped his ear twice.

"Belfort is the next stop," he whispered. "I'm going to get her."

"What are you going to do?" said Tacoma. "Just shoot the guards?"

"No, not yet, anyway. I want to see where she is. According to Beauxchamps, she's up there, but before I start shooting people, I want to be sure."

"How are you going to do that?" said Katie.

"I don't know."

Dewey unzipped the bag at his feet. He pulled a handgun from where he'd tucked it, inside his pants along his right leg. He unscrewed the silencer and stuck it in the bag, then found the shell he'd packed—black, all-weather—along with a pair of gloves. He tucked the gloves, a ski mask, and the gun into a pocket. He glanced back at Beauxchamps, nodding ever so slightly.

He grabbed the walking stick and moved slowly, stooping, toward the front of the car.

Dewey knew he had to get inside the first-class car. He also knew that to get to her, he needed to determine her precise location. He might have to kill the two guards, but that was a last resort. He needed another way.

Dewey placed the walking stick on the shelf above the ski rack and went into the bathroom on the right, locking the door. He untied the shell and put it on. He then reached to the paper towel dispenser, popping the top where a pile of towels was stacked. He removed his glasses and put them on top of the towels. He pulled the gun from his pocket and put it next to the glasses, then shut the top.

Dewey zipped up the shell and pulled the black ski mask over his head. He looked at himself in the mirror. It was like looking at a phantom, his eyes the only thing human, their blue standing out from a veil of black.

He unlocked the door but left it shut. He had to move quickly now. He put on the gloves, then slid the window open. The sound was loud as cold air and snow rushed in. Dewey put one foot on the bottom edge of the opening and climbed up, sticking his head out, then his hand, reaching up above the window for something to grab on to. He found a slat of steel that ran along the edge of the roof. He held tightly to it as he climbed out, pressing his chest against the side of the train, gripping the steel slat for dear life as a hurricane of snow and wind ripped against him. Dewey backed both feet into the open air, so that he was now dangling along the side of the fast-moving train. With his left foot, he kicked at the small round red handle on the window, missing a few times, then nailing it, closing the window. He hoisted himself up, kicking his left leg over the slat and pulling himself onto the roof as wind and snow blinded him.

For several seconds, Dewey lay on the roof just inside the steel slat, near the edge, catching his breath. Then he started to crawl, staying as low to the roof as he could so as not to be blown off. He crawled to the apex of the roof and shimmied forward toward the first-class car. He came to the accordion that enclosed the connection point of the two train cars, being careful not to make any noise. He knew the two gunmen were standing just below the accordion. One false step, too much weight, an accidental grunt, and they would investigate. Dewey slithered over the accordion, like a snake, introducing his weight gradually.

Once he was on top of the first-class car, Dewey crawled to the side, closer and closer to the edge. The roar of the wind mixed with a constant powerful grumble from the locomotive.

He felt as if he were in the middle of a hurricane. He found the steel slat and gripped it. With his left foot, Dewey tried to hold his body steady, pressing the toe of his boot against the steel. Slowly, he inched his head over the edge of the speeding train, trying to get far enough out so that he could see into the windows of the first-class compartments. He started with the first compartment. In the dimmed light he could see two couples, all four people reading. In the next car, a table had been opened and four teenagers were playing a card game. He kept moving forward. Another compartment was occupied by two old men, one reading, the other spread out on the opposite bench asleep. Then he came to the next compartment and saw her.

Her hair was cut short, nearly bald.

She's running.

Katie's cell phone vibrated. It was a text.

FRIEND TO THE MIGHTY

"Mighty" referred to a standard code, one typically used during operations.

Last letter of the first word: D = the 4th letter of the alphabet = 4.

Four men were aboard.

"To" = T means delay. O means time.

"The" was for how long.
Three letters = 3 hours.
The chopper was delayed by three hours.
Katie cursed under her breath.

Dewey remained still atop the car for a few more seconds, then backtracked, going in reverse, knowing that turning around would expose the heaviest part of his body to the wind and possibly result in being blown off the train.

When he found the bathroom window, he stared in. A woman was washing her hands. When she left, he waited. Satisfied there was no one waiting to come in, he swung back to the side of the train, clutching the steel slat for dear life. He kicked the red window latch, opening the window. He stuck a foot on the sill, grabbed the upper edge of the frame, and yanked himself back inside the bathroom.

He pulled off the ski mask as he moved to the door and locked it. He took off his gloves and put them in the pocket of the parka along with the ski mask, then took off the parka. He looked around, seeing a small stainless steel door beneath the sink. He took a pick gun from his pocket, stuck it in the lock, and pressed the trigger. A moment later, the door opened. Pipes from the sink took up some of the space, but there was room. He put his parka inside, reached to the paper towel holder to retrieve his eyeglasses and gun, and put the gun on top of the parka and shut the small door. He put on the eyeglasses and looked into the mirror. He was bright red and sweating. Still, his hair remained for the most part white. It didn't matter anyway; there was nothing he could do at this point.

Dewey found his walking stick and ambled down the aisle to his seat. He glanced at Beauxchamps, then climbed over the man next to him, who was still sleeping.

In silence, Dewey stared out the window as he fought to catch his breath. He tapped his ear.

"I found her," he said. "Let's get ready to move."

"Not so fast," said Katie. "The chopper's three hours away. Mack just texted me."

"Fine," said Dewey. "So we wait."

"There could be a problem with waiting," said Katie. "There are three other men aboard."

"We're not going to make it three hours," said Tacoma. "Dewey's a sitting duck. We need to clear some of these motherfuckers out."

"I have an idea," said Dewey. "Rob, meet me in the restroom. Katie, you watch the first-class car. If she is running—if someone is after her—they can't get in there."

"Roger that."

Dewey stood up and stepped over the sleeping man. He nodded to Beauxchamps, indicating he wanted him to follow him to the front.

• • •

Four cars back, Reema sat alone at a table in the cafeteria car, sipping a cup of tea. She noted Sangar's entrance out of the corner of her eye, though she didn't acknowledge him.

As Sangar passed her table, he placed a small piece of paper down and kept walking toward the front of the train. She waited several minutes and then looked at the paper.

"Come."

Reema walked to the front of the car, looking for Sangar. The restroom was empty. She kept moving, pacing down the dimly lit aisle of the next car. At the front, through the doors, she saw Sangar, smoking a cigarette.

"I saw him," Sangar said quietly, in Persian.

"Where?"

"He's in the second car, disguised as an old man. A sweater with buttons, big glasses. I'm going to kill him."

"I thought we're supposed to try and apprehend him," whispered Reema. "Kill him as a last resort."

Sangar flicked the cigarette to the floor.

"Fuck that. Do you really think we can simply grab him and walk off the train with him? Now, are you coming?"

Reema shook her head.

"No, not yet. So you go up and kill him and then what, get arrested at the next stop? No, thank you. I'll wait back here. If you kill him, I will help you escape. If you fail, I will still be free to try and do what we were supposed to do. Abduct him if possible, kill him if necessary."

70

OFFICE OF THE CHIEF OF STAFF
THE WHITE HOUSE

King leaned an inch or two closer to Bruner. "What was Order Six?" he said.

"There were many programs, Adrian. Many orders. I was preparing to leave the Agency. It was also some time ago."

"It was the only order Casey issued in six years," said King.

"Why don't you have someone pull the file? Surely you didn't bring me here just to ask me about some old CIA operation I was involved with? I was involved in quite a few."

"The files regarding Order Six were scrapped. Even the metadata."

Bruner paused and looked down, deep in thought.

"Well?"

"I'm thinking," said Bruner. "Surely if it was Bill's only order, there's a copy of it somewhere. Have you asked Director Calibrisi?"

"What was Order Six, Charles?" King repeated impatiently.

"Let me see," said Bruner, beginning the lie. "In 1983. You say it was a joint Agency-State program? I vaguely remember an initiative to infiltrate some of the early terror entities using both State Department and Langley people. Go in using diplomacy, but have force backup if necessary. A kinder CIA, if you will. But when I got to State, I wasn't involved. That would've been the Agency. I became an administrator a million miles away from where the action was. It's what I wanted."

"Did you keep any files?"

"Of course not," said Bruner. "It's a felony, as you know. So I answered your questions, now answer mine. Why are you asking about this?"

King reached over to his desk and grabbed a bottle of Poland Spring. He took a large guzzle, wiped his lips, then looked at Bruner.

"They launched a satellite. They needed a closed-loop system so no one knew what they were doing. They launched it in 1994. The program was shut down in '97. But someone's still using it. Someone who was in Toronto the day of the massacre. Another call was made from the Hotel George Cinq—five minutes after Lindsay was killed. *That's* why we're interested."

Bruner nodded heavily, as if suddenly understanding.

"Now I understand why you want to know about this order," he said. "Come to think of it, there was someone. He was chief of station somewhere. I need to remember his name. He was angling to run the program. As I recall, he was put in charge of it. He didn't play by the rules. Keeping a satellite in the air? It's definitely something I could see him doing. I just need to remember his name. Anthony. No Andrew. Andrew something."

King looked down at his desk, reading the list of names Calibrisi had sent over.

"Flaherty," said King.

"Yes, that's it," said Bruner. "Andrew Flaherty. Short, glasses. He used to talk about moving to South America and having his own army, running it for profit. Crazy stuff like that. But an adept agent. A smart man."

71

FRANCE

Dewey entered the restroom, followed by Beauxchamps and quickly thereafter by Tacoma. He locked the door.

"What are we doing?" said Beauxchamps.

Dewey ignored him. He looked at Tacoma.

"Do you have an extra earbud?"

"Yeah." Tacoma handed a small plastic case to Dewey, who gave it to Beauxchamps.

"Put it in your ear," said Dewey. "You tap twice to talk."

Beauxchamps put it in his ear, a confused look on his face.

"What is going on?" he said.

There was a sudden knock on the door, then a deep voice, speaking in French.

"It's the conductor," said Beauxchamps.

"Perfect timing," said Dewey.

Dewey went to the cabinet and removed his gun: Colt M1911A1 .45-caliber semiautomatic. He went to the door, just as the conductor banged again.

Dewey opened the door.

"Excuse me," he said, nodding at the conductor.

Dewey lurched—grabbing the large man by the

tie and heaving him into the bathroom, throwing him down to the floor, at all times training the gun on his head. He locked the door as he kept aim on the conductor.

Tacoma watched, his eyes slightly wide. Beauxchamps looked flummoxed.

Dewey's face was blank, emotionless. The conductor, who looked shocked, immediately threw his arms back, staring up at Dewey.

"Do you speak English?" Dewey asked.

The conductor nodded.

"Don't talk," said Dewey. "If you want to live, do exactly what I say. You press an alarm in your pocket, yell something, you're dead. Do you understand? I have no problem killing you. Frankly, it would be easier. Do you understand?"

The conductor nodded slowly. "Yes, sir."

Dewey scanned him. He had on a blue uniform, along with a cap. He glanced at Beauxchamps. It would be a little baggy.

"Stand up. Take your clothing off," said Dewey. "Put everything on the floor."

The conductor began to get undressed.

Dewey looked at Beauxchamps. "You too. Strip. Put on the conductor's stuff."

Over the next few minutes, Beauxchamps removed his clothing and put on the conductor's uniform. It was too big, but it would suffice. The conductor, meanwhile, pulled on Beauxchamps's clothing, which was several sizes too small.

"Here comes the tough part," said Dewey to the conductor, pointing at the window with the muzzle of the gun. "You can either jump out the window, or I can kill you and throw you out. It's up to you."

"It's . . . it's snowing out. We're already in the mountains."

"I know. I'm sorry."

Dewey pointed at the cabinet.

"There's a jacket in there. Put it on, it'll keep you warm. Now listen, this is important. When you jump, hold your arms around your head, like a helmet. No matter what happens, keep holding on to your head."

The conductor nodded as he put on the parka.

"Once you land, climb back up to the tracks. You know where we are better than I do. Walk to the nearest town."

Dewey pulled the window open. The conductor trudged reluctantly to it. He looked out, climbed to the sill, and hesitated. Then he jumped.

Tacoma started to shut the window, but Dewey stopped him.

"I'm going back out. Listen carefully. This is how it's going to work . . ."

In the first-class dining room, Romy sat down at an empty table. The small brass lamps atop each table cast a golden color through the room, which reflected off the windows. The tablecloth was white and the table was set for two, along with wineglasses, water glasses, and silver.

Romy was hungry. Famished. She hadn't eaten in two days. All she could think about was eating. Yet she couldn't help glancing around the room. Several couples were enjoying a romantic dinner. A pair of children—perhaps seven or eight years old—were enjoying large bowls of ice cream, giggling as they ate.

When the waiter came by Romy's table, she looked up, momentarily startled.

"Good evening, madame," he said. "May I start you off with something to drink?"

"Mademoiselle," Romy corrected him. "A glass of wine, please. Red, a Bordeaux."

"Of course. And will you be dining with us this evening?"

"Yes."

The waiter extended a menu to her.

"I'll be right back with that glass of wine, mademoiselle."

"*Merci.*"

She stared out the window at the swirls of snow. As much as she tried to put it out of her mind, she couldn't. The man on the platform. Why was he there?

Not everything has to do with you.

She smiled for a brief moment at the thought. It's true, she'd fallen into a state of constant paranoia, always looking over her shoulder, and yet not every strange incident, not every odd look, had to do with her.

For a few brief seconds, Romy enjoyed the thought. Maybe the man on the platform was just that, a weird incident. Then she remembered Marseille, and her smile disappeared. She could never rest again. She would never be the same again. This was to be her new life, running from someone or something she didn't understand, running from men sent halfway around the world to kill her, running to places she didn't know, her only protection the simple fact that she didn't know what she was doing, her every move was unpredictable because she didn't know what she was going to do until she had to do it.

Romy's temporary joy at forgetting slipped away and a dark fear reclaimed her.

"Mademoiselle, your wine," said the waiter, placing the glass in front of her.

"Thank you."

"Have you had time to look at the menu?" he asked.

"No. Could you recommend something?"

"Of course. Do you like lamb chops? They're very good, purchased this morning from the market in Avignon."

"That sounds good," she said.

Kyrie looked at Fortuna. "So, what's it going to be?"

"How do I know you don't work with him?"

"Don't be an idiot. If I worked with him, I would've killed you by now. My guess is, he's alone. He works alone."

"I don't need you," said Fortuna. "I can kill him myself. I found him, didn't I?"

"You did? Where is he?"

Fortuna grinned. "He's on the train."

"You haven't found him," Kyrie whispered contemptuously. "You might be on the same train as he is, but there are a thousand passengers. Did you think you'd just waltz down the aisle, identify him, and shoot him? He's highly trained. That's why you only have two men right now instead of four."

"I appreciate your offer, but I don't need you," said Fortuna. "I'll blow up the train if I have to."

"Wrong," Kyrie said.

"What do you mean, wrong?"

"I saw your man at the station," said Kyrie. "Chalon-sur-Saône. It was obvious. If you're going to carry explosives, don't act like it. He carried the suitcase like it was about to explode. No one carries a suitcase that way. I followed him onto the train. He put it in the overhead, and when he sat down, I waited. He was looking at his reflection in the window, making sure he still looked good. I took the suitcase and carried it off the train and put it next to the garbage can. If you don't believe me, go look. I kill people like you for a living, Nebuchar. Blowing up the train is not an option, and by the way, I don't care if Andreas lives or dies. I want what he's after, that's it."

"What is that?" said Fortuna.

"None of your business."

"Someone? *Who?* If we're going to work together, I should know."

"None of your fucking business," said Kyrie. "I don't need your help. You, however, need mine. The deal is simple. I help you find Dewey Andreas, and you and your team of scumbag Muslims kill him and then get off at the next stop. I don't want added complications after Andreas is dead."

"What's in it for you?"

"Distraction," said Kyrie. "Elimination of a competitor. And, frankly, it would be fun to see if you can do it. My money says no—even with my help."

"That's where you're wrong," seethed Fortuna. "There's no greater force than hatred, the desire for revenge. *He killed my father. He killed my brother.*"

"Your brother tried to destroy America. Then your father tried to kill him. I'd want revenge, too, but don't try and tell me they didn't deserve it."

Fortuna stared angrily into Kyrie's eyes.

"Andreas is focused on something else right

now," Kyrie said quietly. "It took something to track him here, I'll give you that. You're already two steps ahead of your father. Your biggest asset right now is that he's distracted. His greatest asset is he knows you're here—that and the fact that you can't identify him. But I can. You and your men will have a tactical advantage. It will only last for a short amount of time. Minutes, not hours. You need to be ready and you need to move quickly."

Dewey pulled on the gloves and went to the window. He looked back at Beauxchamps.

"You said you wanted to tag along," said Dewey. "You're now part of this. Don't fuck up. This might not be the way DGSI does it, but it's the way I do it."

"You don't need to worry about me," said Beauxchamps.

Dewey climbed onto the windowsill and reached up to the roof, lifting himself onto the top of the speeding train.

He heard the window sliding shut beneath him as he clutched the cold steel of the roof.

"COMM check," he said.

"I got you," said Tacoma.

"I can hear you," said Beauxchamps.

"Rob, I'm starting at the car behind the one you're in, right side."

Dewey crabbed along the middle of the roof

to the next car. He crawled carefully to the right window. He moved down along the slat above the windows, leaning over to see inside the car, looking at passengers. Though the light was dim inside the car, he could see clearly. He moved down the entire length of the car, scanning for passengers.

"Nothing on the right," he said as snow and wind tore into his face. "Checking the other side now."

He moved back up the same car, looking for the men who'd been sent to kill him. Again, there was no one, at least no one Dewey suspected enough to send over Conductor Beauxchamps.

"This car's clear," said Dewey, moving on hands and knees farther back. "Let's go to the next car."

Inside, Beauxchamps walked casually down the length of the rail car, occasionally asking to see a ticket. Tacoma waited near the restroom, pretending to talk on a cell phone.

Dewey scanned two more cars, coming up empty. In the third car, he identified someone immediately.

A short young man was looking around suspiciously. He was olive skinned, with a shaved head. He was about a third of the way down the aisle, in a window seat.

"Mark one," said Dewey. "Tenth or eleventh row, right side, against the window, bald."

"Got it," said Beauxchamps.

Beauxchamps moved casually down the aisle. He eyed the man when he was still several rows away. He started asking for tickets a few rows in front of him.

Behind Beauxchamps, Tacoma moved quickly. He reached inside his parka with his left hand—his off hand—and grabbed a silenced SIG Sauer P226, flipping the safety off with his thumb. The gun was already locked and loaded. He kept the weapon inside the coat, shielding it from view as he came up behind Beauxchamps just as Beauxchamps was leaning in to ask the Arab for his ticket.

"*Le billet*, *monsieur*, *s'il vous plaît*."

The man nervously handed Beauxchamps his ticket. Beauxchamps scanned it for a brief second.

Tacoma stood still, pretending to be waiting for Beauxchamps to finish. He studied the woman next to the Arab. She was asleep. Quietly, Tacoma raised the weapon and, from behind the jacket, trained it on the man. Just as Beauxchamps handed him his ticket back, Tacoma fired. A dull *thwack* sounded, though it was drowned out by the steady din of the train. The bullet flew beneath Beauxchamps's outstretched arm, striking the man in the center of his chest. Tacoma kept moving toward the rear of the car as Beauxchamps leaned over the dead

Arab and covered him in the jacket from the floor at his feet.

Dewey kept moving. He was already halfway down the next car by the time Beauxchamps muttered, "All clear."

He saw no one in the car, either side, but in the car after, near the back, he caught him: a gunman in the second to last row. He had a beard and mustache along with a mop of curly black hair. He wore glasses. He was pretending to read a book, but the man's eyes scoured the car. Beside the man's leg, between his thigh and the wall, a handgun was tucked, shielded by the man's leg and the book. The seat next to him was empty.

"Second to last row," said Dewey. "Afro, glasses. Watch it, he has a gun next to his leg. I'm going to stay above him just in case. Rob, he's going to see you if you track. Might want to come at him from the back."

"Roger that."

Dewey removed his .45 from his jacket, flipping off the safety, chambering a round, and clutching it in his right hand above the window.

Beauxchamps spotted the man as soon as he entered the car. He was tall—his head and hair stuck up above the seats, illuminated by a reading light.

"Passing you," whispered Tacoma over commo.

Tacoma walked toward the back of the car, past

the gunman, then waited near the rear door, out of the man's sight line.

Beauxchamps again worked his way down the aisle, asking for tickets, answering the occasional question from a passenger. He started a few rows in front of the man. When he got to him, the man kept reading.

"*Le billet*, *monsieur*," said Beauxchamps.

The Arab continued to read.

"*Monsieur*," said Beauxchamps, louder this time, leaning forward.

"*Je vous ai déjà donné mon billet*," the Arab snapped.

"Rob," said Dewey. "He knows."

Dewey watched from above as the man reached to his pocket, just next to his gun. The man put his hand on the butt of the gun just as Tacoma emerged from the back of the train.

Tacoma stopped at Beauxchamps, pretending to ask him a question, the silenced P226 clutched in his right hand, hot.

"*Pardon*," said Tacoma, interrupting Beauxchamps.

Dewey kept his gun trained on the window. The Arab studied Tacoma for a half second, looking momentarily confused, then he swung the gun out from beside him.

Standing in the aisle, looking at Beauxchamps, Tacoma fired—just as the man's arm swung around. Tacoma's gun made a dull metallic *spit* almost indistinguishable from any number of noises made by the train. The bullet tore through the Arab's heart, then the seat cushion, finally lodging in the wall panel in the next aisle, a few inches from a sleeping man's knee.

Tacoma turned and continued toward the rear of the train as Beauxchamps leaned over and took the weapon from the dead man's hand. He pushed the man's limp neck against the window as the man gurgled his last breath.

"Three down," said Tacoma. "One to go."

Sangar moved ahead, like an ugly wild boar marching slowly through the woods, his short, thick frame taking up most of the aisle. He came to the car before the one where he'd seen the disguised man—a man he believed was Andreas.

He entered the restroom, locking the door. Inside his canvas jacket, beneath his left armpit, was a concealed holster. He removed a pistol: PC-9 ZOAF, an Iranian knockoff of the SIG Sauer P226. Sangar took a silencer from his pants pocket and threaded it into the muzzle, then chambered a round.

Sangar didn't have a well-thought-out escape plan. He hadn't even considered his escape. But Sangar, at forty-seven, was one of the most decorated spies in VEVAK history. Had he wasted time planning for escapes and other such nonsense during his violent, highly successful career, he would not have risen so high within the organization. There would be a way out once the chaos ensued. If not, he trusted Abu Paria to figure out how to find him and free him. And if he died—well, he died doing what he loved, what he was meant to do.

He opened the restroom door and moved into the dimly lit railcar, his hand clutching the weapon in the pocket of his coat, looking for the American named Andreas.

Katie watched as the man entered from the back of the car. Her eyes were nearly shut, her head still, and it was dark. As the man scanned both sides of the aisle, she marked him.

She touched her ear, leaning toward the window in case he looked.

"Rob?"

"What?"

"VEVAK, the incident in Prague three years ago."

"What about it?"

"The man, the Iranian who killed Roger Berl."

"Sangar," whispered Tacoma. "Bardia Sangar."

"He's here," she said. "VEVAK is—"

She felt the cold, hard steel pressing against the side of her head. Katie turned as Sangar eased into the seat next to her, his black eyes glued to her.

"Known accomplices," he said in broken

English as he moved the tip of the silencer to Katie's abdomen. "You are stupid to be on this train." Then Sangar growled, *"Where is he?"*

Tacoma was in the second-to-last car when he heard Sangar's words over his earbud.

"No!" he said aloud, causing a few people to look up.

Tacoma charged up the empty aisle, sprinting through the car, then passed into the next car. Ahead, a woman was stepping into the aisle—Tacoma leapt onto the arm of the seat behind her and jumped over her, using his hand to shield his head from the wall, then landed and kept running.

He passed through the next two cars and entered the dining car at a gallop. There were only a few diners. A middle-aged woman let out a shriek at the sight of Tacoma, desperately running, as if his life was at stake—

The leg came out of nowhere. One of the tables. It was a hard kick just as Tacoma passed by, a martial kick, striking him in the knee and sending him tumbling to the floor, where he smashed awkwardly into a steel wall.

He looked up as blood gushed from his head down his face, into his eyes. She was tall, with dark hair. She wore tight pants, boots, a black sweater. She clutched a silenced handgun, a gold-hued suppressor sticking out from its end. She stepped closer, standing above Tacoma.

The pain was overwhelming now, and he heard

his brain telling his legs to stand up, then telling his arm to sweep the gun around and fire at the woman above him, but he couldn't move.

"No," he grunted.

Everything became crimson as his eyes were washed in blood, and then Tacoma heard—amid a rising decibel of voices and screams from passengers—the metallic *thwack thwack thwack* of the silencer.

72

L'AUBERGE CHEZ FRANÇOIS
GREAT FALLS, VIRGINIA

Berlin was also a long time ago," said Flaherty.

"You lost two agents in a nightclub," said Follett. "They were gunned down. It was blamed on Red Army Faction."

"Yes," said Flaherty. "I remember. John Garrity. Pablo Cashen."

"The satellite was bought from Lockheed's German subsidiary," said Follett. "Their head of European sales also died that night at the club."

Flaherty stood up.

"I don't remember that part," he said. "My sense is, you seem to think I had something to do with the satellite and with Order Six. The truth is, I did. But it was a long time ago."

"Mr. Flaherty, I wanted to ask—"

"I'll be right back," said Flaherty. "I'm just going to the restroom."

In the bathroom, Flaherty splashed cold water on his face. He dried himself off and then stared at his reflection in the mirror.

Flaherty knew he'd handled Follett, misdirected him enough to get through the next two days. That was all they needed. They were now within twenty-four hours of victory.

Yet he felt his heart racing.

"A few more minutes," he whispered to himself.

Then it will all be done. Leave him confused.

He caught a strange light in the mirror coming through the window. He looked at it suspiciously for a moment or two, then his phone vibrated. He looked at his phone. It was from Bruner.

THEY KNOW
GET AWAY NOW

Flaherty went to the window. The lights he'd seen had been from an unmarked vehicle, a black sedan, which pulled to the side of the parking lot. The driver's side door opened and a man climbed out. He wore dark tactical clothing and a flak jacket. The man's eyes were fixed on the front entrance of the restaurant and not on the restroom window.

After the agent moved out of his sight line, Flaherty pushed the window open. Up the road, he counted several police cars coming toward the restaurant, their sirens off. He climbed through the window and got on his stomach. He crawled behind a line of low holly bushes to his car, out of view of the first sedan. He climbed into his car, turned the ignition, and moved slowly out of the parking lot, just another customer leaving for the night.

At the main road, the agents had already taken up position. They were quarantining the restaurant.

Flaherty floored it, gunning past the FBI agent who tried to stop him. The man lurched at the last possible moment; had he not, Flaherty would've run him down. The agent sprinted back to the black sedan.

Flaherty pushed the S550 as fast as it would go. The country road opened up into a series of low hills. Graduated curves became sharper. The up and down of the hills turned steeper. But Flaherty kept the Mercedes floored. In the rearview mirror, he saw the first of the police lights, several hundred yards behind him.

The vehicle swept over a particularly high hill. Flaherty felt weightlessness in his spine for a brief moment. He looked at the speedometer. He was going a hundred and five miles an hour. As the car settled back into the downhill grade,

Flaherty registered a large, dangerous curve a hundred feet away. Just beyond the curve was a large oak tree. Flaherty feathered the brakes as he tried to slow down, but nothing happened. He slammed harder, but nothing happened, and he scrambled to find the emergency brake as the massive tree loomed ahead, becoming larger and larger as the car tore down the steep hill. When, finally, Flaherty found the emergency brake, he yanked back, but nothing happened.

Flaherty jacked the wheel as the car reached the curve. He felt the brutal torque and heard the horrendous screech of tires. Speed won out over physics, and the Mercedes swerved toward the side of the road, its tires unable to maintain grip on the asphalt. The car slid into a rolling tumble, out of control, the tires screeching.

In the moment just before the Mercedes went headfirst into the tree, Flaherty felt no fear, only betrayal. Bruner's face flashed in his mind, and he finally understood. The car slammed with a horrendous torque into the tree, the sound of crushing metal echoing through the dark Virginia night.

73

FRANCE

Kyrie saw the man with the orange ski parka standing near the front of the car. From the second-to-last row, he watched him for more than a minute. Then, with a suddenness that jolted him upright, the man turned and started running, disappearing into the next car.

He looked at Fortuna. "Let's go."

Dewey clung to the roof of the train, halfway down the last car, looking for the final killer, when he heard the chilling low, harsh Iranian accent over his earbud.

Where is he?

He remembered Paria, the monster he'd managed to outwit several years before. The accent was the same, the hatred and anger even more visceral.

Iran.

His hands were numb. His face and hair were caked in snow and ice, which clung to the freezing sweat.

Dewey turned and—slowly, as if calculating the strength of the wind—stood up and started running toward the front of the speeding train.

He had to lean dangerously forward so as to not be blown from the roof. The snow was blinding. But he ran, his eyes focused on nothing but his next step. He leapt over the accordion canopy connecting the cars and kept moving, trying to put the thought of Katie out of his mind, until another sound arose inside his frozen ear. A pained *"No!"* from Tacoma, and then three barely audible shots—three suppressed bullets, and a final horrible grunt—then screams, which echoed out from the car just below.

Beauxchamps heard Katie's words as he came to the rear of the second-to-last car. A few seconds later, Tacoma flew by him, an angry look on his face.

Beauxchamps followed him, running up the aisle, struggling to keep his pants up. Passengers started yelling at him, asking what was going on, but he kept moving.

Tacoma was quickly out of his sight, moving toward the front of the train with speed Beauxchamps couldn't keep up with. He kept running through the second car, pushing people out of his way. In the next car, he heard Tacoma's sudden groan through his earbud. He looked up and saw—through the still open door at the front of the car—the cafeteria car, and a female figure, stepping into the small frame of the opening.

Frantically, Beauxchamps looked around,

scanning the rows of seats as people started yelling and screaming.

Then he saw him. It was the dead Arab, his Afro still protruding above the seats. He was five or six rows back.

Beauxchamps ran for the dead Arab, lunging past a middle-aged man. He found the man's pistol at his feet. Beauxchamps charged toward the front of the car, flipping the safety off as his arms swung through the air. His eyes again found the opening in the door. He saw the female figure and watched in agony as her right arm went slowly, deliberately into the air, her hand holding a gun. He was too late.

Then he heard Tacoma.

No!

Beauxchamps stopped running. He raised the weapon, his hand shaking ever so slightly. He didn't have time to aim.

He pumped the trigger—three rapid pulls—three dull metallic thuds—*thwack thwack thwack*—firing at the woman who was about to shoot Tacoma, firing through the small opening in the door, across a hundred feet of dimly lit, passenger-filled pandemonium. The bullets tore into the killer's back and she dropped to the ground.

As he walked toward the cafeteria car, clutching the gun, Beauxchamps felt elated. He was breathing heavily. The passengers in the front rows of the car cowered in their seats. Several children were crying.

He stepped into the cafeteria car just as he heard the sound of unmuted gunfire behind him. In the same instant, he felt the white hot heat of a bullet, striking him in the middle of the back. He could see Tacoma's orange jacket in the far corner of the dining car, his last sight before he crumpled to the floor and died.

Kyrie clutched his handgun as he walked rapidly through the car, Fortuna just behind him. He pointed at the dead Arab slumped against the glass but kept moving. Kyrie stepped over the man he'd just shot in the back, a man in a conductor's uniform, and entered the cafeteria car.

An eerie silence inhabited the train now as passengers huddled in fear, most with their eyes closed, parents holding children, women crying.

The two men passed quickly through the car, barely looking at the bloody carnage in the front—a woman riddled with bullets piled awkwardly atop the man in the orange jacket, whose head was smashed at a horrible angle into the wall, his face, hair, and jacket covered in blood.

They kept moving toward the front of the train. Kyrie began a fast-paced jog down the aisle as Fortuna trailed him just behind, both men clutching handguns.

In the middle of the next car, Kyrie stopped. He looked around, his eyes darting wildly about, a slightly bewildered look on his face—a look that soon turned maniacal.

He looked at Fortuna.

"I said I would find him," said Kyrie.

"What the hell are you talking about?" said Fortuna.

"Listen," said Kyrie, pointing at the roof of the car as he started walking forward.

"I don't hear anything—"

"Listen!"

It was, at first, nearly impossible to discern, but then Fortuna's face took on a look of recognition. It was the faint clomp of footsteps.

"How do you know it's him?" said Fortuna.

"I don't," said Kyrie. "But I'm guessing that's how they killed your other men. Someone on the roof to mark your men, someone in the car to kill them. Besides, there aren't many people who could get on the roof of a moving train, especially in this weather. It's him."

Fortuna paused, then slowly nodded.

"If you want my advice, take him while he's on the roof," said Kyrie. "It's the last thing he'll expect."

Fortuna entered the next restroom and locked the door. He slid open the window. A wall of wind and cold air struck him. He stuck his gun in a holster attached to his belt, strapping it in. Cold air pummeled his face as he climbed onto the sill and then raised his right hand and reached around to the roof, grabbing a piece of thick steel bracing. As he hoisted himself up, he saw Andreas. He was on the car in front of him, his back to Fortuna, leaning over as he moved slowly toward the front of the speeding train.

It was snowing fiercely and the wind had picked up. Fortuna crawled to the middle of the roof, fighting to keep from being blown off. He paused a few seconds to get acclimated to the wind shear and to the steady gale-force winds. He stood up and removed his gun from the holster. He raised the weapon and aimed it at Dewey.

"Andreas!" he screamed.

Dewey stopped moving. He turned his head around and looked at Fortuna.

Dewey's hair and face were rimmed with white. What skin was visible was red from the wind and physical exertion. He stared at Fortuna, who held him in the crosshairs of the gun.

Fortuna's arm wavered in the wind as he struggled to keep the gun aimed at Dewey.

"Nebuchar," yelled Dewey. *"The ugly one!"*

"You killed my father!" screamed Fortuna. *"You killed my brother!"*

Fortuna fired. The bullet went flying past Dewey, who reached into his jacket pocket and pulled out his gun just as Fortuna fired again, this time hitting Dewey on the left hip. The force of the bullet kicked Dewey to his left and he lost his footing. He let out a pained grunt as he tumbled to the cold steel of the railcar roof. He slid toward the edge, trying to find something—anything—to hold on to. He let the gun go just as he reached the very edge, his two hands, racked with cold, grabbing the slat of steel bracing just as he was about to go tumbling into the mountainous oblivion.

Dewey looked down for a moment as he struggled to catch his breath. He felt the burning of the bullet wound. He looked up at Fortuna, who was inching closer, weapon out and trained on him.

"They deserved to die!" said Dewey.

"It doesn't matter!" screamed Fortuna as he neared. *"A son avenges the killer of his father!"*

Dewey clung to the side of the train, his legs dangling in the air. He glanced behind him, seeing nothing but the tops of pine trees covered in snow and the dark walls of mountains in every direction. The running lights of the train illuminated tracks covered in white, and steep, sharp slopes on both sides.

Dewey felt weak. The pain at his side was horrible. He let his left hand go, moving it down to his hip. He brought it back up. The snow was dark red.

Dewey and Fortuna stared at each other for

several moments. Then Dewey's eyes shot behind Fortuna.

"Duck!" he yelled.

Fortuna swiveled around, looking for what was coming. In the same instant, Dewey swung his right leg back onto the train. Fortuna's sudden movement was met with a brutal wall of wind. He fell backward just as Dewey climbed onto the roof and charged directly at him.

On his back now and sliding, Fortuna grabbed a piece of steel near the middle of the roof with one hand to keep from slipping any farther toward the edge as, with his other hand, he clutched the gun and tried to find Dewey. As Dewey came closer, Fortuna fired—but the bullet missed. Dewey took three running steps and lunged though the air, tackling Fortuna and wrestling him off his mark, both men now skimming down the slippery railcar, Fortuna's gun falling from his hands as he screamed and tried in vain to find something to grab.

The two men were interlocked as they tumbled and slid, Dewey on top of Fortuna, punching Fortuna in the face as Fortuna held Dewey's jacket with both hands now, pulling Dewey with him as they tumbled toward the dark, snowy abyss. They picked up speed, slipping inescapably toward the edge. Fortuna was first to slide over the edge, screaming and clutching Dewey's jacket for dear life.

As Dewey was pulled closer to the edge, his hands grabbed at the roof of the train, searching for something to hold. They found a piece of steel bracing just above the windows. With Fortuna tugging him from below, Dewey clutched the bracing with both hands, even as Fortuna fought to pull him down with him.

The two men now dangled over the side of the fast-moving train as wind and snow pounded and whipped them from all sides, Dewey holding the rail, Fortuna with both hands clutching the neckline of Dewey's jacket. They remained like that for several seconds, until Dewey felt he couldn't hold on any longer. Steeling himself, he took his right hand off the bracing, groaning as he felt his left fingers about to break from his weight and Fortuna's. He reached to his neck with his free hand, numb now, and felt for his zipper. He pulled the zipper down, and the jacket opened up. The material where Fortuna was holding on abruptly slackened, though Dewey's left arm was still inside the jacket.

Dewey let the jacket fall from his right arm.

"No!" screamed Fortuna as he bounced several inches.

Dewey thrust his right hand back to the edge of the roof, grabbing the steel bracing. Fortuna wrapped his legs around Dewey at the knees, struggling to keep hold. Dewey gritted his teeth as he prepared to rely solely on his weak shoulder. Gripping the steel with his right hand, he let his left hand fall. For a few brief moments, the jacket remained tight on his arm. Then it slid off, and with it went Fortuna, who somersaulted into the icy oblivion, his screams echoing until they were gone.

Kyrie grabbed a ski hat someone had left on a seat and pulled it on. He tucked his gun between his belt and waist, inside his pants, then entered the car just behind Romy's. He walked up the aisle, studying the pair of armed guards positioned outside the first-class car.

He came to the front of the car and kept walking toward first class. Both gunmen looked up, though they kept their weapons trained at the ground. As he came closer, Kyrie pulled his gun out and, in one rapid motion, fired two shots. Each man was hit in the center of the forehead, falling as Kyrie reached for the door handle that would lead him into first class.

Romy was taking a sip of wine when the sound of gunfire exploded from the back of the car. Everyone in the dining area looked around in silent shock. Romy stood up and glanced down the aisle. Walking toward the door to first class was a large man, his hair longish and blond. A cold, terrible shiver shot out from the base of her neck.

Kyrie.

She turned and ducked, running to her compartment. She shut the door and stared at it, not knowing what to do. The old woman who shared the compartment looked up at her.

"Is everything all right?" the woman asked.

But Romy didn't answer. She didn't have time to answer.

She went to the window and unlocked it. She held the handle for several moments. Then she heard another gunshot. She slid the window open. Wind and snow poured inside. The woman on the seat shrieked in terror. Romy climbed to the window, standing on the ledge, looking down on trees and snow, and the precipitous edge of the mountain below the tracks.

She looked back. Kyrie was standing in the doorway, his gun trained on her. He had a furious look in his eyes, part anger, but also something else, a look she'd never seen before, as if he might apologize.

That was the look of a monster.

Suddenly, Romy's eyes went wide in horror. Her mouth opened. She pointed behind Kyrie, trying to warn him.

"Behind you!"

He swiveled, leveling the gun, but there was nothing there. When he turned back to the window, Romy was gone.

Kyrie ran to the window and dived through, disappearing into the blackness.

The violent staccato of weapon fire cut above the deafening wind.

Screams could again be heard from inside the train.

Dewey climbed back up on the roof and started running. He got into a low crouch, ignoring the pain at his hip, leaning into the wind, charging toward the gunfire.

Dewey came to the front of the train. He heard screaming—piercing above the howl of the wind—coming from the woman's car. He dived down toward the edge of the roof, grabbing steel just as his feet, legs, and body went sliding over the edge behind him, swinging out. Looking inside the first-class car, he saw chaos. People hiding in their compartments, in the aisles, as a state of panic took over. He looked toward the front of the car. In the space between the two cars, he could see the dead guards. A large splash of blood covered the glass door behind them.

The woman's head suddenly appeared in an open window. He was about to yell, but then she jumped out of the train. Dewey tried to look back to see where she was falling, but her silhouette was quickly lost in the snow and wind.

A moment later, a man soared through the open window, giving chase.

Dewey moved to the next car and climbed back

into the restroom. He removed his gloves and opened the cabinet, grabbing the other weapon. He opened the restroom door and charged left just as he heard his name being yelled from somewhere behind him.

"Andreas!"

A man's voicc, with a thick Middle Eastern accent.

Dewey stopped and turned, sweeping his pistol down the aisle. Katie was standing in the aisle in front of a man, her mouth gagged. The man had dark, oily skin, a ring of gray and black hair around his scalp, and a savage scowl on his round, ugly face.

The man was shielded by Katie. He held a silenced pistol to the side of her head.

"I knew you'd come back," he said. "Now drop the gun, or she dies."

Dewey thought back, for a brief instant, to the range.

"Putting my gun down," he said calmly.

He moved his arm ever so slightly to the right, then fired. The bullet ripped into the Iranian's right eye, kicking off the side and back of his skull.

He walked to Katie and wrapped his arms around her.

"You okay?"

"Yeah. Thanks."

"Go find Rob."

"Where are you going?"

"It's not over. Get that chopper up here as soon as you can."

Dewey turned and ran to the front of the car.

He found the ski bag and removed the skis, placed them on the floor between the two cars, facing out the door at the top of the steps. He kicked his boots off and quickly put on ski boots. He took a tactical jacket from the bag, zipped it up, grabbed the ski poles, then stepped into the ski bindings. He punched a small red button near the door. The door slid open.

He looked back at Katie. Then he leaned low and tilted the ski tips down the steel stairs, pushing off with his feet and the poles, jumping from the speeding train into the dark, precipitous void.

74

RESTON, VIRGINIA

Kopitar stared helplessly at his computer screen. It was 6 A.M.

He was looking at one of the directories in a database which, technically, he didn't have access to. It was a State Department directory—a real-time list of all employees of the Department of Consular Operations.

The list was top secret. While there was little about Consular Operations that warranted such a classification, Bruner had long ago managed to get it classified this way.

Someone was downloading the list.

Kopitar clicked on the user profile of the person or entity doing the download. He was immediately hit with a demand for a password. He typed in a sequence of eight numbers and was let in. The user was someone named Jesus June at Fort Meade, Maryland. NSA.

He picked up his phone.

"Mr. Bruner, it's Hans."

"Yes, Hans."

"Someone is downloading the list of Consular Operations employees. Someone at the NSA."

"It doesn't surprise me," said Bruner. "Is there any way to stop it?"

"No."

"What will they do with it?"

"My guess is, run it against the various NSA algorithms like PRISM. The good news is, they're still on a fishing expedition."

"And the bad news?"

"The bad news is, these programs are state of the art," said Kopitar. "PRISM, DS-300—they use a lot of very cutting-edge technology. AI, context-based parameters—"

"Stop," said Bruner. "Just tell me what it means."

"It's the facial recognition algorithms I'm worried about. Everything else is sanitized. But you can't sanitize someone's bone structure."

"It happens today, Hans," said Bruner. "Hours, not days. Just a little while longer. Is there anything you can think of to slow them down?"

Kopitar paused, watching as his screen became populated with a tile of photographs of a young, handsome Hispanic man. At the top of the screen was his name:

JESUS JUNE
DOB: 9-2-86
ADDRESS: 14 Whitney Avenue,
Apt. 4H
Roslindale, VA

Kopitar glanced at his watch.

"Yes, Mr. Bruner, I have an idea on how to slow them down—for a few hours, anyway."

75

PRIVATE RESIDENCE
THE WHITE HOUSE

The president stepped into the bedroom, wrapping a towel around his waist as he entered. He was barefoot and dripping wet.

The second floor of the White House served as the private residence of the first family. The rooms were luxurious and intimate. On the third floor, a promenade at the perimeter of the roof surrounded the rooms, partly for security and partly to allow for strolls, its outermost edge a seven-foot-high balustrade and railing, preventing anyone from seeing in.

Dellenbaugh toweled off near the window. A pair of pants—khakis—and a shirt—blue-and-red flannel—were on a hanger. Dellenbaugh dressed and crossed to the walk-in closet. The light was already on and Amy Dellenbaugh was standing inside, looking in a drawer.

"Hi," he said, buttoning the shirt. "What are you doing?"

"I'm helping you get dressed," she said, looking at what he was wearing and shaking her head scornfully. She pointed her finger at him and drew it up and down. "No. Definitely not."

"*Why not?* It's Saturday. This is what Americans are wearing today."

"What are you running for?" she said. "President of the lumberjack society?"

Dellenbaugh shook his head, a tad upset.

"I'm not wearing a suit," he said.

"It's an important day, J.P. You're announcing that you're running for reelection. You've never done that before. Millions of people will be watching." She handed him a pair of dark slacks. "Suit pants, white shirt, sleeves rolled up, tie, no jacket. A hint of casual but presidential."

"Fine," said Dellenbaugh, unbuttoning his shirt. He smiled. "The lumberjack society? Maybe I *will* run for that someday."

Amy Dellenbaugh handed him a white button-down shirt.

"Good luck," she said, grinning. "Maybe your second wife will cheer you on?"

76

JOINT BASE ANDREWS
PRINCE GEORGE'S COUNTY, MARYLAND

Air Force Two, a modified Boeing 757, stood with its light blue nose just inside the large hangar. Portable air stairs were positioned next to it, leading to an open door.

For the past hour, a variety of people had been climbing the stairs. This included the flight crew, along with reporters and staff members of the vice president of the United States, Daniel Donato.

At 6:20 A.M., the vice president's limousine pulled up next to the jet. The back door opened and Donato climbed out.

He was dressed in blue suit pants and a white button-down. A couple of senior staff members got out of the limousine as well and followed him toward the stairs.

Donato's family was already in Hawaii—on the Big Island, in a private villa owned by a hedge fund manager whom Donato had become friends with during his time in the Senate, where he served on the Banking Committee. Donato was a few days behind his family, having spent the week raising money for various Republican

House and Senate candidates in Colorado, Washington State, and California. He was a little tired. It would be the Donatos' first family vacation in more than a year.

Donato climbed the stairs and stepped into the cockpit, where three pilots were preparing Air Force Two for takeoff.

"Hi, guys," said Donato, shaking each man's hand.

"Mr. Vice President."

"Thanks for the lift," said Donato. "I hope you guys remembered to fill up the tank."

77

FRANCE

Romy tumbled through the air, instinctively wrapping both arms around her head and clutching tight, trying to curl up into a ball. She landed in a pile of soft snow, which seemed to cascade inward, like a house of cards, falling and falling, tumbling, rolling over and over. Finally, she came to a stop, buried deep beneath the snow. It was as dark as anything she'd ever seen, and then the cold hit her. She was disoriented and surrounded by blackness.

Yet she waited. She knew that if she dug in the wrong direction she would accidentally dig her own grave. She had to find the direction of where she'd dropped from. After almost a minute, she could see a slight variation in light in one direction, a dark, dark gray next to complete slate.

She reached toward the variation in light. She clawed through the snow. Soon, the light grew grayer. Finally, her hands reached out and there was no more snow. She could see everything in the ambient light from the sky. Above, she saw the train tracks cutting across the side of the mountain. There were pine trees along the side of the mountain, but there were also slopes of white in between, which looked dark blue in the light, and they seemed to grow brighter with each passing second as her eyes adjusted.

Romy started moving down the mountain, away from the tracks. The snow grew harder as the sharp incline smoothed into a steep hill. Soon, she was running through deep snow. It was an exhilarating feeling, despite the fact that she knew she was being hunted. She knew Kyrie was behind her and moving just as quickly—no, more quickly—than she was. To kill her.

After almost an hour of running, Romy saw a light through a window in a distant field.

Her hands were frozen, as were her feet and legs, numb as ice. She was, however, sweating. When she saw the light, she broke from a jog into a run, sprinting through the snow. Was someone in the barn? Could they help her? Was it warm?

She came to the open door of the barn and looked in. The barn was empty, abandoned, and yet a lone lightbulb dangled from a high rafter. It smelled of hay and wood.

Suddenly, Romy heard a sound coming from outside. She looked for a weapon, something sharp, anything, as the drumlike echo of footsteps through the snow came from behind her.

Kyrie was not as lucky as he left the train, plummeting into the dark for a second or two before colliding with a tree. The pine punched through his extended arms, his face smashing hard, a small branch stub stabbing into his cheek just below his right eye, puncturing skin, and then his head hit the immovable wood, followed by his collarbone, which snapped. He absorbed the pain, groaning in a low, animal voice, as the spiny branch tore a piece of skin from him and he tumbled to the snow at the base of the tree.

He pressed a handful of snow against his face. He left it there for several seconds and lifted it off, examining it in the dim light. It was soaked in blood.

Kyrie started moving, every step feeling like he was being stabbed between his neck and shoulder. He moved with the train tracks to his right and above him, searching for evidence of where Romy had landed, traveling quickly, before the blizzard covered up her tracks . . . or her body.

After several minutes of struggling through the snow, he saw the ruffed scars of her tracks. He fell into the line of her movements. Groaning with each step, Kyrie started running downhill, following Romy's footprints through thick stands of trees, down sharp crevices of ice, until, in the distance, he saw unnatural light. He still clutched the handgun.

A sloping field lay empty, covered in snow, and her tracks led to a barn. Kyrie walked across the field and approached the corner of the barn. He paused a few moments and stepped around the corner, where a sliding wooden door was partially open. Light spilled out. He glanced down in the light, watching the blood drip from his face like a leaky faucet. Then Kyrie moved to the open door.

He stood still, his eyes scanning the inside of the barn. He saw Romy. She was trying to climb up into the hayloft. As he entered, she heard him, looked back, and fell. She landed on the ground, near the corner opposite Kyrie. She struggled to stand, then started backing up as Kyrie stepped toward her, gun in hand.

As Dewey leapt from the train platform, he flew out on his skis, trying to use the light from the train to guide him. For several moments, he felt air beneath his skis. He kept his legs limber and bouncy, readying himself for the landing. It would be like skiing at Sugarloaf, in Maine, the mountain where he learned to ski.

When Dewey felt the first brush of snow, he let his legs almost completely collapse, absorbing the impact, trying to control the landing. It was steep, and trees dotted the landscape, though there was space enough to maneuver. He landed and crushed through several feet of virgin snow, skidding down the side of the mountain until he could finally gain control. He leaned back, cutting a sharp stop. He looked up at the train as it passed by, then along the illuminated tracks, trying to memorize a path in the darkness. It was a perilously steep descent, dotted with firs, a mountainside in the middle of nowhere, three-quarters of the way up the crest.

The feeling of skis was familiar to Dewey. It had been so long, but when the skis caught the first fast slip of fury, it was like riding a bike.

Dewey cut right, testing his skill against a perilous incline. He stared down at the tops of pine trees a hundred years old, holding a sharp line beneath the artificial mountain that had been built for the train. He dipped down into a sharp slope, then bounced in the skis—catching a moment of air. He could've gone straight, but Dewey wanted to test himself. He slashed beneath the dark overhang of the tracks to his right. After several minutes, he saw the tracks in the snow.

He removed his cell and shone the light at the tracks. They were fresh, someone trudging through the deep snowpack. Mixed into the path was blood.

The tracks ran down the mountain, into a dense stand of trees. Dewey pocketed the cell and lurched left, cutting down the mountain as the fierce blizzard continued to mantle the sky, guided by the tracks and by the ambient blue-black light of the snow.

Romy backed up into the corner, angry at herself for not taking the few seconds available to her to find a weapon. Not that it would have mattered. His face was badly disfigured. The right side was an open wound, skin sideways, purple, with blood trickling down. He favored his right arm and hand. His left dangled awkwardly to the side. He'd broken something. But he held the gun high, aimed at her.

"Stop running from me!" he yelled.

Romy pressed her hands behind her, looking for something, for anything, to save her, as if a magical key were hidden in the corner. She said nothing, her terror obvious.

Kyrie took a step closer.

"I love you, Romy," he said. "I would never harm you."

"You let them put me in a sanitarium," she cried.

"It was the only way to save you, don't you see?"

"Save me? From what? You're a *murderer!* I know what you're doing. I read about the Speaker of the House."

"You don't know what I've seen," cried Kyrie, a tormented look on his face. "I've been within a foot of someone blown up by a suicide vest, Romy! My scars! Where do you think they came from? *The Muslims are evil! They're evil and they're coming! What Charles is doing—what we're doing—is the only way to save humanity!*"

"You're a monster!"

"I want to run away from it all," he said, pleading. "I know I'm a bad man, but I love you. Please. We'll go into town. We'll buy two tickets to wherever you want to go. Tahiti. Buenos Aires. Tokyo. We have enough money to live like royalty. Let's run away, Romy?"

"How can you run away? You're a murderer. A traitor to your own country."

"We're trying to save the country."

"By killing me?"

"That's why I'm saying I want to run away. You and me."

"A sanitarium? I'm not your prisoner. Is that what you call love?"

"It was just until we—"

"Until you kill the president! *I could never love you! You're a monster!*"

Romy felt a large crack in the wood behind her. She inserted her fingertips in it and ripped a long, sharp piece of wood from the board. She held her makeshift dagger behind her back as Kyrie came closer and closer. Romy lunged, slashing her arm from behind her back. The tip of the wood struck Kyrie in the center of his chest, but he turned and ducked, avoiding the impact. He slashed a vicious right fist through the air, hitting Romy below the ear. Her head jerked sharply to the side, then slammed into the wall. Romy fell in a contorted heap, blood surging from her nose.

Dewey stepped into the light of the barn, clutching the ski poles. He felt for his pistol, but then the man turned, his gun trained on Dewey's head. The right side of his face was bloodied. It looked as if it had been clawed by an animal.

Dewey glanced at the woman, facedown in the corner, surrounded by a reservoir of blood, dark and spreading quickly.

Standing above her was the gunman. He stared at Dewey, baring his teeth. Dewey could see he had at least one broken limb.

Dewey looked again at the woman. She was on her stomach, limp against the wall, unconscious and bleeding out. Streaks of blood stained the wood above her head.

Dewey reached to his left calf and pulled out his knife, even though the man took a step forward, pistol in hand, aimed at him. It was a Colt M1911A1, a short, snub-nosed suppressor jutting from the muzzle.

Special Forces.

"Delta?" said Dewey, squaring around calmly, now holding the knife in his right hand, its blade aimed behind him, his trusted SEAL Pup, his best friend, the knife that had gotten him through many hard times.

"Yeah, I was Delta," the man said. "Kyrie Banker, Hamilton, Michigan, 1st SFOD, Tier One."

"I was Delta," said Dewey. "The way to settle this isn't with guns. It's fighting. Shooting isn't fair."

Kyrie grinned for a brief second.

"Funny guy, huh? Fair? What's the first thing they teach you? *Nothing is fair.* Take competitive advantage. When you can hurt, maim. When you can maim, kill."

Kyrie triggered the pistol in the moment Dewey lurched left and down. A split-second *spit* from the gun was followed by a thud as the bullet hit the wall behind Dewey.

But Kyrie still held Dewey, and now Dewey was exposed. Next time, Kyrie wouldn't make the same mistake.

Hit him in the legs, then deliver the kill shot.

Dewey stared at Kyrie. Kyrie took two steps closer and trained the gun on Dewey's torso. Suddenly, Dewey stepped toward Kyrie, thrashing his arm forward just as Kyrie triggered the .45. He fired as Dewey's arm was at it zenith, high over head, like a fastball pitcher. The sound from the pistol was different this time, a dull click as the mag went empty. Dewey's arm continued forward as Kyrie heard the click. He tried to lurch backward as the razor-sharp blade plunged into his chest, just left of center. Kill shot. Kyrie fell to the ground, his arm fumbling weakly for the blade.

Dewey stepped toward him. He pulled a cell phone from his pocket and hit 7, holding it down.

A moment later, there was a brief ring, then a voice.

"This is Calibrisi."

"It's me," said Dewey, his voice hoarse. "I have the woman. I need extraction and a doctor."

"I'm patching in tertiary recon," said Calibrisi.

There were several clicks, and then a female voice came on.

"Two-two-four."

"DCIA," said Calibrisi. "Connect and lock. This is a priority level emergency."

"I'm locking on to you both right now. I have you ninety miles southwest of Frankfurt."

"I need a Trauma Hawk," said Dewey. "Medical suite with immediate access."

Dewey held the phone against his ear as he leaned closer to Kyrie. He pushed Kyrie's weakened hand off the hilt of the knife. He grabbed it and yanked up, then wiped both sides on Kyrie's shirt. He tucked it back into the sheath on his leg. He kept his eyes on Kyrie. Blood seeped over his lips. His eyes looked foggy and listless, though he was still alive.

"Access affirmative," said the woman from CIA logistics. "I'm scrambling DDS one-oh-one right now. We'll be there in less than ten minutes."

"What's the nearest airport?" asked Dewey.

"Frankfurt."

"We'll need one of the flying hospitals, Hector," said Dewey. "Full surgical capabilities."

"I'm one step ahead of you," said Calibrisi. "I thought we were gonna need it for you."

Dewey pocketed the phone. He looked at Kyrie.

"The first thing they teach you," he said, "is know where your weapon is."

Kyrie nodded his head, coughing. "I should've known there was only one bullet left."

"Do you want a soldier's death?" Dewey asked, finding his gun.

Kyrie's chin was drenched in blood. His eyes had tears in them. He turned his head to look at Romy.

"I didn't mean to hurt her," he said.

"Why did you kill Lindsay?"

Kyrie looked up at Dewey, ignoring the question.

"I know you," whispered Kyrie, through words clotted with blood. "I need to tell you something."

Dewey inspected the gun, then chambered a round.

"You need to know something," Kyrie whispered as blood trickled from his nose and ears. "You were on the list. Bruner identified you. You were to be the fourth member of the team."

Dewey was silent. A confused look was on his face.

"I killed your wife," said Kyrie, struggling to complete his words as death approached. "I put the gun in her mouth and I pulled the trigger. She did not commit suicide. It was me. I did it. I thought you would want to know. I'm sorry."

Dewey pointed the gun at Kyrie and fired, sending a bullet into Kyrie's chest. He moved the gun slightly and fired again, at nearly point-blank range, dropping lead into his forehead.

Dewey stared down numbly at Kyrie. Any sounds became silent and a momentary darkness shrouded his vision. A strange feeling came over him, as if night had become day and day night. He suddenly collapsed to his knees as his vision was taken over by Holly, seeing nothing but the photos they made him look at, the pictures of her destroyed face.

What did I do, Holly? Can you ever forgive me?

Dewey clutched the gun in his hand, looking at it as memories and guilt hit him. Was he lying? *Did they kill her because of me?*

Did they murder you because of me?

And then Dewey's attention was awakened by the movement of the dark pool of crimson, spreading out from the corner of the barn, and the woman.

He stood up and walked to the far corner of the barn and knelt next to her. Her neck was bent backward and blood oozed down from her nose and eye. He felt her neck for a pulse. She was alive.

78

THE KENNEDY-WARREN BUILDING
CONNECTICUT AVENUE
WASHINGTON, D.C.

June stayed at NSA until three in the morning, waiting for the results of the Consular Operations scan. It would take several hours, he knew. He decided to drive home and take a shower, feed his turtle, Jeremy, and get some clean clothing.

As he got dressed, June went to his computer and logged on. A square, silver-colored icon was flashing. It was LayerX, one of the NSA software programs designed to correlate and match photographs of individuals against archived electronic databases and media. Facial recognition.

June double-clicked the icon. A tile of eight photos spread across the top of the screen. All were file photos of Consular Operations employees. June clicked a button that said match. Another row of photos appeared below, each one with a line to the file photo above. In every case, the photos on the bottom looked archival, dated, a few in black and white. These were, according to LayerX, matches to the file photos above. An uneasy feeling spread over him as he studied them. The men in the photos on the bottom looked younger, of course, but they were all startlingly similar to the head shots above. He studied the first match, a Consular Operations employee named David Dannaher. When he clicked the photo below Dannaher, a different name appeared.

Kent Zinski
LT., U.S. Navy SEALs
Killed in Action: FEB 6 2004

Zinski had been killed in Afghanistan in 2004. Yet according to LayerX, he was still alive, reincarnated as an agent inside Consular Operations.

June went down the line of photos. In every case, the story was the same: an American soldier, killed in action, still alive.

June logged off and ran for the door.

A man was already in the elevator when June got on. The man nodded politely. June's mind quickly calculated. He was short, with long, greasy brown hair and glasses. He was overweight. Then June realized why he had never become a CIA agent. He realized too late that the man had come to kill him. It was in his eyes.

June reached for the elevator door just as Kopitar thrust a knife into his side, grinding it deep, then ripping it out. June fell. He looked up at Kopitar as blood oozed over the floor.

"Trappe," coughed June as blood seeped over his lips and his eyes fluttered. He looked helplessly up at Kopitar. "Largent. It's a conspiracy . . ."

When the elevator doors opened. Kopitar stepped over June, whose eyes stared glassily, seeing nothing.

79

FRANCE

Dewey remained on his knees next to the woman and again felt for a pulse at her neck. Despite the large quantity of blood on the ground, her pulse remained strong. He leaned down, as if hugging her, and wrapped his arms around her body, beneath her. She was small, no more than five-four or -five. Gently, Dewey lifted her up and carried her closer to the center of the barn, where the light was brighter. He set her down again.

Now Dewey was able to see the blood on the side of her head. She had a massive contusion that bulged like an egg.

Dewey removed his jacket and placed it over her. He stared at her face up close. For several moments, he didn't take his eyes off her. She appeared gentle, even peaceful. He used the sleeve of his shirt to wipe blood from her forehead and cheek.

An electric rumble echoed from somewhere outside, in the distant sky. Rotors from the incoming helicopter.

For the first time, Dewey felt a sharp pain in his hip. He glanced down. His jeans from the belt down were drenched in blood.

Dewey moved to the barn door. The chopper descended from the black sky, cutting a diagonal line toward the ground in front of the barn. Halogen lights abruptly lit up on the nose cone. The air picked up amid the din of rotor chop. It was a light blue Bell H-60ASD, a Trauma Hawk, a minihospital for severe situations. The door to the cabin flew open and two medics leapt out, carrying a stretcher. A moment later, a tall woman with short blond hair emerged. She was calm, with a sharp look in her eyes. She was dressed in bright orange ski pants, a white ski jacket, and leather boots. She walked into the barn, standing at the door, assessing the scene. She crossed her arms and watched as the medics lifted the woman onto the stretcher. She glanced impassively at the dead man in the middle of the barn. She stared for a few moments without emotion, then stepped to Dewey.

"I'm Nina Simonds," she said, extending her hand. "I'm a TC8. Hector called me. I was on vacation, thank you very much. You must be Dewey?"

"Yeah."

She nodded toward Kyrie. "Little disagreement?"

"He liked the Canadiens," said Dewey.

An involuntarily smile crossed her lips.

"I'm going to need a blood sample from him," she said.

"Go for it."

"No, you're going for it," said Simonds. "I'm here to save that woman's life. I'm not here to clean up your mess."

Dewey stared at her, wondering if she was being serious.

"I'm not kidding," she said, anticipating his thoughts. "He hit her and drew blood. We need to know if he was carrying parasites or some sort of unusual bacteria. If he isn't carrying anything, it will let us be more aggressive."

"Aggressive? What does that mean?"

"It means pushing boundaries." Simonds stepped closer and stared into Dewey's eyes. "A tendency toward violence. You are familiar with the concept, from what I've heard."

Dewey glared at her. He turned and went to Kyrie. He knelt and took his blade from its sheath, grabbed Kyrie's hand, and cut off the tip of the index finger. He returned with the piece of finger, blood dripping on the ground.

"Here you go," he said. "There should be enough blood in there to get a sample."

Dr. Simonds looked at the finger stub and then back at Dewey.

"Cute. Give it to one of the medics."

"You didn't answer my question."

"Which was?"

"Why do you need to be aggressive? Isn't she going to live?"

“*Why* do I need to be aggressive?” Simonds said incredulously, nodding toward the woman as the medics lifted her into the air. “Look at her. She’s bleeding out and it looks like her neck is broken. She also has a subdural hematoma. We’ll be lucky to save her life.”

Dr. Simonds’s eyes suddenly shot to Dewey’s hip, which was covered in blood.

“What happened?” she asked in a soft tone.

“I got shot.”

She knelt down and stuck her hand near Dewey’s hip. She pulled a small knife from her pocket, then grabbed Dewey’s blood-soaked pants. She sliced a precise line down the side and pulled the material back. His hip was black and blue, soaked in red. A contusion where the bullet had passed seeped blood with every heart-beat.

Simonds looked at it for a few moments, then stood up.

“That must hurt,” she said.

“I’ll be fine.”

“I’ll get Louie to sew it up. Looks like it went right through you.”

80

NSA

Samantha swiped her pass and entered Signals Intelligence Directorate. She walked past the large bullpen of workstations where she and several dozen other analysts worked and entered Jesus June's large, dimly lit office. Samantha looked around, then walked back into the bullpen.

"Where's Jesus?" she said to everyone.

"He hasn't come in yet."

Samantha put down her bag and took off her coat, then picked up her coffee. She went back to June's office and found the whiteboard where he had diagrammed the various elements that were at play in the ongoing investigation of Order 6. She stared at the board for more than a minute. It was a puzzle. June had started to put the pieces together, but he wasn't done. There was something missing.

One thing was certain, however. There was a threat. The puzzle was about the threat.

She cursed herself for not figuring it out by now.

Samantha picked up her phone. "SID," she said.

A moment later, a male voice came on. "Hey, Sam."

It was Drew Dilworth, an agent inside NSA security.

"Hi, Drew. I need you to send a team to Jesus's apartment. I need you to do it right now."

81

IN THE AIR ABOVE THE PACIFIC OCEAN
AIR FORCE TWO

Air Force Two moved west across the Pacific Ocean toward Hawaii.

Vice President Donato was seated near the front of the luxurious aircraft. A small contingent of his staff surrounded him, each enjoying his or her own row. Several Secret Service agents were aboard. In the back of the plane, a handful of reporters were seated.

The front of Air Force Two was similar to a private jet, with large leather captain's chairs around tables. In front of these work areas were several rows of seats, reserved for staff and Secret Service as well as VIPs, such as elected officials from the state the VP happened to be visiting. In fact, seated across from Donato was the governor of Hawaii, Samantha Bailani, a Democrat. Despite being from different political parties, Donato had invited Bailani to accompany him on the plane trip, knowing that arriving in

Hawaii on Air Force Two would make her look important. Donato was a hard-core conservative, but he nevertheless made it a point to reach out across the political aisle.

Bailani put her iPhone down and stared at Donato. Hawaii's popular, beautiful governor was forty-four years old. She had long black hair and a pretty smile.

"So, Mr. Vice President, may I ask you a question?"

Donato, who'd been looking out the window at the endless blue-black ocean, moved his eyes to her.

"You just did. And call me Danny."

"Good one," she said, then immediately corrected herself. "Sorry. I didn't mean that."

Donato laughed.

"What is it?"

"Why aren't you in Washington? Isn't the president announcing his reelection today?"

"Yes, he is."

"So why aren't you there?"

"It's not complicated. I've been planning this trip for eight months. I could've stayed. I would've stayed, but the president wanted me to go. It's the first vacation I've taken in over a year. My wife is mad at me. I need to do it. Besides, Samantha, I'm irrelevant."

"You are not irrelevant."

"I am. Statistically, less than ten percent of

voters cast their vote based on the vice presidential nominee. Dan Quayle proved that."

"Are you going to run in four years?" asked Bailani.

Donato shrugged. "Maybe."

Bailani smiled. "Well, if I could, I'd support you, you know that," she said.

"You can't and I wouldn't want you to do that, Samantha. But I appreciate it."

82

FRANKFURT, GERMANY

The helicopter flight from the mountain to Frankfurt took twenty minutes. Simonds worked in the cabin of the Trauma Hawk to stabilize the woman. The chopper was single purpose, designed to stem trauma in the early minutes, when time was more valuable than gold. Simonds wanted to keep her alive long enough to get on board the waiting Hospital 777 plane in Frankfurt, where a medical suite on a par with the best surgical units in the world existed, modeled on the Cleveland Clinic and capable of all known disciplines within the advanced surgery spectrum.

The woman was intubated—put on an oxygen machine to do her breathing for her—and injected with a host of drugs designed to keep her alive—antibiotics, coagulants, painkillers, as well as a few more esoteric drugs focused on stimulating brain activity during periods of extreme physical trauma.

Simonds directed the medics how to remove the woman's coat. Within a few seconds, Simonds had pushed them aside and done it herself, exposing the back of the woman's neck. Blood was trickling from her skull.

Simonds leaned in and inspected the wound. She opened a cabinet in the back of the helicopter and a bright light illuminated a variety of jars, tubes, and bottles. She removed two small jars. She handed Dewey one of the jars, which held a tan powder. Simonds twisted off the top of the other jar, which held a white powder. She put a few fingers in her jar and pulled them out, then methodically sprinkled the powder into every part of the woman's neck wound. She handed the jar to Dewey without looking at him and took the jar Dewey had been holding. She looked at her watch and waited. After nearly half a minute, she sprinkled tan powder into the gash, covering it.

She put her hand out, gathering the other jar from Dewey.

"What is it?"

"Cornstarch," she said.

"What's the white stuff?"

"Pharmaceutical cocaine."

• • •

Forty minutes later, the CIA Trauma Hawk set down on the tarmac of a rarely used section of Frankfurt's international airport. Dawn was approaching.

An imposing silver Boeing 777 stood a hundred feet from where the chopper landed, shiny, towering in the floodlights from the tarmac, its engine revving. The plane had the same iconic shape of the 777, but there were only a handful of windows along the sleek fuselage.

A stairway into the plane was already open—it was three times the width of a normal door to accommodate gurneys and other medical equipment. Bright fluorescent light shone from the opening. Flanking both sides of the entrance stood two men in jeans, thigh holsters, and black tactical vests, clutching MP7A1s.

A man approached from the side, meeting the chopper as it touched down. As the doors opened, he stood below, his eyes shooting straight to Dewey. He had a blank expression on his face.

"Dewey, I'm Alberto Ramirez," he said. "Chief of station, Frankfurt."

"Hi."

"There's been a development," said Ramirez. "Hector wants you to call him."

"I'll do it from the plane."

The medics took the woman off the chopper

and hustled to the open door of the jet. Simonds jumped down and stepped to Ramirez.

"What's the situation, Nina?" Ramirez asked.

"It's straightforward. She's got a serious cut and her neck might be broken. She's also got a bad-looking contusion on her head. She's lucky. But she's bleeding to death. I'll do everything I can, but at this point it's up to her."

Simonds kept moving, breaking into a jog toward the Boeing.

Dewey climbed off the helicopter, grimacing as he stepped down to the tarmac.

"You okay?" asked Ramirez.

"No," said Dewey, wincing. He limped toward the plane, then turned. "What about Rob and Katie?"

"We have a team meeting the train," said Ramirez. "Katie found Rob. He's alive. He's being medivacked to Geneva."

Dewey climbed aboard the jet, limping as he ascended the stairs.

The CIA jet took off immediately, climbing to 29,500 feet, flanked by two Navy F/A-18s. A refueling plane was already en route from Andrews AFB. In addition, an Air Force AWACS flew in rough proximity to the CIA jet, a few hundred miles south, eight thousand feet higher, monitoring the flight from above, in a state of constant analysis and monitoring, in case someone tried to come too close.

The woman was carried immediately into the midsection of the fuselage, where an operating room was abuzz, already half filled with nurses, anesthesiologists, and surgeons. The ceiling was high—the operating suite was built all the way down to the bottom of the fuselage, occupying space most jets use for baggage.

An anesthesiologist went to the woman as the gurney was placed next to the operating table and she was lifted off. He placed an oxygen mask over her face as a nurse inserted IVs in both arms.

"I want ten ccs of lidocaine with epinephrine," Simonds told the anesthesiologist. "Start running some propofol, then I want dexamethasone, levetiracetam, and mannitol. Phenytoin too."

Dr. Simonds went to the side of the OR, washing her hands as a nurse tied a surgical jacket around her. Simonds dried her hands, then pulled on surgical gloves and went to the woman. Bright halogen lights shone down from the ceiling.

Simonds pressed the wound on her neck. She remained silent as she inspected the woman. All eyes were on her. Then she examined the woman's skull. She stared for a few pregnant moments and stepped nearer, leaning down and looking close. She removed a thin, high-powered, pencil-shape flashlight from her coat and shone it on the contusion for more than ten seconds.

When she was done, she straightened up, staring down at the woman, thinking. She turned to one of the nurses.

"Number ten scalpel," she said.

Simonds cut an inch-long incision above where the subdural hematoma was, then another nurse tended to the wound, cleaning it and tamping down blood.

"Hudson Brace," said Simonds.

Simonds took the small burr drill and made two tiny holes through the woman's scalp, exposing the dura, the protective membrane around the brain, being careful not to go too deep. She used the scalpel to cut a tiny hole in the dura. Blood shot out. One of the nurses soaked the blood around the incision as Simonds inserted a small, flat Penrose drain into the hole, allowing the blood from the hematoma to flow out.

As she held it there, she looked at another nurse.

"Saline," she said, "with clindamycin. Fifty ccs."

After the flow of blood had eased, Simonds gently pushed the syringe into the opening in the dura, injecting the solution to help evacuate the blood. Finally, she sutured shut the opening in the scalp, leaving the drain between the sutures, still inserted, to continue draining off blood.

Simonds came outside, where Dewey was standing. Her eyes went immediately to his hip.

She looked behind him, at one of the nurses.

"Barb, get this guy into second unit immediately. He needs stitches and antibiotics."

"I'm fine."

"Have you ever had gangrene, Dewey?" she asked.

"Not that I know of."

Simonds grinned.

"Anyway, she lost a lot of blood, but we have that under control."

"How long until we can speak to her?"

Simonds stared into Dewey's eyes.

"I said we have the bleeding under control. The problem is her head. She has a severe contusion. She should be dead by now."

"So what are you going to do?"

"We drained it. Now there's nothing we can do but wait."

"She's going to live, though, right?"

"We're doing everything we can. The problem is, I don't know how extensive the damage to her brain was. We won't know for a while."

Down the hallway from the first OR was another operating room. Dewey limped into the room, where a surgeon and two nurses were waiting for him.

"I'm Louie," said the surgeon. "Have a seat."

One of the nurses cut down the side of his wet jeans, below where Simonds had cut. The pants were soaked in blood and dripping steadily on the ground. Delicately, she pulled the material aside as Dewey winced.

"Ouch," he whispered.

The hip looked raw. The pain was intense as air suddenly hit the wounds. The surgeon reached out with a large needle, aiming it at Dewey's hip.

"I need to stay alert."

"It's local," said Louie. "No morphine. It'll let me inspect the bullet wound. If any bones are broken, tendons or ligaments torn, we're going to need to put you under."

"No," said Dewey. "I'm not going under. If you need to operate, just make sure it's numb."

Louie hit Dewey with the needle at several points along his hip, then dug farther in, his hands gloved, looking for signs of infection or shrapnel. He cleaned the wound for several minutes, then grabbed a threaded surgical needle and started sewing up Dewey's hip.

Ramirez entered the OR. He handed Dewey his phone.

"It's Hector."

"Hi, Dewey."

"Hi, Hector. How's Rob?"

"They're operating on him. He has a broken neck, but he'll live. You should know, Jean Beauxchamps died. He was shot on the train."

Dewey was quiet, watching impassively as the surgeon repaired his hip.

"Do you still think she killed Lindsay?" asked Calibrisi.

"No."

"Who did?"

"I'll tell you who did, that dead guy back in the barn. He was hunting her. He was trying to prevent her from telling Lindsay something. Beauxchamps told me she climbed from the hotel next door. The guy who was supposed to kill her was too late. He realized he needed to eliminate Lindsay."

"It's a stretch," said Calibrisi. "My guess is, she works for a service."

"Who?"

"She could be a merc. We don't know. If you're right, the more important question is, who did *he* work for?"

83

OVAL OFFICE
THE WHITE HOUSE
WASHINGTON, D.C.

President Dellenbaugh stepped into the Oval Office. Several people were already gathered. The mood was ebullient, even excited. John Schmidt, the White House communications director, and Cory Tilley, who was in charge of speechwriting, were seated on one of the two chesterfield sofas in the middle of the room. Adrian King was seated across from them, next to Roger Faust, the head of the Secret Service. Several other staffers were gathered in front of the television cabinet. CNN was already broadcasting live from FedEx Field.

Mike Murphy, the president's top political advisor, was pacing back and forth in front of the French doors that led out to the Rose Garden, speaking to someone on his cell phone. He hung up when he saw the president come into the room.

"Morning, guys," said Dellenbaugh. "Make yourselves at home."

"Mr. President," said Schmidt without looking up. He was reading over the president's speech.

"Good morning, Mr. President," said Tilley. He stood up and handed Dellenbaugh a small stack of papers. "Here's the final draft of the announcement speech. It's already been sent to the teleprompter."

"Thanks, Cory. Have you read it, Mike?"

"Yes," said Murphy.

"And?"

"It's fine."

Tilley shot Murphy an icy stare.

"Fine?" Tilley said. "It's awesome."

"It's pretty good, I must say," added Schmidt.

"Don't get all defensive," said Murphy. "Of

course it's well written. I just think it's too long. There'll be plenty of time to lay out your agenda, Mr. President. I really think we want to leave everyone with one or two big ideas here—not twenty."

"The event starts in a few hours," Schmidt reminded him.

"Well, you should've sent it to me earlier than an hour ago," snapped Murphy. He handed Dellenbaugh a copy of the speech, with hand-written edits. "I basically got rid of page three to page twelve. I also think you need to wing it a little, sir. That's why people like you. You're real."

Dellenbaugh quickly scanned the document. He handed it to Tilley, who also looked at it quickly.

"Why not?" said Tilley, shrugging. "Brevity is the soul of wit. Did you time it out?"

"With all the interruptions from people clapping and cheering, it'll go about twenty minutes," said Murphy.

"How many people do we expect?" said Dellenbaugh.

"It'll be packed," said Murphy. "A hundred thousand." Murphy pointed at the plasma screen on the wall. "In fact, they're already starting to arrive."

"Roger," said Dellenbaugh, looking at Faust. "Is the Secret Service ready?"

"Yes, sir. The field is clean, safe, and protected."

The door to the Oval Office opened and Cecily Vincent, the president's executive assistant, poked her head in. She looked at Dellenbaugh.

"Hector is on line one. He says he needs to speak with you."

"Thanks." Dellenbaugh walked behind his desk and picked up the phone.

"Hi, Hector. Can this wait?"

"No, it can't. It's about the woman."

"Did she survive the surgery?" asked Dellenbaugh.

"She's alive but unconscious. Here's the issue. When she was found in the barn, there was a man with her. Dewey killed him. Dewey believes he was the one who shot Lindsay. He thinks he arrived at the hotel suite where she'd met Lindsay, but she was already gone and so he shot Lindsay."

"This is interesting, Hector, but can we debrief later? I need to focus on the announcement."

"The point is, Mr. President, what if the woman told Lindsay something, something worth killing him over?"

"Or they could've simply wanted him dead," said Dellenbaugh. "Have we run down the connections to foreign intelligence agencies?"

"So far there aren't any."

"Maybe the woman was from the same

agency," said Dellenbaugh. "She got cold feet, didn't kill Lindsay, they brought him in to clean it up. Or she was a decoy."

"You could be right," said Calibrisi. "She screwed up, they sent in a clean-up man, she ran, they tracked her, tried to kill her. Who knows?"

"So what's the problem?"

"The problem is, there's another explanation, and without her being conscious, we don't know what it is. But we have to consider every possible explanation. Because one of the possible explanations has to do with some sort of attack on the United States," said Calibrisi. "A bomb at FedEx Field, for example. She didn't go to the authorities. She went to the *United States* secretary of state."

"What are you suggesting?"

"That we hold off on your reelection announcement until we know more."

"There are going to be a hundred thousand people at FedEx Field. They're already starting to show up."

"I know, sir."

"Have there been any threats? Any chatter?"

"No."

"And say we did cancel the event," said Dellenbaugh, "what would that say about me? About the commander in chief? About the *country?* Are we really going to start allowing threats—which may or may not even exist, and if I had to bet, I would say my explanation is a better one—are we going to just fold up our tent and go home?"

Calibrisi was quiet on the other end of the line.

"I appreciate your concern," said the president. "The stadium has been swept three times. Every square inch. Every employee on site has been vetted."

"But there are a hundred thousand people who *haven't* been vetted."

"There's no way a bomb or any other type of weapon is getting into that stadium," said Dellenbaugh. "I reviewed the security protocols, so did you."

"There's always a way," said Calibrisi. "You know that."

"There are three hundred federal agents inside FedEx Field along with a hundred more outside the stadium. There are dogs, scanners, and a variety of other protective measures. We're not canceling the event, not without something more."

84

FEDEX FIELD

Ellsbury parked his car in Lot B, Section 4, directed there by parking attendants in bright blue windbreakers. He was early, but the lots were already so filled that he needed to park far away.

FedEx Field usually held around eighty-two thousand people, but today the expectation was closer to one hundred thousand. Tickets were free—first come, first served—and the crowds had started gathering at midnight. In the air was the smell of barbecue; many people were tailgating, as if the occasion was a sporting event. Laughter and yelling created a boisterous din. J. P. Dellenbaugh would've loved it.

Banners several stories tall, with the president's face on them, hung from the side of the stadium. Photos of Dellenbaugh speaking somewhere, sleeves rolled up, finger in the air, his slightly tousled brown hair swept back from his handsome face.

FOUR MORE YEARS!!
DELLENBAUGH FOR RE-ELECTION
J.P. & DANNY FOR AMERICA!

Today, as everyone knew, J. P. Dellenbaugh was announcing his reelection campaign. The event's popularity highlighted the simple fact that Dellenbaugh was wildly popular. He was a conservative Republican and yet every blue-collar Democrat in America adored him. The son of parents who both worked on the assembly line at General Motors, Dellenbaugh had a certain set of political beliefs—but he also understood what it meant to have calluses on your hands, to worry about how the electric bill was going to get paid, and he appreciated the hardworking men and women who were the backbone of America. Americans understood this about him. They knew he had their backs.

Ellsbury fell into the groups of people heading for the entrance to Redskins Stadium. Long lines stretched from every entrance. It took almost twenty minutes to get to the entrance and through security, which was bolt tight. In addition to two different total body scanners—one for metal, one for chemicals—an agent scanned people with a wand. A line of FBI agents stood just beyond, along with several dogs, scanning every entrant and pulling aside anyone who appeared suspicious and questioning him or her.

Ellsbury passed through everything, but one of the agents was looking at him. As he started to go left, the agent pointed at him.

"Excuse me. Can I have a word?"

Ellsbury stopped and looked at the agent, who was dressed in dark green tactical gear.

"Yeah?" said Ellsbury.

"Are you a supporter of President Dellenbaugh?"

"Obviously."

"Where are you from?"

"Bethesda."

"What's the name of the high school?" asked the agent, trying to trip up Ellsbury.

"Which one?"

"There's only one."

"There are three. That doesn't include the private ones."

"What are the names?"

"Walt Whitman, Bethesda–Chevy Chase, and Walter Johnson. Any more questions?"

"Enjoy the event," said the agent.

Ellsbury pushed his way through the crowded concourse. He found the nearest elevator and fell into a small crowd, waiting for it to take him up.

Law stood in line at a different entrance just a few minutes after Ellsbury. Law, who was thirty years old, black, and short, looked like an old man. He had colored his hair that morning in a whitish-gray. He had on a Redskins baseball hat and a red windbreaker, and wore baggy slacks and orthopedic shoes. It was a disguise he'd employed before and had fake identification to corroborate the ruse, though as he moved slowly toward the metal detectors he knew he wouldn't need ID. It was too chaotic. The Secret Service was content to let the metal detectors, the chemical detectors, and a slew of FBI agents and dogs do the trick. He passed through both machines and walked slowly past the FBI agents and dogs without raising so much as an eyebrow.

Inside the stadium, Law went right and walked almost three-quarters of the circumference, stopping at a concession to buy a soft pretzel and a Pepsi. He looked at his watch. It was 1:30. A large crowd was gathered at the elevators, so he took a series of escalators to the suite level. He munched on the pretzel as he ambled along the concourse to Suite 26. He removed the key from his pocket and opened the door, locking it behind him.

Law moved to the glass windows at the front of the suite and looked down at the field. In the center, a large rectangular stage had been erected, with a podium at the center. It faced away from where Law was. He would have to shoot the president in the back.

To the side, a thin, roped-off corridor stretched for the president to move down when he entered. In front of the stage, at the side of the field where the seats began, another stage was crowded with cameramen and reporters. Behind the press area, a scaffolding stood at least twenty feet high. Several cameramen were on top of it, seeking a better angle. The tiers of seats as well as the field were packed. Even with the glass shut, the sound of yelling and cheering filled the air. Country music blared from the PA system.

Law noticed people in the seats of the suite next door to him—a man with three children. He looked at the suite to the other side; there was no one there yet, but there would be.

Law removed his jacket and tossed it on the dining table. He propped one of the chairs behind the door to the suite, jamming it tight beneath the knob. He went to the bathroom and retrieved the rifle from the ceiling. He placed it on the floor in front of the wet bar, checking the weapon over to make sure it was ready.

He looked at his watch: 1:48. He found a remote on the wet bar and turned on the large flat-screen television. He put on CNN. Across the bottom of the screen, the ticker read:

DELLENBAUGH ANNOUNCES RE-ELECTION BID

Anderson Cooper's smiling face filled the screen. He was standing somewhere down on the field, interviewing a woman in the audience as, behind them, several people waved at the camera and held up signs. Beyond Cooper and the woman stood the stage where Dellenbaugh would soon speak. Law watched for several minutes, his heart racing.

He went to the rifle and removed the scope. At the window, he looked through it, scanning the roofline. He counted a dozen men in black tactical gear walking slowly along the roof concourse. It took him longer to find the snipers; he was able to count eight, though he knew more were there. He scanned the suites as well, again looking for gunmen. He didn't find any, but he did notice that only four suites were dark and empty. In one of them, he knew, was Ellsbury. Law didn't worry that the other two might be law enforcement. Instead, what concerned him was the fact that so few suites appeared empty. It meant that he stood out, at least a little.

He couldn't worry about that now, however. Now was about calming down. It was about getting in position for the optimal moment, when all eyes would be on the stage ten stories below. It was about taking the shot that would change the world.

Bruner paced in front of the window in his State Department office. Finally, he called his wife. The phone rang several times.

"Hello?"

"Hi, Janie."

There was a long silence. "Are you there?" he said.

"I'm about to leave."

"What's wrong?"

She didn't reply.

"I wanted to say that I'll see you later, for dinner."

"I don't want to hear about it. Not ever."

"Are you saying that what I'm doing is wrong?"

"Of course it's wrong," she cried. "But I support you. It's just so . . . so horrible. Everything. Ever since . . ."

She stopped talking, but he knew what she was trying to say. Ever since their daughter died.

"I know," whispered Bruner. "I don't want to do it. We have to. *I* have to."

"I know. And I love you for it. I just don't ever want to hear about it, not ever again."

Bruner started to hang up the phone, then stopped.

"There's a chance it will not go according to plan," he said. "That . . . some aspect of the plan will go astray."

"What are you saying?" she asked, a hint of emotion in her voice.

"If I don't return . . . if it fails and we're discovered . . . I know how these things work. You'll never see me or hear from me again. It is imperative that you tell them you knew nothing. Do you understand?"

Bruner heard soft sobs from his wife.

"They'll kill me," said Bruner. "But I'll be

waiting for you. I will find our daughter and we will be waiting for you."

Bruner left his office. Outside the main entrance on C Street, an idling black Suburban waited for him. He climbed into the back, behind a pair of State Department security agents. The SUV moved down C Street, heading toward Landover.

He thought of Flaherty. He wanted to be seated next to him, like always. But the seat lay empty.

Traffic was light. Bruner was quiet as he stared out the window. He felt slightly rattled by the conversation with his wife. In many ways, he felt the same horror at what he had done—at what he was about to do—as she did. Bruner admired J. P. Dellenbaugh. Like Bruner, Dellenbaugh had grown up in a blue-collar world. Bruner's father had been killed in Korea and he'd been raised by his mother, who delivered mail in the small Wisconsin town where he grew up. To make ends meet, she worked as a seamstress at a local dry cleaner, going in after coming home from the post office and making dinner for Bruner and his sister. She would toil alone until midnight, sometimes even later, sewing on buttons and putting hems into pants until she was too tired to work any longer. He loved his mother. He watched as she grew old before her time, comforting her when she could no longer carry a mailbag, when arthritis rendered her fingers too clumsy to sew. Yes, Bruner saw in Dellenbaugh the same strength that comes from adversity that has been visited upon one's parents, the same determination of spirit and inner confidence that is the last refuge—the only refuge—of a poor child.

But whatever respect Bruner held for Dellenbaugh paled in comparison to the anger and hatred he felt for the animals who had killed his daughter. It had been more than three decades since he let her go by herself to the gelato shop in the train station in Madrid. The anger had never subsided. The hatred had, if anything, grown into steel purpose. Every day he thought about how much he wished he'd done something different that fateful morning. He should've gone with her, should've held her hand one last time. He wished he had died with her, alongside her. In a way, he *had* died that day. It was what made what he was about to do possible. He was already dead. His very soul was a burning trail of embers that no time, no rational thought, could ever douse. Bruner would be called history's most evil man—worse than bin Laden, worse than Stalin, worse even than Hitler—and yet he didn't care. He didn't care that he would be known as *the man who wiped out Islam.* He didn't care, not because he cared more about avenging his daughter's murder, but because he believed his legacy would be a safer world for all daughters, that killing hundreds of millions, even billions, of Muslims would help ensure a world that would be free.

No president could do what Bruner was about to do. But it was the only solution. Now that it was upon him, he felt the weight of his decisions.

"Do you still believe?" he whispered to himself.

As the Suburban approached FedEx Field, it joined a traffic jam of vehicles entering the stadium proper. Every line of cars had to go through a security perimeter, where three security personnel—FBI agents in black tactical gear, clutching rifles—asked for identification from everyone in each vehicle, scanning licenses on a portable electronic screen the size of an iPad. At the same time, one of the other agents opened trunks, scanned the trunks for explosives, and waved a bomb-detecting wand underneath the chassis.

When the Suburban made it to the front of the line, the two men in front handed their identification to an agent, who scanned their IDs. Bruner opened his window and handed over his ID.

"Mr. Bruner," said the agent, returning the ID. "You have a reserved space near the D entrance."

"Thank you," said Bruner.

85

FEDEX FIELD

The president's limousine entered FedEx Field through the delivery entrance and drove slowly through a phalanx of security, parking well beneath the stadium, where a throng of more than a hundred VIPs were standing. A member of the White House advance team met the limo and opened the back door. Suddenly, the sound from FedEx Field came booming in. Country music—Dellenbaugh's favorite—was playing, a song by Florida Georgia Line, blasting over the perpetual din of people cheering, shouting "Four more years!" and clapping.

A half dozen Secret Service agents flanked the limo.

Amy Dellenbaugh climbed out first, followed by Sally and Summer, the Dellenbaughs' daughters. A crowd of VIPs—members of Congress, governors, large donors, and old friends—let out a cacophonous and sustained cheer.

Dellenbaugh climbed out last. A big smile was on his face as he stepped toward the crowd. For the first time, he noticed his parents. Dellenbaugh let out a loud, "Oh my God!" when he saw them, glancing at Amy, who he knew had arranged the surprise. He stepped toward them. His mother had her hands on her mouth, unable to control her excitement. Dellenbaugh embraced her.

"Hi, Mom," he said, holding her for several moments. "You didn't have to come all this way."

"Are you kidding? My son is announcing that he's running for reelection! You think I'd miss that? Not for the world!"

The president's father stood next to her. Dellenbaugh let go of his mother and wrapped his arms around him.

"Thanks for coming, Dad. Talk about a surprise!"

"I'm very proud of you, J.P."

"I'm proud of you too, Dad."

86

JOINT BASE ANDREWS
PRINCE GEORGE'S COUNTY, MARYLAND

Nina Simonds stood at the side of the woman's bed, checking the various monitors attached to her. She was still unconscious, her head wrapped in bandages down to her eyes.

Simonds leaned over and placed an instrument near the woman's left eye, examining it. She caught Dewey's shadow as he entered.

"How's your hip?"

"Fine."

Simonds touched the woman's arm, which was connected to a variety of tubes and wires.

"She's not going to gain consciousness," said Simonds.

"Until when?"

Simonds stood up.

"What do you mean, 'until when'? Until forever. The operation wasn't successful. Or, perhaps more accurately, the operation was a waste of time. She was already gone by then. I'm sorry. Were you two . . . close?"

Dewey stared at the unconscious woman without responding to the question. Finally, he looked at Simonds.

"I don't know her," said Dewey. "She has information, that's all."

"What sort of information?"

"If we knew that, we wouldn't need to talk to her."

Simonds nodded.

"I don't know what you guys are working on," said Simonds, "but I did find something. I know it's not my job, but we both work for the same agency so I thought I should say something."

"What?" said Dewey.

"She had plastic surgery. Not everyday plastic surgery. The kind we do." Simonds put her index finger to the woman's eyelid. "Both eyes were cut. They removed some material. The incision is almost too small to see. They elongated her eyelashes and her eyelids." She touched the woman's cheek. "They grafted synthetic bone onto her cheekbones, about two millimeters. Went in through her mouth. They also altered her nose. The work was so good that you can't even find where they cut in, but the bone in her nose was broken. Based on the break, it was done by a machine. It's very precise. We're talking about someone whose face was altered, and not just altered. It was done by a professional. By one of us."

"Agency?"

"I'm not saying that. It was done by *an* agency—Langley, or a foreign intelligence service. This is serious surgery, concealment versus enhancement. Whoever did it is like Picasso. It's impressive work."

The wheels on the big plane rumbled to life as the jet arced left and down, beginning its descent into the Washington, D.C., area.

"There has to be more you can do," said Dewey. "Something to wake her up, even if it's just for a few minutes."

Simonds stared at Dewey, an icy look on her face.

"There's nothing," she said. "I wish there was. We'll get her to Bethesda and run a more comprehensive set of diagnostics. There's always a chance I'm missing something, but the instruments don't lie."

87

FEDEX FIELD

Bruner got out of the vehicle and entered FedEx Field at the D entrance, going through the medical and chemical detectors. An FBI agent examined his identification.

"Good afternoon, Mr. Bruner," said the agent.

"Good afternoon."

"Aren't State Department officials supposed to stay out of politics?"

"I suppose they are," said Bruner. "Hopefully, I won't get into too much trouble for coming out and supporting the president."

Bruner took an escalator to the second level and walked around the concourse until he saw the entrance to Section 211. He went into a nearby men's room. A father and his young son were washing their hands. Bruner entered one of the stalls and waited until they had finished. He went to the sink and felt beneath the counter until he found the weapon. He ripped it out of the tape and slipped it into a specially designed pocket beneath his armpit, then walked back to the escalators, descending to the first level and following a line of people who were walking out to the field. The noise was loud. The crowd was excited.

As he came out through the tunnel, sunlight hit his eyes. He scanned the enormous stadium as his eyes adjusted. It was filled to capacity. Red, white, and blue was everywhere—on clothing, on small flags being waved, on signs, on banners hanging from the upper decks. A triangular formation of fighter jets appeared overhead, followed by a violent, earsplitting roar as the formation of F-35s tore just a few hundred feet above the stadium, sending the enormous crowd into pandemonium. A few moments later, a black object appeared in silence out of the sky, behind the wave of F-35s. It was a Stealth Fighter, swooping low. The crowd seemed to quiet as a soft electric purr trailed the sleek plane. The crowd cheered excitedly as it passed overhead, a low rumble shaking the ground.

In the middle of the field, cutting across the fifty-yard line, was the stage. At the center of the stage were a podium and teleprompters. In front of the stage, at approximately the twenty-yard line, was another stage. On it stood dozens of reporters and cameramen.

Bruner walked along the cordon until he came to the VIP entrance just a few feet from where the president would be speaking. He presented a pass and was escorted to the second row, almost directly in front of the podium.

An older woman was already in the seat next to him. Bruner smiled at her as he sat down.

"Hi," he said, extending his hand. "I'm Charles. Are you as excited as I am?"

The woman smiled back.

"More, I would imagine," she said. "I'm Mary Dellenbaugh. He's my nephew."

88

THE KENNEDY-WARREN BUILDING
WASHINGTON, D.C.

The entrance to the Kennedy-Warren was filled with ambulances, police cars, and dark sedans. Blue and red lights flashed in silence. Bruckheimer and Samantha were allowed through the police line.

When they arrived at the elevator, a coroner in a blue uniform was standing in a pool of blood, kneeling over June. Samantha gasped, covering her mouth as tears began to roll down her cheeks.

Bruckheimer put his arm around Samantha's shoulders, trying to comfort her, even as his own eyes became wet.

Samantha took a step toward the body. She leaned over and kissed her fingertips, then placed them on June's chest.

"Good-bye, Jesus," she whispered.

Back at NSA headquarters, Bruckheimer, his voice choked with emotion, announced to everyone in the SID operations theater that June had been killed. Shock and tears swept over the room. Bruckheimer went across the hall to June's vacant office. Samantha was already seated at June's desk, typing.

"Hi," said Samantha. "Sorry. This is what he was working on."

The LayerX matches were spread across the computer screen. Samantha clicked through all eight individuals.

"What does it mean?" said Bruckheimer.

Samantha double-clicked the file on a Consular Operations employee named Simon Smith. According to LayerX, he was a former Delta by the name of Richard Vaughan, killed in Somalia in 1994.

"What about him?" Bruckheimer asked.

The photo of Vaughan was in color. He was standing with three other soldiers in front of a Humvee, somewhere in the desert. Samantha pointed to one of the men in the photo, a tall soldier in camouflage, holding a rifle, standing in back.

"What is it?" said Bruckheimer.

Samantha ran across the hall to her desk and pushed papers aside until she found a folded section of *USA Today*. It was a photo of the newly sworn in Speaker of the House, Bobby Largent. She returned to June's office and held the photo next to the one of the soldier as Bruckheimer looked on.

It was unmistakable. It was the same man.

"Oh my God," said Bruckheimer.

89

FEDEX FIELD

Dellenbaugh spent more than fifteen minutes moving through the crowd of his closest supporters, shaking hands, hugging a few people, as a White House photographer as well as another photographer from the reelection committee took photos.

At some point, one of the members of the White House advance team got his attention.

Dellenbaugh took a few steps back and held up his hand, asking for a little quiet so he could say something.

"Wow," he said, shaking his head in disbelief. "How great is this? Seeing so many old friends, so many loyal supporters, well, it makes me feel humble and grateful. Look over there," he said, pointing. "Senator Hank Rogerson. He was voted the most liberal member of the Senate, but we came into the Senate together. We were roommates up on Tennessee Avenue for almost five years. Thanks for coming. Does this mean you're going to vote Republican, Hank?"

"Damn right," said Rogerson. "I vote for the candidate, not the party. I know if I ever run for president, you'll be there for me."

The crowd erupted into cheers, clapping, and good-hearted laughter.

"You know it," said Dellenbaugh.

Again, laughter rolled over the crowd.

"Thank you all for coming. Thank you for being there for me, through thick and thin. I'm a blessed man, in so many ways, but it wouldn't mean anything if it weren't for all the people who helped me along the way, who supported me, believed in me, put up with my mistakes. I hope I make you all proud. It sounds like a cliché, but I actually believe in all this stuff, in what we're trying to do. I believe in leaving America a better place than we found it. It's never easy, trying to make it better, but we're going to try. That means all of us. So thank you. Now, I'm apparently getting the signal." Dellenbaugh nodded toward the advance man. "I'll see you all in there."

As the small crowd of supporters clapped and cheered once again, Dellenbaugh, his wife, and their two daughters followed the advance man and several Secret Service agents into the long tunnel. Behind them trailed both photographers, who continued to snap pictures.

They walked quickly down the tunnel, toward the field, then they went right, moving beneath the stadium, just off the field. The sound of cheering echoed down through the concrete. Dellenbaugh waited just off the entrance to the field, smiling at his daughters, then at Amy.

The stadium speakers crackled to life.

"Ladies and gentlemen, it is my high privilege and distinct honor to introduce the President of the United States of America, J. P. Dellenbaugh."

Dellenbaugh wrapped both arms around his wife and daughters, like a football huddle, as he got ready to walk across the stage.

"Any last bit of advice?" he asked.

"Ummm, don't fall off the stage?" said Summer.

90

JOINT BASE ANDREWS

The door to the jumbo jet opened just moments after the plane stopped moving on the tarmac. A set of air stairs was driven immediately over. Dewey was the first person down the air stairs. As he stepped to the tarmac, he saw a black helicopter descending toward him. When it landed, the back door opened and Calibrisi climbed out.

"Come on," barked Calibrisi.

Dewey looked back at the jet for a brief moment, then climbed aboard the chopper, taking a seat across from Calibrisi.

"Welcome home," said Calibrisi. "How was the trip?"

Dewey glared without emotion at Calibrisi. "Peachy."

"How is she?"

"She never regained consciousness," said Dewey as the chopper ripped away from the ground, its rotors in a frenetic frenzy of power, soon tearing across the sun-filled sky.

For the first time, Calibrisi noticed Dewey's bloodstained jeans, which a nurse had sewn back up, washed, and dried so he had something to wear. The stains remained.

Calibrisi opened a small cardboard box. Inside were several earbuds. He handed one to Dewey, then stuck one in his own ear.

"Where are we going?"

"Redskins Stadium."

91

IN THE AIR OVER THE NORTHWESTERN HAWAIIAN ISLANDS
AIR FORCE TWO

Vice President Donato entered his suite. He changed from his suit into a green-and-blue-striped golf shirt and khakis.

It would be in the eighties when they landed. He wanted to enjoy every minute of his first vacation in more than a year. He couldn't wait, thinking about playing golf with his son and tennis with his daughter, taking long walks with his wife along the beach. He looked forward to that the most—talking to his wife the way a normal couple talks, as friends, outside the chaotic, programmed world that they were a part of, beyond the reach of the lenses, the cameras, the staff—just being a normal family, a normal couple, at least for a little while.

Donato walked to the cockpit and stuck his head inside. "Hey, guys."

"Mr. Vice President," said Snow, the pilot on the left.

"Hello, sir," said Coleman, the pilot on the right. "I trust the trip has been okay?"

"It's been great. I just wanted to thank you guys."

"You're welcome, Mr. Vice President," said Coleman.

Donato glanced beyond the two pilots, beyond the electronic dashboard, out the window to the gorgeous green silhouettes of the islands, surrounded by ocean.

"How long until we land?" he asked.

"Fifteen minutes, sir. *Sir?*"

Donato's eyes were transfixed as he stared out the front window.

Both pilots followed Donato's stare, turning their heads and looking.

A small spark—a flash of fire—punched

through the peaceful view. It was a small apparition, a tiny orange blaze. As the three men stared in silence, the small burst grew and sharpened. A smoky, white-hot arrow took hold and formed into a bright comet of light just above the orange.

"Oh my God," said Snow.

Coleman hit his headset. "Mayday!" he barked. *"Mayday!"*

Alarm beacons inside the jet roared as the plane's defense systems picked up the incoming warhead. Loud, violent squawks repeated over and over, as an automated female voice boomed from every speaker on the plane:

Warning, take evasive
measures immediately.

Snow lurched up and slammed a button initiating automated air defense systems as Coleman grabbed the plane's controls and pushed hard, down and to the left, trying to move the big jet out of the line of fire.

Warning, take evasive
measures immediately.

Air Force Two made a low, mechanical grinding noise as, in the same moment, it torqued hard to the left. The sound of metal seams stressing, the dull squeak and groans of the plane trying to do something it wasn't meant to do, echoed through the plane, above the robotic monotone of the voice and the loud squawking of the alarm beacons.

Warning, take evasive
measures immediately.

The underside of the fuselage rumbled as undermounted cannons dropped, targeted, and started firing rounds in a high-pitched *rat-a-tat-tat.* A moment later, a different weapon began firing as well—big booms every half second, as the plane's automated defense systems tried to shoot the missile out of the air.

Two low *booms* were followed by rapid hissing noises. The hissing rose above the cacophony as a pair of heat-seeking air-to-surface missiles roared from beneath the plane, targeted on the incoming missile.

The yellow comet of light grew larger. A trail of black exhaust plumed in a wavy line behind the missile as it tore through the sky toward the jet. The confrontation would happen soon—both sides were moving at each other at a blistering speed.

The loud *boom boom boom* of the plane's undermounted miniguns cracked the air a moment later, like a drumbeat, the weapons trained automatically to target the approaching warhead.

Warning, take evasive
measures immediately.

As Donato watched through the window, a sense of deep disbelief struck him and nearly made him faint, but he did not. He could not, for he needed to see, he wanted to know. Would Air Force Two's missiles hit the attacking missile? Would they miss? What about the guns? It's what they were meant to do—he told himself that—but disbelief and surprise turned into fear. It was a fraction of a second, but he saw it as it occurred: the two air-to-surface missiles from the plane passed the incoming missile.

"Fuck," said Coleman.

Donato stared at the incoming warhead. There was a silent fraction of a moment and then the proximity fuse was triggered. The explosion was followed by a wall of shrapnel—white-hot—moving at supersonic speed—striking the plane in a hurricane of ruin and destruction, ripping it to shreds. In a cloudless, azure sky, Air Force Two was torn into dozens of burning pieces. Fuel tanks ignited less than a second after the initial explosion. The plane and everything and everyone in it tumbled in a medley of vapor, smoke, flames and metal, raining toward the black sea below. The vice president of the United States disappeared into the watery oblivion.

92

JOINT BASE ANDREWS

Simonds heard the electric *chirp* from the hallway outside the ICU. When a second chirp occurred, she jerked her head, as if she'd been slapped. A Styrofoam cup full of coffee dropped from her hand to the floor. She sprinted toward the ICU.

A persistent, high-pitched alarm was coming from one of the monitors.

Simonds went to the woman's side, quickly scanning the half dozen diagnostic monitors arrayed next to the bed. The alarm was connected to a device that monitored brain-level activity. Simonds touched the woman's cheek and started rubbing it. Suddenly, one of the woman's eyelids fluttered ever so slightly. For more than a minute, Simonds continued to rub her face. Slowly, the woman's swollen eyes opened. They were beyond bloodshot, the whites turned dark red. She struggled to look around the room. Her eyes found Simonds.

"Listen to me carefully," the woman whispered, reaching for Simonds's hand. "They're going to kill the president and the vice president of the United States."

The woman coughed and lost her grip, struggling to keep her eyes open. A look of pain crossed her face.

"Largent works for them. They murdered the man named Trappe. Largent will be president. Please, it is true. It is why they killed Lindsay. I told him. They killed him because they knew people would listen to him. Please, listen to me. They are taking over your country . . ."

93

FEDEX FIELD

Dellenbaugh stood behind the podium, every sentence causing eruptions of cheers as he announced his plans to seek reelection.

"America was founded by men and women just like you and me," he roared. "All Americans are revolutionaries. The reason this country becomes greater and greater is that we are all revolutionaries, refusing to sit back and allow our freedom to weaken. We are fighters!"

Out of the corner of his eye, Dellenbaugh noticed Chambliss, the lead advance man. He was staring at his phone, an anguished expression on his face.

Dellenbaugh turned back to the teleprompter.

"The fight is not over, my friends," he continued. "The revolution will never be over. Together, if you give me four more years, we will make America better than it's ever been!"

94

JOINT BASE ANDREWS

Simonds nearly tripped as she scrambled frantically toward the cockpit. The two CIA pilots were talking. They looked up at Simonds as she ran toward them, their eyes growing wide.

"I need a phone!" she yelled still halfway down the long passage to the cockpit. *"I need to talk to Hector Calibrisi! This is Emergency Priority!"*

Jonas St. John, the pilot to the left, was momentarily flummoxed, then turned and grabbed a mike.

"This is Captain St. John. This is an Emergency Priority. I need immediate access to DCIA Calibrisi."

"Roger, Captain. Hold on."

The crackle of static hit the air. St. John handed the mike to Dr. Simonds.

"This is Calibrisi."

The cacophony of the crowd at FedEx Field drowned out the noise.

"Hector, it's Nina Simonds. She woke up."

"You have to talk louder," said Calibrisi.

Simonds took a quick breath, despite the panic she now felt, understanding what was happening.

Be strong.

"She spoke," said Simonds, her voice trembling. Her emotions were getting the better of her, but she kept going. "I'm quoting what I remember. She said, 'Listen to me carefully. They're going to kill the president and the vice president.' She said Largent works for them, that they killed Lowell Trappe, that Largent will be president. She said it's why they killed Lindsay, that she told him and they knew people would listen to him, so they killed him. She said they're taking over the country."

95

FEDEX FIELD

The chopper tilted left, cutting from the sky and descending toward FedEx Field in the distance. The stadium grew larger with each passing minute, surrounded by acres and acres of cars glinting in the afternoon sun.

Calibrisi hung up his phone. He tried to process it all as he stared at Dewey, momentarily frozen.

"Oh, no," he whispered, understanding the full meaning of what Dr. Simonds had just told him—at what the woman had said. His heart raced as he looked around, momentarily speechless—paralyzed—helpless.

"Dewey," said Calibrisi. "It's—"

The chopper coursed lower, then landed on a cordoned-off stretch of grass immediately adjacent to the stadium.

"What is it?" said Dewey.

Suddenly a series of loud, insistent beeps came over commo—three long, three short. At the same time, Calibrisi's phone started vibrating and flashing red. He looked at the message scrolling across the phone:

FLASHCON 13:27:40:
SILVER LION DOWN

The vice president of the United States was dead.

Dewey reached for the door handle.

"Hold on," said Calibrisi, barely above a whisper.

Dewey paused.

"The woman spoke. They're going to kill the president."

"What—"

"The vice president is dead. It's a conspiracy. *They're going to kill the president.*"

Dewey waited a half second, then charged to the back wall of the chopper.

Calibrisi tapped his ear twice.

"This is DCIA Calibrisi, voice RECOG."

"Hold please. Voice RECOG." There was a three- or four-second pause. "Affirmative. You're live, Director Calibrisi."

"Requesting Tier One stream into POTUS one-two-nine," said Calibrisi.

"Hold for FBI *Omega*."

A short pause, then: "This is Daniels, Hector," came the deep voice of the FBI in-theater operations commander. "I have *Omega*. We're hot, Hector—POTUS is on stage and speaking."

Dewey opened a cabinet on the back wall, exposing a neatly arrayed, sizable collection of weaponry. He quickly scanned the cabinet, sizing up his options; he was familiar with every rifle, handgun, SAM, explosive, and submachine gun in the large cache. He grabbed a pair of pistols and slammed mags into them. He chambered a round in each gun, then grabbed a few extra mags.

"Listen to me carefully, Nick," said Calibrisi. "You have a *live-shooter scenario.* Assume it's multiple gunmen in some sort of sniper set."

Daniels paused for a brief moment, then panic hit his voice.

"We need to get him off the goddam stage!" he said.

Dewey handed Calibrisi a handgun and an extra mag, then leapt from the chopper.

"One more thing, Nick," Calibrisi said calmly over commo. "This is an inside job. Make sure we have our ducks in a row before you give the go to remove Dellenbaugh. Dewey and I are entering the stadium now—I need an immediate visual black pass."

"Understood," said Daniels. "You got it."

Dewey and Calibrisi moved into the delivery area beneath the stadium. FBI agents clutching carbines registered their entrance but did not attempt to stop them.

"You take the field, I'm going up," said Calibrisi.

Dewey moved into a sprint, despite the pain from the stitches in his hip. He came to a tunnel that emptied out onto the field. A line of armed agents stood at the end of the tunnel, moving aside as Dewey approached.

The crowd was in pandemonium, cheering at everything Dellenbaugh said.

Dewey moved along a steel cordon at the edge of the field. He was met by a pair of armed SWAT agents in tactical gear. Dewey lifted the Velcro patch on his jacket, revealing a plastic ID, which both men quickly examined and then stepped back, nodding at Dewey.

Why aren't they taking him off the stage?

Dewey's eyes scanned the massive crowd. For the first time, he glanced to the stage. In dark pants and a button-down, sleeves rolled up, tie hanging down, his hair slightly messed up, President J. P. Dellenbaugh was pointing to the crowd as he spoke. He had all one hundred thousand of them waiting on his every word as the brilliant midafternoon sun illuminated his big frame in a silhouette.

Dewey reached the side of the stage. It was a mess of bodies, like a rock concert. Everyone was standing and cheering. He instinctively scanned the first several rows in front of President Dellenbaugh, but it seemed pointless. The crowd was a blur of movement—people standing and clapping, arms raised out toward Dellenbaugh, placards in the air, children on the shoulders of parents. Chaos.

But there was something. He saw something. He didn't know what, but it was somewhere. He studied the rows in front of the stage. What was it? Dewey moved behind the stage and slipped between the front row of people and the stage, pushing toward the middle—just behind where Dellenbaugh was now standing and waving at the frenzied crowd.

Law stood near the door of the suite, pacing back and forth. He held his cell phone, waiting for the message. Every minute or so, Law looked out through the peephole in the door to see if anyone was coming.

The sound of President Dellenbaugh's voice echoed through the suite, mixed with the full-throttle cheering of a hundred thousand men and women.

Law told himself he wasn't nervous, but he was. He held up his hands, trying to hold them still. But they trembled, ever so slightly, like leaves on a branch.

Law's sniper rifle was in a fixed position, the bipod atop the waist-high concrete barrier between the main room and the seats at the front that overlooked the playing field. The rifle was covered with a black tablecloth Law had removed from the dining table inside the suite.

Even the tall man in the second row was on his feet, clapping and cheering like everyone else, even as he waited for the moment he knew would soon be there. The moment when Ellsbury or Law killed the president.

Bruner felt a vibration in his pocket and pulled out his cell phone.

FR—8: MISSION SUCCESS

The vice president was dead.

Bruner put the phone back in his pocket as a

surreal sense of light-headedness washed over him, like an epiphany. Bobby Largent was now vice president of the United States.

He looked back up at Dellenbaugh, who stood just feet away from him.

"In four years, we have cut the deficit in half," thundered Dellenbaugh, *"and if America gives me four more years, we will end the deficit forever!"*

Bruner felt the steel skeleton of the gun tucked beneath his left armpit. He glanced above Dellenbaugh. His eyes swept left and right, scanning the suites, waiting for the moment.

Shoot, for God's sake.

Bruner knew he could simply pull out his pistol and fire. The bullet was chambered. The safety was off.

But Bruner also knew it was the final option, a last resort. If he moved on Dellenbaugh, it would be a bittersweet victory. He would be dead in seconds, taken down hard by one of the dozens of FBI shooters arrayed across the roof of the stadium, or by a Secret Service agent nearby, one of the dozens within the envelope of the president.

Bruner was an excellent marksman—he had no doubt he would succeed—but he also had no doubt he would be killed in a hail of bullets within seconds.

The larger objective would be accomplished,

but he would not be there to see it, to witness the reclamation of America, to watch in the coming hours as the Middle East and major parts of Europe were destroyed in thermonuclear heat.

He would not be there to watch as Islam was wiped from the earth in a brutal, inhuman, but *necessary* attack.

He would not be there to feel the power of vengeance for the daughter he loved, the daughter Islam wiped from the earth so many years ago.

Bruner placed his hand inside his jacket as his eyes swept the sides of the stage.

Shoot, he thought, picturing Ellsbury and Law.

His fingers brushed the butt of the pistol. He started to remove the gun from the holster, then paused, glancing again above the crowd to the suites—to Law and Ellsbury. What were they waiting for?

Shoot!

Inside the FBI in-theater command center, located on the roof concourse of FedEx Field, Daniels went to what looked like a black briefcase. He held his thumb against the digital reader until the locks on the case popped open.

Before he could open it, a loud ring came from inside.

The phone was a secure emergency link to FBI CENCOM in Quantico, Virginia.

Daniels opened the case and lifted the phone.

"CENCOM River Two," came a voice. "This is a code nine nine, Daniels. I repeat, *nine nine.*"

"Please advise, River Two."

"Move your teams *now,*" said the man. "Take rules of engagement to an improvise orange scenario. Then—*not before*—remove POTUS."

"Affirmative, CENCOM. Seeking exclusion and process."

"Exclusion and process in place. Get moving, Daniels."

Daniels hung up the phone then triggered commo.

"This is an Emergency Priority command," he said, urgency in his voice. "I have Omega. We are in a *live-shooter scenario.* Squadron Two, you are to *hold.* Shooters: VPOTUS is dead and POTUS is now in imminent danger. I want all snipers locked and loaded! You have in-theater aim-and-fire exclusion. You see something, you shoot. Access points, suites, roof: get looking, and if you believe you see someone targeting POTUS, you *take them down.*"

Daniels exhaled and looked around the small command center, where several agents were working. They looked up, consternation and shock on their faces, aware for the first time of the grave situation.

Daniels continued over commo. "Field teams: Get inside the suites *now!* We are looking for gunmen within line-sight of the president. I want weapons hot when you enter those suites. Now go! *Go!*"

Daniels again: "Squadron Two, prepare to remove POTUS, on my go, not before."

"Roger, Omega, this is Squadron Two, ready on your go, sir."

Dewey moved along the front of the crowd that was gathered behind the stage. The stage came up to his chest. He calmly scanned the rows in front of the stage as he made his way toward the area directly behind Dellenbaugh.

With every step, with every second, his eyes came up empty. There were too many people, too many possibilities—and yet something told him he'd seen something. Some part of him, whether instinct or the trained skills of an operator, had registered a false look, a threatening movement, a face from a file. He didn't know which—didn't have time to know—and a cold shiver bloomed at the base of his spine and shot through him as he realized he might never know.

Then he saw him. It was a tall man in a suit in the second row, standing like everyone else and cheering for Dellenbaugh.

What was it? Think, goddammit!

Dewey pushed aside swarms of people who were pressed up close to the stage, many reaching out toward Dellenbaugh. And then he saw the man's eyes. It was his eyes that gave him away. It was the same flash of movement he'd seen from behind the stage. The man's eyes went from Dellenbaugh to something else—to the sky above. Dewey followed the trajectory. The tall man was scanning the roof, the suites . . .

Scanning with the trained focus of a killer.

Eight two-man FBI tactical teams—spread around the stadium along the roof concourse—charged down fire stairs and started moving suite to suite, opening every door, guns out. Suites that were occupied were left alone.

One of the teams encountered a locked door. The lead agent took a step back and kicked the door, but the lock held. The second agent lifted a compact steel battering ram from across his back as the first agent kicked again, to no avail. The agents stood across from each other and grabbed the battering ram.

"Two, one—" whispered one of the men.

They slammed the battering ram into the door just above the handle, swung it back, and slammed again . . .

Ellsbury, who was across the stadium from Law, was slouched on a chair at the back of the suite, out of sight. He listened as J. P. Dellenbaugh walked onto the stage, the crowd erupting in pandemonium.

"Thank you! Thank you, everyone!"

Then Ellsbury's cell phone vibrated.

FR—8: MISSION SUCCESS

Ellsbury stood. He skulked low toward the front of the suite, carefully setting the Hecate sniper rifle in between two seats in the front row, then lay on his stomach and prepared to fire.

He found Dellenbaugh in the scope, adjusting the optic ever so slightly.

Ellsbury put his right index finger to the safety and slid it off. His finger found the ceramic trigger just as Dellenbaugh took a few steps to his left, taking him out of the crosshairs as he waved to the crowd on that side of the stadium.

Ellsbury held still and steady, waiting for Dellenbaugh to return to the podium.

Law heard a noise from somewhere in the hallway outside. It was a muffled scream from the next suite down, followed by boots pounding along the corridor. They were coming closer.

A low *ding* came from his cell phone.

FR—8: MISSION SUCCESS

Law ran to the front of the suite. He knelt and took up position behind the rifle, then slowly pulled off the tablecloth just as he heard a foot striking the door.

Another kick followed, as Law put his eye to the scope and his left hand found the safety and flicked it off. He adjusted the scope, finding President Dellenbaugh's smiling face within the crosshairs of the sniper rifle.

Then a louder sound jolted him. He recognized the steel-on-steel violence of a battering ram striking the door.

Dewey reached beneath his jacket and shirt, grabbing the butt of his gun. He pulled it out and held it down by his side as he marked the man across the stage.

Dewey moved the safety off, then put his finger on the ceramic trigger.

Suddenly, Dellenbaugh took several steps away from the podium as a fantastic roar erupted from the crowd. It was Dellenbaugh's daughters who caused the commotion as they came running across the stage, followed by Amy Dellenbaugh.

Patriotic music started blaring from the loudspeakers—"Sweet Home Alabama" by Lynyrd Skynyrd. Dewey looked up at Dellenbaugh, who was waving to the crowd.

Dewey saw Secret Service agents charging onto the stage from both sides.

• • •

Special Agent Joel Goggins, one of the FBI snipers, was on his stomach atop a concrete slab on the roof of FedEx Field, at the fifty-yard line. The rifle was on a bipod, its muzzle pointed down and in front of Dellenbaugh—aimed at the luxury suites Goggins guessed would be the choice of the snipers here to kill the president.

Goggins swept the long barrel of the rifle slowly across the row of suites. Most of them were filled with people; only a few were dark and empty. One of those seemingly empty suites—at the far end of the stadium—made him stop. Through the rifle scope, he'd seen something.

"Omega, this is S-one-three," said Goggins into his commo.

"Go, S-one-three."

Goggins adjusted the scope, zooming in as close as the high-powered scope would allow. He studied the empty suite but saw nothing. Without removing his eye from the scope, he pushed a small button on the side of the scope, which initiated the device's thermal-imaging module. A soft, high-pitched electric purr came from the scope as the suite turned a blurry, apocalyptic orange hue. The scope automatically adjusted, and the image sharpened. Within the orange, a light green apparition was visible, indicating the presence of a human being.

"I have a hard ID at two fifteen, a suite on the south face, directly in front of the president."

The person's arm moved. Goggins recognized the man's position. Like Goggins, he was on his stomach, poised over a rifle.

Then he saw the barrel of a gun.

"Take him—"

Goggins didn't wait for Daniels to complete his sentence. He yanked back on the rifle's polymer trigger. The rifle made a low suppressed *boom.* He readjusted the scope and prepared to fire again, but the figure wasn't moving.

"Man down," said Goggins.

Law put his finger to the trigger of the rifle just as the door jamb cracked from the fourth strike of the battering ram.

Stay calm.

Law studied Dellenbaugh in the scope, leveling the president's head in the crosshairs. Then he fired.

A low explosive *boom* echoed as the silenced bullet shot from the sniper rifle.

Dewey heard the woman's scream in the same instant he heard the telltale thud of the rifle, somewhere in the distance. His eyes shot to Dellenbaugh, expecting him to drop, but he continued to speak.

Dewey pivoted, searching the crowd. Several

people were frantically waving their arms. A woman lay on the ground, her neck and chest a riot of blood—hit by the bullet intended for Dellenbaugh.

Several people started screaming and yelling.

Nathaniel knew it would come to this. He knew it the moment Bruner ordered him to cut Flaherty's brakes.

He was atop one of the concrete abutments on the roof of the stadium. He scanned the suites, pretending to be searching for the killers.

Then he heard Goggins over commo: "Man down."

Slowly, Nathaniel tilted the sniper rifle forward, glancing furtively to each side as he did so, making sure nobody was watching. He acquired Dellenbaugh in the scope, adjusting it, then tightening the bipod. He took several deep breaths, then moved his finger to the trigger.

Law knew immediately he'd missed.

"Fuck," he muttered.

He tapped the butt of the rifle ever so slightly, moving its targeting protocol to the right.

Behind him, the door was struck again by the battering ram. Suddenly, the door burst in.

Law chambered another round as he found Dellenbaugh again in the scope. He had time for one more shot . . .

A red laser danced across the concrete to Law's left. Law registered the light in his left eye. He tried to ignore it.

Law concentrated one last time on the target, pulling the trigger just as a metallic *spit spit spit* charged the air behind him. Law saw a blazing white light and felt a millisecond of pain, and that was all.

Bruner registered the woman behind the stage, taken down by Law.

He felt light-headed and euphoric, and yet a horrible sense of sadness came over him. Bruner couldn't have explained the feeling he had in that moment. Everything he'd worked for was now here, and soon it would be gone.

Bruner's eyes went from behind the stage to Dellenbaugh, and then he saw Andreas. He was behind the stage. Bruner's heart skipped a beat as he marked him.

He immediately realized he was about to die.

In that moment, Bruner knew he would have only one chance to avenge his daughter's death. Not two or three, just one. Andreas would kill him, Bruner understood. But he could still kill the president. He could still kill the one man standing between Largent becoming president and then the total annihilation of Islam from the face of the earth.

Bruner looked up at Dellenbaugh and started

clapping and cheering—then moved his right hand beneath his blazer for the gun.

Dewey turned back to the stage. The president's speech was finished. Dellenbaugh was surrounded by his wife and daughters, waving at the crowd.

Across the stage, at eye level, Dewey again found him.

The stadium turned chaotic. Patriotic music blared. The Secret Service was now almost to the Dellenbaughs. It was a mob scene.

But Dewey pushed the chaos aside as he watched the man.

He was older, with neatly combed white hair, nattily attired in a double-breasted suit. It was the way his eyes shifted constantly. Dewey recognized the look, the sharpness, the utter lack of emotion, the objective. The man was scanning.

Operational.

Dewey raised the Colt M1911A1 from his side just as he saw the man's right arm slip nonchalantly into his blazer.

Calibrisi stood at the edge of the rooftop concourse just as the low kick from the FBI marksman's rifle boomed above the din.

The assassin was below him, he knew. Close enough that he heard the shattering glass.

Calibrisi looked across the stadium to where

the FBI sniper was positioned. He could barely see him.

He looked down to the field. From up here, Dellenbaugh was like an ant, discernible only because he was on the stage.

Calibrisi looked around the roof concourse, counting the FBI snipers as they continued to scan the upper levels for gunmen.

Across from where he stood, Calibrisi noticed that one of the FBI marksmen had his weapon pointed down at the field, toward the stage.

Calibrisi tapped his ear three times.

"Nick," he said, "take me off-line."

He heard a click, then Daniels.

"What?"

"Is sniper ROE opened up for envelope-level targeting?"

"Negative," said Daniels. "Why?"

Calibrisi pulled the gun from his coat pocket. He raised it, holding it in his right hand with his left hand underneath for stability. He propped his hands on the concrete barrier and trained the weapon on the sniper.

"One of your gunmen has his weapon aimed at the president."

"Where is he?"

"Five o'clock."

"That's Nathaniel," said Daniels. "Do you have a gun, Hector?"

"Yes."

"I'm going to redeploy," said Daniels. "If he doesn't move, kill him."

A moment later, Daniels came back over commo, speaking this time to the entire FBI field team.

"This is Omega. I need Blair and Nathaniel in command center immediately. *Run.*"

"Omega, this is Blair, be right there."

"Nathaniel, affirmative, Omega. On my way."

Calibrisi watched as the FBI gunman remained on his stomach, his rifle trained down at the stage.

It was, Calibrisi knew, a nearly impossible shot, but there was no other option.

He acquired the gunman along the small steel site atop the muzzle of the pistol. Then Calibrisi fired, three silenced blasts—*thwack thwack thwack*—but the shots missed. Calibrisi paused, adjusted, then fired again—*thwack thwack thwack thwack*—emptying the mag, but every bullet missed the man.

Calibrisi popped out the mag and slammed in a new one and again started firing. Slugs spat from the gun like a drumbeat—*thwack thwack thwack thwack thwack thwack*—and then he saw a spray of red as one of the bullets ripped into the killer's head.

Dewey stepped closer to the stage, his gun out and raised, tracking the man in front of

Dellenbaugh. His hand emerged from his blazer. Dewey had him but paused, knowing it could be a cell phone.

A Secret Service agent at the side of the stage suddenly saw Dewey. The agent pulled a gun from a holster at his waist and started a mad sprint across the stage.

"Get down!"

Dewey vaguely registered the agent's voice. His mind was on the man in the second row. The man directly in front of Dellenbaugh.

Dewey watched, transfixed, as his hand emerged from his coat. He was holding a gun, a short, squat, snub-nosed suppressor screwed into the muzzle.

The Secret Service agent trained his weapon on Dewey and fired—just as Dellenbaugh grabbed his arm, stopping him from killing Dewey.

Dellenbaugh saw Dewey's eyes staring coldly across the stage. He turned to where Dewey was looking.

The white-haired man swept the gun across his chest and trained it at President Dellenbaugh just as Dellenbaugh saw him.

Dewey swung his gun above the stage, tracking the killer. The stage was crowded with people—Dellenbaugh, his daughters, his wife, Secret Service agents—whose legs blocked his view. Then he found him. His arm was now in the air. Amid the panicked shuffling of legs, Dewey tried to take aim, just as the tip of the killer's suppressor swept toward Dellenbaugh. Legs suddenly crossed in front of his view again, but Dewey kept the pistol trained where the man was, putting his finger tighter on the trigger. A glimmer of light emerged, no bigger than a dime, and Dewey fired.

A dull *thwack* as the bullet ripped from Dewey's gun and slammed into the man's forehead. Blood and brains shot across the crowded row of people behind the killer. He was thrown backward, tumbling amid screams and panic to the ground.

Screams and chaos enveloped the area around the stage, even as the cheering continued from the tens of thousands of people who had no idea what was happening. Music blared from the loudspeakers. But panic gripped the hundreds of people closest to the stage. Screams filled Dewey's ears. A block of SWAT-clad agents charged across the stage and leapt down in front of it, scrambling to the dead man. All around Dewey there was screaming and panic, people falling down as they rushed for the exits. Yet it was barely noticeable within the raucous tumult of the crowd.

A swarm of agents rushed Dellenbaugh from the stage, which quickly turned into a scene out of a war zone as SWAT officers stormed onto the platform and created a human barrier between the president and the crowd.

Dewey turned. He searched for the woman who'd been hit just a minute before. She was lying on the ground, alone except for another woman, a brave onlooker, trying to stop the flow of blood from her neck.

Dewey pushed his way back. The woman had short black hair and glasses. A pancake of red covered her chest.

Dewey knelt beside her. With two hands he ripped the woman's sweatshirt at the neck, exposing the bullet wound. The bullet had hit her on the right side, at the base of her neck, and she was bleeding badly, dark red edging out of the bullet hole with every beat of the woman's heart.

Dewey removed his knife from his ankle sheath. He cut away the hood of the woman's sweatshirt and pressed it hard against the bullet hole. She groaned in pain. Her eyes opened. She stared up weakly at Dewey.

"What's your name?" said Dewey as he pressed the hood against the wound, trying to stanch the blood.

The woman's eyes fluttered and shut. Dewey slapped her lightly on the cheek. When her eyes didn't open, he slapped her again, harder this time. She opened her eyes.

"What's your name?" he said, leaning close.

"Lydia," she whispered.

"Lydia? That's a nice name. Do you have any kids, Lydia?"

She nodded. “One.”

“Boy or girl?”

“My daughter,” she whispered, her voice clotted with blood.

“What’s her name?”

Lydia started to drift off. Her eyes fluttered and shut.

“What’s your daughter’s name, Lydia?” Dewey yelled.

He slapped her harder this time, a vicious whack across her cheek. Her cheek flushed red—there would be a bruise—but her eyes opened.

“What’s her name?”

“Caroline.”

“You need to hang on,” said Dewey, getting close to her face. “Caroline needs you. You’re not going to die. But you need to stay with me. Can you do that, Lydia?”

She looked at Dewey.

“Yes,” she said. “I promise.”

96

FBI HEADQUARTERS
J. EDGAR HOOVER BUILDING
WASHINGTON, D.C.

Bruner was laid out on a steel table in the basement-level morgue. His body was stiff. He still had his suit on. Even the holster beneath his left armpit remained on. The right side of his face was purple and black, covered in dried blood. The left side was gone, blown off by a bullet that hit his forehead and splintered Bruner's brittle skull in a craggy line. His brain was exposed, a pasty gray mass of material also coated in a sheen of dried blood.

Calibrisi, Daniels, Polk, and George Kratovil, the FBI director, stood together on one side of the table.

A television on the wall was tuned to CBS, a live report on the attempted assassination of President J. P. Dellenbaugh. Scott Pelley was standing outside FedEx Field.

> "This is Scott Pelley, reporting live from FedEx Field in Landover, Maryland. This stadium, home to the Washington Redskins, is, today, the somber site

of what was—according to several sources—a sophisticated, highly planned, multistage attack on the U.S. presidency. The president, arriving just after noon for what was supposed to be a triumphant announcement for reelection, was targeted for assassination. While details are just beginning to emerge, CBS News has learned that multiple gunmen were inside the stadium and only a combination of the FBI, CIA, and good old-fashioned luck allowed President J. P. Dellenbaugh to survive the attack. We go now live to the White House . . ."

The door to the morgue opened and J. P. Dellenbaugh, accompanied by Amy and Adrian King, his chief of staff, stepped inside.

Dellenbaugh had a blank, dazed expression on his face as he stared down at Bruner's corpse.

King turned off the TV.

Dellenbaugh stared at Bruner's destroyed head. He looked at it for nearly a minute. It was only when his wife stepped behind him and put her hand on his back that he finally looked up. Dellenbaugh looked at Calibrisi, then at Daniels. Dellenbaugh's eyes were cold and angry, yet there was also sadness in them.

Dellenbaugh wanted to thank them. It was why

he came. But he couldn't speak. He turned and left.

It was Amy Dellenbaugh who broke the silence. She was crying.

"Thank you," she said quietly, her voice full with emotion, her eyes moving to each man. "Thank you so much. It's what he wanted to say. Thank you for saving my husband's life."

97

POCAHONTAS COUNTY HOSTERMAN, WEST VIRGINIA

Largent sat in the corner of an old, abandoned lean-to just a few hundred feet from the banks of the Greenbrier River.

He wore a black Carhartt wool-lined bodysuit, old knee-high Gokey leather snake boots, and a long black oilskin duster.

A pump-action Remington 870 12-gauge shotgun lay on the ground next to him.

Largent had been sitting inside the small shack for more than a day now. Other than going to the bathroom, or lying down to catch a few hours of sleep, he hadn't moved.

The moment it failed, Largent had run. He'd stolen a car from the Capitol parking lot, an old Honda Accord, and driven to Dulles Airport, where he abandoned the car and stole another. He might have been Speaker of the U.S. House of Representatives, but before that Largent was a Navy SEAL. He knew how to survive.

Largent knew that in order to survive, he needed time to fade away, blend in, and disappear into the ether. It would get cold soon, but the small wooden shack would work for the winter. It would have to work. He didn't have a choice. If he was caught, he'd be tried for treason in front of a military tribunal and sentenced to death. This way, he had a fighting chance. It would require living like an animal. He would have to kill or steal whatever he was going to eat, at least for the first year or two. Eventually, when memories faded, he could move south—Mexico, Central America, and one day South America.

Largent heard a sound outside the cabin. He remained dead still, except for his right hand, which slowly reached for the 870.

Arching his neck to the right, he glanced through a hole in the wood. Two deer were meandering near the banks of the river, searching for food.

Largent started to stand, moving to kill one of the animals. The meat from even one would last through much of the winter if he rationed it correctly. Then he stopped. As much as he knew he could use the meat, the sound of the gun might alert someone to his presence.

He sat down and watched as the deer moved away. After a few minutes, he shut his eyes, trying to will himself to sleep. Patience was what would enable him to survive. Patience and toughness.

98

OVAL OFFICE
THE WHITE HOUSE

President Dellenbaugh sat in a wooden rocking chair in the middle of the Oval Office. Both leather chesterfield couches were filled. Another rocking chair was to Dellenbaugh's left. In it sat Calibrisi.

Seated on the sofas were members of the National Security Council as well as certain key aides. The meeting was in its second hour. The subject was the conspiracy to take over the U.S. government—a complete and thorough debrief by the CIA, FBI, NSA, and Secret Service of the events surrounding Tim Lindsay's death through Dellenbaugh's speech at FedEx Field.

"We found Harry Black in Bruner's basement," said George Kratovil. "He's on his way to Guantánamo Bay. Unfortunately, Bobby Largent is still at large."

For three days, Bruner's small army of traitors

had been hunted down like dogs. With the help of the NSA, the members of Order 6 were relatively easy to find. Dellenbaugh signed a secret presidential order giving the CIA license to kill any members of the conspiracy. A few came forward and confessed. They were sent to Gitmo.

Dellenbaugh held a large photo of the woman, Romy Banker, without whose help the conspirators would have prevailed. It was an old photo of her, taken at her chalet in the French countryside, found by field agents. Her hair was blond and braided in a simple honeycomb atop her head. She was tan, with small freckles. Her beauty was astonishing—she looked like a young Catherine Deneuve. She appeared shy, as if she didn't want her photo to be taken. But there was the faintest hint of a smile.

"How is Romy doing?" asked Dellenbaugh.

"She's doing better," said King, the White House chief of staff. "I visited her yesterday."

"Does she have any family?" said Dellenbaugh.

"Not that we know of," said King.

"What do we know about her?"

Several heads turned, wondering who would answer.

"We don't know much beyond the file," said Calibrisi. "We've scoured her home in France. We found plenty concerning her husband, but very little on her."

"What is she going to do now?" asked Brubaker, the national security advisor.

"I don't know," said Calibrisi. "She needs to recover. Then I suppose she'll want to go back to France."

"Do they have children?"

"No."

Dellenbaugh continued to hold the photo. Then he placed it on the coffee table.

"The answer to 'What will she do now?' is 'Whatever she wants,' " he said, looking at Calibrisi, then around the room. "If it wasn't for this woman, the United States of America would be gone. It was that close. And the United States of America will never forget it. Romy Banker is going to do whatever she wants and we are going to make sure of that."

"Does that mean money, sir?"

"It means protecting her," said Dellenbaugh. "It might mean money too. If she wants to move to someplace, a villa on the coast of New Zealand, a ranch in Montana, it doesn't matter. It happens. We make it happen. Whoever this woman is, she saved the United States of America."

"I agree," said Calibrisi.

"So do I," said Piper Redgrave, head of the NSA.

"I agree wholeheartedly, Mr. President," said Brubaker.

"Okay, okay, I get it," said Adrian King, "I

get the picture. No need for everyone to say 'I agree.' I really don't feel like listening to all you say 'I agree' for the next half hour."

The room erupted in laughter.

King grinned ever so slightly. "For what it's worth, I agree too. In fact, I've already put into motion a Presidential Commendation and some sort of congressional honor."

"I'll handle setting up the security for her," said Calibrisi. "It will make sense to coordinate it with local law enforcement, so that they understand her safety is important to the White House and the U.S. government. We'll also figure out some sort of twenty-four/seven armed envelope as well as an advanced electronic perimeter connected to us."

The door to the office opened and John Schmidt, the communications director, stuck his head in. Dellenbaugh was giving his first press conference since the events at FedEx Field.

"They're ready, sir. It's live."

"Don't we have a few more minutes?" said Dellenbaugh.

"Actually, it was supposed to start ten minutes ago, Mr. President."

Dellenbaugh stood up. "Oops," he said.

"It's only half a billion people, sir," said Schmidt with a sarcastic grin. "I'm sure they don't mind waiting."

99

WALTER REED MEDICAL CENTER
BETHESDA, MARYLAND

Dewey stepped out of his town house. He walked down the block until he came to the door of a red Ford F-250, which was covered in dust and dirt. He climbed in and drove to Walter Reed Medical Center, just up the road in Bethesda.

Dewey parked and went inside the massive facility. On the fourth floor, past a team of FBI agents, he came to a door and knocked.

"Come in," said the person inside in a soft female voice with a French accent.

"Hi, Romy," he said.

She was in a large bed, with an assortment of tubes and monitors still attached to her. The top of her head was covered in a large white bandage.

"Dewey," said Romy. "I'm so happy to see you, but I feel bad. You don't need to come every day, you know. I feel perhaps I am a headache to you."

Dewey went to the side of Romy's bed. He smiled at her.

"Quite the opposite," he said, putting his hand on hers and holding it for a few moments. "How you feeling?"

"A little better."

Dewey nodded, trying to think of something to say. But she spoke first.

"The news said Bruner was shot."

"Yes."

"Did you do it?" Romy said.

Dewey was quiet. For a few seconds he said nothing.

"You can tell me."

"Yeah."

Dewey's eyes went to the bandage atop her head. She noticed.

"It's not very pretty, is it?"

"It looks fine."

"Thank you."

"So, what will you do now?"

Romy looked at Dewey for a long time, saying nothing.

"I don't know. I don't have anything, really. Everything I thought I had was a lie. I don't know."

"Well, when it's time to get out of here, I'd be glad to show you around a little. Washington, that sort of thing. I have a truck. We can run over some politicians and lobbyists."

She giggled. "It's a plan."

Down the hall, Dewey went to another door. He entered without knocking.

Tacoma's hospital room was bright with

lights and filled with state-of-the-art medical equipment. A multitude of low beeps created a constant rhythm. In the middle, a man lay on the bed. A spaghetti plate worth of tubes and wires ran from various pieces of equipment into his body. The right side of his head was bandaged. A spot of blood colored the outer edge.

He was awake, but barely. His neck was in a large white brace.

Dewey sat down next to the bed and put his feet up on the railing.

"Hey, dickhead," Dewey said. "Bright idea. Trying to stop the train with your head."

Tacoma didn't move, but his eyes grew a little wider. His lips spread into a droopy, heavily sedated smile.

"How's Katie?" he whispered.

"She's fine," said Dewey. "You saved her life."

"No I didn't."

"You almost did. If you hadn't tripped on your shoelaces, I'm guessing you would have saved her."

Tacoma's lips moved into a smile and he laughed.

Dewey stood up. "I need to go. I'll be back in a few days."

"A few days?" whispered Tacoma. "What for?"

"Business trip."

"Where you going?"

"West Virginia."

100

DURBIN, WEST VIRGINIA

Dewey reached Durbin as the sun was setting. He pulled up in front of a small pub called Al's Upper Inn Club.

The pub was dimly lit and mostly empty. A country tune was playing on the jukebox. Dewey took a seat at the bar.

An old, bearded bartender approached.

"Hey," he said. "I get you something?"

"Yeah, I'll take two shots of Jack Daniel's and a beer."

The bartender nodded. "Sounds good."

A few minutes later, he brought Dewey his drinks.

"I need to talk with your dishwasher," said Dewey, hoisting one of the shots and downing it.

Dcwcy placcd a twcnty on thc bar to pay for his drinks.

"Dishwasher? You mean Steve?"

"Kittridge."

"Can I tell him who's here to see him?"

"I wouldn't," said Dewey.

It was Samantha Stout who figured out where Largent was.

The theft of the Honda from Capitol Hill had been easy. Largent took it to Dulles because he wanted everyone to spend time trying to figure out how he got away—which flight, under what alias.

Samantha monitored local police reports from Chantilly, the town Dulles was located in. Sure enough, a woman reported that her car was stolen a few hours after the Honda Largent had driven to Dulles was discovered.

Samantha had entered the vehicle's VIN in a variety of NSA software applications designed to flag activity in real time. Two days after the car—a 1994 Ford Taurus—was reported missing, a seventeen-year-old named Steven Kittridge from Durbin, West Virginia, had attempted to register a 1994 Ford Taurus in his own name. Its VIN was almost exactly the same as the stolen vehicle's, the only difference being the last digit, which, Samantha guessed, had been altered by Kittridge.

A skinny kid with greasy brown hair emerged from the back of the restaurant. He looked at Dewey and slowly approached.

"Yeah?" he said.

"You can keep the fucking car," said Dewey. "But you're going to tell me exactly where you found it."

Dewey downed the other shot of whiskey.

Steven looked momentarily shocked.

"Well . . . I . . . what car?"

Dewey stared at him. "Let's go."

"I'm working," said Steven. "Who the fuck are—"

Dewey reached over the bar and grabbed his arm, lifted him up onto the bar and dragged him over, then hurled him against the wall.

Steven screamed as he hit the wall.

"I said let's go. I work for the U.S. government. That's all you need to know. So you can show me where you found the piece-of-shit Taurus of your own free will, and then keep the piece-of-shit Taurus, or I can make you show me, in which case I guarantee you will not only not keep the fucking car, but you'll also have two broken arms, not to mention I'll turn your ass in for altering the VIN, which is against the law."

"It was down there," said Steven, pointing from the railroad bridge at the Greenbrier River. "We were walking right here. I saw it. It was underwater. I borrowed a tow truck from my uncle. We pulled it out. Am I in trouble, mister?"

Dewey ignored the question.

"You fish?"

"Yeah."

"Are there any old camps along here?"

"Sure, a few."

"I'm talking about old ones. Abandoned."

"Yeah. There's one about a mile from here, down toward Bartow. There's also a few along near Hosterman."

Dewey gave Steven a ride back to Al's. At the bar, he made Steven draw a map, marking the locations of the four camps he could think of.

Dewey had one more beer, one more whiskey, then left.

Dewey parked his truck along a dirt road off the main road down to Hosterman. He looked at his watch. It was four in the morning.

He should've been tired, but he wasn't.

His hair was drenched in sweat. He had already scouted three of the camps Steven identified. To get to them, Dewey was forced to walk for miles along the roiling waters of the Greenbrier. All three had been empty. This was the last one. Yet Dewey had known from the beginning that it was the one where Largent was hiding. After driving the car into the river, it was the closest. Dewey hadn't gone to it first not because he doubted his convictions but, rather, because he was certain of them. He used the other three camps to acclimate himself to the West Virginia night. To remind himself of what it meant to travel alone, in the darkness, in the bitter cold, how to read by the ambient light, then, upon sighting one's target, how to approach, to stalk, to come within a hundred yards without alerting someone, then a hundred feet, and finally a hundred inches. How to make the final silent steps across thrush and bramble, using the patter of the running river to cloak the noise.

Dewey ran in the low grass just above the dark riverbank, his gun at his side, the way a runner grips the baton. Dewey's Colt M1911A1 was locked and loaded, the safety off.

After fifteen minutes of a slow, quiet run, he caught the angular silhouette of the shack, nestled near a tree in the bend of the river.

He moved with a deathlike silence, each step now in slow motion, each breath a hushed whisper. It had taken Dewey fifteen minutes to run two miles from where he'd parked the truck, but now it took him a full hour to move the final fifty feet to the cabin.

He approached the corner of the decrepit structure, looking at the sky. A spectral gray had overtaken the sky as dawn approached. Dewey extended a finger, touching the wood for a brief moment. He raised the gun and aimed it at the opening into the shack—what had once been a doorway. He waited, listening to the sound of the river, watching as the sky moved from gray to muddy blue then to dark tan. He stood as still as stone, the Colt trained at the door.

The creak of the wood came almost two hours after Dewey took up position. It was followed by another creak, this one louder. The footsteps moved along old boards, and then Largent emerged through the doorway. Slowly, he turned and found himself staring down the muzzle of Dewey's gun. Largent remained still as his eyes went from the gun to Dewey.

"FBI?" said Largent.

Dewey said nothing.

"Do you want me to put my hands up?" said Largent.

"I don't care," said Dewey.

"Are you arresting me?"

Dewey shook his head.

Largent nodded slowly.

"Well, go ahead, then."

Dewey fired. The bullet struck Largent in the center of his chest, kicking him backward, though he fought to remain standing. His hand went to his chest, pawing at the bullet hole. He lifted his hand and stared at the blood on his fingers.

"Nineteen eleven . . ." He coughed, the first mouthful of blood coursing over his lips, and he staggered. "That's a good gun."

Then he fell to the ground and died.

Dewey moved over Largent. He kept the gun trained on him as he knelt down and put a finger to his neck. Largent had no pulse. His eyes stared out helplessly, seeing nothing.

Dewey holstered the gun. He went inside and picked up the shotgun. He looked briefly around the abandoned cabin. He came back out and stared down at Largent's corpse, bleeding out all over the ground. After a few moments, Dewey grabbed Largent by the collar of his coat, then hoisted him with a grunt onto his shoulder, fireman style.

Dewey walked back along the river as the sun was just beginning to shine over the blue West Virginia hills to the east. It was a few miles, he knew, and Largent was heavy, and he was a traitor, and he could've just left him there. Someone from the FBI could've come and gotten the body later, yet Dewey knew that he was the one who needed to do it. He was the one who needed to kill him, and he was the one who needed to carry him out. It had nothing to do with Largent. It didn't even have anything to with America. No, Dewey needed to do it for himself.

EPILOGUE

GEORGETOWN

Dewey heard the doorbell and went downstairs. He opened the door. Standing on the brick front steps was a tall man, college or high school age, dressed in a dark blue suit with a bright yellow tie. He was holding a thick envelope.

"Mr. Andreas?" the young man said.

"Yeah."

"I'm Peter Pitchess from the White House. I'm a White House intern. I was sent here to hand-deliver this."

Pitchess handed Dewey the envelope. His name was written across the front in fancy calligraphy. The back of the envelope had a raised emblem, done in gold—a drawing of the White House.

Dewey didn't have a shirt on. His hair was still wet. A drop flipped down onto the envelope, hitting the ink of his name, which immediately started to run.

"What is it?" said Dewey.

"Officially, I'm not supposed to know," said Pitchess. "But it's an invitation to the state dinner."

Dewey nodded, impressed.

"When is it?" Dewey said.

"I think it's on the twenty-seventh," said Pitchess. "You, ah, could open it. It'll probably say the date."

Dewey handed it to Pitchess.

"You open it."

Pitchess excitedly took the envelope. Gingerly, he put a finger at the seam of the envelope and opened it. He pulled out a thick piece of paper. The paper was a subtle mint green, with a thin black line around the border, and the White House at the top, again in gold.

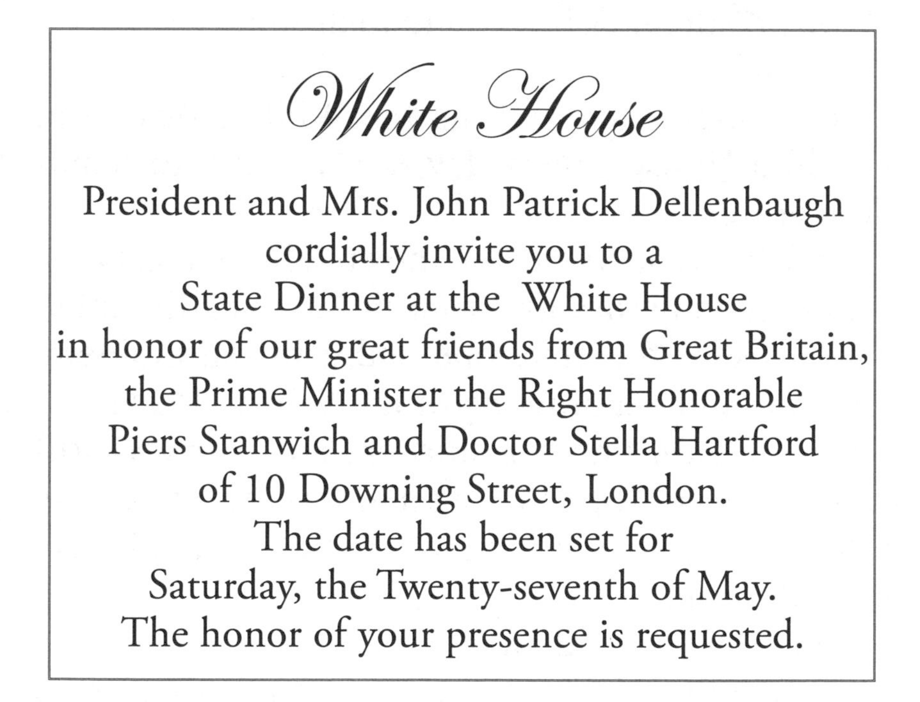

White House

President and Mrs. John Patrick Dellenbaugh
cordially invite you to a
State Dinner at the White House
in honor of our great friends from Great Britain,
the Prime Minister the Right Honorable
Piers Stanwich and Doctor Stella Hartford
of 10 Downing Street, London.
The date has been set for
Saturday, the Twenty-seventh of May.
The honor of your presence is requested.

Pitchess stared at the invitation, his mouth agape. "Wow. Thanks for letting me see that."

"No prob," said Dewey.

"Um, so I'm supposed to ask for an answer. I

mean, I'm sure the answer's yes, but I'm supposed to ask."

Dewey smiled. "I need to check my schedule."

"Seriously?"

Dewey grinned. "Yeah, just tell them to tell the president I need to check my schedule."

Dewey and Daisy decided to walk from Georgetown to the White House, rather than drive or get an Uber—and rather than accept Hector's offer of a ride.

It was Daisy's idea.

"Thanks for inviting me," she said, holding his hand.

"You don't need to thank me."

Daisy was dressed in a white silk dress, simple and racy, ravishing and stunning, her large breasts accentuated—not that they needed to be—her brown legs visible from midthigh down, shapely and captivating. Her long brown hair flowed freely behind her, shimmering in reds and blacks as light hit it, her face sculpted and smooth, large brown eyes, and a nose that on most would be considered too long but was, on her, her most beautiful aspect, and lips that were puffy and seductive. She looked like a young Sophia Loren. For his part, Dewey was dressed in a tuxedo, the largest size the store had had, and his big shoulders and chest pushed against the material. He was clean shaven and his hair was cut to a medium length, parted in the middle, in back still longish, down almost to his shoulders. Dewey's skin was tan, he seemed relaxed, and yet his eyes scanned the streets as they walked.

"A state dinner," said Daisy. "It's sort of exciting."

Dewey smiled. "Yeah."

Dewey suddenly tugged her hand and they came to a stop. He pulled Daisy closer and wrapped his arms around her. They were on an empty sidewalk. The sky was turning black.

He leaned forward and kissed her. Then he reached into his pocket and removed a thin red velvet box. He handed it to her.

She stared at it, speechless.

"Dewey, I . . . I don't know what to say."

She opened the box. Inside was a necklace with small diamonds along the edge and a large ruby hanging down.

"Oh my God," she said.

"I stole it," said Dewey. "You might not want to wear it in public."

Daisy handed the necklace to Dewey, who fastened it around her neck. She smiled bashfully up at him. He was blushing slightly.

"You're adorable, do you know that?" She leaned toward him and stood on her tiptoes. She kissed him on the lips, and they stood on the sidewalk without letting go of each other for a long time, kissing affectionately, even passionately.

Finally, Dewey moved his lips away.

"You think we should maybe bag this dinner and go back and see what happens?"

"No," said Daisy, laughing.

Dewey nodded toward an empty stretch of Rock Creek Park near the road. "What about going behind those bushes over there?"

Daisy looked at him with a slightly disgusted look.

"I'm not a stray dog, Dewey," she said.

GUANTÁNAMO BAY DETENTION CAMP
GUANTÁNAMO BAY, CUBA

Flaherty's cell was made of concrete. The toilet was a hole in the ground. Despite being located in a tropical paradise—just a few miles from several five-star resorts—the cell had only one small window, high enough so that nobody could see in or see out.

Flaherty lay on the ground. He was sweating, not only from the temperature but also from the pain. Other than the night of the accident, he hadn't received any painkillers, not even an aspirin.

He shouldn't have survived. In fact, FBI and CIA investigators shared the same conclusion: nobody could have survived that car crash. But he did. Ultimately, the credit was given to Mercedes and a steel frame designed for the Autobahn, the federal-controlled access highway system in Germany, much of which had no posted speed limits.

Despite his survival, Flaherty wished he were dead.

A thick metal wire was wrapped through his mouth and around the back of his neck. In his mouth—affixed to the wire—was a green rubber gag in the shape of a stick of butter lodged between his teeth. It had been there for so long it was the only thing he knew, the only thing on earth he liked.

Both his legs were in casts, each one dark and filthy. His left arm was also in a cast. He spent all day trying to fall asleep and all night doing the same. Sleep was the only thing he had now, and even that was haunted by memories and nightmares.

He heard the dull clink of his cell door unlocking. He looked up as the thick steel door swung in. A man in a uniform was standing there. In his hand was a cell phone. The officer came to Flaherty and reached behind his neck, unlocking the gag. He lifted Flaherty by his shirt, sitting him up. He handed him the phone.

"You have a phone call."

Flaherty wasn't allowed phone calls at Guantánamo. He stared at the man's hand, and the phone. He hadn't spoken on a cell phone in months.

He took the cell from the officer, who took several steps back and stood in the doorway.

"Andrew Flaherty?"

"Yes," Flaherty coughed in a scratchy voice.

"What if I told you you could walk out of that prison?" the man asked.

Flaherty said nothing.

"You don't believe me, do you? But it's true. You see, we both want the same thing. A better America. I know what you did. I watched you doing it. I was rooting for you."

"Who are you?"

"My name is Joshua Gant."

"Josh Gant, as in the former deputy CIA director?"

"Correct."

"What do you want?"

"To eliminate America's threats, just like you," said Gant. "Promise you'll help me, and you'll walk out of that prison within the hour."

"I'll help you," said Flaherty. "What threats are you talking about?"

Gant let out a high-pitched cackle.

"We're going to kill Dewey Andreas."

1244 PENNSYLVANIA AVENUE
WASHINGTON, D.C.

Dewey woke up early and took a shower. He went to the dresser to find something to wear, pulling out a drawer. It was empty. He pulled out every drawer, but the only thing he found was a pair of paint-covered madras shorts and a sock. He looked around the bedroom. A mountain of dirty clothing was piled in the corner. It came up to his waist and took up a good section of the room. He rifled through it, looking for something that wasn't too obviously dirty. He pulled out various articles—a flannel shirt, a pair of jeans, a Bruins T-shirt—and put them up to his nose. After a good whiff, he dropped each one back onto the pile.

There was a subtle movement beneath the covers of the bed. The top of the blanket moved and Daisy's head appeared.

"Where are you going?" she said sleepily.

"I have an appointment."

"It's Sunday."

"I know. I made coffee. I'll be back in a couple of hours."

With no good options left, Dewey pulled on the tuxedo trousers from the night before, along with the white shirt, which was badly wrinkled. It took him a minute or so, but he finally found the tuxedo jacket where he'd thrown it the night before, on the floor outside the bedroom.

He walked to the building. It was a crisp, cool morning without a cloud in the sky. Only a few people were up and about at this hour. He walked over near Dumbarton Oaks and then down along the bike path that bordered Rock Creek Park, finally cutting over toward Pennsylvania Avenue.

When he got to the office building, a security guard signed him in. He took the elevator to the tenth floor. When he got off, he went left. At the end of the hallway, he saw a small sign.

DR. PAMELA PECK

Dewey knocked.

A moment later, he heard Dr. Peck's voice. "Come in."

Dewey opened the door. Dr. Peck was standing against the glass wall. Over her shoulders, he could see the White House. Dr. Peck's arms were crossed. Her hair was brushed back.

"Hello, Dewey," she said.

"Hi."

"I'm surprised."

"Why?"

"I didn't think you'd come."

Dewey stared at her.

"Won't you sit down?" She pointed to the chair.

"Sure."

Dr. Peck walked to the chair across from him and sat down.

"You didn't need to dress up for me, you know."

Dewey grinned.

"There's lipstick on your shirt," she pointed out.

"It was my only clean shirt. I need to do some laundry."

"Well, I'm not sure I'd call it 'clean,' " said Dr. Peck, smiling.

"I don't even know where the washing machine is. It's Jessica's house. She left it to me. I was thinking maybe I should sell it and move."

"Or you could look for the washing machine."

Dewey stared at her with a blank expression.

"Selling Jessica's town house won't erase what happened, Dewey. Killing Kyrie, killing Charles Bruner—that won't erase what happened to Holly."

"This again," said Dewey with scorn in his voice.

"This again is you, Dewey. These are parts of you. Vital parts. Jessica died in your arms, but you asked her to marry you. You had that moment. You and Holly had a son. He died, too, but you had him. You loved him. Were you in the room when he was born?"

Dewey nodded. His eyes were red.

"What's your point?" he whispered, trying to hold back his emotions. "Are you just trying to torture me?"

Dr. Peck shook her head. "No. Just the opposite."

Dewey was quiet for several minutes. He stared

down at his hands, then looked out the window. He shut his eyes and breathed deeply. Finally, he looked at Dr. Peck.

"I don't understand."

"It's okay. It's not about understanding. It's about feeling. Letting yourself feel. The feeling of watching somebody die who you love. You felt that. You still feel it. It's part of what makes you who you are."

Dewey stood up and walked to the window. He looked out on Pennsylvania Avenue, watching a young couple jogging along the wide sidewalk. He watched them until they disappeared in the distance.

"I shot someone," said Dewey.

"I read the file," said Dr. Peck. "It sounds like you shot a lot of people."

"This one was different. It was like he wanted me to shoot him."

"He was guilty," said Peck.

"I don't think he saw it that way. Even if he did, it doesn't mean you necessarily just give in. I've looked into the eyes of guilty men before, men I'm about to kill. This was different."

Dr. Peck took a deep breath. "You're wondering why he wanted you to shoot him."

"Yeah."

"Why do you care?"

"I don't know. I guess I've been wondering what I would do. If the tables were turned. If I was the one staring down the muzzle of a gun, with no chance for escape. None."

"You want to know what you would do if the gun was pointed at you," she said. "Point-blank. No escape. How you would feel. Is that it?"

"Something like that."

"But don't you already know?"

Dewey turned and shot her an angry look.

"Isn't that why you do it?" she said.

"What the hell are you talking about?"

Dr. Peck was quiet. She glanced at her watch.

"I think that's probably enough for today," she said.

Dewey stepped toward her.

"No fucking way," he said. "Answer me. What do you mean that's why I do it?"

Dr. Peck looked up at Dewey.

"Damascus. Beijing. Moscow. Paris. Perhaps listing them by name would make this easier for you to understand. Fao Bhang. Pyotr Vargarin. Abu Paria. Alexander Fortuna. Aswan Fortuna. Charles Bruner. The list goes on. You do it because you want to know the feeling just before you die. But you already know it. It's what you are. It's the very essence of Dewey Andreas."

ACKNOWLEDGMENTS

I would like to thank my agent, Nicole James. Nicole is not only beautiful, smart, and funny, she's also tough as nails. But then there's something else about Nicole. She's patient and empathetic too. Of course you want to have a tough agent but you have no idea how important it is, when you're stuck, to hear the reassuring words of someone who has your back and who believes in you. Thanks "Nicky."

Thank you also to Keith Kahla, my editor at St. Martin's Press. I don't know how he does it, but Keith can cut to the heart of what's wrong with a book the way a great doctor can diagnose a rare disease (plus Keith charges less).

At St. Martin's Press and Macmillan Audio, I'm grateful to everyone for the tireless effort and enthusiasm you give to my books. Thank you all, and in particular Sally Richardson, Jennifer Enderlin, Hannah Braaten, George Witte, Martin Quinn, Jeff Capshew, Paul Hochman, Justin Velella, Rafal Gibek, Jason Reigal, Ervin Serrano, Robert Allen, Mary Beth Roche, Alison Ziegler, and Joseph Brosnan.

Thanks also to Chris George, Ryan Steck, Adrian King, Michelle Goncalves, and Sam Adams.

Even though she can’t read I want to thank my dog, Mabel, who was at my side for virtually every word I wrote. While Mabel’s snoring can be somewhat of an irritant, I’ve found that the best antidote to it is to simply have Dewey kill someone, which might help explain why he kills so many people in the book.

Finally, thank you to my family: Shannon, Charlie, Teddy, Oscar, and Esmé. One thing that hasn’t changed over all these years and all these books is the love and support you all give to me. Writing can be lonely and having the constant affection, humor, and presence of you all is what makes it so incredibly enjoyable.

Center Point Large Print
600 Brooks Road / PO Box 1
Thorndike, ME 04986-0001 USA

(207) 568-3717

US & Canada:
1 800 929-9108
www.centerpointlargeprint.com